THE POPPY GIRLS

THE POPPY GIRLS

by

Margaret Dickinson

Magna Large Print Books
Long Preston, North Yorkshire,
BD23 4ND, England.

British Library Cataloguing in Publication Data.

A catalogue record of this book is
available from the British Library

ISBN   978-0-7505-4689-8

First published in Great Britain 2018 by Macmillan,
an imprint of Pan Macmillan

Published in Large Print 2019 by arrangement with
Macmillan Publishers International Ltd.

Magna Large Print is an imprint of Library Magna Books Ltd.

Printed and bound in Great Britain by
T.J. (International) Ltd., Cornwall, PL28 8RW

For all my family and friends for their love, encouragement and help through many years.

The Maitland Family

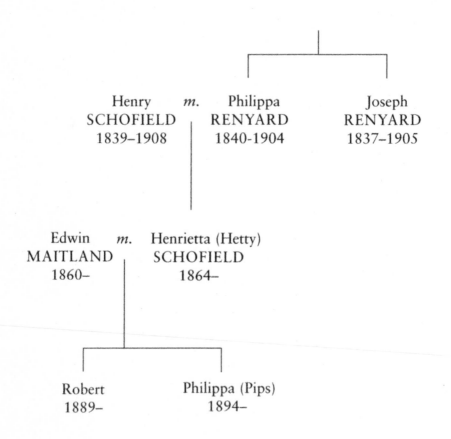

Henry	*m.*	Philippa		Joseph
SCHOFIELD		RENYARD		RENYARD
1839–1908		1840-1904		1837–1905

Edwin	*m.*	Henrietta (Hetty)
MAITLAND		SCHOFIELD
1860–		1864–

| Robert | Philippa (Pips) |
| 1889– | 1894– |

The Dawson Family

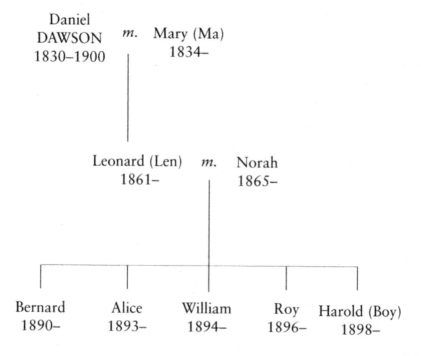

Daniel DAWSON 1830–1900 *m.* Mary (Ma) 1834–

Leonard (Len) 1861– *m.* Norah 1865–

Bernard 1890–   Alice 1893–   William 1894–   Roy 1896–   Harold (Boy) 1898–

ACKNOWLEDGEMENTS

This is a work of fiction; the characters and plot line are all created from my imagination and any resemblance to real people is coincidental.

I am very grateful to James and Claire Birch, of Doddington Hall near Lincoln, for allowing me to use their beautiful home as the setting and inspiration for this story, and also to the members of their team, who have been so helpful with my research.

I am also most grateful to all the staff of Lincoln Central Library, who took the time and trouble to send me lists of suggested areas of research; this was invaluable.

My sincere thanks also to Mike Hodgson, of Thorpe Camp Visitor Centre at Tattershall Thorpe, Lincolnshire, who acted as a guide on one of our coach trips to Belgium. He has so generously shared his knowledge and expertise in answering all my questions, then and since.

A huge thank you, too, to Chris Bassford and Nick Hodgkinson, who organized and led two trips to Ypres, where I was able to do detailed research. Everyone on both trips was so kind, encouraging and helpful; thank you to all of you.

On the second trip to Belgium in 2016, it was wonderful to have my daughter Zoe and niece

Helen with us. They have also read and commented on the early draft of the script, as too have my usual 'first readers': my brother David, my brother-in-law Fred, and my friend Pauline. And, of course, I mustn't forget my lovely husband Dennis, and daughter Mandi, who support and encourage me every step of the way.

And with this, my twenty-fifth novel for Pan Macmillan, I wish to pay tribute to my fantastic agent, Darley Anderson, to my brilliant editor, Trisha Jackson, and to all the superb team at Macmillan. You're the best!

My love and grateful thanks to all of you.

A great many sources have been used in the research for this novel, most notably *Elsie and Mairi Go To War* by Diane Atkinson (Preface Publishing, 2009); *Stretcher Bearer: Fighting for Life in the Trenches* by Charles H. Horton, edited by Dale Le Vack (Lion Books, 2013); *Wounded: The Long Journey Home from the Great War* by Emily Mayhew (Vintage, 2014); *Ypres Diary 1914–1915: The Memoirs of Sir Morgan Crofton*, edited by Gavin Roynon (The History Press, 2004); *World War 1: Day by Day* by Ian Westwell (Snap Productions, 2012); *The History of the Lincolnshire Regiment 1914–1918*, edited by Major-General C. R. Simpson, C.B. (The Naval and Military Press Ltd, 2009) and *Bombardment! The Day the East Coast Bled* by Mark Marsay (Great Northern Publishing, 1999).

One

Lincolnshire, July 1914

'Your daughter will drive me to an early grave. *Now* where is she?'

Dr Edwin Maitland smiled indulgently at his irate wife and said mildly, 'Why is she always my daughter when she's annoying you, but yours when she pleases you?'

'Which isn't very often,' Henrietta snapped.

'Hetty, my love, she is young, healthy and energetic, and a clever girl who is very frustrated by the conventions of the times regarding the expected behaviour of young women. She is envious of her elder brother being able to train as a doctor whilst we' – he paused briefly, for the future that had been mapped out for Philippa had not been his wish, though he must shoulder some of the blame for having tacitly agreed to it – 'have curtailed her ambitions.'

Henrietta spread her hands helplessly. 'Why, oh why can't she just be happy to find a nice husband and settle down? Why does she always have to vie with Robert in everything he does? We gave her a good education. Wasn't that enough?'

'But we didn't allow her to go to university or to medical school as she wanted, did we?'

'What use is a university education to a housewife and mother? And I suspect it was more

15

because Robert had gone rather than that was what she really wanted to do.' There was a pause before Henrietta said, 'You haven't answered my question. Where is she?'

'Out somewhere. Down at the stables, possibly.'

'She'll break her neck on that stallion she rides. He's hard to handle.'

'Not for Pips. Midnight is as docile as a Shetland pony when she's on his back.'

Then, as another thought entered Henrietta's mind, she said, 'Don't tell me she is out on that new contraption of Robert's? Please don't say she is riding pillion on his motorcycle?'

'I really wouldn't know, my love,' Edwin murmured and turned away. He never lied to his wife, but he didn't always tell her the whole truth. Yes, Pips was out with her brother and his new machine, but if Edwin knew his daughter, she wouldn't be riding pillion; she'd be driving it...

The subject of their conversation was at that moment indeed riding her brother's new motorcycle through the village lanes, startling hens, chickens, dogs and cats as well as frightening the life out of the locals.

'There she goes,' Ma Dawson said aloud to no one in particular. 'More spirit and daring than the rest of us put together, that one.'

Ma was sitting in the sunshine in front of the ivy-clad cottage where the Dawson family lived, smoking her clay pipe and watching the world go by, as the machine roared past.

The small village of Doddington, with one

main street and lanes running from it into the surrounding countryside, lay approximately five miles west of Lincoln. At the heart of village life was the hall, a magnificent Elizabethan mansion, and its estate of gardens, park and farmland. The house, completed in 1600, was a symmetrical building, topped by three turrets with leaded cupolas, large windows and spacious rooms. Close by stood St Peter's church, rebuilt in 1771 but keeping its Early English font.

Ma Dawson was probably the oldest person in the village, with pure white hair under her lace bonnet, though she would never reveal her true age. Rumour had it that she wasn't really sure herself just how old she was, though the fact that she had married her soldier husband on his return from the Crimean War meant that she must be eighty at least. Widowed in 1900, she now lived with her son and his family. After leaving the regular army, her husband had learned the trade of carpenter and wheelwright from his uncle and now their son, Leonard, continued the village industry. To Ma's delight, three of her four grandsons were also learning the trade and expanding the family business too. When the village blacksmith had become too old to carry on and had had no one to inherit his business, Leonard and his sons had taken on the workshop, which was only a few yards from their own home and workplace. Now the Dawsons were not only the village's carpenter, wheelwright and undertaker, but also its blacksmith.

As she closed her eyes and lifted her face to the sun, Ma could hear Roy and Harold, the two youngest boys, sawing wood – the trunk of a huge tree they'd felled earlier that day. And from the blacksmith's shop came the sound of Bernard's hammer striking the anvil with a sharp clanging sound that echoed along the village street.

'Here you are, Ma, a nice cup of tea and your favourite biscuit.'

Ma opened her eyes to squint up at her daughter-in-law, Norah.

'Ta, duck. Sit down a minute, why don't you? You've been on the go since dawn.'

'Aye well, Ma. Len and the lads work hard. They have to have a good breakfast inside them before they start in a morning, now don't they?'

'You're a good wife and mother, Norah. I couldn't have wished for anyone better for my son. And you've given me lovely grandchildren too. Four boys and a girl. Who'd have thought it, with me only ever being able to have just the one. I'm proud of all of them.' She paused and smiled toothlessly. 'Even William.'

Norah pulled a face and sighed. 'Maybe he's better employed at the hall for Mrs Maitland as her gardener and handyman. I don't think working with his father and brothers would have been right for him, do you?' Norah was small and thin, with her grey hair pulled back into a bun. She wore a perpetually worried expression for she was always busy looking after the family; her husband, Len, her mother-in-law, who was always called Ma, and five children, though only the four boys still lived at home. Alice, the only girl in the family, worked as a lady's maid at the hall and lived in there. She visited on her days and afternoons off and always tried to give her work-worn mother a helping hand.

Ma was thoughtful for a moment before saying slowly, 'No, I don't, though it would have been nice if they'd all been in the family business. But William is a bit of a black sheep. He's better ploughing his own furrow.' She laughed at her own little joke. 'Literally, sometimes, when he's called in to help out on the farm.'

'I have to admit he's clever with machinery. If owt goes wrong with the threshing gear at harvest, it's William they call for. And he looks after Dr Maitland's new car now.'

For many years, ever since he'd moved into the hall on his marriage to Henrietta Schofield, Edwin Maitland had been the local doctor, holding surgeries in a side room at the hall. Previously, when a home visit to a patient was necessary, he'd travelled around the villages in a pony and trap. But recently, he'd acquired a motor car and now he drove in comparative comfort on his rounds.

Ma nodded down the lane where Pips and the roaring motorcycle had disappeared round the corner. 'And I expect William will be looking after Master Robert's newfangled machine, an' all.'

'I wonder if he's bought that to use when he becomes a partner in his father's practice?'

With a keen interest, the villagers had watched the children at the hall grow and develop. They were devoted to the Maitland family. Henrietta was a firm, but fair, mistress of the house and its estate and many of the locals depended on her for their livelihood from the work that her lands gave them. And, although he was heir to the estate, it had been no surprise when they'd learned that, at eighteen, Robert had gone to medical school.

'Following in his father's footsteps,' they'd agreed.

After qualifying, he'd taken up a post as a junior doctor at Lincoln's County Hospital for a year, but soon – after the approaching August Bank holiday, it was rumoured – he was to become a partner in his father's practice.

The two women were silent for some moments, soaking up the sunshine. For Norah, it was a welcome respite in a busy day.

'What's going to happen, Ma?' she asked softly at last, hardly daring to put her fears into words just in case a malevolent Fate was listening. 'With the assassination of this archduke – whoever he is. Len says there's even talk of it escalating into war.'

Ma shrugged philosophically. 'Out of our hands, duck. If it comes, it comes. I've lived through 'em afore and – God willing – I will again.'

'But the lads would all have to go, wouldn't they?'

'Aye. Certainly Bernard and William and probably Roy too, though Harold at fifteen wouldn't go immediately.'

'He'll be sixteen next month,' Norah murmured. There was a pause before she said, 'What about Len?'

'He'll likely be too old. Besides, they'll need the farms to produce more food and Len's work is mostly for the local farmers, now, isn't it? To say nothing of the work that comes from Mrs

Maitland's lands.'

'It's strange, isn't it, a woman owning a big estate like that?' Norah said.

Ma chuckled. 'It's not as big as some estates, but it's sizeable enough to give local folks a lot of employment – including our family in several ways. And, as for Mrs Maitland owning it, well, there's no one better. I'm only glad it didn't go to some far-off cousin or someone who'd have had no interest in it at all.'

'Was she the only one who could inherit it, then? I thought it usually went to a male, however distantly related.'

'Luckily for us, there wasn't anyone. Mrs Maitland – Hetty, as I still call her, because I've known her since she was a bairn – has lived at the hall all her life. She inherited from her childless uncle who died in – now let me think' – Ma puckered her already wrinkled brow even more – 'about 1905, I think it was, and the estate came straight to Hetty 'cos her mother, who would have inherited, had died the year before.'

'So it didn't go to her father, then?'

'Of course not. He wasn't a blood relative, now was he?'

Norah shook her head and then asked slowly, 'So, who will inherit after Mrs Maitland? Miss Pips?'

Ma shook her head. 'Not when there's a son. It'll be Master Robert. Unless, of course–' She hesitated and then whispered, 'he goes to war.'

They had come full circle, back to the start of the conversation and their fears for their own family. Now, as they sat together in silence, they were both thinking the same thing, but it was Ma who put it into words. 'It'll affect us all, you know, if it does come. All our sons – whatever their class – will have to go.'

To that, Norah had no answer, but it left her wondering and worrying even more.

Two

'That was wonderful,' Pips said, still sitting astride the stationary motorcycle in the stable yard behind the hall. She removed the leather helmet, which Robert had insisted she should wear, and shook out her long auburn hair. Her green eyes were sparkling with excitement. She was tall with a shapely figure and a lovely face.

'You'd better go in by the back door and sneak past Cook, if you can. If Mother gets to hear that you had grime all over your face, she'll know what we've been up to.'

'Oh phooey! Have I?' She scrubbed her face with her fingers but only succeeded in smearing it even more with the dust kicked up by her exhilarating ride.

'Go on with you, I'll put it away.' Robert's brown eyes teased her. He was a good-looking young man with dark brown wavy hair, a broad forehead and strong chin. Pips believed that all his women patients would idolize him.

She swung her leg over the motorcycle and pecked his cheek. 'You're such a dear – most of the time – but I still intend to beat you at chess. I demand a return match after last night.'

Pips scuttled in through the rear entrance and up the servants' staircase at the southern end of the house to the top floor, sped through the Long Gallery and then to the safety of her own bedroom without being seen, except by Alice Dawson, who was lady's maid to both Henrietta and Pips. With a wry shake of her head, the girl followed her young mistress and entered the bedroom close behind her. Alice wore a typical maid's uniform, for she was often required to help out with the housemaid's duties too. Her long black hair was pinned up neatly beneath her white lacy cap. At this moment her dark blue eyes were troubled.

'You'd better get that muck off your face before the mistress sees you. Wherever have you been?'

Without hesitation, for Pips confided in Alice regularly and knew she could trust her with her life, she said, 'Out on Robert's motorcycle.'

Even Alice, inured to Pips's wild ways, was shocked. 'Not – not *driving* it?'

'You *ride* a motorcycle, not drive it, but, yes, of course I was.'

'On your own?'

'Well, yes; they're not really fitted for two people to ride. Now, come on, Alice, don't stand there dithering and asking silly questions. I've got to be cleaned up and got ready for dinner. Are there any guests tonight?'

Alice shook her head. 'Not now. Major Fieldsend and his wife were coming, but evidently he's had to go to London urgently.'

As Pips finished washing and sat down in front of the dressing table, Alice took up the hairbrush and began to brush Pips's hair, which reached below her shoulders, and then to pin it up into an elegant style of the day.

'What a shame. I like old Basil. Considering he used to be such an important figure in the Lincolnshire Regiment before he retired, he's great fun.'

'They're saying in the kitchen,' Alice said, 'that the assassination of this Austrian archduke in Sarajevo could start a war.'

'I presume that's Mr Wainwright talking.' Pips referred to their butler, who was an avid follower of the national and international news and would often discuss politics with Dr Maitland on an equal footing.

'Well, yes,' Alice admitted, 'but he does seem to know what he's talking about.' She grinned impishly. 'Most of the time, anyway.'

Pips caught her maid's glance in the mirror and they both laughed. It was an unusual relationship between Pips and her maid, for she was not really the kind of young woman who needed – or wanted – a lady's maid, but for once, to keep her mother happy, she had bowed to Henrietta's wishes. Pips was a tomboy who would have been happier if she'd been born male. As it was, she was a beautiful, strong-minded and intelligent nineteen-year-old girl who railed against the accident of her birth. Her life wasn't made any easier by her brother, five years her senior, being able – and allowed – to do all the things she longed to do.

She loved Robert dearly – fiercely, it could be said – and he doted on her. And perhaps he was the only one who truly understood and sympathized with the way she felt. He never tried to talk her out of her daring escapades or belittled her intellectual ability, which he recognized easily matched his own. In fact, deep down, he thought it ridiculous that convention would not allow a woman to do everything that a man could do.

'The world's changing, Pips,' he would say softly. 'Soon, girls and women will be able to follow whatever career they want.'

'It's a man's world, Robert, and it'll never change. Women must know their place and be kept in it.'

'Oh, I don't know,' he would say mildly, trying to keep his sister's ready temper in check, 'women are allowed to go to university and to train as doctors now – not just as nurses.' Then he'd add swiftly, 'though I don't mean that to sound derogatory towards the nursing profession. We couldn't manage without them.'

'Do you think that's what I should do, then? Go into nursing? Since Mother and Father won't allow me to become a doctor,' Pips would ask bitterly.

And then Robert would sigh heavily and say, 'Mother would never agree to that either, Pips.'

And there, their conversation would always end.

Three

It was unusual for the Maitlands not to have dinner guests on a Saturday evening. It had always been a ritual in Henrietta's family for as long as she could remember, and certainly for as long as she had been old enough to sit quietly at the table and speak only when spoken to. She'd carried on the tradition when she'd become mistress of Doddington Hall and had tried to instil the same demure behaviour into her own daughter, but it had been impossible and she had quite given up trying. But, she was obliged to admit, ever since Pips had been allowed to join the diners at the age of thirteen, her conversations had been adult and sensible and remarkably well informed.

Though, still anxious as to how her daughter might appear to outsiders, Henrietta had confided in her closest friend, the major's wife, Rosemary Fieldsend.

'Does her chatter irritate you – or anyone else? Philippa is rather – precocious.'

Rosemary had waved her hand dismissively. 'Hetty, dear, you worry too much. She's a delight. So bright and bubbly and entertaining. Basil thinks the world of her. He looks forward to receiving an invitation from you and always asks – without fail, I might add – "Will Pips be allowed to attend?" So there you are, don't you dare stop her dining with us or Basil will go grumpy. And next time you come to us, you must bring her too. She could always go home earlier than you, if you wish. Taylor could take her home in the pony and trap. He's very trustworthy.'

'Oh, I know that. That wouldn't worry me in the slightest, it's just–' She hesitated.

'You're worried that our other guests, who don't know her, would view a thirteen-year-old, who can talk knowledgeably about politics and world affairs, differently to those who know her.'

Henrietta had sighed. 'Yes, something like that.'

'My dear, look at it another way. When she gets to marriageable age and you're looking for a husband for her, she certainly won't bore her suitors.'

'But will she drive them away? Do young men want a wife who, well...?'

'Who is as intelligent and as well informed as they are?'

Rosemary was thoughtful for a moment. 'Some won't, I agree, but any young man with common sense would welcome it. I'm sure that won't be a problem.'

But, almost seven years later, much to Henrietta's disappointment, there was no steady stream of suitors beating a path to the door of the hall.

'So, why has our major not been able to come tonight?' Pips asked as soon as they had all been served and the servants had left the Great Hall where the family always dined. It was a magnificent, long room with antique oak chests, tables and chairs. Mahogany china cabinets held precious family heirlooms and the front windows looked out over the long driveway, down to the

27

gatehouse and beyond. To the left stood the church where the family and villagers worshipped every Sunday.

'I like old Basil,' Pips added, as she picked up her knife and fork.

'Philippa, show some respect, please,' Henrietta admonished, but her mouth twitched with amusement. It was how the whole family thought of the major; a portly figure with a florid face, a grey handlebar moustache and a booming voice that was more suited to the parade ground than a genteel dining room. But he was always such fun and a great favourite with the Maitland family as a dinner guest. 'He's had to go to London, so his wife said in her note. I know officially he's retired, but I understand – though it's all very hush-hush – that the War Office often call on him for advice.'

'Is it to do with the trouble in Bosnia? I mean, it's only a province of the Austro-Hungarian Empire, isn't it? Is it really that serious?'

'I fear so,' Edwin said.

'Why should it affect us? Britain, I mean. I thought they'd caught the Serbian nationalist who did it. Gavrilo Princip. Wasn't that his name?'

'They have,' Robert put in as he picked up his knife and fork. 'But it's not quite as straightforward as that. It's thought that there was a plot to kill the archduke backed by a Serbian secret society called the Black Hand.'

Henrietta tutted. 'It sounds like a tale from *The Boy's Own Paper.*'

Edwin smiled sadly. 'I only wish it were, my love.'

'If it's true what the papers are saying that a

bomb was thrown at the archduke and his wife earlier on the same day, I presume that's why they think it was a plot and not just some lone assassin.'

'It hit the side of the car and the archduke was uninjured, though I believe several of his officers were hurt,' Robert put in.

'You'd have thought they'd have taken that as a warning and abandoned their trip there and then,' Pips said.

'You would have, especially as they'd been foolish enough to visit Bosnia on one of the country's national anniversaries. Something to do with old conflicts with the Turks, I believe.'

'The Balkans has been a tinderbox for some time,' Edwin said. 'All it has needed is a spark to ignite a conflagration and this might well be it.'

'Was Princip killed?'

Robert shook his head. 'No. He's been arrested, but he insists he was working alone and will not reveal any names of other conspirators – if, of course, there were any.'

'Did he throw a grenade too?'

'I don't know, but he certainly used a pistol, though it looks as if there might have been more than just him involved. There are different stories about how the assassin got his opportunity. Some say it was pure coincidence that the royal car drew up beside him on the return journey and Princip got his chance. Others say he was waiting near a sharp turning over a bridge on the route he thought they would take. Whichever the case, the truth is that he shot the archduke and his second shot hit his wife Sofia when she threw herself across her husband. That is the only regret that Princip will admit to; that he was sorry he'd killed the archduchess.'

'But why do you think it might escalate into a war that might even involve Britain?'

'Hopefully, it won't,' Edwin said, 'but there are so many European alliances that would have to be honoured if trouble should break out.'

'First,' Robert took up the explanation, 'Austria is likely to take some sort of retaliation against Serbia. There has already been a demonstration by students in Vienna where they burned the Serbian flag. The archduke was heir to the Austro-Hungarian throne. If they should attack Serbia, Russia is Serbia's ally and, doubtless, will go to her aid.'

'And Austria-Hungary has an alliance with Germany, so...'

'The Kaiser has already reaffirmed his alliance with Austria. It was in the newspapers only a few days after the assassination.'

'And we,' Pips whispered, her eyes widening in horror as she began to see the reason for her father's fears, 'have a Triple Entente with France and Russia, which Germany mistrusts, believing it threatens its power.'

'Understandable, I would say,' Edwin murmured. 'Wouldn't you?'

'And that,' Henrietta said, trying – but failing – to bring the conversation to an end, 'is why our dinner guest has had to go to the War Office. Just in case.'

'Evidently,' Edwin lowered his voice and leaned forward, even though there was no one else in the room, 'though it's not widely known, Basil is well respected as an adviser to the War Office. He was in the regular army for a long time.'

Pips toyed with her food, her eyes downcast on her plate.

'So we could be drawn into a war that is actually none of our making?'

'That's about the size of it, yes.'

Slowly, she raised her head and met her brother's gaze. 'And if we are embroiled in a war, would you go, Robert?'

For a few moments, it seemed as if the four of them were holding their breath. Then, slowly, Robert nodded. 'We had an Officers' Training Corps at medical school. I was a member, but now, I'd probably volunteer to join the Royal Army Medical Corps.'

Pips lifted her chin with a determination that was not lost on any of her family. 'In that case, then so would I.'

Around the supper table in the Dawson household, the atmosphere was much less formal, but the topic of conversation was exactly the same. Len sat at the head of the table with his mother at the opposite end. Norah sat beside him with their four sons seated on either side of the long kitchen table. Only Alice was missing.

'So, d'you think there'll be a war, Father?' Bernard began.

Len wrinkled his brow. He was small in stature and thin, but incredibly strong for his size. He stooped a little now from long hours wielding heavy tools and his grey hair was thinning. 'Hard to say, son. I hope not, though I have to say I haven't much faith in politicians.'

'If there is,' Roy said, 'I shall volunteer for the Lincolns.' He glanced at his grandmother. 'Same as Grandad Dawson.'

'Me too. I'd go,' Harold said.

'You're far too young, Harold, so you can put that thought out of your head this minute,' Norah snapped.

'I'm sixteen,' Harold retorted. 'Well, next month. They'd take me at sixteen, wouldn't they?'

'Only if they were desperate,' Roy teased. Harold, sitting next to him, punched his shoulder.

'Ouch!'

'Now, boys,' Len admonished gently, but beneath their father's soft tone there was always a hint of steel. They knew from experience not to goad him to anger.

'I'm not sure they'd even take you, Roy,' Len went on. 'They might set the age at eighteen or even higher to start with, but at first they'd only call on the regular army and maybe the territorials or university corps like the one Master Robert was in. You know, men who've already had some kind of training.'

'I'll be eighteen in November,' Roy muttered.

'But I'd be old enough at twenty-four, wouldn't I?' Bernard said.

His mother held his gaze across the table. 'And you'd go, would you? You'd volunteer?'

'Like a shot, Mam.'

They stared at each other for a long moment, before Norah smiled thinly, gave a slight nod and murmured huskily, 'Then I'd be very proud of you, son.'

At the opposite end of the table, Ma's eyes rested on William, the only one who'd not spoken. She didn't ask him questions or even draw attention to him for she thought she knew exactly what William's feelings on the matter would be. It would all come out soon enough. There was no need to cause trouble amongst the family now.

Despite the gravity of their discussion, Robert laughed out loud at Pips's firm declaration. Edwin smiled gently whilst Henrietta cast her eyes to the ceiling and shook her head in exasperation. 'Don't be so silly, Philippa. They won't take girls into the RAMC.'

'No, I didn't mean that exactly, but I would volunteer for some kind of war work.'

'They won't want women.'

'I think that's where you're wrong, Mother. They'll need nurses and–'

'I hope you're not suggesting that you should train as a nurse.'

Pips shrugged. 'Whatever it takes to be of service. But they'll need women to take over the men's jobs in this country. Factory workers, bus drivers–'

'Now you are being extraordinarily silly. Women can't do that sort of work.'

Pips and her brother exchanged a glance. Not only had Pips ridden his motorcycle with an inborn expertise that even he had marvelled at, but she had also secretly driven their father's car on several occasions when Robert had borrowed it ostensibly to take her into the city. It would be no problem for Pips to transfer to a larger vehicle. No problem at all.

'Mrs Pankhurst wouldn't agree with you there, Mother,' Pips said.

'That woman!'

'Only yesterday I was reading an article by one of her followers. The writer believes that, should war come, Mrs Pankhurst is likely to decree that all her followers should lay aside their ambitions for the vote and devote their energies to the needs of their country.'

'And not before time,' Henrietta muttered.

'No doubt many of her ladies will volunteer for nursing duties and other such work,' Pips carried on, as if her mother had not spoken. 'And I will be one of them.'

Henrietta glared at her daughter. 'Don't tell me you've joined her movement?'

'Not exactly, Mother. I don't agree with their militant attitude. To me, smashing windows and chaining oneself to railings isn't sending the right message of educated thought and rational behaviour. But what I think might happen is that if women prove themselves reliable, hard-working and undaunted in the face of the horrors they are likely to encounter in war, then they will have demonstrated that they have the right to vote.'

Henrietta did not reply. Instead she stood up, rang the bell for the servants to clear away and marched out of the room, the set of her shoulders displaying her irritation.

Four

As the news became more and more serious each day during the month of July, young men up and down the country were caught up in the fervour of patriotism.

'Mother,' Robert said at breakfast one morning in the middle of July when there were just the two of them sitting down to porridge and kippers, 'I've had a letter from a friend. We got to know each other at medical school, though he was a year ahead of me. He went on to train in surgery and now he's applying for a post at Lincoln County Hospital and will be coming for an interview next week. May I invite him to stay with us?'

Henrietta smiled. 'Of course, my dear. Tell me about him.'

'His name is Giles Kendall and he's from Scarborough. He's a couple of years older than me, tall, with bright blue eyes and fair curly hair. He's very good-looking and comes from a good family. I think his teeth are sound, though I haven't inspected them.'

'Don't tease me, Robert,' Henrietta admonished. But she had the grace to laugh as she added, 'Is he married or betrothed?'

Robert chuckled. 'The inevitable question about any young man who comes within a hundred yards of Pips. But no, actually, he's not. University students, and medical students in particular, are far too busy for courtship and also too poor. He's an only son and his parents dote on him, but his father's a teacher, which, whilst being a genteel and respectable profession, is not the best-paid occupation he might have.'

'There's no disgrace in that. You say this young man specialized in surgery?'

'Yes. That's why he's applying to Lincoln hospital, because I was telling him about how brilliant Father's colleagues are there.' Robert laughed. 'And I've promised I'll send all my patients to him.'

'Please give him time to learn his trade properly first, Robert.' There was a pause before she added, 'You are still planning to start working in the practice after the August Bank Holiday, aren't you? Your father's finding it harder as he gets older, you know.'

'Father, old? Never!'

Edwin was mild-mannered and kindly, a little portly but always smartly dressed in a morning coat and a brightly coloured waistcoat. 'My attire amuses the children and makes the old ladies smile,' he would always explain, peering over his spectacles, his eyes full of mischief.

By contrast, Henrietta was slim and preferred to dress in pastel shades, her sleek grey hair piled up on top of her head.

'He'll be sixty in six years' time and he wants you to be well established in his practice by the time he might wish to retire. And even now, it's time he took a few more days off.'

'Father and I have already discussed it and, yes, I will start straight after the Bank Holiday in two

36

weeks' time.'

Henrietta smiled. 'Good. The room set aside for your surgery next to your father's is all ready.' She stood up. 'And now I must go and talk to Mrs Warren' – Henrietta was referring to the hall's housekeeper – 'and warn her that we will have a guest to stay next week. I can't wait to meet him. You never know, Robert, he might be just the sort of young man that Pips might like...'

'Oh Mother!'

Giles Kendall was everything that Robert had described to his mother – and more. He was charming and courteous and had a lively sense of humour that soon had them all laughing over the dinner table. The two young men were obviously great friends and were not shy in recounting some of their escapades at medical school. Pips listened with growing envy. But her jealousy was not personal; she rather liked Giles. It was just the unfairness of having missed out on all the camaraderie. The boarding school to which she had been sent had been stuffy and snobby; there'd been very little fun under the strict regime of the spinster headmistress.

'Do you ride?' she asked Giles when there was a pause in the conversation.

Giles laughed. 'A motorcycle. It needs looking after, but I'm afraid I'm no mechanic.'

'You'll have to speak to William Dawson whilst you're here,' Edwin said. 'He works for us in the gardens and on the estate. He's a natural with anything mechanical. I never have to take my motor to a garage; William looks after it.'

'I will, sir. Perhaps' – his bright blue gaze was directed at Pips – 'you would introduce me to him?'

Her smile widened. 'Of course,' she answered but did not add, in front of her mother, what was in her mind. *As long as you let me have a ride on your motorcycle.*

Five

'How did you get on?' Pips was watching out for Giles when he returned to the hall following his interview in Lincoln.

He pulled a face. 'Hard to say. The process was rigorous to say the least. They asked a lot of questions that don't seem to have any relevance to the post I'm applying for.'

'What sort of questions?'

Giles waved his hand vaguely. 'Oh, about my background. What my father does ... that sort of thing. Why does that matter? It's me they'd be appointing, not my father.'

'He's a teacher, isn't he? So Robert said. That's an admirable profession. A vocation, I'd say, just like being a doctor.'

'Well, yes, I suppose so,' Giles murmured.

He seemed downcast, so Pips linked her arm through his. Although they'd only just met, she felt at ease with him. 'Well, now you can forget all about it and enjoy the next two days with us. I'll show you around our grounds and perhaps even the sights of Lincoln.'

'I gave them this address as well as my own. I hope that was all right.'

'Of course it is. We're all anxious to hear if you've got the post. But will they let you know as soon as that?'

Giles shrugged. 'I don't know, but with all this talk of war...'

'We'll forget all about that for the moment. I'll show you our beautiful cathedral and the castle. And,' she laughed impishly, 'I'll race you up Steep Hill. But first' – she leaned closer to him – 'you've got to let me have a go on your motorcycle.'

Giles's shocked face made Pips laugh all the louder.

'Is she safe?' he asked Robert worriedly when, the following morning after breakfast, the three of them met in the stable yard.

'As houses,' Robert laughed. 'You just watch her.' He raised his voice. 'Here, Pips, borrow my helmet again.'

'Again?' Giles asked. He glanced from one to the other. 'Have you ridden his motorcycle before, then?'

Pips grinned and nodded, her eyes sparkling.

'I only got mine last week,' Robert said, 'but I think she's spent more time on it than I have.'

'There's William cleaning Father's car. Let's call him over. I'm sure he'd love to see your machine, Giles.'

As she raised her voice and called his name, William Dawson glanced up. He was tall, broad-shouldered and physically very strong, but with mouse-coloured hair and hazel eyes his appearance was rather nondescript and overshadowed by his more vibrant brothers, who were all brown-haired and dark-eyed and ebullient in personality. William was reserved, shy in certain company, though he was a gentle giant and would help anyone in need. As Pips beckoned him, he walked towards them, but even before he reached them, his gaze was on the two motorcycles standing side by side.

'My word – a brand new Bradbury. I never thought to see one of these. Yours, is it, sir?' He glanced briefly at Giles.

Giles nodded, but said modestly, 'But if it needs attention at any time, I'm afraid I'm hopeless with anything mechanical.'

William's eyes shone. 'I'd be happy to take a look at her if needed. That's if you'd trust me, sir.'

'I'd be delighted, William. Thank you. And if you ever need your appendix taken out, then I'm your man.'

The four of them laughed together and then William added, quite seriously, 'If you get the job at the hospital, sir, I'll be happy to help you any time – with or without my appendix.'

It seemed that all the staff at the hall knew about their visitor's interview.

'There are no secrets in this place, Giles,' Robert murmured.

Pips was impatient. 'Let's go round the back of the stables. I don't want anyone from the house seeing me. They'll likely tell Mother.'

The two young men dutifully pushed their

motorcycles out of sight of the windows of the hall with William, intrigued, following them. As Pips mounted the Bradbury and Robert sat astride his own machine, Giles and William watched in fascination, and not without a little awe, as Pips rode away.

'I never thought I'd see the day,' Giles murmured. 'A girl riding a motorcycle.'

William chuckled. 'You obviously don't know Miss Pips very well yet. She's a brilliant horsewoman. She rides the moodiest stallion we've got in the stables. No one can handle him like she can. And now it looks as if she's going to be every bit as good on a motorcycle.'

'Does she drive the car?'

Again William laughed and tapped the side of his nose. 'Not officially, but yes, she does. I think her father suspects, but we try to keep it from her mother. Mrs Maitland's ambitions for her daughter are rather different.'

'Ye-es,' Giles said slowly. 'I expect I can guess what those are.'

No more was said. William was not one to gossip about his employers and his loyalty to Miss Pips was constant. He would willingly lay down his life for her.

Six

'Giles?' Pips knocked on his bedroom door. When it opened she said, 'Would you like to see the grounds before dinner? It's a lovely evening.'

'Indeed I would.'

They left the house by the front door, walked to the left, past the kitchen garden, and came to a smooth square of grass with hoops and mallets.

'This is the croquet lawn,' Pips said.

Giles laughed. 'I haven't ever played that.'

'Then I'll teach you. It's quite easy. D'you see those three lovely sweet chestnut trees on the far side of the lawn? We think they're older than the house. And then, there's the orchard...'

They walked beneath the shade of trees laden with growing fruit and came at last to the end of the gardens where they looked out over the fields. 'We farm all this,' Pips said, waving her arm.

'What a lovely part of the world to live,' Giles murmured.

Over dinner that evening even Henrietta could not prevent the talk of war.

'I think it's getting serious,' Robert remarked.

His father sighed. 'I'm afraid I've thought so ever since the archduke and his wife were assassinated. The last three weeks since it happened have seemed unnaturally quiet. Ominously so, I've thought.'

'Have you seen today's news?' Robert said. 'Austria has made a series of humiliating demands upon Serbia, which they cannot possibly accept. It's almost as if they are forcing Serbia's rejection so that they – Austria, that is – can declare war.'

'And just when there's a real international crisis, half the heads of Europe seem to be on state visits or on holiday, would you believe?' Edwin said.

'What about Britain? What are we going to do?' Pips asked.

Edwin wrinkled his forehead. 'I expect we'll try to be the mediator. I'd love to be a fly on the wall in Sir Edward Grey's Foreign Office, but the closest I can hope to get is a chat with Basil and even that is denied me at the moment. I'm sure he will have some inside information. He's great friends with our local MP too.'

'I don't think they'd listen to the British,' Pips said. 'I think the other countries involved would view anything we tried to do as interference.'

'I bet it won't be long before we've got the British Royal Navy on standby though,' Giles said quietly. He paused and then asked, 'If we do become involved, would you volunteer, Robert?'

Before her brother could answer, Pips said, 'He's going to enlist in the RAMC.'

Robert smiled indulgently at his sister's impetuosity. 'I've decided that I'll wait a while and see what happens. In the meantime, I'll carry on with my career plan, but if I do volunteer, it would be in the medical corps, yes. What about you?'

Giles nodded. 'Me too, though I'd like to get a

little more experience of surgery first. They'll need surgeons and I don't want to be just a butcher.'

Pips saw her mother wince, but Henrietta said nothing.

'Do *you* think they'll have a role for women in the war?' Pips asked, directing her question at Giles.

'I'd be very surprised if they didn't, but doing what – apart from nursing – I wouldn't know.'

After dinner, they all withdrew to the room they called the Brown Parlour near the Great Hall. The windows looked out over the rear gardens and family portraits adorned the panelled walls. It was where the family relaxed after their evening meal when there were no dinner guests and where, each morning, Henrietta planned her day. Edwin would often join her there in the evenings, though he loved to spend time with his books in the library on the opposite side of the hallway. This evening, although Giles was a guest, Henrietta had decided to treat him as one of the family. He walked next to Pips as they followed her mother. 'You could, of course, drive an ambulance,' he murmured.

Pips turned towards him, her green eyes gleaming. 'Abroad, you mean? Actually near the fighting?'

Giles nodded. 'That's where they'll be needed the most and' – his blue gaze looked straight into her eyes – 'if I'm not mistaken, you're not a young lady who would be squeamish.'

Pips chuckled. 'I think my mother would take issue with you about the "young lady" bit, but no, I think I'm quite tough.'

Soberly now, Giles said, 'It would be dangerous work. You'd probably be needed right near the front line to take casualties to first-aid posts or even further back behind the lines to hospitals, depending on the severity of their injuries. None of us know yet quite how they will organize things.'

They paused for a moment and, as she looked into his clear blue eyes, Pips felt a frisson of excitement. 'You really think I'd be *allowed* to do that?'

'I don't think your parents would be too happy–'

'No, no, I don't mean them – would the authorities allow women to do such work?'

Giles sighed. 'I think this war is going to be like no other we've ever known.'

'You seem to know a lot about it. How come?'

'My father served in the Boer War and he believes that things have moved on since then. There have been more inventions that will be used in warfare.'

'I see,' Pips said slowly, but as she opened her mouth to ask more questions Henrietta's voice made them both jump.

'Come along, you two. The coffee's getting cold.' Her admonishment, though, was gentle. She didn't want to put this nice young man off. From what she could see so far, he was perfect husband material for Pips and they seemed to be getting along so well, even though they had only just met.

Henrietta began to hope.

Seven

The Boer War was also the topic of conversation over the Dawsons' supper table.

'What was it like, Dad?' Bernard wanted to know. Bernard, the eldest at twenty-four, was always the one to lead the conversation round the meal table. 'I know you weren't in it yourself, but you must have read about it.'

'It was a messy war,' Len said. 'The British losses were high because of disease as well as actual combat. Typhoid, dysentery and the like were rife. I'm glad I wasn't in it. Some lads from the village – well, they're men now, of course – were involved and they reckoned that the British soldiers were unprepared for the type of countryside they were fighting in and poorly trained for the conditions they faced.'

'Really, Len, must we talk about such things over the supper table and in front of Boy too?' Norah said.

'I'm not a boy, Ma,' Harold said indignantly. 'I'll soon be old enough to fight for my country, just like my brothers. I wish everyone would stop calling me that childish nickname.'

'That's the spirit, Harold,' Ma said and her glance rested for a moment on William, but, yet again, he was taking no part in the conversation. She wondered how long it would be before the rest of the family noticed his reticence, but at present the excitement amongst the other three boys masked his silence.

Bernard was still talking animatedly. He was of average height but muscular from his work at the anvil, for it was he who had taken on the black-smithing, helped by Harold, who was learning the trade under his guidance. He had brown hair and twinkling eyes and a ready smile, though his expression could darken in a trice, for he had a swift temper. He was a great favourite with the village girls, though at present he did not have a serious girlfriend.

Roy, however, who helped his father in the carpenter's workshop, was walking out with Betty Cooper, the daughter of the farm manager on Mrs Maitland's estate. Betty worked in the dairy and their courtship was approved of by both families. Even Ma, who was very choosy about who her grandchildren should keep company with, approved of the quietly spoken, well-mannered girl. Betty was a pretty girl with fair hair, a clear skin and she openly adored Roy. Roy resembled his father; he was thin and wiry with light brown hair.

'Though you're far too young to be thinking of marriage yet,' Ma, who still had some sway in the family, had pronounced when the blossoming romance had become common knowledge. 'I don't believe in women working once they are married. They should be in the home caring for their husband and any children that might come along. And they will come along, so, Roy, you need to be earning enough to keep both of you, and don't tell me the old adage "two can live as cheaply as one", because it's nonsense.'

But the brother who had a real roving eye was young Harold. Tall for his age, Harold was a good-looking, cheeky sixteen-year-old – well, almost – and the village girls of the same age simpered and blushed whenever he winked saucily at them.

William had never shown any interest in the village girls; he knew that if anyone found out about the girl who held his heart in the palm of her hand, he would be mocked and ridiculed. So, he kept silent, just as he was keeping quiet now whilst the talk of war – and his brothers' excitement – raged around him. He was the quiet one in the family. He could see his grandmother glancing at him now and again. Thankfully, she seemed to be the only one who had noticed his reluctance to join in the conversation and he was grateful to her for not trying to engage him in the discussions. But just as William was thinking he was being overlooked, Bernard suddenly became aware of his brother's silence.

'What about you, William?' he asked his brother directly. 'Will you volunteer?'

There was a waiting stillness around the table, as if all the other members of the family now realized that William had not yet voiced his opinion about the threat of war. Colour flooded William's face, but he said steadily and firmly, 'No, I wouldn't.'

Eight

Now the gaze of every member of his family was upon him.

Bernard was frowning. 'Whatever do you mean?'

'Exactly what I say. I wouldn't volunteer.'

'But you'd have to go if they brought in conscription,' Roy put in.

'Not necessarily.'

His three brothers rounded on him.

'So you wouldn't defend your country?' Bernard said.

'He's a bloody coward, that's what he is,' Harold spat.

'Harold! I will not have you using language like that,' Norah snapped.

Quietly, William said, 'I don't believe in killing another human being.'

'It's a praiseworthy sentiment, William,' Len said softly, 'but it's not a luxury you can afford when your homeland is threatened. You have to be prepared to fight for king and country.'

'And I would,' William said at once, 'if we were attacked. Of course I would. But we're not being invaded. We're talking about us *declaring* war on other countries. That's totally different.'

'It's all to do with the alliances that were put in place to try to keep the peace in Europe.'

'Well, it's not working, is it?'

'Sadly, no,' Len was forced to agree. 'But we

49

have to keep our promises at national level just as we do in our own lives.'

'I didn't make any such promises.'

'No, but the Government did on our behalf and we voted for the Government.'

'No, I didn't vote and, even if I had been able to, I wouldn't have voted for this Government and I certainly wouldn't have voted to plunge our country into a war that is nothing to do with us.'

'Of course it's to do with us.'

William shook his head as if he didn't understand their reasoning. 'Not unless this country is attacked,' he said stubbornly.

Bernard cast a glance at their father. 'Can't you make him understand, Dad? I don't want everyone thinking we've a coward in the family.'

Len stared down the table at William. There was disappointment and anger in his eyes, yet when he spoke his tone was quiet. 'Son, alliances, treaties between countries – call them what you will – must be kept. Maybe we don't agree with everything that our Government does, but, as a nation, we have to abide by their decisions. Right now, our treaty is with Russia and France and if they go to war, then we are honour bound to support them and possibly go to war alongside them. I think we also have an understanding that if Belgium, a neutral country, were to be attacked, we'd go to her aid.'

'I believe,' Ma said softly, 'that there are certain religious groups who refuse to go to war. The Quakers, for example.'

'Oh, going to become Quaker now, is he?' Harold scoffed, 'so that he doesn't have to fight?'

'No, I'm just pointing out that there are people whose personal decisions are respected.'

'Well, I don't like it and the rest of the village won't either when they find out,' Harold said and Bernard and Roy nodded their agreement.

'And how are they going to know?'

Harold glared at William. 'Because I'm going to make damn sure they will.'

Nine

There was no such talk of pacifism at the hall, though there was caution in rushing to volunteer, at least by the two young men. Pips was not so ready to wait; she was eager to do something right now. The following morning she pounced on the newspaper as soon as it was delivered and scoured its front page for news.

'They're still dithering,' she said, throwing the paper onto the breakfast table in disgust.

'Thank you, Pips,' Edwin said mildly as he picked up the discarded paper and rearranged the pages back into their right order.

'Sorry, Father. It's just – why can't they get on with it? Make some decisions.'

'Because,' Henrietta said as she sat down at the table, 'they're not as foolhardy as you to precipitate their countries into a war. Now, my dear, sit down and eat your breakfast and – please – let's have no more talk of war, at least not for a while.'

'I've eaten, thank you, Mother. I'm going riding. Midnight could do with a gallop. Robert, Giles, are you coming?'

'Not this morning, Pips. I need to shadow Father today if I'm to start working in the practice properly after the Bank Holiday. But maybe Giles would...'

Giles pulled an apologetic face. 'I'm sorry, I don't ride. Being an academic, my father didn't approve of what he saw as the extravagance of riding lessons for my sister and me.' He smiled ruefully. 'Particularly since we didn't have a horse.'

For a brief moment Pips stared at him in astonishment. Then she blinked and colour suffused her face. She hadn't meant to embarrass him. 'Oh – I'm sorry, I didn't think.'

'That's your trouble, Philippa,' Henrietta murmured.

'It's quite all right, Pips,' Giles said smoothly. 'You weren't to know, but I do,' he added impishly, 'play chess.'

Pips's eyes gleamed. 'Ah, then I challenge you to a match this evening.'

Giles glanced uncertainly towards Henrietta. 'I really ought to leave today. I don't want to outstay my welcome. You've been wonderfully kind.'

'Nonsense,' Henrietta said briskly and smiled at him. 'You couldn't outstay your welcome, as you put it. Please – stay as long as you wish and certainly over the weekend, if you'd like to.'

'I'll see you at luncheon, then,' Pips said and, with a swift smile, she was gone.

Henrietta sighed inwardly. She hoped her daughter's waywardness wasn't putting off this nice young man. She glanced at him to see that

Giles was still staring at the door, through which Pips had disappeared, with a thoughtful expression.

'Midnight's all ready for you, Miss Pips,' William greeted her. 'I guessed you'd be riding this morning.'

Pips rewarded him with a bright smile. 'Thank you, William. I need a good gallop too. I'm so fed up of all this hesitating by the Government. Why don't they get on with making a decision? Are we going to war or not?'

Colour suffused William's face and his head dropped.

Ever observant, Pips said, 'What is it, William? I can see something's wrong.'

He was silent for a moment, then slowly he raised his head, his eyes anguished. 'It's all this talk of war. My brothers – even Harold – can't wait to volunteer. And I' – he pulled in a deep, shuddering breath – 'I can't agree with them.'

'You mean you wouldn't volunteer?'

Miserably, William shook his head. He knew he was going to lose Pips's respect and the thought was like a dagger through his heart, but his principles were stronger even than his devotion to her.

But her voice was soft as she asked, 'And you'd be prepared to stand up against everyone to stick to your guns? Oh, sorry' – she grinned sheepishly – 'no pun intended.'

He shrugged off her apology. 'Yes, I would. I can't face the thought of taking another man's life, even if they are our supposed enemy.'

'I admire your...' She hesitated, searching for the right word.

'Foolishness,' William finished for her.

Pips shook her head. 'No, no, I wasn't going to say that. Courage, that's the word.'

'Courage?' William laughed wryly. 'My family think I'm a coward.'

'Have they said that?'

He nodded.

'They're wrong. It takes a special kind of bravery to be the only one standing up against everyone else. But it won't be just your family, you know, who'll disapprove.'

'I know.' He paused and then asked, tentatively, 'So – so you don't think I'm a coward?'

'Most definitely not, but what I think you should do, William, is find some other way to serve your country in a time of war, if it does come to that.'

'How?'

Pips wrinkled her brow. 'I don't know, but I'll give it some thought.'

Ten

As Pips galloped across the fields, the wind streaming through her flowing hair, the farm labourers stopped their work to watch her. 'There she goes,' they said, smiling, for they were all, without exception, fond of the feisty, outspoken young woman. 'It's a pity,' they'd say, 'that she won't be the one to inherit the estate, though the son will be a good master, no doubt. But there's just something about Miss Pips that has us all eating out of her hand.'

'And just look at her on that horse. He's a wild one.'

'He matches her spirit,' they'd laugh together and then return to their work with a smile on their faces for having seen her that morning.

Pips reined in, dismounted and walked beside Midnight for a while. It was unusually cool and breezy for July, but it was still not, Pips thought, a day for anyone to be thinking about plunging their country into conflict. Her thoughts turned to William. Whilst she did not agree with him, she could respect his feelings. He was a gentle soul and though he worked for the estate, his main work now was in the gardens of the house, the parkland and the stables when he was needed. She remembered how, as a youngster, he'd run from the sight of a pig being killed. They hadn't been able to find him for hours and even now, he never wanted to be around when animals were killed or sent for slaughter. And war was a slaughter, however much anyone tried to glorify it. But there was one thing that William was good at and no one could deny it. He was clever with machinery of any kind and was in his element at harvest time when he was in sole charge of keeping the threshing engine going. He also kept Dr Maitland's car in reliable working order and his eyes had lit up the day that Robert had ridden his Phelon & Moore motorcycle into the yard.

But what to do about him now? If his family didn't understand him, then there was little chance that anyone else in the village would either. He was in for a tough time.

'Oh, Midnight,' she said, resting her cheek against the horse's neck. 'What are we to do about William? You'd tell me if you could, wouldn't you, my beautiful boy?'

With a sigh, Pips mounted and turned her horse towards home.

Back in the yard, the stable lad was waiting for them.

'I'll groom him, Jake. I have some thinking to do and it always helps. Besides, it helps me bond with him.'

Jake, a thin, gawky boy, grinned. 'I dun't reckon you and this horse could be any closer. He idolizes you, Miss Pips.' The young boy could have added, 'Like we all do', but was too shy to make such a bold remark. Instead, he said, 'You're the only one he'll do anything for. He plays us up summat rotten when you're not about.'

'Do you, Midnight?' she pretended to scold her horse. 'We can't have that sort of behaviour. Now, you be a good boy for Jake. You hear me?'

The horse harrumphed and pawed the ground, just as if he understood.

'D'you want me to hold the rope for you, Miss?'

'He'll be fine. He'll just stand, won't you, boy?'

With a hoof pick, Pips removed all the dirt and small stones from Midnight's hooves. Then, using different brushes in turn, she groomed him until his black coat was smooth and shining. She sponged his face and then gently combed his mane and his tail.

'There. You'll do.' She stood back to admire her handiwork. 'What a handsome fellow you are. Jake will look after you now.'

With a final pat on the horse's neck and a nod of thanks to Jake, Pips turned towards the house.

'Giles has had a letter delivered this morning – by hand,' Robert whispered on the Saturday morning, 'but he's disappeared up to his room to read it. I don't like to ask.'

'Well, I will,' Pips said. She ran lightly up the central staircase to the first floor and turned to the left to the guest room where Giles was sleeping. It was the bedroom they called the Tiger Room, with a four-poster bed, red drapes and curtains and a patterned carpet. Nearby was a dressing room for the comfort of their guests. She rapped sharply on the door.

'Giles – are you there?'

She heard movement in the room and a few seconds later, the door opened. He was holding a sheet of paper in his hand but, because his face was in shadow from the window behind him, she was unable to read his expression. As forthright as ever, she asked, 'Have you had news about your position at the hospital?'

'Yes – I have.'

'And?'

'I've been appointed to the post.'

Pips clapped her hands. 'Oh, that's marvellous. Congratulations. We must celebrate tonight.' She paused, as he remained silent. 'Aren't you pleased?'

'Yes – yes, of course I am.'

'I feel there's a "but".'

'It's just that I can't feel celebratory when there's the threat of war hanging over us all.'

She put her head on one side and regarded him thoughtfully. 'You know, what Robert said the other night sounds eminently sensible to me. Perhaps you should both carry on with your careers as planned until we know exactly what is happening. Even if war is declared, it might well be over in a few months, weeks even.'

He smiled thinly. 'You're right, of course.'

'Please come down and tell the others about your success. They'll be delighted.' She held out her hand towards him and he took it. Together, still holding hands, they went downstairs and into the parlour where Henrietta was planning the day's meals with Mrs Bentley, the cook. Edwin was opening up his Saturday morning surgery and three patients had already arrived at the rear door of the house.

'Mother—'

Henrietta glanced up to see her daughter and their young house guest holding hands. Though not displeased, she was startled to see how quickly their friendship had developed. Could it be a real romance?

'Sorry to interrupt, but Giles has wonderful news. He's got the position at the hospital. Where's Robert? We must tell him. I thought he was waiting for us in the hall, but he seems to have disappeared.'

Giles seemed slightly embarrassed by Pips's enthusiasm, but was relieved when Henrietta smiled and said, 'Then this calls for a celebration, my dears. As for Robert, he's sitting in on your father's surgery this morning. High time he got to know his future patients.'

Pips giggled. 'He's known most of them all his life.'

'Yes.' Henrietta pulled a face. 'I suppose, in some ways, that might prove to be a disadvantage. Still, never mind about that now. We shall see in due course, no doubt, how it all works out.' She turned to Giles. 'Congratulations. I am delighted for you. And please, you must stay here as long as you want. When do you take up your position? You could live here, if you wanted.'

'That's very kind of you, Mrs Maitland, but I shall get lodgings near to the hospital, though I would very much like to visit you now and again on my days off.'

'You'll always be very welcome.'

Suddenly becoming aware that they were still holding hands, Pips and Giles let go of each other; reluctantly, it seemed to the hopeful mother.

Eleven

'So, what are we doing on the Bank Holiday weekend?' Pips asked as they sat at dinner that evening. 'It's only just over a week away now.'

Champagne in honour of Giles's good news was being served and tonight, at least, all talk of war had been banned by Henrietta, even though, over the last few days, the news had become ever more serious.

'I thought we'd take Giles on a tour of the city that is now to become his home,' Robert suggested. 'We'll play at being tourists. Perhaps, you would lend us the car, Father, if you don't need it.'

Edwin smiled. 'No. I don't mind. If I get an urgent call out, I can always take the pony and trap like I did in the old days.'

'That's settled, then,' Pips said firmly. 'I hope you'll be here for the weekend – unless, of course, you want to go home to Scarborough.' She couldn't keep the note of regret out of her tone at the thought that Giles might not spend the time with them.

But Giles smiled. 'No, my parents are visiting my married sister in Northumberland that weekend. I'd be delighted to come here. Thank you.'

But during the week that followed the fear of war escalated. Serbia rejected Austria's unreasonable demands and any hope of a diplomatic resolution between the two countries lay in tatters. The following day, Serbia mobilized its army and at the same time letters flew between the Czar of Russia and his distant cousin Kaiser Wilhelm of Germany. Nicholas warned the Kaiser that he could not remain uninvolved if Serbia was attacked.

'Have you seen the news?' Pips came running into the Great Hall flourishing the morning's paper.

'How can we, my dear, when you're holding it?' Edwin said mildly, and he held out his hand to take it from her and read the news for himself.

But Pips couldn't wait. 'It's Austria. They've invaded Serbia.'

'What's that?' Robert asked, entering the room at that moment. 'They're at war? Austria and Serbia?'

The family glanced at one another with sober faces.

'This is it, then,' Robert said, 'because unless someone backs down pretty quickly, it's going to drag a whole lot more countries into the fray.' He sat down and helped himself to his breakfast, but his mouth was set in a grim line. If what he suspected happened, he would have some very difficult decisions to make over the coming weeks.

Each day the news was even more worrying. In Russia, the Czar mobilized his troops and, in response, the Kaiser warned him that unless he ceased this action, Germany would put her troops on a war footing. All Britain's attempts at mediation were met with contempt and on Saturday, 1 August, Kaiser Wilhelm declared war on his Russian relative.

But on the August Bank Holiday Monday, determined to put all thoughts of war behind them at least for one day, the three young people set off in high spirits.

From the centre of the city, they walked up Steep Hill.

'I promise you, it's worth the effort,' Pips laughed, as Giles puffed his way to the top. 'You'll love our cathedral.'

It was cool and quiet inside and Giles sank into the nearest pew and gazed around him. 'Magnificent,' he murmured.

'You must see the two rose windows and St Hugh's Choirs. Oh, and the Chapter House. And we mustn't forget the imp. I bet you can't find him.'

'The what?' Giles laughed.

'The Lincoln Imp. He's famous. Haven't you heard of him?'

Giles shook his head.

'Legend has it that he was turned to stone by angels because he was causing havoc in the cathedral. He sits high up in the Angel Choir. Come on, I'll show you...'

Whilst her young mistress did not need her and Henrietta had given permission, Alice had the day off. She went home to her family, but it was not the happy day she had hoped for. She walked into a strained atmosphere and it was left to her grandmother to explain.

'They're all at loggerheads over this threat of war,' Ma said. 'Bernard, Roy and even Boy are all determined to volunteer, but William is adamant he'll take no part in the fighting. It's causing a rift in the family, Alice, and I don't like it. We've always been close-knit. There've never been rows like we're getting now.'

'Rows?' Alice was shocked. Whilst siblings in other families fell out constantly, the Dawsons never quarrelled; they were renowned throughout the village for being the happiest, most united family for miles.

'Oh yes,' Ma said firmly. 'The others are hardly speaking to William and when they do, it's to criticize him for his beliefs.'

'His beliefs?' Alice was puzzled. 'I don't under-stand.'

Ma sighed. 'He says he can't be a party to the killing, that he can't bring himself to kill another human being.'

'I see,' Alice said slowly. 'Well, I'm not surprised, he's always been...' She hesitated, not sure of the right word to use.

'Cowardly,' Ma suggested.

'No, no,' Alice said swiftly. 'Not that. Sensitive. I suppose that's the word I'm looking for.'

'We can't afford to be soft when it comes to defending our island from invaders.'

Alice stared at her as she whispered, 'Is that what's going to happen?'

'Don't you hear – or read – the news at the hall?'

'Not really. Mr Wainwright keeps us servants informed, though I think he adds his own view of things on to what the newspapers are saying, so I'm not quite sure what's *actually* happening.' She paused and then added, 'You really think there's going to be a war, Ma?' Mrs Dawson senior was called 'Ma' throughout the family and even one or two of the villagers had adopted the name. She was one of the oldest – and most respected – inhabitants of the small village.

'I'm sure of it and if there is, then two, if not three, of your brothers will go.'

Twelve

Whilst everyone was enjoying the Bank Holiday, Germany declared war on France. On the following day, 4 August, Germany invaded Belgium, ignoring the seventy-five-year-old treaty guaranteeing its neutrality. The British Government sent an ultimatum to Germany that they should recall their troops from Belgium by midnight. At 10.45 that evening, the King held a Council to declare war on Germany. In stark contrast to the happy holiday weekend they had enjoyed, people awoke the following morning to find themselves at war. That evening, over dinner, when Henrietta could no longer ban any such talk, Edwin read out the statement printed in the newspapers that war had been declared upon Germany.

'I wouldn't want to be in Herbert Asquith's shoes right now,' Edwin murmured, referring to the Prime Minister, who shouldered the burden of taking the country into war.

'So what happens now?' Pips asked eagerly.

'We're the only European country not to have conscription, so, initially, it will be left to our regular army, who, though smaller, are highly trained.'

'But will they have enough artillery?'

'Very doubtful,' Edwin said, 'but what we do have in our favour is a much larger navy with battleships and cruisers.'

'They won't be much use if we're to stop Germany marching through Belgium to get to France,' Robert said. 'I really don't like the sound of it. What are they calling it? The Schlieffen Plan? I don't see how our regular army could cope. Surely, they'll be calling for volunteers.'

'What's the Schlieffen Plan?' Pips was intrigued and, as always, wanted to understand everything that was happening.

'Way back in 1905, General Schlieffen devised a plan to launch a surprise attack by sweeping through Belgium into France before their allies – Russia in particular – had time to mobilize. They banked on being able to defeat France in six weeks.'

Horrified, Pips said, 'But – but how can they do that? March through Belgium, I mean. Has Belgium agreed? Surely not?'

Robert shook his head. 'Of course they haven't. That's what's causing all the trouble and pulling us into the war. We guaranteed Belgium's neutrality about seventy-five years ago, but Germany was gambling on us ignoring that old promise and not supporting Belgium now. But they've misread British loyalty. The German Army is already marching through Belgium towards France and we have to help stop them.'

'But how do you know all this? About the Schlieffen Plan? Surely it was top secret – for the Germans, I mean.'

Edwin gave a wry smile but as he opened his mouth to speak, Pips pointed her finger at him and took the word from his lips. 'Old Basil! It was him, wasn't it?'

Edwin nodded and now he chuckled openly. 'The major has a rare way with people. They think of him as something of a buffoon. But he is a wily old bird. He appears to drink copious amounts of whisky and pretends to be sharing secrets, which, of course, he is not. But, drawn in by his affable, loquacious manner, others find themselves opening up to him and telling him all sorts of things they shouldn't.'

'And he and Mrs Fieldsend have lived all over the world following his army career,' Henrietta put in, 'and have met a great many people from the military, from Government and from high society.'

'And that is precisely why he has been called to London,' Edwin said, his eyes twinkling, 'and why we are deprived of his entertaining and, I might say, informative company.'

Pips blinked. 'Oh,' was all she could think of to say.

The conversation followed much the same pattern in the Dawson household.

'I shall go as soon as they ask for volunteers,' Bernard said and Roy echoed his declaration.

'Me too,' Harold said stoutly, but was told, yet again, that he wasn't old enough. The boy pouted, but said no more. William, as always, said nothing, and now the rest of the family merely ignored him. He came and went from home to his work, facing resentful silence at home and questions at work, which he was not prepared to answer. Inwardly, he hoped and prayed that the skirmish would be just that and that it would indeed 'all be over by

Christmas', as was being said.

The day after the official declaration of war, Robert took up his position as junior partner in his father's general practice. A consulting room, adjacent to his father's, had been equipped and the young man welcomed his first patient. This was not a success; Mrs Bess Cooper, the wife of the estate's farm manager, came into the room. She was a big woman; tall and well built, and somewhat overweight. She presented a formidable figure and there were not many in the village who dared to cross her. But if there was one person in the community whom she did revere – other than Mrs Maitland – then it was someone with the title Doctor in front of his name.

'Oh, it's you, Master Robert. Is your father not here?'

'He is here, Mrs Cooper, but I have started in the practice today. How may I help you?'

'Ah well now, I don't rightly know if I should see you, Master Robert. I've known you since you were a little lad in britches.' The woman smiled, but she was obviously ill at ease. 'It don't seem right that you should be doctoring me.' Bess couldn't quite come to terms with the thought that he was now to become familiar with intimate parts of her body.

Robert hid his smile; he'd rather suspected that he was going to encounter this attitude frequently. Perhaps it had been a mistake to start work in the village where he'd grown up. But he could understand and sympathize with the woman's reluctance.

'If it's nothing too personal, Mrs Cooper, then perhaps I can help. But if you'd rather see my father, then we can make another appointment for you. First, tell me what the problem is.'

'I don't want to be unfair to you. After all, you've done your training, we all know that. And you've done well.' She was moving slowly towards the chair set for the patients to sit in. She sat down and pulled in a deep breath, as if coming to a decision. 'It's my chest, Master Robert. Your dad always listens to me chest when I get one of me coughs. Then he gives me his special linctus, he calls it, and it works a treat. Maybe you could just give me a bottle of that, could you?'

'I really ought to listen to your chest and your back, Mrs Cooper. Just to be sure.'

'Oh.' Her face fell as she deliberated and then said hesitantly, 'Well, all right, then.'

'You needn't undress entirely, Mrs Cooper,' Robert said gently. 'As long as I can get to your back and the upper part of your chest, that should be fine.'

Moments later, Robert sat back down in his chair whilst Mrs Cooper hastily adjusted her clothing.

'There's certainly a rattle in there. Do you normally get a cough this time of the year?'

'Always coming up to harvest time, Master Robert. Me breathing gets that bad.'

'I see. Now just let me check what my father normally prescribes...' Robert consulted the notes Edwin had made in his neat, spidery handwriting. 'Ah yes, I see. I'll make sure this is made up for you by this afternoon. Maybe your husband could pick it up for you later.'

'Or one of the girls will. Betty or our Peggy. My Charlie sometimes doesn't get home till late this time of year.'

'Very well, then.'

As she rose and went towards the door, Mrs Cooper smiled and, over her shoulder, said, 'Thank you, doctor.'

As the door closed behind her, Robert felt he could claim a small victory. If Bess Cooper was on his side, then the rest of the villagers would follow her lead like lambs following the ewe.

Thirteen

The rest of that first day passed in much the same manner; the women of the village were at first reluctant, but all of them, except one, finally capitulated and allowed Robert to attend to them. The men, however, posed no problems at all, though they teased him a little, having known him since childhood. Perhaps the best compliment he received all morning was from Mr Walsh, a bluff local farmer, who had a nasty carbuncle on his neck that required lancing. As he left the room, he nodded and said in his brusque manner, 'You'll do, Master Robert, you'll do.'

'The only lady who wouldn't succumb to my charm,' Robert told them over luncheon, 'was old Mrs Watkins.'

Edwin, at the head of the table, chuckled. 'Ah

69

yes, she returned to the waiting room and insisted on seeing me. Said she would wait all day, if she had to. Anyway, I was able to fit her in when another patient was late arriving for their appointment. Now, this afternoon we'll do the house calls together, Robert. You can drive.'

'I wonder how Giles is getting on?' Pips murmured. It was his first day in his new post too.

They didn't have too long to find out, for Giles took advantage of Henrietta's open invitation to visit the hall and stay any time he liked. He arrived on his motorcycle on the Friday evening in time for dinner with the family. This evening, once again, there were no other guests.

'It doesn't look as if our friends will be able to dine with us for some time. Rosemary has written to say that they are staying in London for the time being. I'm guessing – though she doesn't say so – that the War Office need the major as some sort of adviser,' Henrietta explained as they sat down. She glanced at Giles. 'But it's nice that you could join us.'

'I fully expected to be on duty for the whole of the first weekend, Mrs Maitland, but no, I've been given the day off tomorrow.'

Robert laughed. 'No such luck for me. I'm on call because it's high time Father had some time off. But Pips will look after you.'

'What are things like in the city?' Edwin asked.

'There's an air of excitement and young men are already clamouring to volunteer. Have you seen the "call to arms" advertisement in the newspapers today, placed there by the newly appointed Secretary for War, Lord Kitchener? He's calling

70

for one hundred thousand men to volunteer. That'll bring them flocking to enlist.'

'What about young women?' Pips asked. 'What sort of work are they needed for? I must do *something.*'

Now, Henrietta was powerless to stop the talk of war at mealtimes.

'Just calm down, Philippa,' her mother remonstrated. 'I'm sure there will be plenty of opportunity for some kind of useful occupation for us. I plan to set up a knitting and sewing circle in the village. You could help me with that.'

For a moment Pips's face was a picture of disgust, but she managed to bite back a ready retort and say dutifully, 'I'd be happy to help in any way I can.' But no one around the table – including her mother – was left in any doubt that knitting socks, scarves and balaclavas was not Pips's idea of helping the war effort.

But her escape from such boredom came from an unexpected quarter. The following morning at breakfast, Robert and Giles were poring over the newspaper headlines.

'It says here that Austria declared war on Russia two days ago and Serbia declared against Germany. It's certainly escalating very fast now,' Robert said.

Giles murmured. 'What do you think we should do?'

'Stick to what we decided for the moment. If, like they're saying, it'll all be over for Christmas, there is little point in us disrupting our careers just yet.'

'You're right, of course, but I am very much

71

afraid that it will last a lot longer than four months or so.'

'Good morning,' Pips said, entering the room and taking her place at the breakfast table. 'And what are you two looking so serious about?'

'See for yourself,' Robert said and he passed over the newspaper, jabbing his finger at the article he had just been reading.

Pips read it swiftly, but before she could ask, Robert said, 'Giles and I are both agreed that we shouldn't go just yet.'

'I think you're right. I just wish–'

At that moment, Edwin entered the room with his wife. He was holding a letter in his hand as he sat down at the head of the table. 'I think this is something that we should all discuss as a family.'

Giles half-rose from his chair. 'If you'd like me to...'

'No, no, it isn't private, my boy. Please stay. I've received a letter from an old friend of mine in London, Dr John Hazelwood. We were at medical school together and we've kept in touch ever since. He writes to say that he is planning to form what he calls a flying ambulance corps to help the wounded. Of course, he will work closely with the authorities and will ensure that he has their full approval and co-operation, but it will be a voluntary, independent unit that he can take to wherever the need is the greatest. He is looking for applicants to do a variety of jobs. As well as doctors and nurses, he'll need drivers, cooks, medical orderlies and stretcher bearers and probably a few general dogsbodies as well. It will take him a few weeks to get everything organized and, of course, it might all be over by then.'

'We've just said the same thing, but I'm beginning to doubt it now,' Robert murmured.

'So am I,' Edwin agreed, looking up from the letter in his hand. 'I was just wondering if it was an alternative for you, Robert, rather than joining the RAMC, for which you might have to sign on for years. This way – with an independent organization – you wouldn't be so tied.'

'But what about here? The practice?'

Edwin shrugged. 'I can manage on my own for a while longer, if you really want to go.'

'Is he taking women? Other than qualified nurses, I mean?' Pips asked.

'Now, Philippa,' Henrietta began. 'I don't really think–'

'Hetty, my love,' Edwin said gently, 'Pips is determined to do something. She is one of the reasons I brought this letter in here this morning. If she were to go with someone like John, I'd be a lot happier.'

'I wouldn't mind being a dogsbody, as you call it, and I can drive,' Pips said eagerly. 'I'm sure I could drive an ambulance.'

Edwin chuckled. 'And where, might I ask, did you learn to drive a vehicle?' His eyes twinkled at his daughter as he added, 'As if I didn't know.'

'So I was right,' Henrietta said. 'You *have* been riding Robert's motorcycle. Robert, I'm surprised at you. How could you let your sister endanger herself – and others?'

'Pips is perfectly safe, Mother,' Robert said smoothly. 'She's better at riding it than I am.'

Pips shot him a grateful glance then turned

back to her father. 'So, what do I have to do to apply to Dr Hazelwood?'

'Write him a letter telling him all about yourself and what you are prepared to do...'

'Anything. I'll do anything.'

'And I will write to him too,' Edwin continued, 'and let him know you go with our blessing. And I'll mention, too, that Robert and Giles might also be interested. That's if you're both agreeable?'

Robert and Giles exchanged a glance and then nodded.

'Just a minute, Edwin,' Henrietta said. 'I haven't said I agree to Pips going.'

'My love, she will go anyway. Wouldn't it be better if we support her and give her our permission? You don't want to part on bad terms with your daughter, now do you?' He sighed. 'I'm afraid there is going to be a lot of heartache in this village – in fact, throughout the whole country – before this war is over, however long or short it may be. The young are feverish with patriotism. Nothing and no one will stand in their way and – particularly where young men are concerned – if they don't come back, just think how their families are going to feel if the last time they saw them they quarrelled. Besides, I don't think Pips will be in much danger. Any work she is involved in will be way behind the front lines, I'm sure.'

'Will you write to your friend, then, and ask him exactly what work she would have to do? If he agrees to take her, that is. Will you at least do that for me?'

'Of course I will, Hetty, my love.'

Pips, sensing that her mother was capitulating,

jumped up and ran to the end of the table where she hugged her. 'Thank you, Mother, thank you.'

'I haven't agreed entirely yet. I need your father to make more enquiries first, but' – she sighed – 'I can see that you are keen to help, and I wouldn't want to stand in your way. I'm just concerned for your safety, that's all.'

'I know, and I do understand, but knitting socks and gloves isn't really me, is it, Mother?'

Henrietta was gracious enough to smile wryly. 'No, my dear, I am obliged to agree with you there.'

'I don't know how William can do it,' Norah said to Ma, when they were alone in the kitchen on the Saturday morning. 'A strapping lad like him not wanting to volunteer. What will folks say?'

'Aye, he's a big lad, stronger than the rest of 'em put together, I'd say. And Boy has the makings of being the same when he grows a bit. He looks a lot older than his age, you know, Norah.'

Norah glanced at her mother-in-law and her eyes widened. 'You reckon they might take him because he *looks* older?'

'I wouldn't put it past them.'

'The boys are going to volunteer today – Bernard and Roy, that is,' she added. There was a bitterness in her tone that she could not include William's name. 'It's all arranged with some of the other lads in the village, but I've had a word with them and told them they're not to let Boy go with them.'

Early that afternoon, the two Dawson brothers, dressed in their Sunday best, stepped out of the cottage. Already gathered outside were several other young men from the village and another – Sam Nuttall – was coming towards them further down the street, but his progress was hampered by the hysterical woman clinging to his arm.

Her cries carried shrilly through the morning air. 'You're not to go, Samuel. I won't let you go. You *can't* go. It'll kill me. Is that what you want?'

Her husband, Bert, was trying to prise her grasp from their son's arm. At last Samuel shook her free and marched towards his friends without looking back.

Ma, who had come outside with Norah to wave her grandsons off, nodded towards the distraught woman. 'Looks like poor Clara's taking it badly.'

Norah's lip curled with disdain. 'She should think 'ersen lucky she hasn't got a coward skulking indoors.'

'I thought William must've gone to work early. I haven't seen him today.'

'Neither have I. To be honest, I haven't seen him since yesterday. I don't think he came home last night.'

'Maybe he's stayed at the hall.'

'You think they'd harbour a coward, Ma?'

Ma didn't answer as the seven or eight young men fell into line and began to march proudly up the lane towards the road leading to the city. Relatives and friends lined their route and cheered loudly.

'Where's Boy?' Norah said suddenly. 'I thought he'd have come to wave 'em off.'

Ma smiled sadly. 'Norah, duck, Boy will be waiting round the corner, well out of your sight, to join them. He'll go all the way to Lincoln with them. You mark my words.'

Norah gave a wry laugh. 'Well, he's wasting his time. Bernard'll make sure the recruiting officers know his real age.'

Ma said nothing. She had a shrewd suspicion that somehow Boy would manage to join up. Maybe not today, maybe not for a while. But in the end, young Harold Dawson would go to war.

Fourteen

Pips dressed with care for dinner that evening. Alice had not appeared to help her, but Pips was not the sort of young woman to throw a tantrum because she had to manage without her lady's maid. Besides, Alice looked after both Henrietta and Pips. No doubt she was helping her mother. Pips was thinking about Giles. She liked him, she decided. She liked him very much. After dinner, Giles intended to return to his lodgings in the city.

'I'm on call tomorrow,' he had explained.

They had enjoyed the day together, endlessly discussing the war on their walks and over meals, though they had paused that afternoon to engage in a game of chess.

'Unless you're as good as a world champion, Giles,' Robert had teased, 'she'll beat you hands down. But at least if she's playing you, she's not beating me.'

'I don't stand a chance, then,' Giles had laughed, 'because when we play you always beat me.'

'I don't always win,' Pips had said modestly.

'No, true,' Robert had laughed. 'Just most of the time.'

As she ran down the stairs to the first floor, Henrietta opened her bedroom door and called to her. 'If you're ready, Philippa, please ask Alice to come to my room. I can't get my hair right this evening and she has such a way...'

'Alice isn't with me, Mother. I thought she was helping you.'

Henrietta blinked. 'No, I haven't seen her. She had the afternoon off. I thought she should go home to be with her family for an hour or two if her brothers have volunteered. Hasn't she come back?'

'I've no idea. I'll go to the kitchen and find out.'

When Pips entered the kitchen, she found Alice sitting at the table, her head in her hands, being comforted by Cook and Sarah, the housemaid. Even Joan, the scullery maid, was standing close by. Alice raised her tear-streaked face. 'Oh miss, I'm sorry, I should have come up to you and the mistress, but...'

'No matter.' Pips waved aside her apology. 'But whatever's wrong?'

'It's William. He's disappeared.'

Pips sat down at the table and reached across to take Alice's hand. 'Are you sure he's not here – at the hall? He sometimes feeds the horses when the stable lad has an afternoon off.'

Alice shook her head. 'No, I've asked Jake and he hasn't seen him.'

'When was he last seen?'

'Yesterday.'

'Yesterday!' Pips was shocked. 'Have your brothers been out looking for him?'

Alice buried her face in her hands again and her sobs increased. At last she wailed, 'They refuse to search for him.'

'Why?'

'Because – because he wouldn't go with them this morning into Lincoln to volunteer.'

'Ah.' Pips was beginning to understand. She stood up. 'Cook, can you hold back dinner for half an hour? My parents and Robert should hear about this.'

'Of course, Miss Pips.'

'Alice, come with me.'

'Oh miss, I can't let the rest of the family see me looking like this. Whatever would your mother say?'

'Mother will say nothing – in the circumstances.'

Pips led Alice through into the Great Hall where the family and Giles were already waiting.

'I've asked Cook to put dinner back for half an hour, Mother. We have a problem.'

'Oh Alice, my dear, what's wrong?' Henrietta came at once to the girl's side.

'It's William,' Pips explained. 'He's missing. The family haven't seen him since yesterday.'

Robert now moved towards Alice and put his arm around her shoulders. 'Come and sit down and tell us all you know.'

'Bernard and Roy went into the city this morning to enlist in the Lincolnshire Regiment. Yesterday, they tried to persuade William to promise to go with them, but he refused. They – they were horrible to him, Ma told me. They called him a coward and Harold picked up a white feather from the ground and threw it at him. William turned and ran up the road and he hasn't been seen since. I've asked everyone here and they haven't seen him either.'

'D'you think he could've changed his mind and gone to enlist?' Robert asked.

Alice shook her head. 'No, he won't do that. He's adamant he won't kill people.'

There was silence in the room and everyone glanced at each other. Then their focus came back to Alice. Robert was the one to take charge. 'We'll have our dinner quickly and then I'll organize a search party. You run back home to make sure he's not come back, and get your father and brothers to come to the hall to help. All right?'

Alice nodded, but said tentatively, 'I'll ask them, but I don't think they'll come to help. They're all ashamed of him.'

An unusually hurried dinner was over in half an hour and Robert and Pips rose from the table before coffee was served. 'Please excuse us, Mother. We must look for William.'

She nodded her understanding and Giles got up too. 'I'll help.'

'Shouldn't you be getting back?'

He shrugged. 'Another hour or so won't hurt.'

The three young people hastened from the room leaving Edwin and Henrietta staring at each other down the length of the table.

'Is there anything we ought to do?'

'Leave it to Robert and Pips. They'll get to the bottom of whatever's been going on. But, I have to say, I don't like the sound of it, Hetty, my love. I don't like the sound of it at all.'

Fifteen

The stable lad, Jake Goodall, was checking the horses for the final time that night when Robert, Pips and Giles hurried into the yard. At only fourteen and small in stature, he was far too young to volunteer.

'Have you seen William?' Robert asked.

'No, sir. Not since yesterday morning when he started work at the normal time. I took the 'osses out for a ride in the afternoon and when I came back, he'd gone. I just thought he'd knocked off early an' gone home. It wasn't till Alice came to work this morning and said he was missing that I thought it odd. T'ain't like him to just go off and not say owt.'

'Jake, is that all you know? Are you sure?'

'Yes, sir. I don't know no more. Except...' The young boy hesitated.

'Go on,' Pips prompted.

'Well, there's summat funny happened. Look, I'll show you.'

He led the way round the back of the stables and stopped to point at the ground. There were splashes of yellow paint and a scattering of white feathers.

Robert's face was grim. 'You know what this is, don't you? Someone has tarred and feathered him, only they've used yellow paint as a sign of cowardice instead of tar.'

As they walked back to the yard once more, Pips asked, 'But where can he be?'

'Hiding, I shouldn't wonder.' Robert turned to Jake. 'Have you searched the stables and barns?'

'No, sir.'

'Is there anyone else who will help us?' He glanced across the yard to see Alice walking towards them from the house. 'Because it doesn't look as if any of his family are coming.'

'I could go and ask the local farmers, if you like.'

Robert thought quickly. If what he suspected might have happened, he didn't want the incident to be widely known. 'We'll look first – the five of us – and then, if we don't find him, you can seek help. Right, Pips – Giles – we'll start with the lofts above the stables and then the barns.' He turned as Alice drew near. 'Any news?'

She shook her head. 'I think my brothers know something, but they won't say, only that he's no longer their brother.'

There was a shocked silence before Robert said, 'Come on, let's get going.'

They searched the stables and barns thoroughly, but there was no sign of him.

'Well, I'm stumped.' Robert scratched his head. 'I can't think of anywhere else to look. He wouldn't go into the house, would he?'

Alice shook her head.

'Then he can't be here.'

'There is one place we haven't looked, Master Robert,' Jake said tentatively.

'Is there, Jake? Where?'

'The rooms above the gatehouse. There's a steep staircase leading up there. I've never been up, mind. William told me the floor might not be safe. It's a very old building, isn't it?'

Robert nodded. 'Older than the house, we be-ieve. It's worth a look, though.'

The five of them hurried round the end of the house to the gatehouse standing halfway down the long drive.

'I'll go up,' Robert said.

They heard him step carefully onto the floor above and then his footsteps crossing the room.

'He's here. Come up, all of you, but be careful.'

William was cowering in the furthest dark corner. He was a mess of yellow paint, covered with white feathers.

Robert squatted down in front of him. 'Come on, old chap, let's get you cleaned up.'

William drew his knees up and bent his head forward, covering his head with his arms. 'Leave me, Master Robert. I aren't worth it.'

Pips moved forward. 'Nonsense, William. You've nothing to be ashamed of. You're only standing up for what you believe is right. Now, come on. Let us help you and then you can go home.'

'No!' William's head shot up. 'No, miss. I aren't going home. I can't. They've turned me out.'

'Your father's head of the house, not your brothers.'

William's head dropped again, his voice muffled.

83

'It was him what told me to go, so I came here. I thought I could sleep in the hayloft, but my brothers followed me and – and did this.'

'When did this happen?'

'Last night. They came and found me and dragged me out behind the stables so no one could see.'

'They must have planned it to have got hold of yellow paint and all these feathers,' Giles said, appalled at what had happened.

'Ever since the war was declared, they've been on at me to go with them to enlist as soon as the call came for volunteers. And it came on Friday morning – in the papers. But I can't – I really can't – shoot people, even if they are classed as our enemy. I know my whole family are disgusted with me, but I never thought they'd do something like this.'

Now, Alice moved forward. 'I'm not, William. I understand how you feel. If anything, I'm shocked at just how eager our brothers are to join the killing, even though they say its patriotism. I'll stand by you, but come home. Please, come home.'

'No, Alice, I can't.'

'But where will you go?'

William shrugged and the paint and feathers on his clothes shifted. 'I don't know.'

Jake moved from the shadows. 'If the mistress says it's all right, he can stay with me. They'll not touch me.'

Jake had a room above the stables to be close to his beloved horses. Henrietta had made sure that it was warm in winter and adequately furnished.

Orphaned as a baby, Jake had been raised in a boys' home for pauper children, operated by the Lincoln Union. At the age of twelve, he'd run away from the home and had scoured the countryside around Lincoln, sleeping rough and looking for work. Henrietta had taken pity on him and had employed him. Housed, clothed and fed, the young boy had thought he'd found Heaven. His loyalty to Henrietta was deep and lasting. Now, sensing that his employers wanted to help William, he made the suggestion.

'Thank you, Jake, that sounds very sensible,' Robert said. 'We'll see that he's provided with a bed. Now, up with you, William. Let's get you down and changed out of these clothes.'

'I haven't got any others, Master Robert.'

'Then Alice will go home and fetch all your belongings. Jake, you go too, and if any protest is made, tell them I've sent you.'

'I'll go with them,' Pips said. 'They'll not argue with me.'

Pips, Alice and Jake set off in the darkness whilst Robert and Giles took William to Jake's room and helped him out of his ruined clothes. They washed as much of the paint from his face and hands as they could.

'I'm afraid it'll take a while for all trace to disappear,' Robert said.

William sighed. 'No doubt I'll get similar treatment when the locals find out about me.'

'You've no need to go into the village. Stay here in the grounds of the hall. You'll be safe here.'

Sixteen

'And what brings you three here at this time of night?' Bernard's tone was insolent.

Alice had led the others in through the back door, hoping her family were in bed, but her older brother met them in the scullery.

Pips pushed to the front, standing protectively in front of the other two. 'We've come for all William's possessions. I trust your parents will have no objection to us taking them.' Her voice was like ice and her eyes flashed with anger in the light of the oil lamp on the table.

'You'd better ask them.'

As Pips passed in front of him towards the living room, he grasped her arm and thrust his face close to hers. 'If you help that – that coward, then you're no better than he is.'

Unafraid, Pips glared back at him. 'Take your hand from my arm this minute,' she spat, 'and stand aside. It's your father and mother I wish to speak to – not you.'

Bernard smirked but he released her arm, though Pips was not done yet. Now it was she who lowered her voice and, still close to him, hissed, 'Just remember, there are other wheel-wrights and blacksmiths in the area.'

Bernard gave a bark of laughter. 'Are you threatening me, Miss Pips?'

'I most certainly am. Any more disgraceful

behaviour like you've shown to your brother and you'll find that your family business will be ostracized by everyone in the district. I'll make sure of it.'

She turned away and stepped through into the room beyond to see the rest of the family. She glanced at each of them in turn. Ma Dawson was sitting in her usual chair in front of the range, whilst Len sat on the opposite side of the hearth. Norah sat at the table. She had been darning socks, but these now lay untouched on the table in front of her. Roy and Harold were sitting on either side of the table, a board game of draughts between them. Len and Norah got to their feet and Norah nudged her sons to do the same. They obeyed, though reluctantly, Pips could see. Only Ma Dawson remained in her chair.

'I've come for William's possessions. He's staying' – she hesitated, unwilling to give away William's exact whereabouts – 'at the hall.' Now she sought and held Norah's gaze. 'I presume you are aware of what's happened to him?'

'You – you've found him? Where was he? What's happened?'

'Your sons – your other sons – daubed him with yellow paint and threw white feathers over him. He tells me' – her gaze now sought Len's – 'that you have thrown him out. Is that true?'

'It is.'

Norah gasped and Ma pursed her lips and frowned, but they said nothing. They would not go against the head of the house.

'Then you have no objection to us removing all his possessions?'

87

'None. He's no longer my son.'

For a moment, Pips stared at him, unable to comprehend what she was hearing. With a slight disbelieving shake of her head, she beckoned a tentative Alice forward. 'Can you get all his things together?'

Alice nodded and with a fearful glance at her father scuttled up the stairs to the bedroom William had shared with his brothers. There was an awkward silence in the room whilst they heard her moving about upstairs and no one offered to help her. Pips sought Ma's eyes.

'Mrs Dawson, do you agree with what's happening?'

Ma glanced at Len. With a slight sigh she said heavily, 'I'm old, Miss Pips, and I rely on the charity of my son and daughter-in-law. It is owing to them that I have a roof over my head.' Then, as if some of her old spirit returned for a brief moment, she met Pips's gaze and said firmly, 'No, I don't agree with it – certainly not what the boys have done to him. We've always stuck together as a family through thick and thin and whilst I don't agree with William's sentiments, I wouldn't disown him. In fact, I don't, he's still my grandson, but I'm powerless to help him, as you can see.'

Pips smiled and nodded. She turned to Norah to ask her the same question, but before the woman could answer, Ma butted in, 'Please don't ask her, Miss Pips. T'aint fair to cause trouble between husband and wife.'

'You're right. I'm sorry. Perhaps I shouldn't have asked you either.'

Ma shrugged. 'If they put me in the workhouse, I'll let you know.'

She wouldn't put it past them if these last few hours were anything to go by, Pips thought, but she said nothing more as, only a few moments later, Alice appeared carrying a bundle wrapped in a sheet. Jake took it from her and carried it outside.

'Thank you.' Pips's voice was heavy with sarcasm and, as she turned to leave, she met Bernard's belligerent gaze. 'Remember what I said, because I meant it.'

When the two young women and Jake returned to the hall, they found that Robert and Giles had put William's clothes to be burned the next morning. They'd managed to wash off much of the yellow paint, but traces still clung to his hair. They'd fetched an unused single bed from the servants' attic bedrooms in the hall and had installed it in Jake's room above the stables. William was sitting wrapped in a blanket awaiting his fresh clothes to be brought. He was shivering, but it was more from shock – and perhaps fear, too – than from the cold for the summer night was warm.

'Here we are, William,' Pips said, far more cheerfully than she was feeling. She was still outraged at how his family had treated him. 'Go into the bedroom and put these on. You'll feel much better once you're dressed again.'

'I think it would be a good idea if he went straight to bed,' Robert said. 'He's had a nasty shock. And Alice, you can bring him some hot milk from the house liberally laced with whisky and something to eat too.'

'Yes, Master Robert.' And she hurried away to do his bidding and to help her brother.

'Perhaps you're right,' Pips agreed and added gently to William, 'I expect you didn't get any sleep last night.'

His teeth chattered as he said, 'Not much, Miss Pips, no.'

'Then we'll go and leave Jake to help you. I'd light a fire, Jake. Keep him warm. Alice will be back very soon, and then you should try to get some rest.'

As they all turned to leave, Pips put her hand on Jake's shoulder. 'Thank you. You're a good-hearted young man. We won't forget this and we'll see you have everything you need. I'll talk to my mother.'

Jake glowed beneath her praise.

A little later, Pips walked with Giles to the end of the driveway before he started his motorcycle.

'Thank you for your help tonight. I hope it hasn't made you too late getting back home.'

'I was glad to be of service,' he said softly. 'Poor young feller. He's only standing up for what he believes in.'

'It was courageous of him to go against his own family.'

'Indeed. I don't know if I'd have had the strength to oppose my nearest and dearest.' They were silent for a moment, as if delaying the parting for as long as possible.

'Come again as soon as you can – if – if you want to, that is.'

'I'd like that very much. As long as I'm not imposing.'

Despite the trauma of the evening, Pips laughed. 'Oh you're not, I promise you, but you mustn't mind Mother's loaded remarks and leading questions.'

'I don't mind them one bit. In fact...' He hesitated and Pips wondered what he'd been about to say. Instead he said, 'Let me know if you hear anything from your father's friend. I would miss you if you went away, but I know we all have to do what we feel is right. And' – he chuckled – 'it's quite likely that Robert and I won't be far behind you.'

He took her hand and raised it briefly to his lips, whispering, 'Good night, Pips. Sweet dreams.' Then he started his motorcycle and rode off into the night, leaving Pips standing at the gate until she could no longer hear the sound of his engine.

Seventeen

The letter from Dr Hazelwood came back by return. Edwin read it aloud over breakfast:

'...I should be delighted to have your son and his colleague join me. Although your daughter has no nursing experience, the fact that she is willing to do anything – and that she could drive an ambulance – will be a valuable asset. Please reassure your wife that we will be well behind the front lines and not expected* *to be in real danger. If any – or all three – decide to come along, I will let them know when they need to be ready. There is still a lot to prepare before we are ready to go abroad. I will keep you informed and I look forward to hearing further from you...'*

'I shall definitely go,' Pips said. 'What about you, Robert?'

'I intend to talk to Giles again at the weekend,' Robert replied. He glanced at Edwin. 'Are you sure you wouldn't mind me going, Father?'

Edwin glanced at his wife before saying slowly, 'We have discussed this and though we are both reluctant to see you go into danger – because despite what John says, it will be dangerous – we give you both our blessing. We are proud that you want to do your patriotic duty.'

Pips leapt up from her chair and hugged first her father and then her mother. 'Oh thank you, thank you. I didn't want to go against your wishes, but I *have* to go.'

'There's just one thing, Philippa,' Henrietta said. 'We wondered if you would ask Alice if she is willing to go with you. We'd feel so much better if you had another young woman with you.'

For a moment, Pips stared at her mother and then a slow smile spread across her face. 'Now that is good thinking, Mother, and you've given me another idea too.'

'But of course, her parents might not let her go.'

'I don't think there's much fear of that happening, not after the way they've treated their son.'

'But they might see it differently for a girl.'

'I doubt it,' Pips said wryly. 'I think they'd leap at anything to restore their family's credibility in the eyes of the villagers.'

Edwin and Henrietta now knew all that had happened and they too had been appalled.

'Of course William must stay here,' Henrietta had said at once. 'Is he all right living with Jake?'

'They'll be fine,' Pips reassured her. 'I think they'll be company for each other, if truth be known.'

'I'll see them both later today and find out if there's anything else they need. Poor boy. How anyone can treat their son – or brother – like that is quite beyond me.'

Not for the first time, Pips realized that her mother's severe manner hid a kind and generous heart.

After breakfast, Pips went in search of Alice and found her in Henrietta's bedroom sorting out the laundry. The bedroom where Henrietta and Edwin slept was known as the Holly Room, with a four-poster bed with patterned curtains. But the most impressive feature of the room was the old tapestries that lined all the walls. Henrietta was a clever needle-woman and kept them in an excellent state of repair. She had tried to teach Pips the same skill, but Pips had no talent for embroidery.

'You could do it if you applied yourself.'

'I haven't the patience, Mother. Why don't you teach Alice? She has all the patience in the world.'

Henrietta's mouth had twitched as she'd remarked drily, 'She has to have, being your lady's maid.'

Pips had laughed and agreed.

And so it had been Alice whom Henrietta had taught to repair the delicate works of art and even to embark on creating new tapestry chair-seat covers. But at this moment, the young girl was fulfilling her duties as their maid. Swiftly, Pips told her all about Dr Hazelwood and his flying ambulance corps. 'I don't exactly know yet what it will entail, but I'm going to go. Alice, will you come with me?'

Alice's eyes sparkled. 'Oh miss, yes, of course I will. I wouldn't let you go on your own and I'd be doing my bit too, wouldn't I?'

Pips hardly ever cried; in fact, her family couldn't remember the last time they'd seen her shed tears, but now she felt a lump at the back of her throat and tears prickle behind her eyelids. She'd never doubted Alice's devotion to her, indeed to all the Maitland family, but if ever proof were needed, here it was.

Her voice was husky as she said, 'You certainly would, Alice. But you must realize that it could be very dangerous.'

Alice shrugged. 'That doesn't worry me – not too much, anyway. The soldiers are likely to face far worse than we would, Miss Pips.'

'I'm thinking of asking William if he'd like to go with us. Dr Hazelwood needs all sorts of helpers. Maybe William could be a stretcher bearer, because it's highly likely that I'm going to be asked to drive an ambulance. That way he could stay with us.'

'I can't answer for him, miss, but you can certainly ask him.'

94

'I'll go this minute...' And like the whirlwind she was, Pips ran from the room and down the stairs leaving Alice smiling and shaking her head fondly over her young mistress's impetuosity.

Pips found Jake cleaning out Midnight's stable. She paused briefly to pat the horse's head. 'No gallop today, old feller. I have work to do.' The horse harrumphed his understanding.

'Jake, is William around?'

'He's still in bed, miss. I didn't like to wake him. He's still suffering from what happened to him.' He looked anxious for a moment. 'But I'll get him up if—'

'No, no, let him rest. He obviously needs it. But when he does get up, please tell him I'd like a word.'

Pips returned indoors. She could hardly wait until the weekend to find out if Robert and Giles would go too, but she intended to join Dr Hazelwood's venture anyway. She had Alice's promise that she would go with her, so now there was nothing standing in her way.

Later that morning, word came from the kitchen that William was waiting at the back door to speak to Pips. She went down immediately.

'Come into the kitchen,' she said.

'I'll stay out here, miss, if it's all the same to you. I'm not sure what the others—'

'Nonsense, William, come in. Cook, please will you make us a cup of tea? Here, sit down at the table, William.'

As the young man moved hesitantly inside, Pips glanced at the members of staff and was relieved

95

to see that, taking their lead from Mr Wainwright, they were all smiling a welcome at William.

As they sat down at one corner of the table, Pips once more explained swiftly about Dr Hazelwood's idea. 'I intend to join him and I shall offer to drive an ambulance. Alice has agreed to go with me and I wondered if you would come too. It's a private venture, so there's nothing military about it. I don't think we'll even carry weapons, though we'll probably have to go into the danger zones to pick up wounded, but I understand that Dr Hazelwood has cleared it with the authorities that we'll all be allowed to wear white arm bands with a red cross, so it will be obvious to everyone what we're doing. It'll not be easy. We'll be working in all sorts of difficult conditions; rain, snow – whatever the weather – and there will be some dreadful sights and awful wounds to dress. To say nothing of the hard physical work of carrying heavy stretchers for hours.' She smiled and her glance roamed over his tall frame and his muscular shoulders. 'But if anyone can do that, William, you can. What do you say? You'd be doing something very worthwhile.'

He stared at her. 'I'm not afraid of the danger, miss. I just don't want to kill folk. Yes, of course I'll come.'

Of course he'd go, he thought. He'd follow Miss Pips to the end of the world and into whatever hell she chose to go.

'Good,' Pips said briskly. 'Do you want to go home and tell your parents?'

William shook his head vehemently. 'I aren't ever going home again.'

'In that case, I shall take great pleasure in telling them.'

In the late afternoon, just before dinner, Pips walked into the village. The blacksmith's workshop was silent and Len was just closing up the wheelwright's.

'May I have a word with you and the rest of your family, Mr Dawson?'

His eyes narrowed as he regarded her warily, but then he shrugged, walked the short distance to his home with her and ushered her inside.

'Miss Maitland has something to say to us,' he said bluntly and, by the use of her formal name instead of the usual 'Miss Pips', she knew she was unwelcome in their home. The family were all gathered in the kitchen, waiting for their evening meal to be served.

'This is not to seek your permission, but just to inform you. I am joining a private flying ambulance corps which is being formed in London to go out to the war front. Alice is coming with me – and so is William.'

Norah turned from the range. 'I won't let Alice go. Len, you have to stop her.'

Her husband shrugged. 'She's twenty-one, Norah. I couldn't prevent her going even if I wanted to – and I'm not sure I do.'

Norah gasped and turned white. She reached for the nearest chair and sat down as Len added, 'The only person I can – and will – stop, is Boy.'

Harold said nothing. But behind his eyes, Pips thought she could see a mutinous and calculating look. He'll go, she thought, he'll keep volunteering until they take him and there won't be anything Len can do about it. But she kept her thoughts to herself. Instead she said quietly, 'And William?'

Len glared at her. 'I've told you 'afore, he's nowt to do with us. I don't care what he does.'

In her chair by the fire, Ma lowered her head.

'Very well.' Pips turned and left the house.

Eighteen

The Dawson family – apart from Len – were united in their efforts to dissuade Alice from accompanying her young mistress. But the young woman was surprisingly adamant. Alice had always been thought to be shy and biddable.

Only Ma was not surprised. 'She's got a stubborn streak in her that you've all failed to notice,' she told her family. 'I saw it in her when she was a little girl. She'll be all right, Norah. You shouldn't worry too much.'

'But out there, Ma, in danger and helping to nurse wounded soldiers. You know what they say about men and their nurses.'

Ma tried to make light of Norah's worries. 'Then maybe she'll find herself a nice young officer as a husband. She doesn't seem to like any of the village lads. She's certainly different to her brothers. They seem to have the local girls swarming around them like bees around a honeypot. I hear that Boy has been seen walking hand in hand with Betty's sister.'

Norah turned from kneading bread. 'Peggy? Oh surely not. She's only fifteen.'

'She looks older, though, and she's a forward little madam. He ought to be careful.'

'I'll get his dad to have a word with him.' There was silence between them as Norah returned to her bread making.

At last, Ma asked softly, 'What about William?'

It was a long time before Norah replied. She pounded the dough before saying flatly, 'There's nowt I can do about it and I'm not sure I want to anyway. Len and the boys are right. He's a coward and I'm ashamed of him. Mind you, just between us, Ma, mebbe I wouldn't have gone as far as throwing him out of his home, but I have to go along with my husband's decision.'

Ma sighed heavily. She leaned her head against the back of her chair and closed her eyes. 'Aye, I know. Once upon a time, I could have overruled my son, but not now. I haven't got the strength left.' After a pause she murmured, 'You know, I reckon Alice is siding with William. I think that's part of the reason she's going with Miss Pips.'

'Then he's responsible for the break-up of this family,' Norah said bitterly, 'and for putting his sister in danger. And for that, I'll never forgive him.'

During the following week, Britain and France declared war on Austria-Hungary and French troops had entered Lorraine. When Giles visited for the day on the Sunday, the talk was of nothing else but Dr Hazelwood's flying ambulance corps. Edwin had already written to him to say that he

99

had three recruits for his enterprise:

You already know a little about my daughter, but with her will be her lady's maid, Alice Dawson. She is devoted to Philippa and is a strong, capable village girl who is willing to do anything asked of her. Also with them will be Alice's brother, William. He is a very skilled mechanic and would prove a useful addition to your team, I think. He is also willing to act as a stretcher bearer. You may wonder why he is not volunteering for Kitchener's army as his two brothers have done; I should tell you that he does not want to fight, but is willing to serve his country by helping to save lives rather than take them. I hope his reasons will be acceptable to you.

My son, Robert, and his friend, Giles Kendall, have both recently qualified as doctors; Giles as a surgeon. They are at the present time still debating whether to join you. I hope to have news on this for you very soon.

'Father,' Robert began over dinner, 'if you're really sure I'm not letting you down as regards the practice, I would like to accompany Dr Hazelwood.'

'Me too,' Giles said. 'I've spoken to my superior at the hospital and he has generously agreed that I can have leave of absence from my post for as long as is needed.'

'We all hope it will be over swiftly, but it could go on for several months, years, even. Does he realize that?'

Giles nodded. 'He does and he has promised that there will always be a post for me there whenever I come back.'

'That's good to know.'

100

'And there's something else. The War Office has commandeered three wards at the County and they're also planning to set up a military hospital here, in the buildings of the Lincoln Grammar School, I believe. They'll be erecting huts on the playing fields too, I shouldn't wonder. The boys are to be moved elsewhere for the duration. It will be the Fourth Northern General Hospital, Lincoln.'

Suddenly, the talk of casualties being carried to their city brought the reality of what was happening home to all of them.

'Then I will write to John and let him know that he has five young people ready and willing to join him.' Edwin raised his wine glass and his voice was a little husky as he added, 'Godspeed to all of you.'

Nineteen

News soon arrived that, despite fierce resistance from the Belgians, the German army had captured the fortress at Liège.

'Have British forces left for France yet?' Pips asked her father and brother over breakfast.

'Strange you should ask that, Pips. It's here in today's paper that Lord Kitchener has authorized the announcement that the British Expeditionary Force has landed in France. And,' Edwin went on, picking up a letter from beside his plate, 'I have also heard from John Hazelwood. I'll read his letter to you:

'I shall be delighted to have all five join the corps. In addition, there will be a fully qualified sister and a nurse, both Belgian, who speak English as well as French and German, two London bus drivers, who are willing to act as stretcher bearers, and one of whom wouldn't mind undertaking cooking duties. Please be aware that stretcher bearers have an extremely dangerous job; they will be exposed to shellfire in taking the wounded from the front line to the advanced first-aid posts, one of which will be ours.

'Also with us will be Mrs Marigold Parrott, the wife of an army colonel, who is likely to go to the front with his regiment very soon. She has already contributed £100 to this venture and will take charge of the accounting and the ordering of supplies. Mrs Parrott will also act as something of a war correspondent in an effort to raise much-needed funds back home. She speaks French fluently and has a smattering of German.'

Edwin glanced up. 'I presume, Pips and Robert, that you still remember some of your French and German from your schooling.' They both nodded as Edwin continued to read from the letter.

'Sadly, at the outset, we cannot expect to receive any funding from either the British, French or Belgian authorities, so each member must pay their own way. Although we do have the promise of an ambulance from the British Red Cross.'

Here Edwin broke off again. 'Initially, Hetty and I will fund you all.'

'I shall begin fund-raising locally at once,' Henrietta promised. 'I have lots of ideas and I have several friends and acquaintances who I know will join me. People will be only too willing to support a local venture. Rosemary has come home and I have already spoken to her. She is already rallying fund-raising troops.'

'There's just one more thing,' Edwin said, picking up the letter again.

'It is unlikely that we shall be ready to leave for Belgium much before the end of September and, in the meantime, if your two young ladies would agree to undertake an intensive first-aid and home-nursing course, that would be very helpful.'

Edwin glanced up, looking to Robert for suggestions.

'I think that might be possible at the hospital,' Robert said. 'Giles told me at the weekend that he'd heard one of the sisters talking about the need for such a course to be run. I'll go into Lincoln myself after surgery and make some enquiries.'

'If not,' Edwin said, waving the sheet of paper in his hand, 'John says he can arrange for them to attend a course in London, though it would mean them finding accommodation there.'

'Would William be able to go with us?' Pips asked. 'It would be so useful, if he's to be a stretcher bearer.'

Edwin wrinkled his brow. 'I don't see why not. Perhaps you could ask that question too, Robert? Who would be allowed to attend?'

'I'll see what I can find out.'

With the interest of three more people, Sister Jenkins, who planned to run such a course in her spare time at the County Hospital, was able to start the training sessions. Edwin lent Pips his car to drive the three of them to the hospital and back each day.

'It'll give you some driving practice,' he chuckled.

'But what about your rounds, Father?'

Edwin waved her protestations aside. 'I can manage with the pony and trap, if need be, like I did before we got the car. No, you take it. Just be careful, though, or I'll have your mother to answer to.'

But Henrietta made no protest; she was far too busy organizing fund-raising events in the village and further afield to worry about what Pips was doing. As well as Rosemary Fieldsend, she enlisted the help of their wide circle of well-to-do ladies in the district.

'You know, I ought to involve the village women,' Henrietta said, as she and Edwin enjoyed their usual nightcap together.

'I'm sure you'd find them very willing,' Edwin murmured, swirling his whisky in his glass. 'There are several young men gone from the village already, including the two oldest Dawson boys.'

'Ma Dawson might be the one to approach. She is well respected.'

'Mm. I just wonder how things stand now over the William issue. With the Dawsons and the rest of the village, I mean.'

Henrietta wriggled her shoulders impatiently.

'Such a lot of nonsense. The young man has a right to do whatever he thinks is his duty. Perhaps their attitude has changed now he's going with Dr Hazelwood.'

'I doubt it,' Edwin said sadly.

On 20 August, the same day the news came through that the Germans had captured Brussels, Henrietta walked down the road to the Dawsons' cottage.

She sat opposite Ma near the range. She was sorry to see that the older woman seemed to have sunk into misery. As she drew off her gloves, Henrietta came straight to the point of her visit. 'I wondered if you would be interested in helping me set up a knitting and sewing circle in the village, Mrs Dawson.' She glanced up at Norah, who was standing near the kitchen table, twisting her fingers nervously. She wasn't used to having what she considered 'grand company' sitting in her kitchen. 'I know you are always busy, Norah, looking after your family, but perhaps you could find a few minutes sometimes to help too?'

'What d'you think, Ma?' Norah looked at her mother-in-law.

'I'm too old and tired to organize it, Mrs Maitland, but I don't mind doing a bit of knitting. It'll help take me mind off...' Her voice trailed away.

'Ma's taken the boys going and the trouble we've had very hard, Mrs Maitland. It's caused a rift in the family.'

'I think you're the perfect person to organize it, Mrs Dawson,' Henrietta said briskly, trying to pull the woman out of her despondency. 'You're regarded as the matriarch of the village.'

Ma smiled wryly. 'I think that title has passed to Bess Cooper. You'd do better to ask her.'

'Couldn't you work together? You get along, don't you?'

'Aye, sort of. Roy was – is – walking out with Betty.' Ma bit her lip to stop herself referring to Harold's friendship with the younger sister, Peggy. She wasn't sure if Bess approved of it or even knew about it. 'But we'll give it a try, ma'am. I'll get Norah to ask Bess to call in and I'll talk to her.'

'Thank you,' Henrietta said as she stood up to take her leave. 'That's all I'm asking.'

'I think they'll do it,' Henrietta told her family over dinner that evening. 'It'll help all the women of the village to feel that they're helping their boys.'

'I've had another letter from John,' Edwin said. 'He's delighted to hear that you're undertaking a first-aid course, Pips. He plans to design his own uniforms for what he calls his "Hazelwood Nurses", to distinguish them – if possible – from other nursing organisations.'

'That sounds like a very good idea,' Pips said.

'So, what's all this about, then, Ma?'

Frowning, Bess Cooper stood in front of Ma, her arms folded across her ample bosom. But Ma had no fear of the big woman, whom she had known as a little girl in pinafores, running barefoot through the fields. Ma was probably the only person amongst the villagers whom Bess really respected.

'Mrs Maitland wants us to form a knitting circle to send socks, balaclavas and the like to the troops.'

Bess blinked. 'But I thought they're all saying it's going to be over afore Christmas.' She grinned suddenly, showing uneven teeth. 'Specially now your lads are out there.'

'They're not there yet,' Norah said tartly. She was in awe of Bess, even if Ma wasn't. 'They're still training.' Though she would never have voiced it aloud, she hoped that the war would, as everyone said, be over in a few months and that her boys would not have to go abroad. Of course, she'd cheered them on their way, proud that they'd volunteered, but if it came to the time that they really might have to go into the thick of the fighting, she would know every mother's fear. And buried deep within her, so deep that she would never acknowledge it even to herself, she had a sneaking empathy with William's beliefs.

'All to the good if it is,' Ma said, 'but if it isn't, we need to have clothing ready to send out to the lads when winter comes.'

'But it's abroad. It's warm out there, isn't it?'

Ma eyed her neighbour with pity. It seemed Bess's elementary education was sadly lacking. Gently, she said, 'I think the climate in Belgium and northern France is similar to ours. You're thinking of the countries near the equator.'

'Ah. Right.' Bess shook her shoulders, unwilling to admit that she hadn't got a clue what Ma was talking about. But she'd take the older woman's word for it. 'So, what do you want me to do?'

'Go round the village and ask all the women to

107

help. We can have a meeting at the hall, Mrs Maitland said. She suggested we form a committee to organize it all.' Ma smiled at Bess. 'I suggested you should be Chairman of it.'

Bess was startled. 'Me? Oh, I couldn't do owt like that. I wouldn't know where to start. You'd be much better at that sort of thing, Ma. Or Mrs Maitland.'

'She's forming another Committee for fund-raising, so I don't think she'd want to lead this one too.'

Bess shrugged. 'She's nowt else to do wi' her time. Not like the rest of us. She's servants to look after her family.'

Ma smiled. 'Do I detect a note of bitterness, Bess?'

Bess had the grace to laugh. 'Not really. I sometimes think it'd be nice to be well off, but then I suppose it has its own problems.'

Sometimes, Ma thought, though she lacked a formal education, Bess could be remarkably astute.

The first-aid course at the hospital was going well. At the end of the month, the newspapers were filled with the news that the British forces, fighting alongside their French and Belgian allies, had suffered heavy casualties in the struggle for the town of Mons.

'In under a month,' Edwin said, 'the enemy have swept through most of Belgium, forcing the Allies to retreat to the Somme.'

'That's regarded as the last barrier before Paris,' Robert murmured.

'We must get out there,' Pips said impatiently. 'Why doesn't Dr Hazelwood hurry things up?'

'It's taking a lot of organizing, my dear,' her father said mildly. 'It's not quite as easy to set up as your mother's knitting circle, admirable though that is,' he added hastily, smiling at his wife.

Henrietta had the grace to laugh. 'Our efforts will be useful and welcomed, I'm sure, but no, Pips, your father is quite right. A flying ambulance corps must take an awful lot of organization, to say nothing of raising the necessary funds.'

'You just concentrate on learning everything you can,' her father said seriously. 'How's Alice doing?'

'Very well – so far. But we haven't had to dress real wounds yet. I just wonder if she'll be a bit squeamish then.'

Robert teased. 'And of course *you* won't be.'

Pips glared at him. 'Most certainly not.'

Twenty

They didn't have very long to wait to find out if Pips's vehement denial was true. On 12 September, the sister leading their first-aid course said, 'We have the first convoy of casualties arriving tomorrow. Miss Maitland and Miss Dawson, I am assigning you to one of the wards. It will be valuable experience for you.'

Sister Jenkins omitted to say, although she was thinking it, that it would prove whether these young women would be able to face what un-doubtedly lay in wait for them across the Channel. 'You will take instruction from the staff nurse in charge, but on no account must you undertake any physical care of the wounded without super-vision. And you, Mr Dawson, will you act as an orderly on the ward?'

'Yes, sister,' Pips and Alice chorused and William nodded.

The next day their patients arrived in a motley collection of vehicles. Some stretcher cases were even transported in a furniture van. Others, not so seriously injured, came in private cars driven there by willing volunteers from the city and surrounding district. Edwin was amongst them, though he was careful not to divulge that he was a local doctor.

Pips and Alice dispensed hot cocoa and sand-wiches and told them they were to have a bath before being shown to their beds.

'I'll need help, nurse,' one soldier, whose fore-arm was heavily bandaged, said. 'I would like a bath but I'm – er' – suddenly, he was very apolo-getic – 'crawling with lice. I thought we'd got rid of them before we was shipped back home. But I reckon some of the eggs must've been hiding in the seams of our clothes and have hatched since.'

'We'll soon get rid of those little blighters,' Pips said cheerfully, not in the least fazed. 'I'll just check with sister if I'm allowed to help you. You see, I'm not a proper nurse, just a volunteer.'

Swiftly, she explained to Sister Jenkins, who nodded her agreement. 'Just mind you don't get his bandages wet. Let me know when you're done and I'll see to his dressing. Has he had something to eat and drink?'

'Yes, sister.'

'Give his uniform to the orderlies, then. They'll deal with that.'

'Now, tell me your name,' Pips asked as she helped the man to bathe, turning her head away now and again more to spare his embarrassment than her own. But she was happy to wash his back and to help him dry himself.

'Wilson, miss. Private Alan Wilson.'

'Where were you injured?' she asked, trying to take both their minds off his nakedness. Though it didn't trouble Pips in the slightest, she felt for the man's modesty.

'At Mons, miss.' His expression was bleak as he added huskily, 'We was forced to retreat. We don't like that, miss, not us British soldiers, but we had no choice. Worst of it was, some of the townsfolk – men, women and children – were caught in the crossfire when they attended church.'

He sank into silence and, after a short pause, she held out a shapeless nightshirt. 'I'm afraid you'll have to put this rather natty little number on,' she laughed. 'I think the hospital are going to try to get some sort of day clothes for the walking wounded, but they haven't arrived yet.'

It raised a smile and they giggled together as she helped him into the garment. 'Now, let's go and find sister and get that arm looked at by a professional.'

'You'd do for me, miss. I'm sure you're capable, but I wouldn't like you to be in trouble.' He leaned closer. 'Is she the one with two red stripes on her arm?' When Pips nodded, he added, 'Is she a bit of a tartar?'

'No, she's lovely, actually. She's the one who's been leading the first-aid course for those of us preparing to go to the front.'

Alan's thin, unshaven face was shocked. 'You're not going out there, miss, are you?'

'I'm hoping to, yes.'

She could see the fear in his eyes and knew it was not for himself now, but for her. Slowly he shook his head. 'It's bad out there, and it'll get worse. Ne'er mind what they're saying – that it'll be over in a few weeks. This war's going to go on a long time and it'll be a bloody one, an' all. 'Scuse my language.' He held her gaze. 'Don't go, miss. Stay here and nurse the ones that get back here, if you must, but don't go out there.'

'I've given my word,' Pips said solemnly and ex-plained about Dr Hazelwood's plans.

Alan seemed to relax a little. 'Maybe you'll be well behind the lines, then, miss. Away from the shelling. I hope so.'

Pips smiled, but she did not disillusion him. She knew that John Hazelwood's plan was to get as close as possible to the fighting in order to be able to help the wounded quickly. Instead, she said briskly, 'Now, would you like me to shave you and cut your hair?'

'Don't they have a barber visit?'

'I don't think so. It's been part of our training. Sister said it would come in useful.' She grinned. 'I've been practising on my father and brother at home, though I wasn't allowed to trim my father's bushy moustache. He's very proud of it.'

112

Half an hour later, Alan was declaring that it was the best shave he'd had in a long time and advising all his fellow soldiers to book Pips to shave them and cut their hair.

The following day, Pips and Alice experienced their first death of a badly wounded soldier. They felt the staff nurse watching them closely and were determined to show the right amount of concern and sympathy, but not undue emotion. But once in the refuge of their room, the two young women clung to each other. Alice sobbed on Pips's shoulder.

'I – I've never seen a dead b-body before and – and he was so – so mutilated. Oh Pips, it was awful.'

Pips did not allow her own tears to fall, but she held Alice tightly. 'Are you sure you want to carry on?' she murmured gently. 'It'll get worse, you know.'

Resolutely, Alice dried her tears. 'I'm not giving up. Whatever happens, I'll never give up.'

The next convoy was even larger than the first and had more men who were seriously wounded. There were several deaths and Pips and Alice soon learned to care for the deceased tenderly, but then get on with caring for the living.

'You've done well – all three of you,' Sister Jenkins told Pips, Alice and William during the last days of September. 'And you've all had your inoculations, so you're ready to go whenever the call comes.'

Twenty-One

News of the Battle of the Aisne had filled the newspapers during the previous week.

'We should be out there *now*,' Pips fretted.

It was only two days later that they received news that everything was ready for their departure to Belgium and that they should go to London.

'At last,' Pips said, as if they'd been waiting for months. To the impatient girl, it felt as if they had. There was a sudden flurry of activity as last-minute packing was done. Robert and Giles took as many medical supplies as the five of them could carry between them.

On their last evening at home, the family sat around the dinner table. Alice helped the house-maid to serve the meal, as she usually did, under Mr Wainwright's watchful eyes, but at the end of the meal, Edwin rose to his feet.

'Wainwright, would you be good enough to see if William is available to join us in the drawing room.' He glanced at Alice. 'You too, Alice. There is something I wish to say to all of you. And Wainwright, would you open that champagne I've been saving, please. In fact, please ask all the staff to join us on this special occasion. Jake too.'

Ten minutes later, they all trooped into the drawing room, looking ill at ease and somewhat out of place whilst Wainwright deftly poured drinks for everyone. Alice handed them round.

Edwin stood in front of the fireplace and raised his glass. 'I want us all to drink to the health of Dr Hazelwood's flying ambulance corps.'

They all repeated Edwin's toast and then he added, 'And there's something else I would like to add. My wife and I have been discussing the matter and, Robert, we would like you to take our car. I know they are desperately short of vehicles and, whilst it won't be an ambulance exactly, I'm sure you will be able to put it to good use.'

'Are you sure, Father?' Robert frowned. 'What about your rounds?'

Edwin shrugged. 'I managed with a pony and trap for many years and with Jake's help' – he raised his glass to the youth standing awkwardly at the back of the gathering – 'I'm sure we can keep it in working order.'

Red in the face with embarrassment, Jake nevertheless moved forward a few inches and nodded enthusiastically. 'We can, Mr Maitland. I'll get her polished up and looking as good as new.'

'Excellent, excellent.' Edwin beamed. 'So you have no need to worry, Robert.'

'Thank you, Father. The car will be a godsend, I'm sure.'

'And I have some news too,' Henrietta said. 'My fund-raising ladies have been doing such a sterling job that we have raised enough money already to buy and equip a Talbot motor ambulance. It will be waiting for you to collect at Dover. I'm sure you'll be able to arrange for its transportation across the Channel somehow.'

'Mother,' Pips clapped her hands, 'that's amazing.'

'And the ladies' knitting circle in the village is in full swing, led, I might add' – she cast a sympathetic glance at William – 'by your grandmother, William. I think it's given her a new lease of life, though she won't take the credit and insists that Bess Cooper is really in charge.'

As the servants took their leave and scurried back to the kitchen, Henrietta said softly, 'William, you will go and see your family before you leave, won't you?'

William stared at her for a moment before saying quietly but firmly, 'I'm sorry, ma'am, but I can't.'

Henrietta sighed and laid her hand gently on his arm. 'I'm sorry you feel that way, but I do understand. You do realize, don't you, William, that the work for which you have volunteered will be every bit as dangerous – if not more so – as being a soldier? You will not even be allowed to carry a gun to defend yourself.'

'It's what I want to do, ma'am.'

She stared at him for a long moment before saying softly, 'Then may God go with you, my dear boy.'

It was the same heartfelt wish that she was to repeat the following morning as the five of them set off.

Pips felt a little guilty that the hardest farewell was to her horse; it was harder than saying goodbye to members of her family. She knew she would still have communication with them, but with Midnight, there could be nothing.

'Look after him for me, Jake, won't you?' she

said softly as she stroked the animal's neck.

'I'll do me best, miss, but I dun't reckon he'll let me ride him.'

'Then take him into the park or to a field so that he can have a good gallop. He'll always come home, Jake. You needn't worry about him running off.'

For a moment she rested her cheek against his neck and whispered, 'Goodbye, old fella. You be a good boy for Jake. You hear me?'

Then she turned and hurried away, before the tears in her eyes fell.

William said goodbye to Jake, but he did not visit his family. The five spent a night in London and departed the next day for Ostend. Dr Hazelwood, a small, rotund, jovial man with rimless spectacles and a bristling moustache, was waiting for them when the ship docked.

'Have you had a good trip across? No enemy submarines lurking outside the harbour or in the English Channel?'

Robert assured him that their crossing had been uneventful and that none of them had even suffered seasickness.

'Good, good. Now, I will take you to the hotel where you'll spend the night. The other members of the unit will be joining us this evening for dinner. I thought it would be nice for us all to get to know each other. Have a rest after your journey and I will see you later. And be warned, we have an early start tomorrow.'

They congregated in the hotel lounge before dinner, where Dr Hazelwood made the introductions. 'This is Sister Leonore Martens and Nurse Brigitta Dupont. They are both Belgian and speak excellent English.'

The sister was a middle-aged woman, tall and slim and still dressed in her nursing uniform. Oh dear, Pips thought, she looked a tartar. But, to her surprise, as the sister was introduced, her severe expression disappeared when she smiled. Her eyes sparkled with mischief. The nurse was much younger; a fair-haired, pretty girl with blue eyes and smooth, pink skin. She was slight in build and Pips wondered how she would cope with the rigours she guessed would face them all.

'And these two reprobates are brothers, Hugh and Peter Enderby, former London bus drivers, who are willing to do whatever is asked of them. Oh, and I mustn't forget to mention Mrs Parrott. She can't be here tonight but will join us tomorrow morning before we set off. Now, I understand your father has sent his car, Robert?' John's eyes twinkled over his spectacles. 'That is most generous of him, because I can't promise to return it to him in its present condition. And I understand we have a motorcycle and sidecar too. Is that correct?'

At the last moment Giles had decided to bring his own machine along and had had a sidecar fitted.

'I thought it might be useful, sir,' he murmured.

'My dear boy, it most certainly will be.'

'And there's one other thing, Dr Hazelwood,' Robert said. 'My mother's fund-raising has enabled us to bring a fully equipped motor ambulance. Admittedly, it's second-hand, but it's been serviced and declared mechanically sound. It's on its way and should be here by tomorrow morning.'

John Hazelwood's eyes sparkled again. 'Capital, capital, my boy. How generous the people of Lincoln must be. I must write to your mother myself.' Dr Hazelwood was no fool and he suspected that, to have been able to make an ambulance available in such a short space of time, Henrietta had put a great deal of her own money into the fund. But he voiced none of these thoughts to her son. Instead, he said, 'Now, I think they're ready for us in the dining room.'

After dinner, in halting English, the proprietor warned them that the hotel had been shelled the previous evening, but the new arrivals merely shrugged and went to their beds, tired after the four-hour crossing. There would be worse to come, they all knew.

No one questioned each other as to why they were there. William was no longer alone in not having volunteered to fight and, as he went to sleep that night in a strange land and a long way from home, he felt the happiest he had been for several weeks.

Twenty-Two

At breakfast the following morning, Dr Hazelwood laid out his plans. 'We are going to Ghent to start with, but because we are a mobile unit, we will go where we are needed the most, wherever that might be.' For a moment, his face sobered. 'But I have to tell you, my friends, that is always going to be where the fighting is at its most fierce. I want you all to understand that now.' He glanced around at them. 'Because if anyone is unsure, now is the time to say so.' No one said a word and he smiled and nodded. 'Good, good. So, we will proceed. I intend to get you settled, and once I see that you are functioning satisfactorily' – he smiled benignly at them over his rimless spectacles – 'and I do not anticipate any problems on that score, then I shall return to England to set up another unit. Now, you must decide who's driving what vehicle and we can be on our way.'

The two Enderby brothers chose to drive the ambulance donated by the Red Cross, which was waiting for them in Ostend. William drove the ambulance which had been paid for by Henrietta's magnificent fund-raising, taking Nurse Brigitta with him in case he should lose sight of the other vehicles. Dr Hazelwood drove his own car, which he had brought but which he would no doubt take back with him when he returned to England. Mrs Parrott sat beside him. Most probably they wished to discuss financial matters as they travelled. Robert drove Edwin's car with Alice beside him and Sister Leonore in the back seat. Giles rode his motorcycle with Pips in his sidecar.

'We have done very well for vehicles,' Dr Hazelwood said, beaming, as the party set off for Ghent.

'I can't believe how flat it is,' Alice remarked as they covered the miles. 'It's just like Lincolnshire. I feel at home already.'

Robert chuckled, but added seriously, 'Now, I need you to help me, Alice. I'm not used to driving on the right-hand side of the road. You must keep an eye on me and tell me at once if I start to veer to the left.'

'Right you are, Master Robert.'

'Oh, I think we could dispense with the "Master" bit now, don't you?'

Alice blushed. 'I'll try,' was all she could promise.

As they drove into Ghent and found their way to the military hospital, their route was lined with cheering people. 'Is this for us?' Alice asked in wonderment.

'Perhaps they think it's someone important arriving,' Robert said, 'with cars and ambulances and a motorcycle. I wish I'd brought mine too.'

Sister Leonore leaned forward. 'We are important to them, Dr Maitland,' she said. She spoke excellent English with an appealing accent. 'Many of them will be refugees, trying to escape the shelling. They have had to leave their homes, bringing with them only what they can carry. They are happy to see more help arriving and the red crosses on the side of the ambulances will give them hope of medical help, which I am sure will be badly needed.'

'Will we be able to help them?' Robert frowned, thinking of the drain on their medical supplies. 'I mean, we're here to tend military personnel, aren't we?'

'Primarily, yes, but I think you will find that Dr Hazelwood will never turn anyone away –

whoever they are – if they need help.' She paused and then, leaning forward even further, added, 'And you must be prepared to treat German soldiers in just the same way that you treat our own forces. There is no barrier – no *enemy* – when it comes to an injured man, woman or child.'

Robert mulled this over for a few moments before saying, 'I'm glad to hear it. I have to admit that had been worrying me; what to do if a civilian or even, like you say, an enemy, needed our care. You've set my mind at rest, sister. Thank you.'

'I think we will all work very well together. And don't disturb yourself about Nurse Dupont. She is much stronger than she looks, both physically and emotionally. She will cope with whatever she has to face.'

Beside him, Alice murmured, 'I just hope I will,' but only loud enough for Robert to hear.

The staff at the hospital made them very welcome and gave them refreshments on their arrival. Then they were taken on a tour of the wards to meet some of the wounded. For the first time, they all experienced the ravages of the war at first hand. Stoically, Pips and Alice spoke to the injured but, once away from the wards, Alice was white-faced and shaking. 'I didn't realize it would be quite so bad. I mean, we had a taste of it at the Lincoln County, but their injuries were nothing like this. Did you see that poor boy with half his face blown away? I wonder he is still alive.'

'Are you sure you're going to be able to cope?'

Firmly, Alice nodded. 'Yes, I will, Miss Pips. I'm glad we've seen it because now I know what to expect.'

Alice didn't ask Pips if she would be all right; she knew her young mistress. Pips would handle anything.

For the first few days, the unit would be engaged in travelling twenty miles or so to bring wounded from the battlefield to the hospital. Mrs Parrott was given a corner of an office and at once began her bookkeeping and fund-raising. Letters flew from her pen to her contacts back home. The resident doctors at the hospital welcomed the two English doctors, even though they knew the additional help they brought would only be temporary. Sister Leonore and Nurse Brigitta, as they asked to be called, assisted Robert and Giles, whilst the rest of the team were divided between the two ambulances: the Enderby brothers and Alice in one, and Pips and William in the other. They would go to the front line to pick up the wounded.

On the first morning, Robert gathered his team together. 'Now, I just want to know that you have all the medical supplies you need in one of these.'

He handed out a canvas satchel with a red cross on the side to William and the two Enderby brothers. He also gave one to Pips and smiled at her. 'You should have one too, Pips, because I can't see you not going to the front to fetch in the wounded and putting all your first-aid knowledge to the test. What about you, Alice?'

'I'd like one, please. I expect I'll be going too.'

'Now, let's check you've got everything. You should have a water bottle – two, if you can carry them. A tin of morphine tablets, but if you give them to anyone, make sure you write on their

123

forehead in crayon so that the medics know what they've already been given. But only use them in extreme circumstances. And make sure you fill up your bag with as many dressings as you can. Stuff them into every corner. And don't forget a small pair of scissors. I'll get Mrs Parrott to send for some more. And you'll need to try to take care of your hands. You're bound to get blisters.'

'Oh William,' Pips said as they drove out on that first morning, leading the way with the second ambulance following them, 'just look at all these poor refugees fleeing from the danger. But where are they going? Where *can* they go?'

She slowed the vehicle as they passed between lines of refugees trudging along both sides of the road: old men, young boys, women and small children.

'I suppose all the able-bodied men are at the front,' William murmured.

As they journeyed on, they saw just what the people were fleeing from; burned-out houses and buildings, craters caused by the shelling and mounds of debris everywhere.

'Fancy this happening to your homeland. However are they going to recover? Just look at the devastation, William, and the war has only been going a couple of months. Whatever will it look like if it goes on for a long time?'

The vehicle hit a small shell hole in the road and the ambulance jolted, almost throwing William against the windscreen.

'Sorry,' Pips muttered, 'I didn't see it. It's going to be a nightmare driving the seriously wounded back along this road.' Before William could answer, Pips added, 'Ah, this looks like where we want to be. I'll pull over.'

In a bombed-out barn a short distance from the roadside, twenty-three injured soldiers were sitting or lying on the floor. Many had open wounds, others had dirty, makeshift bandages. Pips glanced around; there was no one who appeared to be a doctor or a nurse. None of the wounded seemed to have received any proper medical attention. A feeling of helplessness swept over her. She approached one of the men leaning against the dusty wall.

'Who brought you here?'

'The stretcher bearers,' he whispered. He closed his eyes and rested his head against the wall. Agony was etched into his face and Pips looked down to see a gaping wound in his right leg, so deep that she could see the bone. Far from revolting her, it made her angry. This man would probably lose his leg at the very least because of lack of immediate attention. Infection would set in. She wanted to scoop him up in her arms and rush him back to the hospital that instant. But common sense came to her rescue. She must be practical, she told herself. As her gaze swept around the rest of the barn, she could see that this man was by no means the worst. Men lay groaning, some were obviously unconscious.

'We can't take all of you at once, but we will assess the worst cases and then come back for others as soon as we can.'

Without opening his eyes, and clamping his teeth onto his bottom lip, the soldier nodded.

'William, have the others got here?'

'Just.'

Pips hurried outside to see Alice and the two brothers climbing down from their vehicle and folding back the canvas flaps at the rear in readiness to receive the stretchers.

'There are over twenty wounded in there. Alice, you and I will assess the worst cases. They must be taken back first. Hugh, Peter and you, William, will carry them out to the ambulances. When you have as many as you can take, go back to the hospital, but come back as quickly as you can. There are a lot of stretcher cases, so it will take several journeys to transport them all.'

The three men organized the transfer of the wounded between them and the first trip for both ambulances was made up solely of stretcher cases. Alice went back with William, the two vehicles travelling in tandem, whilst Pips, keeping some medical supplies with her, did what she could to clean up wounds, apply pads of cotton wool covered in gauze and to administer what painkillers she had.

'Mam, I want me mam,' a young soldier – Pips thought he couldn't be older than sixteen – moaned. He was delirious with fever and the gaping edges of the open wound in his thigh were swollen and the flesh was turning a strange grey colour.

'That's bad, that is,' the soldier sitting next to the boy said. 'He'll likely have to have his leg amputated.'

'D'you know how long it is since he was wounded?'

The soldier shifted his position a little and

winced as he did so. 'Three days ago, I reckon. He was lying between the trenches for a day at least.'

'I don't understand. What do you mean "between the trenches"?'

'In some places, both sides are starting to dig in now. They're constructing trenches and we call the piece of land between them "no-man's-land". It's the bit we're both fighting for, I suppose. It's usually about two hundred and fifty yards across, sometimes less, sometimes more. The lad was shot when we went over the top about three days ago.' He wrinkled his forehead. 'Aye, that'd be when he copped it. It's taken us two days to be brought here.'

'How – how long was he out there?'

'Couldn't get him in until night. Both sides allow the wounded to be fetched in after dark. At least, where we are, they do. I don't reckon it's official, of course. It's something that just – happens.'

'We'll get him in the next ambulance. They've just got back.' She turned and called, 'William, over here!'

Gently, she helped William lift the young boy onto a stretcher and then to carry him out to the ambulance. Returning, she said to the soldier, who was still sitting in the same place, 'What about you?'

'I'll be fine till they come back again' – he lowered his voice – 'if they do.'

'Oh, they'll come back.' Pips glanced around at all the wounded still waiting. She marvelled at their stoicism. Not one of them had demanded to be taken first. 'They have to.'

Twenty-Three

'Have you heard from the lads?' Ma asked Norah on the last Tuesday in September as her daughter-in-law ironed the weekly wash.

'No, Ma, I haven't. I'd tell you if I had.'

'No need to snap, love.'

'Sorry, but I'm just so worried about all of them.'

Ma was on the point of saying 'even William', but she bit down on the tip of her tongue to stop herself uttering the words.

Weeks had passed since Bernard and Roy had proudly marched away to report for duty. Ma, Len and Norah had waved to them from the front doorway, but Boy had marched alongside them, pretending that he was going too. Only much later did he return home in a foul mood.

'I thought I could get on the train with 'em, but our Bernard told an officer and he sent me off with a flea in me ear. I *hate* our Bernard,' he'd said, before stamping upstairs to his room and not appearing until the next morning.

After a moment, Ma said, 'What about Alice?'

Norah shook her head. 'No, nothing. But they've only been gone a few days.'

'If I was you, I'd go to the hall and ask Mrs Maitland. She'll be hearing regularly from Miss Pips, no doubt.'

'I could do, I suppose.' Norah sounded doubtful. 'Mebbe I'll send Boy to have a word

128

with Jake. He'll know if owt's been heard.'

Ma laughed wryly. 'All the staff will. I reckon household staff know more about what's going on than their masters do.' She paused and then added slyly, 'You could see Mrs Warren if you don't want to trouble the mistress.'

'No, I aren't going anywhere near there. I'll send Boy tonight.'

But that evening, Harold did not arrive home.

'Where is he, Len? Where's he gone?'

'Stop panicking, woman. He's likely out with young Peggy. He left the workshop at the normal time. I've heard he's been seeing a lot of her since the lads went.'

'I'm surprised her mam lets her keep company with boys.'

'They're only kids. Leave 'em be, Norah. They won't come to no harm.'

Norah glared at him. 'Kids, you say? Huh! Our Harold thinks he's old enough to go to war. Oh my!' She clapped her hand over her mouth and stared at her husband with wide eyes. 'Oh Len, you don't think he's gone to try and join up again? The boys aren't there this time to stop it happening.'

'He's only sixteen, Norah. Of course they won't take him.'

'He looks older, though, and he'll lie. He'll do anything to get in.'

'Just get the supper on the table, Norah, and stop fussing.'

Norah did as her husband asked, but her own appetite deserted her. As she was clearing away the remnants of the meal, a knock came at the back door and she opened it to find Peggy Cooper standing there. The young girl – fair-haired like her elder sister, Betty, but smaller in stature – stared wide-eyed at Norah.

'Is Harold here?' she asked.

'Hello, love. No, he's not.'

'That's why I've come.' The girl was fearful; something was obviously troubling her. 'Can – can I come in?'

'Oh yes, of course. Sorry, love.' Norah opened the door wider and ushered the girl through the back scullery and into the kitchen. For a moment the girl seemed terrified at having to face the three of them. Sensing her nervousness, Ma said kindly, 'Come in, duck, we don't bite.'

Peggy twisted her fingers together. 'You might – when you know what I've come to tell you.'

Now, all three stared at her.

'What? What is it?' Norah's voice was high-pitched, almost, as if she guessed what the girl was about to say.

Peggy pulled in a deep breath and said in a rush, 'He's gone to enlist. He went after work so's you wouldn't suspect and he asked me to come and tell you if he wasn't home by nine o'clock tonight.' She glanced at the bracket clock on Norah's mantelpiece. The time showed ten minutes past nine.

For a long moment there was silence in the room and then Norah collapsed into a chair near the table and rested her head in her hands. 'I knew it,' she muttered. 'I knew he'd find a way to do it.' She raised her head and her anguished eyes sought Len's face. 'You'll have to go into the city and stop it. It might not be too late.'

But Len only shrugged. 'I aren't even going to try. At least Boy's no coward.' The words hung heavily in the room.

'So,' Norah said flatly, 'that's all of them gone. All my children. I might lose them all, every one of them.'

'Don't be silly, woman. Alice won't be in danger. She'll be well behind the lines. Miss Pips will see to that.' His tone was heavy with sarcasm as he added, 'They just want to play at being nurses, smooth the wounded soldier's fevered brow and write letters home for them. They won't be anywhere near the fighting. You mark my words. And as for – *him'* – Len could not even bring himself to utter his son's name – 'you can be sure he'll keep well out of danger, coward that he is.'

Twenty-Four

As the two ambulances drew away from the now empty barn, the shelling started. It had taken them all day and the night too, for as soon as they thought they had loaded the last of the wounded, another seventeen, who had just been retrieved from the area between the trenches under cover of darkness, were brought into the barn. And then, with the first light of dawn, the bombardment had started. Now, almost dropping with fatigue, dishevelled and hungry, the team headed back to the hospital with shells exploding all around them.

'Want me to drive, Miss Pips?' William asked.

Pips shook her head. 'You're exhausted, but you've done a grand job today, William.'

'You must be tired an' all.'

'A bit,' was all Pips would admit. 'Robert says we must get some sleep whenever and wherever we can. And eat, William. You must eat and drink whenever you can too.'

'I will, but first I need to mend my jacket. One poor feller clutched at it and tore my sleeve.'

In their spare moments, the stretcher bearers sat together and swapped stories whilst they mended their uniforms. Talking about their experiences together helped to deal with the horrors they were now witnessing.

The hospital was overwhelmed with the new arrivals and there was no rest for anyone yet. After a quick wash and something to eat, Pips and Alice went into the wards to help. Robert and Giles had remained on duty too through the night, helping their colleagues wherever they could. Their eyes were dark with exhaustion, but whilst there were still wounded to attend to, they kept on working. The two nurses, Sister Leonore and Brigitta, were still at their sides.

When at last they were able to leave their patients they fell into bed without even talking to one another, so great was their weariness, but later that morning, over a hurried meal before they set out again, Pips wanted to know how those they had already brought back had fared.

'The young boy with the bad thigh wound? How is he?'

'There were several of them, Pips,' Robert said.

'Which one do you mean?'

'He was a very young boy – probably not even old enough to be fighting, but his wound was swollen and turning grey.'

'Ah yes, I know the one you mean. It was gas gangrene.'

'Gas? You mean – the enemy are using gas?'

Robert shook his head. 'No, nothing to do with that. It's that the wound creates a kind of gas within it and bubbles. You can actually hear it crackling. We think it's caused by infection from lying on the open ground or in muddy shell holes for hours before being rescued. There's still so much we don't know yet.' He looked straight into her eyes. 'There's little we can do once they've got it and I'm sorry to tell you, Pips, that the boy died early this morning.'

Pips brushed away the tears that sprang to her eyes. She must not cry, she told herself fiercely. She would have to face this sort of thing every day from now on. 'Would – would it have helped if we could have got to him sooner?'

'I expect so, yes.' Trying to divert her away from thoughts of the boy, Robert said, 'And talking of using gas as a weapon, it's not widely known but the French used tear gas grenades against the Germans in August. I think we can expect retaliation from them and I fully expect they will come up with something even more deadly.'

Pips was silent for a few moments before saying softly, 'This isn't going to be over by Christmas, is it?'

Grimly, Robert shook his head. 'No, Pips, it isn't.'

Twenty-Five

'Well, if you won't go, then I will,' Norah said. It wasn't often she deliberately disobeyed her husband, or even argued with him, but this was too important to her to give way to him. And, though she'd said nothing yet, Norah believed that Ma agreed with her.

For a moment Len glared at her. His mouth tightened and his eyes glittered, but then he shrugged and turned away to leave the cottage. 'Do what you like,' he muttered over his shoulder.

Norah glanced helplessly at her mother-in-law.

'He'll not speak to you for a day or two, Norah, but you go, duck. You'll likely get a lift from a carrier, mebbe, or someone going into the city. You need to know where Boy is. I'd go mesen if I could walk that far, but I can't. I'll do the vegetables and see to Len's dinner. I can do that for you. There's only him left now,' she added sadly, 'and how he's going to cope with all the work on his own, I don't know.'

'He'll have to employ someone from the village. Someone who's either too old or too young to go. I'd thought Harold was too young...' Her voice faded away in hopelessness, and to keep herself from bursting into tears, she hurried about her housework.

About mid-morning, wearing her best Sunday hat and coat, Norah set off to walk towards

Lincoln. She'd gone about a mile when a pony and trap drew up alongside her and Jake said, 'Want a lift, missus? Oh, it's you, Mrs Dawson.' He hesitated a moment, unwilling to get into any arguments with her about William, but he could hardly drive past her. 'Want a lift into town?'

'Thank you, Jake. That's good of you.' As she settled herself and Jake flicked the reins for the horse to move on, she added, 'Our Harold's disappeared and we think he's gone to volunteer. He tried when the lads went, but they told the recruiting officer that he was too young and put a stop to it.'

Jake, who was small and slight and looked nothing like his fourteen years, said, 'He looks older than sixteen, missus. I reckon they might tek him. Besides, I heard they don't ask too many questions if a lad's willing.'

Norah sighed. 'That's what I'm afraid of.' She glanced at the solemn face of the boy beside her. 'You don't know anything, do you, Jake? He didn't come to you like–' She broke off, just as unwilling to raise the subject of William between them as Jake was.

'No, missus, he didn't.'

As they approached the outskirts of the city, Jake said, 'I'll take you to the barracks on Burton Road. Or to the Drill Hall. I hear that's a recruiting centre, an' all. He'll have gone to one of 'em. Which one d'you want to try first?'

'Let's go to the Drill Hall. It'll save going up the hill if I can find something out there.'

As they drew close, they could see a line of men waiting at the door.

'Looks like they're still joining up,' Jake said. 'It'll be this Kitchener poster that's plastered everywhere that's doing it. He makes you think he's pointing directly at you.'

'Huh! Harold didn't need no poster to tell him. He couldn't wait to go the minute war was declared. Before, if truth be told.' As she climbed down from the trap, Norah said, 'Thanks for the lift, Jake. You're a good lad.' She met his gaze, trying to communicate silently her thanks to him for having helped William. She didn't dare to speak the words aloud, but she hoped he understood. She had very mixed feelings about her William. Whilst she was ashamed of him that he had not shown more courage, she did not agree with her husband in throwing him out of his home. And she certainly didn't like what his brothers had done to him, even though Len had shown no sign of disapproval. Maybe, if he'd been allowed to stay within the family circle, they could have persuaded him to do his duty.

'I'll call round this way when I'm ready to leave,' Jake offered. 'Then I can take you back.'

Norah nodded and turned away to join the end of the long line of men. They were all in a merry mood, laughing and joking and excited at the prospect of a fine adventure.

'You come to enlist, missus?' the man at the end of the queue asked.

'No, I've come to see if they've accepted my sixteen-year-old son. If they have, I want to stop him going.'

The man sobered and shook his head. 'They'll not let you do that. If he's signed up and taken

136

the King's Shilling, that'll be it.'

'We'll see,' Norah said, her mouth pursed with determination.

It took over an hour for her to reach the head of the line, and by that time there were as many standing behind her as there had been in front of her. At last she found herself standing in front of a burly recruiting officer. Swiftly she explained her mission, but was met with a steely, disapproving stare. Nevertheless, he asked curtly, 'When do you think he might have come here?'

'Yesterday. Late afternoon or early evening.'

Grudgingly, he said, 'I'll check the lists for you, but I doubt I can do much. If he's signed up, he's committed.'

'But he's only sixteen. He's too young. He came with his brothers when they enlisted, but they told the recruiting officer his age and he was refused.'

The sergeant turned to a fellow officer. 'Hold the fort, will you, Martin? I'd better check this out. Just stand aside, missus, and let the next volunteer forward. I'll see what I can do.'

He was gone ten minutes and Norah wondered if he'd really had time to check the lists thoroughly, especially when he said, 'Sorry, missus, no name of Harold Dawson on the list of names we took yesterday. Can't help you, I'm afraid.'

Can't or won't, Norah thought bitterly. As she was about to turn away the other officer, whose name was Martin – though whether that was his Christian name or his surname Norah couldn't be sure – said, 'If he's that keen to join up and we refused him, sergeant, he might have gone to

137

Newark, where nobody would know him. They're recruiting for the Sherwood Foresters there.'

'Oh, but he wanted to be in the Lincolns,' Norah said. 'Like his brothers.'

'But which did he want the most, missus? To be with his brothers or to volunteer to be a soldier?'

For a long moment, Norah stared at him, feeling as if her heart turned over in her chest as she realized the truth.

More than anything, Harold wanted to be a soldier.

Twenty-Six

'We're a bit short of petrol at the moment,' Giles told Pips, 'so we can't make quite so many trips to the front lines. How about we take an afternoon off? I've found a nice little tea shop. Do say you'll come.'

'Of course. It'd be lovely to get out of this uniform for an hour or two – much as I'm proud to wear it.'

As they walked from the hospital to seek out the tea shop, they paused to buy souvenirs and postcards to send home.

'Oh look, there's a hairdresser's. I must come and have my hair trimmed and washed properly.'

'Why don't you go in and see if they can see you later this afternoon?' Giles smiled. 'No time like the present. You might not get another chance. I know you girls like to have your hair done.'

'And how do you know so much about girls?' she teased, pretending indignation.

'I have an older sister,' he said promptly. 'Now, go on.'

She made an appointment for an hour later. As she emerged from the salon, she spotted a photographer's studio on the opposite side of the street. 'Do let's have our photograph taken, Giles.'

'You should be in your uniform for that, shouldn't you?'

'Oh phooey! Yes, I suppose so.'

'We'll come back another day. Now, let's find this tea shop. I'm starving.'

They sat opposite one another and talked about their lives before the war.

'Did you always want to be a doctor – a surgeon?'

'Yes, I did. Right from being a small boy.'

'So did I,' she sighed. 'Well, a doctor, but my parents – no, that's not quite right – my *mother* wouldn't hear of it. I think I could have got round my father, but...' She shrugged. 'There was no persuading Mother. I'm lucky to be even here doing a bit of nursing.'

Giles reached across the table and touched her hand. 'It's much more than "a bit of nursing", Pips. You're doing a wonderful job.'

'It's a team effort, isn't it? We couldn't do it without each other.'

'That's true.'

'Tell me about your family. You know so much about mine, but all you've said so far is that your father's a teacher and you have a married sister. Has she any children?'

'Not yet, but we're hopeful. My mother can't wait to be a grandmother.'

Pips pulled a face. 'Are they all like that? Mothers?'

'Probably. I know it was our mother's prime motive in life to find a suitable husband for Mary. Now that's been accomplished, she's turned her attention to me.'

'I know the feeling.'

'Maybe we should put them both out of their misery and marry each other,' he said lightly.

Pips chuckled. 'You're certainly "suitable" in my mother's eyes, but what would your mother think of me?'

'She'd adore you – like we all do. I tell you what, let's persuade the others to come and have their photos taken tomorrow too so that we can send them home.'

'That's a lovely idea.'

Alice and Robert agreed to go too, but William was adamant.

'No, Miss Pips. I've no one I wish to send a photo to. They wouldn't want one anyway.'

'Well, if you change your mind...'

'I won't,' he said firmly. 'But – thank you for asking me. It's nice of you to include me.'

'You're part of the team, William, a very important part. Don't ever forget it.'

It was a merry party that set out to visit the photographer's studio. For an hour or so, they could forget the war, except that Pips and Alice were dressed in their nurse's uniforms, with clean aprons, caps and cuffs over their grey dresses.

'We should wear our capes, too,' Pips said, 'turned back to show the red lining.'

'It'll only be black and white, though, won't it?'

'The photographer said he can tint them. We'll pick the best ones out and just have those done.'

They had photographs taken singly and then in groups.

'I want a picture of you and Alice together, Pips – Dr Hazelwood's nurses – so that we can send them home to our families,' Robert said. 'It really is a lovely uniform Dr Hazelwood has designed.'

'You speak English very well,' Giles remarked to the photographer as they stood waiting for him to organize the poses he wanted.

The man shrugged. 'It is the second language here. Now, miss,' he addressed Pips, 'you stand so, and you, miss,' he turned to Alice, 'stand at her side, put your hands on her shoulders and lean in a little towards her.'

The girls giggled together, their heads almost touching.

'Perfect,' the man said. 'So beautiful!'

As they walked home, Giles said softly, 'Pips, may I have a copy of one of the photographs of you on your own?'

'If you want one, of course.'

'I do.'

Their few days of respite were short-lived.

'There've been heavy casualties at Antwerp. The town is under siege,' Robert told the team. 'We're to expect a train of badly injured Belgian soldiers. We must ask the hospital what they want us to do.'

'We can go to the station and help to ferry them back here,' Pips suggested. 'If they're agreeable.'

The doctors and nurses at the hospital were grateful to accept any help they could get; they knew they were going to be stretched to the limits yet again. Dr Hazelwood and his team used all the vehicles at their disposal and Pips and Alice were waiting on the platform when the train drew in. They were appalled by the seriousness of the soldiers' injuries and moved quickly amongst them to administer whatever first aid they could there and then. When the platform was crowded with stretchers and walking wounded, another train pulled in.

'Oh, not another one,' Alice murmured. 'We haven't got these patients moved yet.'

'It's not one from the front,' Pips said, worriedly. 'It's British soldiers on their way there. Oh dear, they really oughtn't to see this. It's hardly good for morale, is it?'

But as the new arrivals jumped down from the train, the Belgian soldiers called cheery greetings to them. Some British soldiers, after a moment's hesitation, moved amongst the lines of stretchers, squatting down to talk to their comrades. Several gave the wounded men cigarettes, lighting them and then placing them between their lips. Hugh, Peter and William loaded the two ambulances and drove back to the hospital. Dr Hazelwood and Pips took the cars with as many non-stretcher cases as they could fit into them, leaving Alice with the casualties. Local women provided tea and sandwiches, their faces solemn. Some were close to tears, though they tried to hide their sorrow bravely. These were their men and their defeat cut them deeply. And now there was fear. The enemy was moving ever closer. Could no one stop them?

Everyone at the hospital worked until the early hours and then, with only a couple of hours' sleep, were up again to receive yet more wounded.

'I will stay a few days more,' John Hazelwood said, 'but then I really think I must go back to England and try to form more units. The need is even greater than I had envisaged.'

'I don't think we're in the right place,' Pips said to Robert and Giles over dinner three days later when the numbers of casualties they were bringing into the hospital showed no sign of diminishing. 'We're supposed to be a mobile unit – a "flying" ambulance. So, why aren't we moving to where the fighting is? The injuries of the wounded are so bad that, after a train journey, there's little hope of saving some of them.'

Robert shrugged, reaching for the bread. 'At the moment, whilst he's here, we do what Dr Hazelwood tells us.'

'But–'

'Pips, we can't argue' – he leaned forward – 'yet. But he's obviously itching to get back to England to set up another unit. He thinks we're working very well.' Robert winked at her. 'But once he's gone...'

'Yes, but when? We should be where the main battle is going on and as near to the front as possible, not here in Ghent. Do you know what's happening elsewhere?'

'We were too late arriving here for the battle at

Mons,' Giles said, 'from which, sadly, the British eventually had to retreat a couple of hundred miles as far as the River Marne. But then the Allies forced the Germans back across the river and both sides dug in for a while. Now, though, Antwerp seems to be their focus, but they'll move south-westwards from there. Already there's fighting at towns only about twelve miles to the east from here.'

Pips stared at him. 'They're coming towards us, then, aren't they?'

Solemnly, Robert nodded. 'You see, Pips, there isn't just one area of fighting. It's going on along a front that stretches from Switzerland all along the border between France and Germany and through Belgium. Both sides are trying to get to the coast to occupy the Channel ports,' Robert went on, 'particularly Calais.'

Giles laughed wryly. 'A sort of race to get to the sea first, eh?'

'Something like that.'

'And that's what they're doing now?' Pips said. 'So they're not actually fighting each other so much as moving their troops.'

'Oh no, they're fighting each other every step of the way.'

'Where are they now?'

'Heading towards Ypres and, if the Germans take Antwerp and move towards Ghent, then we'll have to move.'

'So, are we all going to converge at Ypres, then?'

'It looks like it.'

'Why don't we go there now?'

Giles said, 'Maybe we should. Not wait to be

driven back by the Germans. I intend to have a word with Dr Hazelwood.'

'Then you're a braver man than I am,' Robert laughed.

But, as it turned out, Dr Hazelwood entirely agreed with them. 'That is the sole purpose of having a flying ambulance corps; to be able to travel to where we are needed the most. However, I am on the point of departing for England. Do you think you can arrange to move to Ypres yourselves?'

'Of course,' Robert and Giles chorused, and Robert added, 'Leave it to us, sir. We'll organize everything.'

'If you are to be truly mobile, you will need tents. I have ordered six large ones from England and a few smaller ones for the team to sleep in, together with more equipment. It should all be arriving any day now.' He smiled benignly at Robert. 'Thanks to Mrs Parrot's contacts in England and your mother's sterling fund-raising back in Lincolnshire. And of course, wherever you end up, if you can find empty barns or houses that haven't been completely destroyed by shells, then use them by all means.'

'Mother will be delighted. Did you know that a huge parcel of balaclavas, socks and gloves arrived yesterday from my home village?'

'I did. They will be most useful in the approaching winter.' His face clouded. 'I shudder to think what will happen when the weather gets bitterly cold.' Then he seemed to shake himself out of his melancholy thoughts. 'Still, all we can do is our best. Now, are you sure you can cope with the number we have in the corps, or do you want me to recruit one or two more when I get back home?'

The two young doctors exchanged a glance before Giles said, 'I think we can manage at the moment, sir.'

The older man nodded. 'Very good, but if you should find yourselves overstretched, do let me know. Tired doctors and nurses are not going to be of much use to seriously wounded and sick men. You mustn't think of it as weakness to get plenty of rest and even a day or so off when you can. And now, I must ready myself for my departure. I'll see you when I get back. Somewhere near Ypres, I expect.'

Twenty-Seven

After John Hazelwood had left, the team lingered in Ghent another day or two. There were still wounded being brought in and both Robert and Giles were reluctant to leave.

'I know we'll have to go, but the hospital can't cope with the influx of casualties,' Robert said. 'We can hardly just up sticks and move and leave them in the lurch.'

'Don't let's leave it too long,' Pips said. 'I don't fancy being captured.'

Robert said, 'You're right, we'll go tomorrow. It's obvious where they're heading. I don't think it'll be long before Antwerp falls and then they'll be heading towards Ghent. Rumour has it that there's already fighting near Ypres, and we need to get to a place where we can establish ourselves as a semi-permanent fixture.'

They set up camp to the west of Ypres on 6 October, near Brandhoek. It was an ideal place for their medical unit. Situated on the main road between Ypres and Poperinghe, it was fairly safe from enemy shellfire and casualties could be received from the front lines, treated and then sent on by road or rail to Poperinghe and thence to base hospitals on the French coast.

The Enderby brothers and William erected the tents; three small tents for the women and the two doctors to sleep in, two to a tent, and a slightly larger one for the brothers and William, sleeping in a circle with their feet to the central pole. Mrs Parrott was billeted in a nearby cottage. Then there were six large tents, one of which would act as a treatment room, one as an emergency operating theatre, and three of which would become hospital 'wards' for medical and surgical cases. The last one would be the moribund ward, where those beyond all help would be placed and kept as comfortable as possible.

'We're here not a moment too soon,' Giles told them the following morning. 'I've just heard that there are thousands of enemy troops marching along the road from Menin towards Ypres.'

'Will they come here?' Brigitta asked fearfully. So much had been heard about the atrocities committed by enemy soldiers in the early days of the war as they'd begun their march through Belgium to reach France. It was understandable that any Belgian girl would fear for her safety. William

147

moved to her side.

'I'll look after you,' he whispered. The girl glanced up at him with a grateful smile.

'I think they might be content – for the time being – to occupy the town.' Giles sighed. 'No doubt they'll take everything the townsfolk have in the way of food, certainly.'

That night Hugh and Peter Enderby, together with William, set out towards the town. They told no one of their venture, fearing that they would be stopped, so it wasn't until the following morning that they were missed.

'D'you think they've been captured?' Brigitta asked, her voice high-pitched with fear. 'Did the Germans come in the night and take them?' The young girl looked close to tears until Sister Leonore said briskly, 'Pull yourself together, nurse. If the Germans had come here, we'd all have known about it.'

The girl seemed to calm down at once under the sister's stern common sense.

'She's right,' Pips said, 'but where can they be?'

'I've a shrewd suspicion they might have gone into the town to see what's happening.'

'Oh Giles, no. They'll be in danger.'

Giles shrugged. 'They're not in uniform. They might be able to pass themselves off as townsfolk.'

'But they can't speak the language, can they? What will happen if they're questioned?'

To this, Giles had no answer, but Robert said, 'I shall give them a dressing-down when they do get back. We can't have any of our party just disappearing without warning. We need to stay together.'

The trio returned about mid-afternoon bringing useful news. Robert decided to say little for the present.

'They've virtually ransacked the town,' William began and Hugh and Peter joined in eagerly.

'They've taken over Cloth Hall as a billet, the railway station and–'

'Schools, and they've descended on people's homes demanding to be fed and accommodated.'

'The local bakers were up all night to provide bread for all of them.'

'How many do you think are there?' Robert asked.

'Several thousand, I'd say. The town's crammed with soldiers, horses, carts, guns – everything an army takes with it.'

'And they're taking anything they want. More horses and carts – and food, of course – promising the people they'll be paid, but they won't be, will they?'

'Have they – done anything?' Brigitta asked. 'I mean, how have they treated the people?'

William moved to her side at once. 'Apart from stealing from them, they've treated the townsfolk quite well. They haven't harmed anyone. Not that we've heard.'

'But at midday, they started to move out,' Hugh said.

'Are they coming this way?' Pips asked, even before the young nurse could voice the question.

'We stayed long enough to see where they were going,' Hugh said. 'The soldiers began to march on the road to the south-west, but the cavalry were heading this way. Have you seen anything?'

'No,' Robert said, 'nor heard anything.'

'Was there any fighting?' Giles asked. 'Are there wounded to be helped?'

'Not that we know of. The townsfolk didn't put up any resistance.'

'How could they?' William said. 'Sensibly, the mayor told them to stay in their homes.'

'So what happens now?' Pips demanded. 'What do we do?'

'Stay here for the moment,' Robert said. Then he glanced at each of the three men. 'You've brought us useful information, but please, don't disappear again without telling us. We didn't know what had happened to you.'

William looked upon Robert as the natural leader of the corps, now that Dr Hazelwood had left them. 'Yes, we should have told you. I'm sorry, sir.'

Robert smiled and murmured, 'Robert now, William. Just Robert.'

Twenty-Eight

'At last!' Norah came into the kitchen waving a letter. Every day since Bernard and Roy had left, she had watched out for the postman and this morning her persistence – it could not be said to be patience – had been rewarded.

She tore open the envelope and sat down in

Len's chair to read it.

'Are they all right?'

After a moment's pause whilst Norah finished reading it for herself, she said, 'I'll read it to you:

'*Dear Mam, Dad, Ma and Boy,*

Well, here we are at last with a few lines to you. We are both well and are in Belton Park, near Grantham. We believe we're the first service battalion to be raised after Lord Kitchener's call for volunteers. Now that's something to be proud of, isn't it? The other lads are all great and we're having a lot of fun, though the training is hard, but not for me and Roy. We're a couple of tough nuts! Things are improving now, but when we first got here there were no uniforms or rifles for us. Target practice was with air guns. Of course, we're well used to them, as you know, so me and Roy were "top of the class".'

'They sound as if they're enjoying it all, as if they're on holiday,' Ma sniffed. 'Have they forgotten what it's all about?'

Norah sighed. 'Ma, from the beginning, all these young men seem to think it's a big adventure.'

'Maybe they haven't seen the papers about the defeat at Mons and the pictures of the wounded like we have,' Ma murmured.

Norah nodded and said quietly, 'That was when it started to come home to me, Ma, exactly what they'd let themselves in for.'

The two women stared at each other.

'And that's what Boy has gone into, an' all.'

Norah jumped up. 'I've got to try and find out about him. I'll do what you suggested. I'll go to

151

the hall. I'll go this very minute before I lose me nerve.'

'Ivy,' Norah, sitting in the kitchen at the hall, addressed the cook, 'do you think the mistress would help me?'

Ivy Bentley eyed her visitor sceptically. She'd heard all about the shenanigans over William and if she were truthful – which she always was – she couldn't really decide whose side, if sides there were to be taken, she was on. But one thing she did know; she did not approve of how William's brothers had treated him.

Rotund and bustling, she made a cup of tea and set it down in front of Norah. Sitting down herself with a sigh – it was a relief for her aching feet to have an excuse to sit for a few moments – she said abruptly, ''Pends what it is, Norah.'

'It's young Harold. He's disappeared.'

Ivy was about to ask sarcastically if he was hiding somewhere covered in yellow paint and feathers, but one look at Norah's distraught face silenced the remark. 'How do you think the mistress could help you?'

'We think he's gone to enlist. He went with the boys the first time but they made sure the recruiting officers knew his age.'

'And now you think he might have gone back on his own?'

'Yes. I've asked at the Drill Hall and then young Jake took me up the hill to the barracks, but the answer was just the same. They can't – or won't – tell me anything. They did say they haven't a record of him going to either place, but one

152

officer suggested he might have gone to Newark to enlist in the Sherwoods.'

'But he's underage, Norah. No one should take him.'

'I know,' Norah said bleakly, 'but that doesn't stop them. There's a lad we've heard of in the village who's got in and he's only a few months older than Harold.'

'Did he go to Newark?'

Norah nodded miserably. 'We reckon Harold must've been talking to him and maybe that's what gave him the idea.'

'But how do you think the mistress could help?'

'She's got influence. She could write to the authorities and point out his age. He should never have been accepted.'

'But you're not sure that he has been, are you?'

'No, but – where else can he be?'

'Mm, I see your point.'

The two women sat in silence, each busy with her thoughts. At last Ivy said, 'I'll send young Sarah to see if Mrs Maitland will see you, but I don't hold out much hope that she can do much.' She smiled wryly. 'Even Mrs Maitland can't tell the army what to do.'

Ten minutes later, Norah was again explaining her dilemma to Henrietta.

'I'm willing to try, Mrs Dawson, but I'm very much afraid that, if he has enlisted as you think, it'll be too late.'

'If only he'd said something, we could have let him go with Miss Pips and Alice if he'd wanted to be involved in some way.'

153

Henrietta raised her eyebrows. Even now, no mention was made of William. It really seemed as if, for his family, William no longer existed.

'What does his father say?'

'The same as you've just said, ma'am. That if he's joined up, they won't release him.'

'I'll do what I can, Mrs Dawson.'

That evening Henrietta discussed the matter with Edwin and together they composed a letter addressed to the Commanding Officer at the Newark Recruiting Centre. It was sent the next day, but a week later a terse reply was received stating that Harold had indeed enlisted in the Sherwood Foresters and was already at basic training camp. Henrietta went herself to break the news to Norah and Ma Dawson.

'I'm so sorry, Mrs Dawson.' She seemed to address both women who bore the name 'Mrs Dawson'.

'You did your best, ma'am,' Norah said flatly. 'Thank you for trying.'

'If only young Peggy had told us what she knew earlier,' Ma said harshly, 'we might have been able to stop him.'

'You can't blame her, Ma. She was being loyal to Harold. But, at least,' Norah said, trying to smile at Mrs Maitland, 'we know for certain now where he is.'

'Although they've accepted him,' Henrietta said, trying to comfort the two women whose anguish was written plainly on their faces, 'they'll realize his youth and perhaps they won't send him overseas for some while.'

Norah nodded, but could not speak now. Instead, she clung to the hope that Mrs Maitland was right. Maybe he wouldn't be sent to France yet, maybe not at all.

The subject of their concern was, at that moment, enjoying himself in a way he'd never have thought possible. He was in the company of men who treated him as an equal, who called him by his proper name, either 'Harold' or 'Dawson', and who even admired him for his skills.

'By 'eck, Dawson, tha's a fine shot for a young 'un,' a volunteer like himself whose name he'd learned was Jim Leatham, remarked. 'Where did tha learn to shoot like that?'

Careful not to give too much away about himself, Harold grinned and said, 'I grew up in the countryside. My brothers taught me to shoot.'

The older man guffawed. 'Teach tha to do a spot of poaching, did they?'

Harold frowned. 'No. Our village owes its livelihood to the estate. We wouldn't do that to Mrs–' He clamped his mouth shut, afraid that already he'd said too much.

'Where's tha from, then?'

Harold grinned. 'Now that'd be telling, wouldn't it?'

Smiling knowingly, with his head on one side, Leatham eyed him. 'I'd say tha's a Lincolnshire yeller-belly.'

Harold's jaw dropped and before he could stop himself he asked, 'How'd you know that?'

'It's the accent, lad. It's a dead giveaway.'

'Where are you from, then?' Harold asked,

155

trying to divert attention from himself.

Jim Leatham puffed out his chest. 'Yorkshire. The biggest and best county in the British Isles.'

'Lincolnshire's not far behind you, mate. I learned that at school.'

'Aye, well, you're right there, lad. I'll give you that. Now...' he leaned closer to Harold and dropped his voice – 'you stick with me, young 'un, 'cos if I'm not much mistaken, tha's underage.' He tapped the side of his nose. 'But we'll say nowt about it, eh? Us northerners must stick together.'

Harold grinned. 'Thanks.'

'I don't reckon they'd boot you out anyway, 'specially as you're such a fine shot, but they might hold you back from the rest of us when we get sent over there. Mind you, I don't reckon any of us are going anywhere yet. They're sending the territorials afore they let us loose on the enemy.'

'D'you think so?' Harold was crestfallen. He wanted to get 'stuck in'.

'Sure of it. So, it's just a lot of marching and shooting and bayonet practice for us. But it's not a bad life, is it, lad?'

'It's a great life. I reckon I'll sign on as a regular when it's all over.'

Leatham's smile faded. He patted Harold's shoulder and his voice was a little husky as he said, 'Aye, lad, that's a good idea. You just hold on to that, eh?'

The older man did not add, 'if you come back'. He guessed the young boy, who shouldn't even be here, had been caught up in the patriotic fever to enlist. Perhaps others in the village where he lived, maybe even his family – the brothers he'd spoken of – had volunteered and the young lad had felt left out. No doubt over the coming weeks, in snatches of conversation, he'd find out. Leatham felt – rather than knew at this moment – that Harold didn't really understand it all, but he did. At least, he knew a little of what they had to expect if and when they were sent to the front. He'd read the papers about the bloodbath at Mons at the end of August and the battles that were going on this very minute.

Breaking into the man's thoughts, Harold asked, 'How come, if you're such a proud Yorkshireman, you've joined the Sherwoods?'

'Ah, now, that'd be telling.'

Harold grinned. So, he thought, he wasn't the only one with secrets.

Twenty-Nine

The battle for Ypres, the town that both sides of the conflict looked upon as the gateway to the sea ports, was still raging throughout October. The unit worked day after day fetching the wounded from the battlefronts, but still the journey to get back to the dressing station was too far; many died on the way or, in need of first-aid treatment much sooner, suffered or died unnecessarily.

'I know that we can't move the whole unit close, but surely we could establish an advanced first-aid post much nearer to the front lines,' Pips said for the umpteenth time to Giles.

'I agree with you. I had two patients yesterday who, if only they'd had even basic medical attention hours earlier, I might have managed to save. As it was...' His voice faded away and for a moment his face was bleak. Pips touched his arm, but could find no words of comfort; there were none.

'I'm sure Dr Hazelwood meant us to be nearer the front,' she said at last. 'That's why he called us a flying ambulance corps. We should be within a mile of the firing line. Some of the RAMC advanced dressing stations are positioned between the field artillery and the trenches. That's where we should be.'

'Let's talk to Robert. But first, there's a lull in the arrival of wounded and there's no sound of shelling. I know it's a bit cold, but let's go for a walk.'

'We'd better tell someone.' Pips smiled. 'We don't want to be in trouble for disappearing.'

'You really wouldn't think there was a war on,' Giles said as they stood arm in arm beneath the shelter of a copse. 'The land here is hardly touched and there are even a few birds about.'

'D'you know, that's the first thing I noticed when we were near the trenches. Even when the guns fell silent, there was no birdsong. It was eerie.'

'They've more sense than to stay in such a place. More sense than we have.'

'How long's it going to go on, d'you think?'

'There's no chance of it being over by Christmas like they all said. I'm sorry to say that neither side seems to be making any real headway. And now winter's almost here, both sides are digging in where they are. We'll reach a sort of stalemate, so it could go on for years.'

They walked a little further beneath the trees until Pips said reluctantly, 'We'd better go back.'

As they turned to retrace their steps, Giles took her hands in his and gently turned her to face him. 'Pips, I know this isn't the time or the place, but I have to say it. Well, just in case...'

'Go on,' she prompted.

'You must know I've fallen in love with you.'

Pips chuckled softly. 'A girl doesn't like to presume.'

'Well, I have. Dare I hope that – that you could feel the same one day?'

'I already do, Giles. I think I've loved you from the moment Robert first brought you to meet us. But don't you dare tell my mother.'

His arms slipped around her waist and he drew her close but, just as he was about to kiss her for the first time, they heard the distant shelling begin again.

He took her hand. 'Come, we'd better go back. They'll be worried.'

As they ran, Giles panted, 'Darling Pips, say you'll marry me when all this is over.'

'Of course I will.'

And amidst the sound of enemy gunfire, they couldn't help but laugh out loud at the incongruity of it all.

Back at the post, they joined in the preparations for receiving more wounded. When everything was ready, Pips said, 'Right, William, you drive my father's car this time. There are bound to be walking wounded. You'll be able to transport five or six in that, I should think. I'll take the motor ambulance. Alice – you come with me. Let's go.'

'Where exactly are we going?'

'Haven't a clue, but we'll just head towards where the gunfire is.'

A shell exploded nearby and rocked the vehicle.

'I think you ought to stop here, Miss Pips,' Alice said, trying to keep the fear from her voice. 'Look.' She pointed ahead of them. 'They're carrying the wounded out of the trenches. We can pick them up from here.'

Pips halted the vehicle and leapt down. She cupped her hands around her mouth and shouted, but, above the noise, the stretcher bearers couldn't hear her. With a wry smile, remembering how much trouble she'd been in with her mother when Henrietta had got to know that Pips had learned to do it, she stuck two fingers in her mouth and gave a shrill whistle. The four stretcher bearers carrying a casualty towards her looked up and then glanced at each other.

Pips beckoned them towards her, pointing at the ambulance. As they reached her, one said, 'Was that you whistling, nurse?'

Pips nodded. 'I shouted, but you didn't hear me.'

'For God's sake, woman,' one of the other men said. 'Don't whistle around here. That's the signal to go over the top. You'll have even more casualties than we've already got if they don't realize it's a false alarm.'

Pips was at once contrite. 'I'm so sorry. I had no idea.'

160

'Aye well, happen you weren't to know.' The man was slightly mollified, but he was still serious as he added, but take my word for it. Right, lads, let's get him in the back. Where's your driver, nurse?'

'Er, that's me. I brought the ambulance and William has driven the car here.' She turned to gesture towards the vehicle that had just pulled up. 'We thought there might be less serious cases we could take in that. I think it'll take five or maybe six.'

'By heck! That's a beauty. Shame to have it out here. It'll end up ruined. Who owns it? Some bigwig in the army?'

'No, it was my father's.'

The man pulled a face. 'Well off, is he?'

'He's a doctor. He couldn't come out here himself, so he felt this was a contribution he could make.'

'He's a generous man, then.' The soldier looked her up and down, insolently. 'Letting both his prize possessions come into this hellhole.'

Despite the incongruity of their surroundings, Pips threw back her head and laughed aloud. 'Believe me, soldier, I'm nobody's possession, I assure you. Now, get this poor lad on board my ambulance and fetch me three more.'

'Right, m'lady.' The man touched his forelock, but did as she bade.

When the first casualty was settled in the ambulance, the four stretcher bearers headed back towards the trench system.

'Don't mind old Bob,' one of the others said in a low voice. 'Being a bit brusque is his way of coping. We're all real glad to see you, nurse.'

Pips nodded. 'I know.' She turned and raised her voice. 'Alice, you stay here with the wounded. William, we'll go and see if we can bring some of those who can walk to the car.'

When both vehicles held as many as they could take, they turned and set off back to the first-aid post.

'This is awful,' Pips muttered as she leaned forward over the steering wheel, trying to negotiate the deep ruts and shell holes in the road. From the rear of the vehicle, she could hear the screams of her patients as each bump in the road caused them greater pain, but she could not slow down. There were just over five miles to travel before they would reach the unit, but it felt like twenty-five and she doubted that all the wounded soldiers she was carrying would survive the journey. She'd never thought to see such wounds. The first-aid training course, though thorough, had not prepared them for the horrific injuries that the new weapons of war were inflicting; ripped flesh that bled profusely, shattered bones, shrapnel buried deep within torn bodies and wounds infected by dirt. One soldier had had his lower jaw shattered and it was already infected. If only medical aid was even closer to the trenches. And then she was obliged to halt as a line of horse-drawn gun carriages, heading to the battlefront, passed them. Pips swallowed hard as she saw the filthy condition of the horses. Their coats were matted with mud and they trudged along, stumbling into shell holes, and yet they were still whipped by their drivers to go ever faster. Pips felt a surge of anger; she empathized with the wounded soldiers – of course she did – but at least they were here by choice, the animals certainly were not. She blinked rapidly and brushed the back of her hand across her eyes as she tried not to compare these sad creatures with her own beautiful Midnight. As soon as the convoy had passed, she moved on, but then the screams of pain began again.

'It's ridiculous,' Pips ranted to Giles when the wounded had been carried into the tents and Brigitta and Leonore were assessing the needs of each patient. To add to her distress, one of the soldiers, who'd had a dreadful stomach wound, had not survived the journey and she felt his loss keenly as if, somehow, it had been her fault because she had failed to transport him to safety. 'Our unit should be so much closer to the front line. If it had been, I might have saved him.'

'I must go,' Giles said. 'I'm needed to help Robert. There are at least three of those you've just brought in needing immediate surgery. We'll talk again about this, but you look exhausted, Pips. You should rest.'

She shook her head. 'No, I must go back. There are more to bring.'

'There'll always be more to bring, but you have to rest sometime. You'll be no good to anyone if you make yourself ill.'

Pips smiled weakly. 'One more trip, Giles, and then I'll stop.'

But she was not able to keep her promise. She made three more trips before even she was forced to admit that she could do no more, but it wrenched at her heart to remember the silent pleading in the eyes of those who still awaited rescue.

'I'll go back,' William said, as Pips swayed on her feet with weariness. 'You must get a drink and something to eat, Pips. Perhaps Brigitta could come with me. I'll ask the sister.'

'Of course,' Leonore agreed at once when William explained. 'Alice and I can manage here now.'

As he drove back towards the battleground with the petite nurse beside him, William worried that he should not have asked her. If she should be injured, he fretted, he would never forgive himself. But Brigitta sat beside him, remarkably composed as she looked out upon the devastation of her homeland and saw the refugees – her compatriots – traipsing along the road, carrying pathetically small bundles of their belongings, their tired and bedraggled children trailing in their wake.

'Where can they all go?' she murmured. 'How will they find safety from all this carnage?'

'I wish we could help them all – especially the little ones – but our duty is to the wounded,' William said.

'I know.'

'Are your family safe? I don't know where you live.'

'My parents are both dead. I was brought up by my maternal grandparents. They live just outside Lijssenthoek, near Poperinghe.'

'D'you know if they are safe?'

For a brief moment, Brigitta's face crumpled,

but then she steadied herself. 'I – don't know. I wish I did, but I don't.'

'Then we must try to find out for you. Perhaps,' William added, feeling that he was being greatly daring, 'if we could get some time off together we could visit them and find out if they are all right. It can't be far away from us. At least, not if we could borrow a vehicle.'

'It isn't.' Brigitta turned her lovely blue eyes towards him and, briefly, as he risked a glance at her, he saw the unshed tears shining in them. 'You'd do that for me?'

'Of course,' he said huskily. There was so much more he'd have liked to say to her, but now was not the time and certainly not the place.

Although they were committed to the wounded in their own immediate vicinity, the team were aware of what was happening not far away.

At the very end of October, Robert told them all, 'There's a dreadful battle going on to the north of here. The Belgians have opened the sluice gates and flooded the land between Nieuwpoort and Diksmuide to halt the German advance.'

They stared at him with solemn faces. 'That must have been an awful decision to have to make,' Pips murmured. 'It'd be like breaking down our sea defences and flooding half of Lincolnshire. Can you imagine what devastation it must have caused?'

No one answered her as their hearts went out to all the poor Belgians who must have been affected.

'I expect,' Giles said reasonably at last, 'they felt

165

it preferable to their land being occupied by the enemy.'

'But you know what might happen now, don't you?' Robert said. 'The fighting might well be pushed further south towards us. The battle for Ypres will intensify. If the town falls, it leaves the way to the coast wide open and the Allies will fight to the bitter end to make sure that doesn't happen.'

The weeks passed, each one much the same as the last as the battle for the town continued. The weather was now damp and cold and, on some days, there was snow. The members of the team were weary with the constant stream of wounded that passed through their hands. And still it irked all of them that if only some of the wounds they saw could have been dressed much sooner, there would have been a much higher rate of recovery, even survival.

'Where is the heavy fighting?' Pips asked, 'because that's where we ought to be.'

'Hugh and Peter have set out towards a village called Zillebeke, just to the south-east of Ypres. We've heard there's intense action there. Our forces are being pushed back, though in other places, we're advancing. It's all a bit mad, really.'

'Then that's where we should set up an advanced first-aid post. Alice and I will go.'

'Not on your own,' Giles said sharply. He turned to Robert. 'Can you manage with Sister Leonore and Brigitta if I go with William, Pips and Alice?'

Robert frowned, but something in Giles's eyes

told him there had been a shift in the relationship between him and Pips. Ever sensitive where his sister was concerned, Robert nodded. 'It'd be even better if there's a doctor in a forward post. I'm sure we can manage here. But I think it'd be good if Brigitta went instead of Alice – if she's willing. That way you'd have a trained nurse too.'

'Yes, I can see the logic of that.'

The four of them set out to follow the route which Hugh and Peter had taken earlier, William driving the motor ambulance. On the road they passed more refugees fleeing from the fighting, rickety carts loaded with their few possessions pulled by scrawny, tired horses. Amongst them came horse-drawn ambulances carrying wounded men.

'There's Hugh and Peter's vehicle coming back,' William said suddenly, drawing to a halt. Peter stopped alongside them.

'There's a field about two miles ahead of you, just behind the fighting where they've started digging a network of trenches,' he shouted. 'You can set up the tents there, mate. It should be behind the shelling, but near enough for the wounded to get treated more quickly.'

Peter was a burly London bus driver in his forties, tall, broad and amazingly strong with a craggy face that broke into ready smiles. His brother was shorter, stockier but equally as strong. He was quieter than the ebullient Peter, but just as friendly. They'd left wives and families at home to come.

'We're too old to enlist,' Peter had explained, 'but we want to do our bit.'

167

They both spoke pure cockney, and often used the famous rhyming slang, which mystified Leonore and Brigitta until the two brothers laughingly translated. To everyone's amusement, Brigitta was soon talking about soldiers having been wounded in their 'boat race' and their 'plates of meat' being affected by trench foot. It sounded so comical in her engaging accent. Peter and Hugh loved it and roared with laughter, making it their mission to teach her a new saying every day.

'No rude ones, boys,' she told them coyly. But it brought fun and laughter not only to the members of the unit, but also to the wounded in an otherwise sorry situation.

But now as the two ambulances passed each other on the shell-pitted road, sadly there was no time for levity.

'We'll be back...' Peter promised as the two vehicles pulled away from each other.

Thirty

The noise of gunfire grew louder and they could see shells landing not far ahead of them, earth being thrown into the air leaving huge craters in the land.

'D'you think I should stop here?'

'Just a little further, William,' Pips said. 'We must be as near as possible to the front line.'

No one argued with her; they understood her reasoning and yet...

After another half a mile, Giles said firmly, 'This is near enough.'

'I think that's the field the boys talked about,' William said, nodding to the left. 'It looks relatively unscathed.'

'At the moment,' Giles murmured. 'Let's just hope they don't increase the elevation of their guns.'

William drove into the field and at once they all began to unload the ambulance and to erect the two bell tents they'd brought.

'Thank goodness for Mrs Parrott's wonderful fund-raising,' Pips remarked. The unit was well provided with equipment and medical supplies.

'To say nothing of your mother's superb efforts too,' Giles said. Weekly, parcels arrived from Henrietta. 'And the beauty of it is,' he added as he hammered a tent peg into the ground, 'with your father's advice, she knows exactly what's needed.' He stood up and arched his back, grimacing a little.

Pips glanced around her. 'Right, I think we're ready. Let's get up there and see what we can do. Are you and Brigitta staying here, Giles, ready to receive the wounded?'

'We'll come with you on this first trip and then we'll stay behind when we have patients to attend to. Right, let's go.'

As they neared the line, they could see wounded being carried towards them by their fellow soldiers. William pulled the vehicle to a halt and, as they climbed down, a man with a captain's insignia on his uniform came towards them. He held out his hand to Giles and nodded to the rest of the party.

'Captain George Allender,' he said briefly. He was distinguished-looking, tall and straight-backed, with dark hair and a small, neat moustache.

Pips judged him to be in his early forties. He had lovely dark blue eyes, she thought, but they looked so sad. He looked as if he was carrying the whole weight of the war on his shoulders. As she glanced around her, at his men furiously digging trenches, at others carrying the wounded away from the front line, she could see exactly why he must feel like that.

'We've set up an advanced first-aid post about half a mile behind your artillery,' Giles told him. 'We're ready to take your most seriously wounded first.'

The captain stared at him for a moment before saying tersely, 'I'm sorry, doctor, that's not what my orders are. Minor wounds are to be treated first.'

Overhearing, Pips could not hold back. 'Whatever do you mean?'

His gaze found hers, and his mouth was tight as he said, 'It's the army's way, nurse. The whole object is to return men to the front as soon as they are fit. The more seriously wounded have to wait. Those not likely to recover at all must be – left.'

'That's diabolical,' Pips said heatedly, but she felt Giles's warning hand on her arm.

'Leave it, Pips. We must do what we're told.'

She turned to face him, her eyes blazing. 'No, we mustn't. We're an independent flying ambulance corps. Are you telling me that that is what Dr

Hazelwood would want us to do?'

Giles shrugged. 'I really don't know and he's not here to ask. So, we ought to follow the army's guidelines. Don't you think so, captain?'

George Allender hesitated. His penetrating eyes met Pips's belligerent gaze. 'I'm sorry,' he said and at that moment he seemed to be speaking to her alone. 'I understand how you feel – and I sympathize. Those are the army's rulings, but' – the corner of his mouth twitched ever so slightly as he added with a touch of dry humour – 'you, of course, are not in the army nor subject to its orders.'

Now he saw and felt the fullness of Pips's beaming smile as she realized he was passing the decision-making to the nursing team. 'No, captain, we are not,' she said softly.

'There is one thing I'd like you to remember, though,' he added, a note of caution in his tone. 'Out here, left unattended for several hours, days even, the slightest wound can very quickly turn into a serious one. The onset of blood poisoning can be swift in these dreadful conditions. The ground itself is saturated with infection.'

'I understand what you're saying, but we can only do our best and what we think is right,' Pips said, willing to be more reasonable now that she felt he was unbending a little.

The captain nodded and gestured towards three wounded men lying in the back of a horse-drawn cart. 'They're ready to go, but I can't spare men to take them...'

'I will,' Pips said, and she turned to Giles. 'You and the others stay here and load the ambulance.

171

I can manage the horse and you'll be back before me, anyway.'

Without waiting for a reply, Pips went to the horse's head, patted him briefly and then, with soothing words, urged him forward. He was black with a white star on his forehead and reminded her painfully of Midnight.

'Now, boy,' she murmured soothingly, 'walk on. We have work to do.'

She led the horse carefully forward, trying to steer him around the holes in the roadway, but the cart still jolted and she winced at the cries from the wounded men lying in the back. The half-mile back to the post they had set up seemed ten times longer. Peter and Hugh had been on the point of returning to the front when they saw her leading the horse into the field. They stayed to help her unload the three casualties into the care of Giles and Brigitta, who had already arrived back at the post.

'You can ride back with us in the ambulance,' Peter said.

'No, I'll bring the horse and cart. It'll be needed again.'

The brothers set off without her and Pips, still walking beside the horse, followed. With a few moments' respite, she thought of her parents and a wave of homesickness threatened to engulf her. However tired she was later, she promised herself, she would write to them tonight. But how, she wondered, as she glanced about at the devastation around her, was she ever to explain all this? Houses and cottages lay in crumbling ruins, so damaged by the enemy's shells they weren't even fit to use as makeshift first-aid posts. Land, once tilled and burgeoning with golden corn in the summer months, now lay ravaged. It would take a generation to bring it back to its former glory.

Thirty-One

'There's a letter from Pips,' Henrietta said, handing it across the table to her husband as they took luncheon together. 'She doesn't say exactly where they are...'

'I don't expect she can,' Edwin said. 'The censor and all that.'

'But, reading between the lines – and I'm very good at doing that where Philippa is concerned – I think they're working a lot nearer the front line than we were led to believe before they went.'

Edwin chuckled. 'That wouldn't surprise me one bit.' Then his face clouded as he shared his wife's concern. 'I know how you feel, Hetty, my love. I feel exactly the same, but they've gone out there to do their best to help the wounded and that, I'm afraid, probably means being in the thick of it, particularly as they are a mobile unit and go where they're needed.'

Henrietta shuddered. 'I know and I admire them all for what they're doing. I'm proud of them all – including,' she said firmly, 'William Dawson, but it doesn't stop me worrying, Edwin.'

'I know, I know.' He sighed. 'And, sadly, there are countless thousands feeling exactly as we are and several of them are in this village. Poor Mrs Nuttall has taken to her bed since her only son – her only child – volunteered. I'm at my wit's end to know how to help her. There's nothing physically wrong with her, at least, not yet. But her emotional state is making her ill.'

Henrietta was thoughtful. 'Mm, perhaps I can help. Would you allow me to try?'

'Of course, my love. But I don't know how.'

'Leave it with me. I'll have a word with Ma. See how they're coping too.'

'Have they heard anything from their boys?'

'I think they get the odd letter from Bernard and Roy – and Norah says she writes every week to them, but there's been no word from Harold. They still have no idea exactly where he is.'

Henrietta called frequently at the Dawsons' cottage to help Ma and Bess Cooper organize the knitting and sewing circle amongst the women of the village. But today, she had another mission. As she sat down opposite Ma and accepted the cup of tea Norah offered her, she came straight to the point. 'Have you heard about Mrs Nuttall?'

'Aye, poor woman. Taken her Sam going very hard, hasn't she?'

'Will you come with me to see her?'

Ma hesitated. 'I don't get about much, now, Mrs Maitland. I couldn't walk that far.'

'Then I'll bring the pony and trap when my husband doesn't need it.' Henrietta was not about to be defeated. 'Jake can drive us.'

Ma still hesitated, but the lady from the hall was hard to refuse. 'Will tomorrow afternoon

174

about two suit you, Mrs Dawson?'

Ma sighed softly, but nodded.

The following afternoon was bright for November, but cool. Henrietta helped Ma into the trap and tucked a rug warmly round her knees. Climbing in herself she instructed Jake to drive on until they came to the low cottage where Mr and Mrs Nuttall lived. Bert Nuttall was digging his vegetable patch at the side of the cottage and he looked up in surprise when he saw that the pony and trap had stopped outside his gate. He was even more shocked to see who was climbing out of it and heading towards his front door. He threw down his fork and came to greet them.

Taking off his cap, he greeted the two women and then addressed Henrietta, 'The wife's in bed, ma'am.'

'We know, Mr Nuttall. That's exactly why we're here.'

'Ah,' Bert said, understanding at once. 'Your husband's mentioned it, I expect.'

'The doctor never discusses his patient's ailments with me, Mr Nuttall, I promise you, but I understand that your wife is not exactly – ill.'

'No, ma'am.' He touched his forehead. 'It's in here. She's taken our Samuel going to heart and I'm afraid she will make hersen' really ill if she goes on like it.'

'I think we might be able to help.'

'I'd be so grateful if you could, ma'am. Just let me go in and make sure she's – well – decent.'

Henrietta smiled and nodded.

'Of course.'

He returned after what seemed a long time as they stood waiting in the cold. 'I had a job to persuade her, ma'am, but do come in.'

He held open the door and then led them through to the back of the cottage. As they passed through, both women noticed the dank, dusty air. Mrs Nuttall, once as house-proud as any of the women in the village, had let the condition of her home deteriorate. They entered the stuffy bedroom and approached the side of the bed. Clara Nuttall's eyes were red, her face blotchy and her grey hair wild and unkempt. She looked as if she had neither washed nor brushed her hair for several days, and the front of her flannelette nightdress was stained.

'Mrs Nuttall,' Henrietta began, 'we're sorry to see you this way, but we need your help.'

Clara turned her head to look at them. Her eyes were dull, lifeless almost.

'My – my help?'

'That's right. All the women in the village have formed a knitting and sewing circle to make items of clothing for our boys at the front.'

At her words, tears rolled down Clara's cheeks. 'I – can't. My boy...'

'Yes, Mrs Nuttall, we know all about young Samuel volunteering. You must be very proud of him.'

'Proud? Proud, you say? Proud of him going to get hissen killed? What a foolish woman you are, Mrs Maitland.' Her voice rose shrilly.

'Now, Clara, don't speak to Mrs Maitland like that,' Bert said, shooting an apologetic look at Henrietta.

'I'll speak to her how I like if she's come to tell me that I should be rejoicing that my boy's gone to be killed.'

There was an uncomfortable pause before Ma said quietly, 'All my family's gone. All five of 'em.'

For a moment, Clara stared at her. 'Even William? I thought he'd refused to go. I thought he was the only one with any sense.'

'He's gone with Master Robert and Miss Pips to act as a stretcher bearer at the first-aid post they're setting up. Alice has gone too.'

'Oh well, they'll be all right, then. They'll make sure they're miles behind the front line, won't they?'

Neither Henrietta nor Ma knew exactly where their loved ones were so they remained silent.

'Bernard and Roy have volunteered and even Boy has disappeared,' Ma said. 'He's enlisted, an' all. He went to Newark without telling us, where no one would know him and try to stop him. Mrs Maitland found out for us.'

'More fool him, then. He had no need to go.'

'I'd agree with you there, Clara,' Ma said. 'But he didn't want to be branded a coward, like William has been.'

Clara winced, then muttered, 'And you think that's what my boy would have been thought of if he hadn't gone?'

'Not necessarily,' Henrietta said. 'The authorities haven't brought in conscription yet.'

'What's that?'

'When they call up all able-bodied men between certain ages. They have to go then, unless there's a good reason why they could apply for exemption.'

177

'So what you're saying,' Clara said slowly, 'is that if they eventually bring in this – conscription, my boy would've had to've gone then?'

'Most certainly.'

'Oh.' Clara was thoughtful whilst Henrietta added craftily, 'At least, because he's volunteered, he's been able to choose what regiment he joined. I expect he went with some of the other village lads, did he?'

Clara glanced at Ma. 'He went with your Bernard and Roy. Same day.'

'Ah, so at least he's with his pals. And speaking of pals, I've heard that several of the larger cities have already formed "pals' battalions", where men from the same city or town, or even the same workplace, all go together. I think Lord Derby was one of the first to instigate this in answer to Kitchener's call for volunteers by suggesting that the commercial workers in Liverpool, such as clerks and the like, might like to form a "battalion of comrades". I hear that other places are following suit. So you see, our boys from Doddington will more than likely be able to stay together and look out for each other.'

'Our Bernard and Roy are still at training camp,' Ma put in, 'though where Boy is, I couldn't tell you.'

For a brief moment, Clara's face showed sympathy for someone other than herself. 'That must be awful for you, Ma. At least we hear regularly from Samuel, don't we, Bert?'

'We do, duck, yes. And we know he's still in training too.' He glanced at Ma. 'Let's hope they're all together, eh? I'll mind to ask our lad next time

178

I write to him.'

Clara glanced away and sighed and seemed to be lost in thought. As the silence lengthened in the room, Henrietta said, 'We'll be going. But please, Mrs Nuttall, think about what we've said, will you?'

Clara's only reply was to lie back against her pillows and close her eyes.

Outside the cottage, Henrietta breathed in the fresh air thankfully. Bert held out his hand. 'I don't know how to thank you, ma'am. At least you've tried, but I'm so afraid she's going to stay in her bed until Sam comes home again.'

Henrietta shook his hand, holding it for a moment between both her own. 'May God keep him safe and bring him back to you, Mr Nuttall.'

The man seemed close to tears himself now and could only nod in acknowledgement.

The following morning, Bert awoke to find his wife already out of bed and getting dressed.

'You're right, Bert. I need to stir mesen. Get the copper going, will you? I need a bath. And then I'd better get this place cleaned. You won't have lifted a finger to do women's work, I'll be bound.'

Later that afternoon, Clara walked down the lane to find Ma Dawson sitting in her usual place outside the Dawsons' cottage. The old lady puffed contentedly on her pipe and managed to show no surprise at Clara's arrival.

'Thanks for coming yesterday, Ma. I've been doing a lot of thinking – most of the night, actually – and you're all right. I shouldn't be lying in me

179

bed feeling sorry for mesen when there's others suffering as much or more. I'll be pleased to help with the sewing and knitting.'

'That's good, Clara, 'cos our lads out there need all the help we can give 'em. Now, duck, let's go in and see if Norah can find us a cuppa.'

Thirty-Two

'Roy...' Bernard found his brother polishing his boots. 'I've had a letter from home.'

The brothers were still at training camp and kitted out in what was called 'Kitchener's blue'. This was not so much because they were still 'rookie' soldiers, but because there was a shortage of khaki uniforms. Reveille at 6 a.m., on parade at seven before breakfast at eight, was no hardship for them. They were, though, getting rather tired of the constant drill, though they were obliged to admit that now they were beginning to look like real soldiers.

Roy looked up to see the single sheet of paper in his brother's hand.

'Mam's written. Harold's disappeared. He went a while back.'

'What d'you mean "disappeared"?'

'He ran away to enlist.'

Roy spat on his boot and scrubbed at it fiercely. 'That's all William's fault. If he hadn't been such a bloody coward, Harold wouldn't have been so keen to prove that he wasn't.'

180

'Mm.' Bernard's murmur was non-committal. 'Did they go after him?'

'Mam tried, but he didn't enlist in Lincoln. He went to Newark.'

Roy looked up sharply now. 'He won't be in the Lincolns, then?'

Bernard shook his head. 'He's in the Sherwood Foresters, Mam says.'

'So, we're not likely to run into him?'

'Shouldn't think so.'

'Silly little hothead,' Roy muttered. 'Why didn't he give it another year or so? It might all be over by then.'

Astutely, Bernard said, 'That's probably exactly why he didn't want to wait. He doesn't want to miss the action. He wants to be a war hero.'

'Don't we all,' Roy muttered, rubbing at his boot even harder.

'I wish now we'd let him join up with us. At least we'd have been able to keep an eye on him. But he'll be with strangers now.'

The two brothers exchanged a glance.

'There's nowt we can do, Bernard. Stuck here just hanging about. Why don't they send us out there? Surely there's nowt left for us to learn now. As if a couple of country lads can't shoot straight.'

'Aye well, we'll all have to go together, I expect.'

'Does Mam say owt else? Does she mention Alice?'

'Yes, she's doing fine, but Mam says she doesn't tell them much in her letters.'

Roy paused and looked thoughtful for a moment. 'I wonder why.'

'Mebbe it's because *he's* with her.' Bernard

glanced down again at his mother's letter. There was no mention of William. 'I expect it's difficult not to speak of him when they're working together.'

'Aye,' Roy said sarcastically, taking up his boot brush once more. 'Safely behind the lines and well out of any danger. I tell you one thing, Bernard, if we ever come across William when we do get out there, I'll shoot him mesen.'

Back at the advanced first-aid post, Giles was still worried.

'I still think we're a bit too close. If the enemy should alter the trajectory of their shelling, we might well be in the firing line.'

'Nonsense, Giles. They're only trying to hit our trenches. They're not going to fire beyond them, surely,' Pips said.

'They might be trying to take out our supplies as they come up to the line.'

They glanced at the road where lines of horse-drawn carts and motor vehicles were transporting supplies to the front. Shells burst about half a mile away, but none fell near where they'd pitched the first-aid post.

'I'm sure we'll be all right here. You have to admit that you'll be able to treat injuries so much earlier here, won't you?'

Giles smiled wryly. 'I can't deny that. And it will make a difference to their chance of recovery.'

'There you are, then,' Pips said triumphantly, but then she smiled and tucked her arm through his. 'I love you for wanting to take care of us all, but we need to be nearer the wounded. You do agree about that, don't you?'

'Wholeheartedly, but I don't think Dr Hazelwood would want us to put ourselves in danger to do so. We're no good to anyone then, are we?'

'True.' Pips glanced about her again. They watched as the bangs were followed by clouds of smoke rising into the sky.

'It looks like we're going to be busy,' she murmured. 'I must go with William.' She squeezed his arm. 'I'll see you later.'

Briefly, he gripped her hand. 'Do take care, darling. Please.'

'You drive the ambulance today, William,' Pips said, early the following morning. 'I'll bring the car.'

Hugh and Peter had already set out again. They were helping to bring the wounded to the advanced first-aid post and then taking those who could be moved further, back to Robert.

They headed, in convoy with Pips leading, towards the gunfire and the rising puffs of smoke, the noise of shellfire getting louder as they approached.

'Oh dear,' Pips murmured to herself. 'It looks as if it's going to be bad.'

She drove the car as near to the system of trenches as she dared, William following her faithfully. Already she could see stretcher bearers congregating in readiness to go into the trenches.

'Let's go with them,' Pips said impulsively, when William joined her.

'I will, Miss Pips, but I don't think you should.'

'Phooey.' Pips flapped her hand at him and they

183

both dissolved into laughter. Her favourite expression, used so often in her growing years, reminded them of home and of all the years they'd known each other.

He met her gaze and said softly, 'Never thought we'd find ourselves in a place like this, did we, miss?'

'No, William, we didn't, but come on.'

They walked beyond the long-range artillery placements to the reserve trench, then through the network of communication and support trenches until they came to the front line. They arrived in time to see the soldiers standing on the fire step, leaning against the sides of the trench, their rifles at the ready. The officer was walking up and down behind them and, at the back of the trench, stood the stretcher bearers. No one spoke to them; it was as if, by ignoring the very men who would fetch them if they were wounded, the soldiers were denying the fact that they might, in a few minutes, become a casualty.

'What are you doing here?' the officer patrolling the trench barked at Pips.

'Good morning, Captain Allender. We meet again. We're here to help, if we're needed.'

'You should go back, nurse. You can stay' – he nodded at William – 'but I'd be obliged...'

Further down the line, a whistle sounded and the captain turned away sharply, shouted to his men, and then blew his own whistle. Immediately the trench was alive with activity. The men clambered up the side and went over the parapet. At once, the sound of gunfire was all around them and bullets pinged into the walls of the trench.

'In here...' George Allender grabbed Pips's arm and pulled her into a dugout. 'Stay there...' And then he was gone, over the top after his men.

The stretcher bearers now mounted the fire step and peered cautiously over the edge. The sound of gunfire died away a little.

'There's several down already,' one murmured.

'Give it a few minutes till our lads get a bit further in, then we'll go.'

It seemed an age before the word was given and the men lifted their stretchers up and over the side and then climbed up too. William went with them.

'You stay here, Miss Pips.'

Though she longed to follow, she knew there was no point in deliberately disobeying the captain's orders. She didn't want to add to his worries.

It was only a few minutes, though, before the first casualty was carried back into the trench and she had work to do.

'Didn't even get to the bloody wire,' the man said, 'before I was hit in the knee.'

The two men carrying him set him down in the bottom of the trench and climbed back out.

'Let's see what I can do,' Pips said, squatting down beside him and opening her medical bag.

'Lord, I thought I was seeing things, nurse. I thought I'd died and gone to heaven and you was an angel.'

'No angel, I assure you. Now let's look at that knee.' She dressed his wound, which was still clean.

'It's missed your kneecap, thank goodness, though I think it's shattered your tibia just below the knee.'

'It bloody well hurts, nurse. Sorry for the language.'

'Don't think about it. I've heard far worse since I've been out here, I can assure you. Now, if you can stand and lean on me, we might be able to get you back to the car we've got waiting just behind your reserve trench.'

He gaped at her. 'Have you come in front of our long-range artillery, nurse?'

'I expect so. I did see a few big guns, but they're trained on the enemy, surely.'

'Well, yes, but I didn't think you'd've been allowed to come that close.'

She chuckled. 'We didn't ask permission, soldier. We just came.'

'Well, bugger me. You're a brave lass and no mistake. Sorry for the language.'

'Please don't apologize any more. It's water off a duck's back. Now, what's your name?'

'Hawkins, nurse.'

She was just about to hoist him onto his one good foot and have him lean on her, when two more casualties arrived, one yelling in dreadful pain. Again they were set on the floor of the trench.

'Sorry, I can't leave now,' she said to her first patient. 'Look, let's get you into that dugout. You sit there and don't get that dressing dirty, whatever you do.'

With him in comparative safety, Pips tended the other two, but soon she was overwhelmed with more and more arriving every minute.

After about half an hour, the floor of the trench, as far as she could see to the first corner, was covered with wounded men sitting or lying and she suspected that there'd be more beyond that.

William slithered into the trench, his eyes wild, his cap askew. 'By heck, miss, it's hairy out there. The lads said I'd to come back and help you move as many out as we can. I've got the stretcher.'

Carefully, he reached up and pulled the stretcher down into the trench, just as a bullet hit the ground close to him, showering earth into his face.

'Keep down, Miss Pips, for God's sake, keep down.'

Thirty-Three

They worked tirelessly, staunching bleeding wounds and bandaging shattered limbs, all the time talking quietly to the casualties, trying to ooze confidence even when they knew a case was hopeless. Then, as the attack seemed to be over and men returned to the trench, they began to carry the wounded down the system of trenches to the waiting ambulances. More had appeared, mostly horse-drawn, but Pips and William loaded their two vehicles.

'William, you go first in the car, you'll be quicker, and I'll bring the ambulance. Take Private Hawkins with you. His leg is wounded, but he can sit upright. And there are five more, who are walking wounded, if you can fit them in,' Pips said, as she appeared out of the trench with the first soldier she had helped leaning heavily on her.

187

'It'll be a squeeze, miss, but I don't reckon they'll mind.'

William set off in front of her, but halfway back, the ambulance's engine made a peculiar noise and then stopped. Pips clambered out and went round to the back. As she opened the door, voices greeted her.

'What's happened?'

'Why have we stopped?'

'I knew we shouldn't have a woman driving us.'

'Sorry, boys. The engine's died on me.'

'T'ain't the only thing that'll die if you don't get us back to a first-aid post.'

'Anyone need a drink of water? I have some in the cab.' Ignoring the grumbling, she handed out water and then looked at their wounds. One seriously injured soldier was now unconscious. Pips bit her lip. There was nothing she could do until help arrived. She hoped William would come straight back.

It seemed an age before she heard the sound of the car, though in fact it was only about ten minutes. But to those in dreadful pain, it seemed an eternity. William pulled up in front of her, leaving space for other vehicles to pass.

'What's happened, Pips?'

'The engine just died.'

'Let's take a look...'

William disappeared under the bonnet whilst Pips still tried to reassure the wounded. Mentally crossing her fingers, she told them, 'William's a mechanical genius. He'll have us going in no time.'

Five minutes later, her silent prayers were answered as the engine burst into life. Grinning at her, William slammed the bonnet cover. 'There you are, as good as new. It was just a plug lead worked loose on these rough roads.'

'Thank you, William. Right, lads, hold tight. We're off again.' To William she said, 'I'll come straight back. Where are Hugh and Peter? D'you know?'

'They're taking the ones that can be moved straight away back to Robert and perhaps even to the nearest casualty-clearing station.' He shook his head. 'There's that many being brought to our advanced unit, we can't cope. We've got to move them out as soon as we can.'

Pips nodded, imagining how their first-aid post was already being overwhelmed.

Fifteen minutes later, after crawling the rest of the way along the pitted road and trying to ignore the cries of pain from the back of her ambulance, she could see for herself the enormity of the task Dr Hazelwood's team had. The wounded were lying everywhere, awaiting their turn for attention. Brigitta moved quietly amongst them and Giles worked in the tent set up to deal with the worst of the wounded. As she pulled up just inside the field, Hugh and Peter drew in beside her and came at once to help unload her casualties.

'We ought to concentrate on getting all these moved back to Robert,' Hugh told her as he helped her carry the men off the vehicle.

'I can't, Hugh. I must go back. At least if we can get them back here, we can deal with the worst cases.'

He glanced at her. 'You know that's not what we're supposed to do, don't you? You ought to bring the slightly wounded first, miss.'

Grimly, her mouth tight, Pips said, 'I'm fully aware of what the army wants, but I can't leave seriously injured men to bring back those with little more than a scratch first. I can't instruct you what to do – you must do what your conscience tells you – but I'm doing it my way.'

Hugh grinned at her. 'I hope, if I get hurt, miss, that you're on hand to come and get me.'

She smiled back at him. She liked the two cockney brothers; their humour kept the whole team buoyed up even in the darkest times.

'You can bet your life on it, Hugh.'

He roared with laughter, the welcome sound floating across the field. 'I probably would be, miss. Now, off you go. Stay safe.' It was Hugh's 'goodbye' phrase.

When she got back to the trenches, she found some of the soldiers close to panic.

'It's the captain. He's been hurt.'

'Where is he?'

'Still out in no-man's-land. But as soon as we put our heads above the parapet, they fire at us. We can't get him.'

'We've got to get him. He's our talisman. If he gets killed, then we're all done for.'

Pips glanced around her. The wounded looked up at her with pleading eyes, yet what they said was the opposite. 'Go and find the captain, miss. We're fine.'

They were anything but 'fine', she could see that, but she could also feel that the rescue of their captain meant far more to them.

She turned to one of the able-bodied men.

'Show me.'

He led her back to the front line and helped her up onto the fire step. 'We reckon he's in that shell hole just to the left, nurse.'

'How can we get to him?'

'We can't. We've tried and there's a sniper just waiting for us to poke our heads up. He'll just have to wait until nightfall. Then both sides fetch their wounded in. It's like a bit of an unspoken truce. You know?'

'Are there many more out there along with the captain?'

'I don't know.'

'How far away are the enemy trenches?'

'Not far. You can hear them talking and laughing when the wind's in the right direction.'

'Find me a stick.'

'Eh?'

'A stick or a pole. Something I can hoist a white flag up on.'

'You can't do that, miss. They'll think we're surrendering.'

'Just find me something.'

A few moments later the soldier returned with a pole he'd pulled out of a stretcher. 'I don't like this, miss.'

Pips removed her white nurse's cap. Then, standing on the fire step again, she raised her voice and in her schoolgirl German shouted, 'German soldiers, can you hear me?'

There was a moment's silence before a voice said, 'Yes, we hear you.'

'I am a British nurse. I wish to fetch a wounded man in from a' – she paused, not knowing the

German for 'shell hole' – 'from the land between us. I will have a soldier with me, but he will not have a gun.'

There was silence for several moments before the voice came again. 'Hold up a white flag and we will not shoot you. We don't shoot women.'

'That's not what I've heard,' the soldier beside her muttered. 'Just ask the poor Belgians.'

Ignoring him, Pips wrapped her cap around the end of the pole and held it aloft. The German shouted again. 'We see it. We will not fire.'

'Don't go, miss, the captain'll have my guts for garters if I let you.'

'This isn't your responsibility, soldier. By the way, what's your name? I can't keep calling you "soldier".'

'Smith, miss.'

'I'll go up first, Private Smith, and if they don't shoot, will you follow me?'

After a moment's hesitation, he nodded, but his eyes were fearful.

Slowly, holding her white flag aloft, Pips climbed up the ladder and stepped onto the parapet. Her heart was pounding as she stood up, but no shots were fired. She glanced back down into the trench. 'I think it's all right. Come on.'

Reluctantly, the soldier climbed up and together they made for the hole in the barbed wire. One or two bodies lay against it, obviously beyond Pips's help.

'Over here,' the soldier pointed, still glancing fearfully towards the enemy's trenches. But they reached the shell hole and slithered into it. George Allender gaped at them as if he were seeing an apparition. Beside him lay another soldier, moaning, 'My eyes – my eyes. I can't see.'

Without preamble, Pips said to the captain, 'Where are you hurt?'

'My leg.' Still mesmerized, George showed her. It was a flesh wound – the bullet had not hit the bone – but it was bleeding profusely and in danger of becoming infected as he lay there in the blood-soaked mud.

Swiftly, Pips dressed it and wound a bandage around it.

'You shouldn't have done this, Miss Maitland.' He glanced at Smith. 'And you shouldn't have let her.'

'Begging your pardon, captain, but you try stopping her. I couldn't.'

The captain smiled wryly. 'I don't doubt it, Smith.'

'Can you stand?' Pips asked, ignoring their conversation.

Private Smith helped the captain to his feet.

'Take him back to the trench. I'll bring this other soldier.'

He was only a boy. Pips doubted he was old enough to be here. He reminded her sharply of Harold Dawson. Briefly, she wondered where he was now. Her mother had written to tell her that he had disappeared and the family believed he had enlisted. It had been hard to tell Alice and William the news.

As they began to climb the side of the hole, Pips said, 'Wait!' Then she raised her voice and shouted, 'We are coming out now. There are four of us. We have two wounded. Don't shoot.'

The German shouted to them again. 'Hold your flag up and we will hold our fire. But no more, now. You cannot fetch any more until tonight.'

Pips sighed, but she shouted, 'Understood.'

The short journey back to their own trench was tortuous. Any moment they expected a bullet in their backs, but the German kept his word and they reached the ladder safely. Once below the parapet, they all breathed a sigh of relief, yet there was still a long way to go to get the two casualties back to the waiting ambulance.

'Just let me see to this boy's eyes, captain.'

It was an ugly sight as she gently eased the boy's hands from his face. He had a shrapnel wound in his left eye and his right eye was caked with mud. At this moment, he was completely blind, though she couldn't see if his right eye was permanently damaged. Gently, she bathed away the earth, but his eye was closed and he screamed in pain. She bandaged his eyes and then helped him to stand.

'Lean on me. We'll get you back to the first-aid post and get you some real help. I'm sorry I can't do more here.'

They struggled through the trench system and finally reached Pips's ambulance. She took the captain, the young boy and four others in her ambulance, George Allender sitting in the cab beside her.

'You shouldn't have done it, you know,' he said, as she negotiated the ruts and holes in the road.

Pips chuckled. 'Thankfully, captain, I am not under your command. You can't court-martial me. And I very much hope you won't take any action over Private Smith. I left him little choice.'

George smiled. 'If I do report the incident, Miss Maitland, it will be to recommend him for a medal.'

'Good. He certainly deserves it. He was clearly petrified, but he came anyway.'

George nodded and said seriously, 'Yes, that's what real bravery is.'

When they got back to the advanced unit, Pips could see that a great many had been moved on by Hugh and Peter and there were only a few being brought in now. No doubt there would be another influx that night, when the wounded could be fetched in from what the men called no-man's-land. Pips shuddered thinking of men lying for hours in muddy shell holes or on the open ground. Their wounds, whatever they were now, would be so much worse by the time they could be rescued.

Pips handed the captain and the rest of the casualties over to Brigitta. 'I must go back. There are nine more to bring, but I might be able to get them all in one more journey if some of them can sit upright.'

As Pips completed her final trip, the weariness washed over her. They all went back to the main post near Brandhoek for a few hours. All the casualties had been brought here too. She stumbled across the grass to the small tent she shared with the other women and fell onto her bed. She was quickly asleep and didn't wake until she felt Alice shaking her.

'I've brought you a cup of tea.'

Outside the tent, Pips could see it was already dark.

'You should have woken me, Alice. I have to get back to the advanced post. They'll be bringing the wounded in.'

'You're to do no more tonight. You're exhausted.'

'Nonsense, Alice. I have to go. There are wounded men still out there.'

'Hugh, Peter and William are coping with that, Miss Pips. And I'll go with them too.'

'Alice, just do as I say. Fetch me a bowl of hot water and a clean uniform.'

Alice stood up as if to do Pips's bidding, but then she stood very still for a moment.

'Alice...' Pips began impatiently.

Slowly Alice turned back to look down at her. Standing with her hands on her hips, she said, 'This is the last time I'm going to call you "Miss Pips". I'm not your lady's maid any more. Out here, we're equals. I even did the same first-aid course as you, so I'm just as qualified – apart from the fact that I can't drive or speak foreign languages. I'll gladly and willingly do what you *ask* me to do, but not what you *order* me to do.'

Without waiting for Pips to reply, Alice left the tent and hurried away.

Open-mouthed, Pips stared after her. Then a smile spread slowly across her mouth as she murmured, 'Well, well, well. Who'd have thought it, but good for you, Alice Dawson. Good for you.'

Thirty-Four

'November already,' Ma said dolefully as she cast off the second sock of a pair she was knitting. 'I don't know about you, Norah, but I can't get in the mood for Christmas this year.'

'I'm just going through the motions, Ma. Making puddings, mince pies and preparing to cook a goose as usual.'

'There'll be no one here to eat it except us three.'

'Mebbe the lads'll get home. Surely – if they're still in training camp – they'll let them have some leave.'

'Aye, mebbe,' Ma said listlessly, but she couldn't inject hope into her tone.

She glanced up as a knock sounded at the back door and Bess, followed by Clara, came into the kitchen.

'Nah then, ladies,' Bess greeted them and Clara nodded. She was smiling.

'What's up with you, Clara Nuttall?' Ma asked. 'You look like the cat that's found the cream in the larder.'

'Samuel's coming home for Christmas. He's got seventy-two hours' leave.'

'Aw, lass, that's grand,' Ma said, genuinely pleased for the little woman who had taken her son's departure so hard.

'I'm going to try to persuade him to stay at home

197

– not to go back.'

The other three women in the room were shocked. They glanced at each other uncomfortably.

'You can't do that, duck,' Ma said. 'He'd be in serious trouble. He'd be classed as a deserter. And you know what they do to them, don't you?'

Clara bit her lip and shook her head.

Bess snorted with contempt. 'They put 'em up against a wall and shoot 'em, that's what.' Clara gasped and turned white, feeling for the nearest chair to sink into. 'Couldn't I – keep him hidden for the rest of the war?'

'No, duck, you couldn't,' Ma said gently, with a warning glance at Bess. 'They'd come looking for him and then they'd court-martial him and, yes, his punishment would be – severe.'

Clara's eyes filled with tears. 'I was so happy when I got his letter saying that he was coming for Christmas. I thought I could get him to stay...' Her voice trailed away.

'You mustn't even try, Clara,' Bess said bluntly. 'He's joined the army and that's an end to it. Oh, I know I've no right to talk, only having two daughters and them safely at home, but I do know that if I'd've had lads, I'd've backed 'em in whatever they wanted to do, even...' she glared at Ma, 'if they'd refused to go.' She nodded as if agreeing with herself. 'Aye, I know it's the un-mentionable subject in this house, but I've always been one to speak my mind, you all know that, and I'll say it now; I'd not've turned me back on me son. I'd've respected his wishes and stood by him. It took a lot of courage for your William to stand up agin his family and the whole village. I admire him, if no one else does. And when he comes back, I'll be the first to shek his hand.'

Ma and Norah avoided meeting the woman's gaze. They had very mixed feelings, none of which they dared to voice aloud for fear that Len would get to hear about it. Good-hearted in many ways though Bess was, she was better than a town crier when it came to spreading gossip.

'Now,' Bess said, changing the subject, 'me and Clara have brought you several pairs of socks, a couple of balaclavas and two Christmas cakes. We reckoned you'd be taking things up to the hall for Mrs Maitland to send out to Miss Pips. She'll see they get to the right place, now won't she?'

'I hope Mrs Maitland knows where to send it all,' Ma said. 'She was telling me that in her last letter home, Miss Pips said they were moving about a lot. They keep going to where the fighting's the heaviest.'

'Really?' Norah frowned. 'You didn't tell me that, Ma.'

Ma could have bitten off the end of her tongue. When Henrietta had told her the news, they'd decided not to tell Norah. Now Ma had let it out.

'I thought everyone said they'd be staying well behind the front lines, that Alice wouldn't be in any danger,' Norah said.

Or William, they were both thinking, though neither spoke his name aloud.

'Miss Pips explained it,' Ma said gently, as Bess pulled out a chair and sat down too. She wasn't going to miss this piece of juicy gossip. Already she could imagine herself telling the rest of the

199

villagers whether they wanted to hear it or not. 'You all reckon William Dawson's a coward,' she could hear herself saying. 'Well, he isn't. He's up there, right at the front, fetching in the wounded and liable to get shot at himself. And, from what I've heard, stretcher bearers don't carry a weapon, so he's nowt to defend hissen with.' She wasn't beyond embroidering a good tale. Even though she really had no idea exactly what William would be doing, it sounded good. And she didn't know if it was true about him not carrying a gun, but it sounded like common sense to her. You couldn't wield a gun if you were carrying stretchers. Bess Cooper might not have had much book learning, but she certainly wasn't lacking in common sense.

'They need to be as near to the front as they can get, you see,' Ma went on now, 'to aid the casualties as soon as possible. Long delays cause more problems for the wounded.'

'Stands to reason,' Bess sniffed. 'They could bleed to death, else.'

'But Alice, what about Alice?' Norah asked.

'She'll be all right, Norah, duck. She'll be back at the first-aid post,' Bess said. 'They'll not have sited that where the enemy's guns can reach 'em.'

'I just hope you're right, Bess,' Norah murmured.

About William, she still said nothing.

Thirty-Five

'If you're insisting on going back to Zillebeke, then I'm coming with you this time, Pips,' Alice said firmly and, without waiting for a refusal, she climbed into the motor ambulance. 'Robert says he can manage without me for a few hours.'

The team had slipped into a routine of working amicably and smoothly together. Pips and William brought the wounded from the trenches to the advanced post, where their needs were assessed. They were either treated there or passed on to Robert or Giles at the main post still at Brandhoek for more serious procedures.

With more and more wounded arriving, Giles had been forced to stay at the main post to carry out operations alongside Robert, with Leonore assisting them both. Now the forward post was manned only by Pips, William and one other nurse; sometimes Brigitta, sometimes Alice. Hugh and Peter still worked between the front line, the advanced post and the main first-aid post – and even the nearest casualty-clearing station – ferrying casualties to the best place for them.

Giles and Robert were the ones to say which patients were ready to be taken further inland, then on to a larger hospital near the coast and even home to England, if their recovery was going to be prolonged.

Pips grinned at Alice. 'Come on, then. You're a

glutton for punishment, Alice Dawson, I'll say that for you.'

'So are you,' Alice retorted and they laughed together, their easy friendship restored.

As dawn broke, they brought the last of the casualties in – those who were still alive – from no-man's-land. It had been a difficult night, but, when she got back to the main post, weary though she was, Pips felt she owed it to Captain Allender to give him news of his men.

'We wanted to send him on, but he refused,' Leonore told her. 'He wants to get back to the front as soon as he can.'

Pips nodded. 'The army's his life. Is he married, d'you know?'

'I think so. One of his men brought his belongings from the dugout and I helped him sort them out and repack them. There was a photograph of a sweet-faced young woman with a little girl on her knee.'

'Where is he now?'

Leonore pointed the way to the tent where the less wounded waited for transport to take them wherever they were going. In the captain's case, it was back to the front line.

'Good morning, Captain Allender,' Pips greeted him. He was sitting near the tent flap, his kit and belongings packed.

'Good morning, Miss Maitland. Have you come to take me back?'

'I hadn't. I've had a long night, but if you really want to go as soon as possible...'

'I do.'

'...and you've been discharged by the doctor, then yes, I'll drive you back.'

He stood up. 'I'd be most grateful. My men shouldn't really have sent all my belongings here. But I suppose they thought I wouldn't be going back yet. No matter...' He hoisted his kit bag onto his shoulder and began to reach down for another bag.

'Here, let me.'

Pips observed him shrewdly as he limped towards the ambulance, but she made no comment. Whoever had dressed his wound would have made sure that it was well covered.

'I don't suppose it's any good me telling you that you ought to go behind the lines until it's healed?'

'Not a bit. I want to be – need to be – with my men.'

'I can understand that,' she murmured. 'They seem to look upon you as some sort of talisman.'

'Unfortunately for me, yes. It's not a comfortable position, I can assure you. But I'm saddled with it and so must do my best.' As she climbed in beside him, he laughed wryly, 'Though perhaps now I've been injured, they'll view me as a little more human.'

'Where are you from, captain?' Pips asked conversationally as she negotiated the pitted road.

'Leeds.'

'Really? I'm surprised you're not in a Yorkshire regiment, then.'

George laughed, a low, infectious chuckle. 'I ran away from home at fifteen to join the army. I thought the county regimental headquarters would be the first place my parents would look. In peacetime, they might have been able to extricate me, as I was underage. I'm not sure they would have been, but that's how I thought then. To a fifteen-year-old, who hadn't then seen much of the world, parents were omnipotent.'

'Were they angry?'

'At first, yes, but it was my paternal grandfather who talked them round. He'd been a soldier in the Crimea and he told them there was no better life for a young man.'

'D'you know, it's strange but there's a family in our village with much the same sort of story as yours.' Pips related the events of the last few months ending, 'The youngest son, who's only just sixteen, has run away to enlist.'

What she omitted to tell him, quite deliberately, was that William, who'd already carried many of the captain's men to safety, was also from the same family.

'It's unlikely he'll be sent out here yet,' George said. 'We'll be in a sorry state if we have to start sending sixteen-year-olds to the front.'

'Here we are,' she said, pulling to a halt just behind the heavy artillery placements. 'Can you manage?'

'I'll be fine – and thanks.' He paused a moment, his hand on the door as he met her gaze. 'Take care of yourself, Miss Maitland, won't you? Au revoir,' he said softly and then he was gone.

As she watched him limp away she realized that his farewell had been the French words for 'until we meet again'.

Thirty-Six

'The three of us'd like to go into Ypres, sir, if you've no objection.'

They had now brought the tents and medical supplies back from the field where they'd sited the advanced post near Zillebeke, and were all back at Brandhoek together.

'D'you think it's safe, Peter?'

'It's been a bit quieter for the last few days and we'll be careful. We plan to go in civvies and carry no weapons. We've just seen some British cavalry heading that way and mean to tag on to them.'

Reluctantly, Robert nodded. 'All right then, but for heaven's sake be careful.'

Peter, Hugh and William set off. The other members of the team watched them go.

'I don't like it,' Pips murmured.

Giles put his arm around her waist and chuckled. 'Only because you'd like to go with them.'

Pips grinned. 'How well you know me already.'

The three men walked slowly towards the town.

'It's been shelled constantly just recently,' William murmured. 'I wonder how it's fared.'

They didn't have long to wait to find out. Houses and buildings lay in ruins, the belongings of former occupants scattered amidst the rubble. The streets were deserted and the men's footsteps echoed eerily in the dusk of early evening.

'Folks can't still be living here, surely,' Hugh said.

'We've seen the refugees on the road to Poperinghe. But I reckon there are still folks in some of the houses – even damaged ones,' Peter said.

They reached the square and were surprised to see not only some French cavalry, but also one or two English ambulances.

'That officer over there,' Hugh nodded towards a soldier with a sergeant's insignia who seemed to be issuing orders to stretcher bearers, 'he looks like he's in charge. Let's see if we can help.'

'Evening, sergeant,' Peter said. 'Can we be of assistance?'

The man turned, drew his pistol and pointed it at them. Automatically, the three raised their hands above their heads.

'We're stretcher bearers with a flying ambulance corps camped at Brandhoek,' Hugh explained, sounding much calmer than he was feeling inside. 'Can we help your lads?'

The man lowered his pistol and grinned at them. 'Watcha, mate. What are you doin' out here?'

The three men laughed to hear his broad cockney accent. They lowered their arms and moved forward to shake the man's hand.

For a brief moment, they laughed and joked and then Peter said again, seriously, 'Can we help you?' He nodded towards two men who were carrying wounded out from a large building on one side of the square.

'We're moving German wounded out. Some of 'em are goners. There's been no one to look after them and nearly all of 'em have got gangrene. Pitiful sight, they are, even if they are the enemy. 'Course, they're our prisoners now.'

'Where are you taking them?'

'Poperinghe, if they can survive the journey.'

The three men looked at each other and Peter said what was in all their minds. 'Give two of us a lift back to our post and we'll fetch two more ambulances.'

'Great. We can use all the help we can get. Don't mind telling you, I don't like this place. There's hardly anyone here. It's as if it's died.'

'It was a lovely town,' William said wistfully.

The first ambulance, loaded with casualties, was ready to leave and William and Peter climbed into the cab.

'I reckon Miss Pips'll get her wish now,' William laughed above the noise of the engine.

'Eh? What d'you mean?'

'I know that look she had on her face when we were leaving. For two pins, she'd have come with us.'

'Never known a woman like her, I haven't. Cockney lasses are pretty strong and resilient, but her...' Peter shook his head in wonderment.

William was right. When they explained why they had come back, Pips was the first to say, 'I'll go. I'll take the car. William and Peter can drive the two motor ambulances.'

'Pips, I don't think...' Giles began, then sighed and shrugged. Pips wasn't listening; she was already running towards the car.

'I'll go with her.'

'Alice, no...' Robert began, but she too, if she

heard him, took no notice.

It was a soul-destroying and thankless task.

'Most of them won't survive,' Pips whispered to Alice as they moved amongst the wounded, 'but there are just one or two young boys over there I'd like Giles and Robert to take a look at. If they were to amputate straight away, those boys might have a chance.'

'You'd better speak to the sergeant.'

'Yes, I'll have a word.'

'I'll leave one of my soldiers with you until they're able to be moved on,' the sergeant said when she explained what she had in mind.

'Of course, sergeant,' Pips said stiffly. 'But they're hardly going to run far, are they?'

'You're right there, miss, but orders is orders.'

'Yes, I keep hearing that a lot,' Pips said drily.

Giles, with Robert's assistance, operated on three of the four young German soldiers whom Pips had decided could be treated. He shook his head over the fourth. 'He wouldn't survive the op, but we won't subject him to the tortuous journey to Poperinghe. Put him in the moribund tent. I doubt he'll last till morning anyway.'

Pips sat beside the soldier for the remainder of the night, holding his hand and murmuring to him in German now and again.

Just before dawn, he seemed to rouse himself and asked her to feel in the pocket of his jacket.

'My wallet,' he said in German. 'Please...'

She took it out and opened it.

'Picture of my mother and father,' he whispered.

She searched amongst the pieces of paper in his wallet and took out a small, crumpled photograph. How often, she wondered, had this young boy pored over the likeness of his parents?

He held it between trembling fingers and a tear slipped from his eye.

'You will write to them for me – after the war? The address is in my wallet. You will tell them I didn't suffer? Please.'

A lump in her throat threatened to choke her. Even as he lay dying, his thoughts were for the feelings of his loved ones. He was no different from all the dying English soldiers she had nursed. They, too, always wanted their families to believe they had died quickly and without pain.

'Of course, I will,' Pips promised, deciding that before she handed over his belongings to the sergeant, she would take a note of his parents' address.

As dawn broke over the ravaged land, the young German soldier died, still holding her hand and clutching the photograph.

Thirty-Seven

The sound of shelling disturbed their sleep for several nights.

'They mean to obliterate Ypres,' William mourned. 'How can they destroy such beautiful buildings?'

On 22 November there was more bad news.

Hugh, Peter and William visited the town yet again and returned to the post with solemn faces.

'That delightful town,' Hugh's voice was unsteady. 'It's in ruins and Cloth Hall is on fire. They can't save it.'

'It's just a heap of rubble now,' Peter added. 'I really don't know what was so important about it that both sides want to hold this particular town.'

'To my mind, it'd make more sense to straighten out the front line,' Robert said, 'perhaps along the route of the canal, but then I'm not a military man.'

'I expect,' Pips said reasonably, 'we don't want to give up so much as an inch to the enemy. After all, it's been hard won over these last few weeks. Didn't you say it holds the key to the coastal ports? I'll have to ask George what he thinks.'

'Ours not to reason why...' William began to quote and then faltered, but they all knew the next line. And many had certainly died in the effort to keep Ypres in Allied hands.

Two days later, the battle for the town was deemed to be at an end, but it was still in Allied hands. There had been a high number of casualties on both sides, but now, with the onset of harsh winter weather, both sides dug in deep and prepared to sit it out and wait for spring. There were no plans for any offensives before the weather improved, which wasn't likely until the following year.

'We're still needed here through the winter, though,' Robert said. 'Disease and trench foot will rise dramatically and many, because of poor nutrition, will get ill.'

'And no doubt snipers will still take pot shots at our trenches when they see movement,' Pips said wryly. 'And if they get too bored, they'll likely send a few shells our way.'

In an effort to raise their spirits, Robert said, 'But we could take some leave in turn. I'll draw up a rota.'

'I don't want to go away over Christmas,' Pips said promptly. 'I want to go to the trenches and give out presents.'

Two days later, she called the other members of the unit together. 'Just look at all these parcels my mother has sent.

They gazed around in awe at the piles of boxes and parcels stacked in Pips's tent. She'd had to push the camp beds where she and Alice slept close together to accommodate all the gifts.

'I've had word,' Robert said, 'that Dr Hazelwood will be paying us a visit just before Christmas and will bring more supplies and gifts for the troops.'

'I'm not surprised. I expect he wants to check up on us,' Pips said reasonably.

'Well, yes, but I gather he's put together another unit that will be coming out and he'll want to get them settled like he did us.'

'Will they be here with us?'

Robert shook his head. 'I don't think so. There are a few pockets of fighting still going on – albeit half-heartedly – and he'll place them where he thinks they'll be of most use.'

'Do you think all hostilities will cease at least for Christmas Day?' Alice asked. 'I mean, aren't the Germans supposed to love the festivities as much as we do? Wasn't it Prince Albert who brought the idea of Christmas trees to Britain?'

'He generally gets the credit,' Giles laughed, 'but I read somewhere that it was the German wife of George the Third, Queen Charlotte, who first brought the idea to this country way back in the early 1800s. But the tradition certainly came from Germany, so let's hope they revere the day as much as we do.'

'It'd be nice if they did, but anyway, we'll have to distribute all these parcels and not only amongst the wounded. We ought to get some to the trenches. That's where they'll be the most welcome.'

'We'll load them into the motor ambulance and the car,' William suggested, 'and take them as far as the reserve trenches.'

'We'll go on Christmas Eve. It'll be a nice surprise for the lads at the front.'

Dr Hazelwood arrived on 19 December. There were still casualties arriving, but not as many as when a major battle was in progress.

'As I suspected would happen,' Robert said, as he took the doctor on a tour of the tented first-aid post, 'at the moment our patients are mainly those with trench foot or frostbite or illness of some kind.'

Dr Hazelwood nodded his agreement. 'You're doing a grand job here. I hope the unit I've just brought out here does as well. And I understand you're going to take parcels to the trenches on Christmas Eve. I'd like to go with you. I've brought a carload of more gifts from home. Mrs

Parrott's sterling work in fund-raising is reaping its rewards.'

'Mrs Parrott isn't here at the post. She's in Poperinghe just now. She will come with us if we all move, of course, but we'll always ensure that she's billeted in the nearest village or town in what we hope is comparative safety. But she visits us often, usually about once a week, to see what we need. She's marvellous at organizing and obtaining supplies for us. I don't know how she does it.'

'She has built up an excellent line of communication stretching back to England, where she has a network of fund-raisers beavering away for her. I believe your mother is one of her contacts.'

Robert smiled. 'I'm delighted to hear it. Mother started fund-raising and organizing a local knitting circle the moment war was declared. She'll be in her element.'

'Now we're alone, Robert, there's something I must tell you, but I'm going to leave you to break the news to Giles.'

Minutes later, a solemn-faced Robert sought out his friend. 'Giles, old chap,' Robert began, 'there's something you ought to know. Dr Hazelwood has brought news from home. Scarborough has been bombarded. It happened last Wednesday.'

Giles stared at Robert. 'I don't understand. What d'you mean, "bombarded"? D'you mean bombed from an aircraft or a Zeppelin?'

Robert shook his head. 'No, from German ships out at sea.'

Giles's mouth dropped open. 'From – from the sea?'

Robert nodded. 'Evidently, one or two ships engaged with the fortress at West Hartlepool, whilst a cruiser attacked Scarborough and then Whitby on its return journey. They had two cracks at Scarborough. The first hit the foreshore and the esplanade and the second hit targets further inland in the town.'

Giles sat down suddenly. 'You don't know exactly where, though?'

'No, sorry. But Dr Hazelwood brought this for you to see.' Robert handed him a national newspaper dated the day after the incident. 'It might give you more details.' On the front page there were pictures of the devastation and, on the inside pages, accounts given by various residents of what had happened to them.

'It says here two battle cruisers and one armoured cruiser took part.' Giles paused as he scanned the words and absorbed the photographs. 'The lighthouse has been hit,' he murmured, pointing at a picture. 'And that house in Lonsdale Road that's been damaged – I know it.'

'It's not near where you live, is it?'

Giles shook his head. 'But I do wonder if my parents are all right.' He looked up suddenly. 'There have been several fatalities. That's not what you're trying to tell me, is it? That you think they might have been killed?'

'No, no,' Robert said swiftly. 'How could I? I don't even know exactly where they live. You've only ever told us that they live in Scarborough. But if you want to go home, we'd all understand.'

For a moment, Giles hesitated. 'I can't leave. I'm the only surgeon attached to this unit. I'm needed here.'

'Dr Hazelwood has said he will organize a replacement if you want to visit your parents. He tried to find out if they were all right, but he didn't know their address. He did ask the authorities if they had the name "Kendall" on their casualty list, but they confirmed that they hadn't. Nor was there any record of anyone of that name being in hospital. But it still doesn't confirm that they're unharmed, Giles. You know, not for definite.'

Giles shook his head adamantly. 'No, I'll stay here. They wouldn't expect me to rush home.'

'Then we must try to get further news. I'll ask Captain Allender – I think he's still in the area – if he can find out anything through his channels of communication...'

'No,' Giles said harshly. 'I don't want to be indebted to that man.'

Robert stared at him for a moment, and then understanding began to filter into his mind. Giles was jealous of Captain Allender where Pips was concerned. Maybe that was the real reason he didn't want to leave. Robert turned away and, for the first time since he had become friends with him, he was disgusted at Giles.

Did he really have so little trust in Pips that he was refusing to take compassionate leave to find out if his parents were unhurt in what must have been a dreadful shock for his home town? And did he also care so little for them?

Three days later, Giles received a letter. 'They're all right,' he told Robert.

'I'm glad,' Robert said, but his tone was stiff.

'Their house was untouched but eighteen people

215

died as a result of the attack – some immediately, others later of their wounds.'

'Anyone you knew?' Robert's tone softened a little. Perhaps Giles had been right not to go after all, though Robert was sure that in the same circumstances, he would have rushed home.

'Father doesn't say. I expect he doesn't know all the names yet. The whole town's in a state of shock, though, and fearful that it will happen again.'

'What about Whitby?'

'There were a few killed there, but not as many.'

'Are you sure you don't want to take leave?' Robert asked again. 'We could manage somehow. The surgical cases could be taken further on to the nearest casualty-clearing station.'

Giles shook his head as he folded the letter and tucked it into his pocket. 'No, my father says it would serve no useful purpose and, besides, he knows I'm needed here.'

'I can't deny that,' Robert sighed as he saw William's ambulance approaching. No doubt there would be several patients needing their attention.

Thirty-Eight

'Hello – anyone at home?'

Norah and Ma exchanged a glance. 'That's our Bernard's voice.' Norah dropped the spoon she was holding onto the kitchen table with a clatter and rushed towards the scullery, flinging the

216

door open wide. 'Bernard! And Roy too! Oh, this is wonderful! Why didn't you let us know you were coming?'

'Didn't know oursens until yesterday, Mam,' Bernard said, giving her a bear hug.

'Nah, then, Ma,' he said, moving into the kitchen. He bent to kiss her forehead and, when he straightened up, he noticed all the knitting wool at the side of her chair. 'What's all this, then?'

'Socks and balaclavas for the soldiers. We've got all the women in the village making them. Then Mrs Maitland collects them and parcels 'em up to send out to Miss Pips and Alice.'

'So, they're still there, then?'

Ma nodded and explained.

'I only wish we were out there,' Roy said, as he joined them, greeted his grandmother and then dropped into the chair opposite her. 'Where's Dad?'

'Where d'you think? At work.'

'Got enough to keep him busy?'

'More than enough. Too much,' Norah said, and there was a hint of resentment in her tone that Len had been left with the work of three men, to say nothing of the help Boy had started to be.

'We'll give him a hand whilst we're home.'

'How long have you got?'

The two young men grinned at each other. 'Nearly two weeks, Mam. We don't have to report back until Monday the fourth of January. There's several of us from the village come home. Sam Nuttall was on the same train as us.'

'Thank goodness for that,' Ma said. 'I don't

217

know what Clara would have done if he hadn't come home.'

'Taken to her bed again, I shouldn't wonder,' Norah said drily.

'Right, then,' Roy said, dropping his kit bag in the corner of the kitchen. 'I'm off to give Betty a bit of a surprise, an' all. I just hope she hasn't been swept off her feet by some yokel who hasn't had the guts to enlist.'

There was a brief silence in the kitchen and then everyone spoke at once to cover the embarrassment. The thought of William was like a spectre in the room.

As Roy left, Bernard said quietly, 'Have you heard anything from Boy?'

Norah pursed her lips. 'Not a word.'

'Maybe he'll get leave for Christmas.'

'Maybe,' Norah said listlessly. She hadn't much hope, but at least tomorrow would be a much brighter Christmas Day than she'd thought it would be, now that Bernard and Roy had come home on leave.

If only she could have had all her family – including William – around her table just one more time. But sadly, with a mother's intuition, she knew with certainty that it would never happen again.

'So, we'll go to the front this afternoon,' Dr Hazelwood said on Christmas Eve. 'Who will you take? I can drive my car myself, though I'd like a little help the other end to unload it all.'

'Of course.' Robert thought for a moment and then said, 'William wants to drive our motor ambulance and Pips and Alice will want to go, as do Giles and I. I suggest we leave Sister Leonore and Nurse Brigitta here to look after the wounded we still have here. Hugh and Peter can bring the other ambulance and help us distribute the parcels.'

Before he could stop himself, William said, 'Couldn't Brigitta come with me? I mean – I think...' He was stammering now in embarrassment. 'She'd like to see the soldiers in happier circumstances.'

Robert hid his smile; he had witnessed William's growing fondness for the pretty nurse.

'I don't see why not,' he said, 'if sister doesn't mind managing on her own and gives her permission.'

The convoy set out in the afternoon. It had been a cold, frosty day – the kind of weather that heralded Christmas – and as dusk closed in, it began to snow. There had been no shelling that day, as if both sides relished a little quiet. When the party reached the reserve trenches they were greeted by a resounding cheer when the soldiers realized what their vehicles carried and soon they were handing out wine, plum puddings, mince pies and tins of Tickler's jam. 'They come from my home county,' Pips told the men. 'It's a firm in Grimsby.'

There was laughter around her. 'Aye, an' when we've eaten t'jam, miss, we'll use t'tins for home-made grenades.'

'It seems pretty quiet at the moment,' Pips remarked, glancing about her. 'D'you think they'd let us take some parcels to the support trenches and the front line ourselves? We'd like to.'

'You'd better ask the captain, nurse. I'll fetch him.'

'Captain Allender,' she smiled as he approached, 'I'd like to introduce you to Dr Hazelwood, who formed our flying ambulance corps.'

The man held out his hand. 'I'm very pleased to meet you, Dr Hazelwood. I can't tell you how much your unit being so close means to us. The survival rate of my wounded is so much better since their arrival.'

'I think you know everyone else, having been to the post.'

George shook hands with Robert and Giles and nodded towards the others, who were already unloading the vehicles. The captain called some of his men forward to help carry parcels through the communication trenches towards the front line.

'It's quiet just now, if you all want to see the forward trenches,' George offered. They all followed him, each of them taking as much as they could carry.

To Pips's surprise, the soldiers were amazingly cheerful and their delight in the simple gifts was touching.

'Socks! Fellers, I've got some socks at last.' One had already torn open his small parcel and was holding a pair of brown socks. 'Best Christmas present I've ever had in me life, miss.' He grasped Pips's shoulders and kissed her soundly on both cheeks. 'That's the French way of greeting.' He guffawed loudly. 'They've got some nice ways. That's one tradition I'll tek back home to Blighty with me.'

220

Pips laughed with him. 'Then I'll warn all the girls.'

As dusk came, the soldiers performed their usual 'stand to' at that time.

'We'll dispense with the usual maintenance of the trenches activity just for tonight,' Captain Allender said. 'Though we'll need to fetch water and rations. Corporal Brown, can you find some rum for our visitors. I'm sure you know where some can be found.'

Captain Allender stayed with them the whole time, warning them of the dangers as they moved along the forward trench to hand out presents and take a drink with the men.

'We should be going,' Robert murmured, but there was such a party atmosphere now in the trench that he was loathe to break it up.

'Ssh,' Giles said suddenly. 'Listen.'

Those around him fell silent and in the quiet of the night they heard singing. 'Is it our lads,' a soldier whispered, 'further down the line?'

'No,' George Allender said. 'It's coming from the German trenches. We're quite close here. They're only a few yards away.'

Pips made a move as if she would peer over the side of the trench, but George caught hold of her arm. 'Keep down. It might be a trap to get us to poke our heads above the parapet.'

But the soldier who'd been given the socks climbed the ladder and looked carefully over the top. 'Sir, they've got lighted candles all along the top of their trench and it *is* them singing.'

'*Stille Nacht! Heilige Nacht!*' Pips murmured and added swiftly, 'I was taught a little German.

It comes in useful now and then.'

'As I very well know,' George said softly, and Pips looked up to see him smiling down at her.

As the hymn came to an end, further down their own trench an English voice began to sing, 'It Came Upon the Midnight Clear'. Soon, the singing rippled along the trench as others joined in. Even Pips couldn't stop herself humming the tune and murmuring, 'That's an apt choice.'

As the voices died away, they heard a German voice shouting.

'Hey, Tommy, you want a present? I give you present, yes.'

'Careful, lads,' their captain warned. 'Pass it along, sergeant. Keep down. It might be a trap.'

But the soldier still on the ladder said incredulously, 'They're getting out of their trenches, captain. They're walking towards us.'

'Are they armed?'

'Dun't look like it, sir. They're carrying candles.'

'Hold your fire,' George shouted and the order went down the line. Now he too climbed a nearby ladder to look over the parapet.

'Well, I'll be damned,' Pips heard him mutter. 'It doesn't look like an ambush, but we'd better be careful...'

His warning went unheeded as soldiers from both sides now began to climb up the ladders and over the top of the trench side. Cutting holes in the barbed wire, they passed into no-man's-land and walked towards each other.

'Ha, Tommy, I bring you chocolate? You give me tobacco, ya?'

The soldier who'd first looked out glanced down

at Pips. 'You got any more of them socks, miss? I bet they need them as much as we do.'

'Of course, here you are. And take these biscuits too. And cake. There's a cake here we haven't touched yet.'

'I don't think we should be doing this,' George said worriedly. 'It'll be frowned upon by the brass. Fraternizing in a time of war, they'd say.'

Robert and Giles were climbing the ladders cautiously. 'It looks safe enough. They've met up in the middle,' Robert said. 'They're exchanging gifts. And now someone's started a snowball fight.'

The sound of laughter echoed across the strip of land between the two trenches that was now filled with soldiers from both sides.

'If I hadn't seen this with my own eyes,' Giles said incredulously, 'I wouldn't have believed it. They'll never believe it back home.'

'I hope they don't get to hear about it,' George muttered and then, hearing the laughter floating across the strip of land between the two lines of trenches, he suddenly said, 'Oh, what the hell,' and he held out his hand to help Pips up the ladder. 'I can only be court-martialled.'

Thirty-Nine

The following morning, Pips said, 'I don't know about you, but I'm going back to the trenches. I want to spend Christmas Day with the lads. And it'll be interesting to see what happens with the Germans after last night.'

The meeting between the two sides had gone on until the early hours of the morning and now Pips was intrigued to see what the atmosphere would be like today.

'Right, we'll all go,' Robert said. 'That's if Dr Hazelwood approves.'

The doctor not only approved, but he also joined them, and they arrived to find the British soldiers cooking two geese on a spit over a fire and a team setting up a makeshift table in a shell hole behind the front lines.

'Morning, captain,' Pips greeted George Allender. 'What's happening?'

He was smiling, but there was still a tinge of anxiety in his eyes. 'You'll have to see for yourself.'

He led them all down the series of trenches until they climbed the ladders and stepped over the parapet.

'Oh my!'

There was a boisterous game of football in progress between the two sides.

'So, remind me, captain,' Pips murmured as they stood together watching the two sides in the bitter conflict now playing football in no-man's-land, on ground already soaked with the blood of their comrades, 'why are we at war?'

He was silent for a moment before saying drily, 'One wonders – when you look at this – but I've always thought that ordinary German men and women don't want a war any more than we do. Left to the likes of these men' – he waved his arm to encompass both sides – 'we wouldn't have one. We'd play them at football. One would emerge the winner, then we'd all shake hands, slap each other on the back and go home.'

They stood watching as the men from their first-aid unit joined in the rough and tumble of the game and it seemed to Pips that Robert and Giles were the most enthusiastic. Dr Hazelwood joined Pips and the captain.

'I need your advice,' he murmured, standing beside them, his gaze still on the game. 'A young soldier from their side has approached me. In halting English he has asked for help for a friend of his who, he says, is very sick in their trench over there.'

'What's the matter with him? Does he know?'

'He pointed to his feet. I guess the poor boy has trench foot.'

'Have they no medical supplies?'

'He says not. But I think it's more that they don't know what to do about it.'

'Surely their own medical people will. Why hasn't he been taken back to one of their first-aid posts?'

'I don't know.' The doctor was obviously troubled. His calling, his Hippocratic oath and his instinct, was to help anyone in trouble, no matter who they were.

'We could take a look at him,' Pips suggested.

Dr Hazelwood smiled at her. 'I knew you'd say that, but I didn't know what the captain would think.'

George was obviously struggling to decide. He sighed. 'Very well, but we must find his superior first and see what he wants us to do.'

The doctor hurried away and returned with the young soldier who had approached him, followed by a smiling captain who clicked his heels and bowed politely to Pips. In very good English he said, 'You have medicine for my man?'

'I may have, captain, but I need to see him first.'

'He cannot be moved. You will come to our trench, yes?'

'I don't think that's a good idea,' George said at once. 'They might take you prisoner.'

The German officer said stiffly, 'We would never harm a nurse, and look' – he waved behind him – 'we are friends today, yes.' Then he grinned widely. 'Tomorrow, I kill you.'

They all laughed.

'I'll get Giles or Robert to come with me,' Pips said. 'It's best you don't go, Captain Allender. That really might cause trouble for you.'

She crossed the uneven ground to where the football game was still in progress and, standing on the sideline, she beckoned to Giles, who had seen her already. He kicked the ball to Robert and then ran towards her. Swiftly, she explained what had been asked of them.

'Right,' he said at once. 'I'll come with you.'

They followed the German captain into the enemy's trench.

'Good Lord,' Giles said in a low voice. 'Just look at this. I'd heard their trenches were much better constructed than ours, but this is a mess.'

'Maybe they're only considered to be temporary,' Pips whispered back. 'Come on, we'd better find this boy. The captain's beckoning.'

The young boy – Pips was sure he couldn't be much more than fifteen, sixteen at the most – was lying in a dugout. His friend stood looking on whilst Giles examined him.

'What's your name?' Pips asked the boy gently.

He didn't answer; he was feverish and seemed to be rambling. 'It's Hans, Fräulein.'

Giles stood up and turned to the officer. 'He needs that foot amputated if you're to save his life. Can you get him back to your first-aid posts?'

'Not today. Our stretcher bearers are...' He made a drinking motion with his hand.

Giles glanced at Pips. 'Then we will take him back to our first-aid post. I am a surgeon and I can do the operation right away. It's the only chance he has. But what I can't promise, is to return him to you. He'll need nursing – proper care – for some time. He may have to become our prisoner and be taken to a hospital. But he won't be alone. We already have prisoners of war who are being treated in our hospitals.'

The captain shrugged. 'He is no use to us now, anyway. But his friend here seems determined to get help for him.'

'Can you find us a stretcher?'

Before his superior could speak, the young soldier who'd asked for their help said, 'Yes. I know where there's one.'

He hurried out of the dugout and returned only minutes later, struggling with a stretcher. He laid it on the ground and Pips and Giles gently lifted the casualty onto it. It was awkward, manoeuvring it out of the dugout and the trench but, as they were carrying it across the ground towards their own trench, William came running across to take one end.

'Here, Pips, let me.'

The two captains from opposing sides stood with Dr Hazelwood watching.

'I'm afraid he will have to be our prisoner,' Captain Allender said. 'I really dare not return him to you, even though I'd like to.'

'But he will be well cared for. I give you my personal promise,' Dr Hazelwood said.

The German sounded unsure. 'You won't – shoot him?'

'Heavens, no!' Dr Hazelwood was shocked. 'He may be sent back to England as a prisoner of war, but he will not be harmed. In fact, we will do everything we can to save his life.'

'And yet,' the German murmured, 'tomorrow we will begin killing each other again.'

'Ridiculous, isn't it?' George Allender muttered as his gaze followed William and one of his own men carrying the casualty to an ambulance.

William and Brigitta set off at once back to the first-aid post.

'I should go too,' Giles said. 'He'll need an operation as soon as we can do it.'

Reluctant though she was to leave this miracle of camaraderie being acted out before her eyes, Pips said, 'I'll come with you.'

She shook hands with George and nodded to the German captain and then she and Giles hurried back to the ambulance in which they had arrived.

As she drove carefully, Giles murmured. 'This Captain Allender chap – have you known him longer than I'm aware of?' There was an unusual tightness in Giles's tone.

'No, why?'

'You just seem – very friendly with him.'

Pips chuckled. 'Could you, my darling Giles, be just a tiny bit jealous?'

Giles had the grace to laugh. 'Of course I am.'

Pips took her left hand off the wheel and grasped his hand. 'You've no need, my love. I promise you, you've really no need.'

Giles, with Leonore assisting him and Pips standing by, amputated the boy's foot just above his ankle. When it was over and the young soldier was sleeping in the recovery tent, Giles said, 'I still can't understand why his comrades didn't take him to their own first-aid posts. Surely they must be well organized.'

'Their captain indicated that they'd all been drinking – possibly heavily. Presumably he feared they'd be in no fit state to operate.' She paused and then asked, 'What are we to do with him once he's well enough to be moved, Giles?'

'He should be fit enough in a couple of days; besides, we can't keep him here long, any more than we do our own chaps.' He smiled at her. 'Maybe your friend Captain Allender will decide what should be done.'

'I don't think...' she began and then stopped.

'What? Go on, say it.'

'I don't think he wants to be involved. He wasn't too happy about what he termed fraternization. There could be trouble.'

Giles grimaced. 'Then we'd better take the decision. At least, we'll discuss it with Dr Hazelwood. After all, it was he who set the ball rolling, as it were.'

Pips stayed beside the boy through the day. She heard Dr Hazelwood, Robert and the two Enderby brothers return later in the afternoon.

'How is he now?' Giles said, visiting the tent during the evening.

'He's sleeping surprisingly well,' Pips said.

'But not you. You should go and get some rest, Pips. You weren't thinking of sitting with him all night too, were you?'

'I'm all right. I've catnapped.'

'Maybe, but that's not proper rest. Go and get some sleep whilst you can. And that's an order. I'll get Brigitta to keep an eye on Hans.'

For once, Pips did as he bade her. She wouldn't have admitted it, but the events of the previous night and of the day had left her drained, though it was nothing that a few hours' sleep wouldn't rectify. Pips was blessed with a strong constitution, and never had she needed it more than now.

Forty

'Just look at this in the paper,' Len said, as the remnants of the Dawson family sat down to breakfast on the last morning of the boys' leave. He jabbed his finger at a front-page article. 'It says here that the two sides played football in no-man's-land on Christmas Day and even exchanged gifts.'

'There you are, Ma,' Bernard teased. 'Some Hun could be wearing the socks you've knitted.'

For a brief moment, Ma's face was a picture of indignation and then her expression softened. 'Ah well, he's some mother's son.'

Bernard guffawed. 'Typical woman's remark, in't it, Roy?'

'Don't cheek your grandmother, Bernard,' Norah said sharply. 'It's not easy for us with *all* our family in danger.' She glared at him and no one in the room was in any doubt that, for once, she was including William in the remark.

Len cleared his throat and brought the topic of conversation back to the newspaper. 'I reckon it'll cause trouble for some of the officers who let it happen – or even took part themselves. They might even be court-martialled.'

'Quite right too,' Roy said. 'Killing 'em one minute and then playing football with 'em the next. It's ridiculous.'

'This whole war's ridiculous, if you ask me,'

231

Norah said and crashed the pots together as she cleared the table.

But, it seemed, no one was asking her opinion.

After a moment's silence, Bernard got up. 'Come on, Roy, time we was going if we're to cadge a lift into Lincoln with the carrier's cart.'

Len stood up and held out his hand towards his two sons in turn. 'Good luck, lads. Keep in touch. Yar mam and Ma like to get letters from you.'

'I'm not much of a letter writer, Dad. Nor is Roy, but we'll send you a line or two every week, just to let you know what's happening. Give our love to Alice when you write next to her and tell that young rascal, Boy, when you see him, that we'll clip his ear when we catch up with him.' Bernard grinned. 'But tell him we're proud of him an' all.'

In a flurry of 'goodbyes' the two young men left to return to training camp. And still no mention had been made of their brother, William.

'Where's William?' Robert asked.

'Just arrived back with casualties. It's very light at the moment. I don't think the soldiers on this section have the heart for killing now, not after Christmas Day,' Pips replied.

The New Year of 1915 had passed and fighting had resumed but, in the section where they were, in a desultory fashion.

'Young Hans is ready to be moved on,' Robert said. 'But where to, I don't know. Back to his comrades or as our prisoner of war. Dr Hazelwood said we ought to keep him here as long as possible, but we'll soon be needing the space.'

'Mm. We ought to ask Captain Allender. Tell you what, I'll take Giles's motorcycle and see if I can find him. I'll even borrow his leathers.'

'Of course, but you ought to ask Giles first,' Robert murmured.

Pips blinked. 'Why? I'm sure he won't mind. He knows how good I am at riding it.'

Robert smiled. 'Oh, not that, but I think he has – concerns about the captain.'

'Oh phooey!' She flapped her hand at him and turned away to change her clothing.

A few minutes later, she was roaring out of the field and down the rough track towards the front lines.

'Where's Pips going?' Giles wanted to know.

'To ask the captain what we should do about Hans. He's ready to be moved.'

Giles stared after the receding motorcycle. 'Has she now?' he murmured.

'Good Lord!' George Allender exclaimed, as he saw the figure dismount from the noisy machine, take off the leather helmet and shake her long hair free. 'You!' He came towards her, smiling. 'Is there anything you can't do?'

'Plenty.' She grinned. 'I never learned to shoot straight.' She laughed at herself, acknowledging aloud for the first time what her parents had always suspected. 'And it's always riled me that Robert can.'

Intuitively, George said, 'Are you competitive with your brother?'

'Oh yes – in everything. I wanted to go to university or to medical school like he did, but my

233

parents – well, to be fair, my mother – wouldn't hear of it. She had my life mapped out for me. Married to a nice, well-to-do man and producing a barrow-load of grandchildren for her. At least the war has put a stop to that.'

He chuckled. 'Maybe only a temporary halt, because, if I'm not mistaken, there's something between you and Dr Kendall, isn't there?'

Pips felt the colour rising in her face. 'I'd like to think so, but the war distorts things. It's not like ordinary life, is it?'

'It certainly isn't,' he said softly. After a moment's pause he added, 'Anyway, what brings you here?'

'The young German boy we took back to operate on his foot. Hans. He's well enough to be moved and we can't keep him any longer. What do you want us to do with him?'

'Send him down the usual route of casualty-clearing stations and hospitals, but making sure everyone knows he is a prisoner of war. The authorities will know what to do. I don't imagine for one minute that he will be the only German soldier they've treated in Allied hospitals. He may be sent to England, but eventually he will end up in a POW camp somewhere.'

Pips returned to the first-aid post and reported to Robert and Giles what Captain Allender had advised. 'William can take him first thing tomorrow morning.'

'Good,' Robert said. 'Two of the casualties he brought in today are ready to go too, though how they'll take to being in the company of an enemy,

I don't know.'

There were tears in the boy's eyes as William and Hugh lifted Hans into the back of the ambulance the following morning. Luckily, the two soldiers travelling with him bore no malice towards him.

'We were there, playing football with 'em on Christmas Day,' one told Pips. 'How can you hate a young lad like that when you've been playing football with his mates? I didn't want to start the shooting again, nurse, if I'm honest. I'd've sooner turned tail and gone home, but you have to obey the orders of those who reckon they know best. But do they, nurse? Do they really?'

It was a question Pips could not answer.

Before his departure, Dr Hazelwood had left strict instructions with Robert and Giles, who shared the responsibility for the unit, that they were all to take time off when they could.

'Overtired doctors and nurses and even stretcher bearers are no use to anyone if they fall sick themselves,' he had said firmly. 'Make sure everyone – including both of you – gets some rest. If you can, get right away from the post. Make use of your father's car, Robert. It is not an indulgence, it is a necessity to keep you all fit and well.'

'Things are pretty quiet just now,' Robert said to Giles. 'I don't think there'll be much until spring, so I think all of us should take some leave in turn.'

'Go home, you mean? Back to England?'

'I wasn't thinking of that, but if you'd like to go to see your parents after the dreadful news Dr Hazelwood brought...'

235

Giles shook his head. 'No, I've had long letters from them both now, assuring me that they are fine. The shells didn't fall anywhere near our home. They're both shocked, of course, and they knew one or two of the people who were injured, but thankfully no one amongst their friends or acquaintances was killed. But I would like to take Pips to the coast where we could both enjoy some time together. Would you have any objection, as her big brother?'

'None at all, old chap. Besides, Pips will decide what she wants to do.' He laughed. 'She wouldn't take a scrap of notice of me anyway.'

'Won't your parents be expecting you to keep an eye on her?'

Robert shook his head. 'They know what Pips is like. I don't think they *understand* her, but they do recognize her rather unusual qualities. Unusual, that is, for a woman. I would just ask one thing of you, Giles.'

'What's that?'

'Don't hurt her.'

Giles shook his head. 'I wouldn't do that for the world, Robert.'

'Where are we going?'

'It's a surprise.'

Pips pulled a face. 'I'm not too keen on surprises. I like to know exactly what I'm doing.'

They'd packed a small suitcase each of civilian clothes. 'No doctor's or nurse's uniforms,' was all Giles would tell her, and so Pips was wearing the civilian suit she had arrived in and had packed her one dress suitable for an evening meal in a hotel.

236

They drove to a small coastal village just across the French border. As they pulled into the car park of the only hotel, Giles switched off the engine and turned to face her. 'Now, you have a decision to make and I am not putting any pressure on you. The choice is yours. Are we booking in as Mr and Mrs Kendall in one room – or Mr Kendall and Miss Maitland in two?'

Pips gasped and stared at him wide-eyed. This was something she had not expected. She glanced away, thinking quickly. She'd seen so much death and mutilation – people's lives altered in seconds. Young men, no more than boys really, who, she guessed, had died without knowing what it was to love and be loved.

She loved and trusted Giles. She turned back to face him, smiling. 'Oh, just one, I think, Giles. Don't you?'

'My darling.' His voice was husky as he took her hand and raised her fingers to his lips.

As they entered the hotel, her heart was racing with pent-up excitement and emotion and not a little trepidation. Of course, she knew what happened between a man and a woman, but it would be her first time. Swiftly, she pushed aside all thoughts of her strait-laced mother, who would be horrified. But Henrietta was not out here, not living with the thought that, although they were supposed to be safely behind the lines, a stray shell could wipe them all out in a second. If you live with danger, Pips thought, you have to live dangerously...

A little nervously, she said, 'You – you do know that it'll be my first time?'

Now he leaned across and kissed her cheek. 'I know. I'll be very gentle – and careful. I'd never hurt you, my love.'

As they climbed out of the car and headed into the reception of the hotel, Pips couldn't help being a little disappointed that his reply to her admission of virginity had not been, 'Me too.'

'Oh Pips, you look so much better,' Alice greeted her. 'I don't need to ask if you've had a nice time. Where did you go? What did you do?'

'We went just across the border on the coast and stayed in a nice hotel on the seafront. The meals were very good – considering there's a war on – and we walked along the beach and–'

'In this weather? It's winter.'

Pips smiled to herself. They hadn't felt the cold as they'd walked, talking, laughing and making plans.

'What shall we do after the war?' she'd asked him.

'Get married,' he'd said promptly. 'We'll have a lovely wedding in the church right next to your home. Your mother will be in her element. It'll be one of the happiest days of her life. And I hope it will be your very happiest, my darling Pips.'

She'd rested her head against his shoulder. 'But where shall we live? Near the hospital? I presume you'll be going back to Lincoln.'

'Either that or at the hall. Won't your parents want you to live there?'

'I wouldn't think so. I'm not the heir. Robert is.'

'Oh. I see.'

'You sound a little disappointed,' she teased.

238

'Heavens, no!' he said swiftly. 'I just thought your parents would want you there and would perhaps put aside rooms for us, that's all.'

Pips chuckled. 'I want to get out from under my mother's thumb, Giles. I want to be my own mistress.' She smiled coyly. 'Even though, at the moment, I'm just yours.'

At night, they'd lain together in the big, soft, four-poster bed, making gentle love, cocooned for a few precious hours in a little world of their own making. And then they'd slept wrapped in each other's arms.

But now it was back to harsh reality, and there was a tacit understanding that nothing should happen between them when they were at the post, except perhaps for a brief, snatched kiss. They would conduct themselves in a completely professional manner, even though it would be so difficult now that they had tasted the heights of joyful union.

'So,' Pips asked, 'what's been happening?'

'Nothing much,' Alice said. 'Not many wounded coming in just now. The captain came one day. He seemed a bit put out when I said you weren't here and that you and Giles had gone away for a couple of nights. He's not been again. Oh, and by the way, there's a letter for you. I think it's from your father.' Alice chuckled. 'It's in his doctor's spidery handwriting.'

Pips laughed and slipped it into the pocket of her apron. She always looked forward to hearing from her father; they were long, rambling, newsy letters all about the people in the village she

239

knew. She would savour it later...

'Robert! Robert!' Alice flew from tent to tent in the dusk of evening searching for him.

'Whatever's the matter, Alice?' He went to her at once and clasped hold of her shoulders.

'You must come at once – you too, Dr Kendall.' Whilst she now felt comfortable calling both Pips and Robert by their Christian names, she could not yet bring herself to address Giles as anything but Dr Kendall. 'It's Pips. She's crying, and I've never known her to cry, Robert. Never! And I've known her a long time. It must be bad news. There was a letter from your father.'

'Where is she?'

'In our tent.'

The three of them hurried across the grass towards the women's tent.

'What's wrong, Pips?' Robert sat down on the bed beside her and put his arm around her shoulders. Giles squatted down in front of her and Alice stood near the opening to the tent, wringing her hands.

'It's Midnight. My beautiful, beautiful Midnight. They've commandeered him for the front. He's – he's already been taken.'

'Oh Pips, I'm so sorry, but you must have known it was a possibility. He's not even a farm horse that's needed for work.'

'Father says poor Jake's heartbroken and fearing I will blame him for letting them take Midnight.'

'The lad wouldn't have had a choice.'

'I know,' Pips sniffed miserably.

'You must write to Jake and reassure him that

you fully understand there was nothing that could have been done to stop it, not by him or by anyone else.'

'I shouldn't be crying over a horse – an animal – when there are thousands of men being killed every day. It's just that we've seen such terrible sights out here of the poor creatures, how they're ill-used and die in agony. They didn't ask for all this and yet they're suffering.'

'Neither did the men,' Robert reminded her softly. 'Oh, they all rushed to volunteer, but now they see the cruel reality, I bet most of them wish they hadn't been so hasty. What about Jake's position at the hall if the horses have gone?'

'They've not taken the pony – too small, I expect – so he still has that to care for and Father says he's taken on much of the work that William used to do in the grounds.'

'D'you think he'll try and volunteer? How old is he now?'

'About fifteen, we think. Mother was never very sure of his age and he didn't seem to know either. Although he's strong and wiry, he's very small. I don't think they'd take him.'

'Don't you be too sure. They'll soon be taking anyone they can get, and if they bring in conscription eventually... Anyway, let's not think about that now.' He turned and smiled at Alice, still hovering near the tent opening. 'D'you think you could make us all a cup of tea, please?'

'Of course.' Alice hurried away whilst, stoically, Pips dried her tears and allowed herself to be led out of the tent. Though it was still Robert who had his arm about her, Giles touched her shoulder.

241

'I'm so sorry, darling,' he murmured. She clasped his hand tightly, drawing strength from his love and concern.

Forty-One

Before any plans for a spring offensive could begin, Robert made sure all the members of the team took some leave. William and Brigitta were the last to go. Their friendship was blossoming and he took her hand and said, 'Where would you like to go? Robert says we can take Dr Maitland's car.'

Shyly, she said, 'Could we go to see my grandparents? I have had no recent news and I would like to know if they're all right.'

'Of course.' Then he grinned. 'As long as you know the way. Apart from going backwards and forwards between our post, the clearing stations and hospitals, I haven't been anywhere else. You told me it's somewhere near Poperinghe, but in which direction? You know, we could have gone before now. It can't be far away.'

She shrugged. 'I didn't like to ask, at least not until Dr Robert said we can all take some leave.'

He nodded understandingly.

'We'd be able to stay with them.' She blushed prettily. 'They have two spare rooms.'

'I wouldn't expect anything else,' he said gallantly.

And so, on an unusually beautiful day in early

242

February, William and Brigitta set off to visit her grandparents.

'Now, where am I heading?' William smiled at her sitting beside him. Today she was dressed in a smart blue costume and matching hat. Her white blouse was frilled at the neck, framing her face. She was like a beautiful porcelain doll, and just as precious to William. He never ceased to marvel that such a delicate-looking girl could have such physical and inner strength to deal with the terrible sights they all encountered day after day. Whilst he'd admired and adored Pips for as long as he could remember – and he believed he always would – Brigitta was a girl whom he could love and be loved by in return. Dare he begin to hope that even amid all the horror, love could find a way? He'd seen for himself the blossoming romance between Pips and Giles, so why not for him too? She was smiling up at him now, her pink cheeks dimpling prettily.

'My grandparents have a farm just to the southwest of Poperinghe at a place called Lijssenthoek.'

'Fancy, I've been backwards and forwards to "Pop", as our soldiers call it, taking the wounded to the casualty-clearing stations there so many times I've lost count, and I never knew about your family living so close. I do wish you'd told me before, Brigitta. I'm sure Robert would have let us go.'

'Poperinghe is used by the Allied military now, being so near the Ypres battlefield. A lot of soldiers are billeted there and, of course, supplies come there by rail. And the troops stay there both before they go to the front and when they come back.' In a soft voice she added, '*If* they come back.' In a stronger voice, she went on. 'So, you see, it's in an ideal position. Far enough behind the front line so as not to be shelled – at least that's what we hope – but near enough for the wounded to be taken there and for soldiers to have rest when they are relieved at the front.'

'The people – the residents – haven't left, then? They haven't become refugees?'

'No. We got a lot of refugees passing through fleeing from the advancing Germans, but Poperinghe's townsfolk have stayed, though they're worried, obviously, that the war will end up on their doorstep one day. In the meantime, it's becoming a sort of haven for everyone – military, wounded, refugees...' She smiled. 'But we still have cinemas and clubs and cafes open. It's good for the soldiers to be able to relax.'

'And your grandparents?'

'I've heard from some of the soldiers that they're still trying to run the farm as best they can and that they've got nurses billeted with them now. But they'll squeeze us in,' she added hastily.

William was silent for a few moments before he asked quietly, 'And what do they think about you nursing so near the front? Wouldn't they prefer you to stay with them and work locally?'

Brigitta smiled. 'Perhaps, but they've never said so. I'm their only grandchild and, since they brought me up, we're very close, but all they've said to me is that–' She hesitated and William prompted, 'Go on.'

'That they're very proud of what I'm doing. They're very patriotic and are horrified by what's happening to their lovely country.'

'I can only guess at how it must feel to be occupied by an enemy. Let's hope Poperinghe continues to enjoy a kind of freedom.'

'Turn left here,' Brigitta said suddenly. 'It's not far down this road.'

About five minutes later, William was turning the car into a farmyard.

'There's Grandpa,' Brigitta cried, scrambling out of the car and running across the yard, her arms wide.

An old man turned to greet her, enveloping her in his arms and holding her close for several moments before, over her shoulder, his gaze met William's.

Brigitta released herself from his embrace and shyly introduced William. Mr Dupont held out his gnarled hand and grasped William's warmly.

'I am pleased to meet you, William. Please come in and meet my wife.'

Just like Brigitta, her grandparents both spoke English well, but with a strong accent. Mrs Dupont was small and round, like one of her own bread buns, William thought with an inward smile. She bustled about her large kitchen preparing food and drink for them. Husband and wife were both talkative and carried on each other's sentences so that there was little break in the conversation for either Brigitta or William. They fired questions at them, but never waited for an answer before hurrying on to ask another question. At last they all sat down at the table and Mrs Dupont ordered, 'Eat, eat, please.' Then she beamed at

William. 'You are very welcome in our home. Your mother will be thankful that we look after you, yes?'

William smiled weakly and nodded his head in acknowledgement, but made no comment. For the moment, it seemed that the old couple's questions were exhausted, for they listened to Brigitta telling them about their work, but William noticed that she skirted round the gory details and the many wounded who did not survive. Instead, she concentrated on those they'd helped and who had been transported further down the line either to hospitals nearer the coast or even home to their native countries.

'And you work together?' Mrs Dupont asked, glancing between them with her bright blue gaze.

'William's a stretcher bearer,' Brigitta said. She knew all about his home life and what had happened, and she seemed to be trying to steer her grandparents away from asking him too many sensitive questions. He sighed inwardly. If it was necessary, he would tell them the truth. He wanted no secrets between them.

Her grandfather was eyeing William shrewdly. 'That's a very dangerous job, young man,' he said quietly and in the long pause that followed, William took a deep breath. 'I volunteered to do it.'

'You have a medical condition that renders you unfit for military service?'

William shook his head. 'No, sir, I wanted to help save lives, not take them.'

There was a pause before the old man asked quietly, 'And if you were required to rescue a German soldier, how would you feel about that?'

246

William faced him squarely, meeting the old man's gaze steadily. His answer, he felt, would determine any future he might have with Brigitta. He could see the love the old couple had for their granddaughter, and she for them. In that brief moment, William decided that he would not break up their family. If they disapproved of him, then he would never declare his growing fondness for Brigitta.

'We already have, sir.' And he went on to explain to the old couple what had happened on Christmas Day. 'Of course, he had to become our prisoner of war, but he will be treated with humanity, I'm certain of that.'

There was silence in the room, filled with tension. It felt as if each one of them was holding their breath. Then William, almost to his surprise, saw the old man begin to smile as he said softly, 'As would any one of our boys, I trust, if they were captured by those we must call our enemy. I have great admiration for you, young man. It cannot have been easy for you to take that decision.'

Beside him, Brigitta said nothing, but he could feel her sympathetic gaze on him as he decided the time was right to be completely honest with her family. 'I come from a family of four boys and one girl. Alice came with the unit. She is out here too, but two of my brothers – the ones that are old enough – volunteered at once for the Lincolnshire regiment. My family do not approve of my decision, Mr Dupont. In fact, they have disowned me.'

'That is terrible.' Mrs Dupont wiped her eyes with the corner of her copious apron. 'They should be proud of you.'

'The job you're doing,' Mr Dupont said slowly, 'is in some ways far more dangerous than that of a soldier. You go out to pick up the wounded all the time, don't you, whereas a soldier will only spend so many days at a time in the trenches when his life is truly at risk? No, my boy, you are to be congratulated and honoured, not censured.'

'It's kind of you to say so, sir.' William's voice was husky. He was overcome with emotion at their kindness and understanding.

'I don't approve of war,' Mr Dupont went on, 'but it is necessary when an enemy invades your country. We have to fight then, William.'

'Of course, I understand that. If – if my homeland were invaded, then I know I would feel differently.'

The old man smiled, a little impishly, William thought, as he glanced at his granddaughter and said softly, 'Perhaps, one day, this country might become your country, eh?'

A little later, two of the nurses billeted with the Duponts arrived home off duty. They were eager to hear all that Brigitta was doing, but they gabbled away so rapidly in their own tongue, that William could understand none of it.

'They were at school with Brigitta,' her grandfather explained to him. 'They have much to say to one another. Come, I will show you around the farm, such as it is now. We manage to scratch a living, but it is not what it once was.'

Having looked around the farm buildings, they stood together, gazing out across the fields. 'It is very like home,' William murmured, and he could not keep the wistfulness from his voice.

'It is flat like this, where you live?'

William nodded. 'Yes, Lincolnshire in England is mostly flat, though we have the Wolds, but near the sea and to the south of the county, where the fens begin, it is very flat but very fertile.'

There was silence between the two men until Mr Dupont said, 'You will do your best to watch over our Brigitta, yes?'

William nodded solemnly. 'I will.'

'You are growing fond of her?'

'Yes, sir. I am.' He turned to look at the old man. 'You – you don't mind?'

'Not at all. I am glad.' He turned and held out his hand. 'Come back to us safely – both of you.'

William shook his hand in a warm grasp. It was a promise made, one he prayed he would be able to keep.

Forty-Two

'Norah! Norah!'

Ma was sitting outside in front of their cottage. It was hardly suitable weather, so early in March, but she was well wrapped up.

'I can't stay cooped up indoors all day. I need some fresh air, even if it is cold,' she'd say every day that it wasn't actually raining or snowing.

Norah came running, fearful that the old lady had fallen or been taken ill suddenly. 'What is it? What's wrong?'

Ma was still sitting where Norah had left her.

She didn't seem ill, but she was pointing up the lane with a trembling finger. 'There's a soldier coming down the road, but I can't see who it is. Is it – is it one of our lads?'

Norah squinted as the young man, dressed in khaki uniform and carrying his heavy kit, marched towards them.

'Oh Ma,' Norah breathed at last, 'it's Boy. It's our Boy.' And then she was running towards him, her arms outstretched as Ma surreptitiously wiped a tear of joy from her eyes. She watched as Norah flung her arms around her son. Harold submitted to her embrace with a smile, but then Norah stood back and slapped his face hard.

'What's that for, Mam?'

'What d'you think it's for? Going off without a word and then not letting us know where you were for months on end. Not one word have you sent in all this time.'

'You'd have tried to stop me if you'd known where I was.'

'I did try. Believe me, I did. But it seems the army, once you'd signed up, wouldn't let you go even though you were underage. Still are, if it comes to that. Anyway, it's done now and I've had to come to terms with it, but it'll be a long time until I can forgive you for what you did.'

'Aye, and it'll be a long time before I forgive William for what he did, an' all.'

They'd continued to walk towards Ma, who'd pulled herself up to greet her grandson. She overheard Norah's words as she said, 'You mean, you volunteered because William wouldn't?'

Before Harold could answer, Ma said, 'Don't lay

the blame at William's door, Boy. What he's doing now is just as dangerous – if not more so – than being a soldier, so just you remember that.' It was the first time Ma had openly stuck up for William, and Norah and Harold stared at her in surprise.

'I wouldn't let Len hear you talking like that, Ma,' Norah said softly. 'He'll never forgive William or own him as his son.'

But Ma noticed that for the first time Norah did not add 'And neither will I'.

There was muted celebration at Harold's homecoming. They were happy to see that he was fit and well, but they were concerned when he told them that this might be an embarkation leave. 'When I go back, we're likely to be sent to France any time soon. How're the lads? Have you heard from them?'

'We get letters from both of them, though not very often. We think they're still in this country, but they're not allowed to say where. We got a letter with a place name heavily scored out. We couldn't read it. But they're together. We do know that.'

'That's good, then.'

'I wish you'd gone with them,' Norah blurted out, 'if you had to go at all. They could have looked out for you.'

Harold grimaced and then laughed. 'It'd have been good, yes, but it was their fault I didn't get in the Lincolns. They kept telling the officers that I was underage. Mind you, it's good in the Sherwoods; they're a great bunch of lads. We all look out for each other. I've got a special mate called

251

Jim Leatham. He's from Yorkshire. He's a bit older than me.' He grinned. 'But it's like having one of me brothers with me.'

He spent his first evening at home, but the following morning, dressed in his uniform to show the world that he was no coward, Harold set off down the street.

'I'm sure he's grown, Norah,' Ma said, sitting in her usual seat outside the front door for a few minutes as she watched him go.

'He's certainly filled out. He's broader in the shoulders. He looks more like...' Here Norah stopped and bit down on the end of her tongue. Boy had grown more like William in stature during the weeks he'd been gone. Instead, she asked, 'Where's he off to?'

Ma sniffed. 'To see young Peggy, I shouldn't wonder.'

'I expect that's why he's come back, really,' Norah said, unhappily. 'To see her. I don't suppose he's come back to see us.'

'That's very perceptive of you, Norah duck, and, sadly, I think you're right.'

Harold spent most of his leave with Peggy, coming home late at night after the rest of his family were in bed.

'He'd do better to give you a hand whilst he's here,' Norah said.

'Let the lad have a bit of fun,' was all Len would say. 'He's only young and he's about to do a man's job.'

On the last night of his leave, Harold did not come home at all. He turned up early the next morning

252

to pick up his kit, bid a swift and somewhat sheep-ish farewell to his parents and grandmother, and then he headed towards Lincoln on the carrier's cart.

Forty-Three

On 10 March an offensive by the British in the region around Neuve Chapelle began.

'We must move,' Robert decided. 'We must be where the fighting is.'

'We should let Captain Allender know that we're going,' Pips said. 'William, would you and Brigitta like to take one of the ambulances and visit the trenches? Ask for the captain and let him know that we're moving to where the action is.'

They were gone two hours and when they returned, George was following them on a motor-cycle. In the ambulance, William had two casualties suffering from trench foot.

'The mud is dreadful,' he told Pips. 'The trenches are ankle-deep in water – deeper in some parts. It's a wonder they haven't all got problems with their feet. The captain told us they have a daily foot inspection and these two were found to be starting with it this morning, so here they are. What shall I do with them?'

'We're packing up here. You'd better take them to the CCS in Pop.'

'How will I find where you've gone?'

'Take Brigitta with you. She'll know roughly

where we're going. It's about forty kilometres away.' She wrinkled her forehead. 'That's about twenty-four miles.' Then she turned and smiled at George as he approached. 'Good morning, Captain Allender.'

He was smiling at her. 'That's very clever of you.'

She frowned. 'What is?'

'Being able to convert kilometres into miles in your head. I can never get the hang of it.'

Pips shrugged off his compliment.

'I thought I'd just come and say goodbye,' George went on.

'That's very good of you,' Giles said, as he came up behind Pips and put his arm possessively around her waist. 'It's been good to know you, but we have to move on to where we're needed the most.'

'Of course,' George said, 'but there was just something I wanted to warn you all about.'

'Oh, what's that?'

'We've heard some disturbing news. At the beginning of January in a battle at a place called Bulimov on the Eastern Front, the Germans used tear gas, but there are strong rumours that they're developing the use of chlorine. That can actually kill. It damages the eyes, nose, throat and lungs and can cause death by asphyxiation.'

'Oh my,' Pips murmured, but it was Giles who said, 'And you think they might try it here – on the Western Front – too?'

George shrugged. 'No one knows what they'll do, but it's a possibility. In fact, I'd say a strong probability.'

'Have our boys been supplied with any kind of

254

gas mask?' Giles asked.

The captain shook his head. 'No. I don't think anyone ever considered such a cruel weapon would be used by either side.'

'Has poison gas ever been used before that?' Pips asked.

'Not that I've heard, though we do know the French first used tear gas last August, but we think, this time, they'll use something far more deadly.'

The battle lasted only three days and ended without a definite victory for either side, although the British consolidated the ground they had captured.

'So what do we do now?' Pips asked when all the casualties had been either returned to the front or shipped down the line to hospitals.

'Enjoy the warmer weather and wait for the next offensive, which, I'm sure, won't be long in coming, but in the meantime,' Giles smiled, 'if Robert doesn't mind, we'll take a trip to the coast, shall we?'

Pips glanced around her, saw that they were alone, wound her arms around his neck and kissed him soundly. 'Absolutely,' she murmured against his mouth.

By 22 April they were on the move again, back to the position they'd so recently left at Brandhoek.

'This is becoming like home,' Pips said. A battle was again in progress. Across the flat land of Flanders fields, the guns boomed, whistles sounded and the team waited for the inevitable; the arrival of wounded and dying men. 'I wonder why they seem to keep coming back to fight for Ypres?'

'Both sides seem to regard it as the gateway to the Channel ports,' Giles said.

They stood watching as, in the distance, they could see the town being heavily shelled. On the nearby road, refugees were fleeing from their homes. Wagons stacked with household goods were pulled by scrawny, terrified horses that looked as if at the next shell burst they would bolt. Old men pushed handcarts and women carried bundles of clothes and bedding. Beside them, children, some of them crying in fear, stumbled along the road, clutching their favourite toy.

'I wish we could help them all, but we can't, can we?' Pips said.

Sadly, Giles shook his head. 'No, our duty is to the wounded.'

'We'd better take our ambulances as near as we can,' Hugh said as the day wore on. 'Where are we going, exactly?'

'To a place called Mouse Trap Farm,' Robert said. 'It's towards Saint Julien. It's about five miles away. If you think we should move an advanced post there, let us know.'

'I know where that is. I'd better go too,' William said. 'Pips, can you bring the car? No doubt there'll be some walking wounded.'

As they all drew near, they could see a curious greenish mist floating over the trenches. They halted the three vehicles and stood together.

'What is it?' Pips said. 'Fog?'

At that moment, a line of men stumbled out of the support trench towards them. The one in the front seemed unharmed, but those behind him, each with one hand on the shoulder of the man in front of him, were coughing and holding their other hand across their eyes.

'Whatever's the matter with them?' As they came closer Pips automatically stepped forward to help them, but she hesitated when a strange smell emanated from them and stung her throat and made her eyes water.

'Keep back, nurse,' the man leading the line shouted. 'It's gas. Poor devils have been gassed.'

Pips turned and ran back to the ambulances. 'Quick,' she shouted to the other three. 'Get cloths to cover your mouths. Don't forget to do what Robert told you.'

She ran behind one of the vehicles out of sight of the others, lifted up her skirts and urinated on the piece of cloth. Then she tied it over her mouth and nose. It was disgusting, but she knew it would help stave off the worst effects of the gas that was now billowing stealthily towards them.

Returning, she saw that the other three had followed Robert's suggestion too. With as many of the casualties loaded into the car as possible, she set off back towards the post. It was a very different kind of injury that they were now dealing with. It was pitiful to see the blinded men, crying and gasping for breath. It was likely that those who survived – if any did – would be maimed for life.

'If the wind changes direction,' she told Giles and Robert, 'and blows this way, we might have to move again. We can't risk all the medical team being affected.'

'This is a wicked weapon,' Robert muttered. 'It

ought to be banned on both sides. We must get in touch with Mrs Parrott and ask her to find out about some form of gas mask.'

'But, as always, the authorities are too late,' Pips said grimly. 'I must go back.'

They spent the whole day ferrying casualties back to the post. By nightfall they were overwhelmed with the numbers and Hugh, Peter and William had to drive backwards and forwards through the night to move them on to the nearest clearing station.

The following day, it all happened again, but on the next day, the unit had a surprise visitor.

'Hello, Mrs Parrott, what are you doing here?' Pips greeted her.

The tall, grey-haired woman smiled. How Marigold Parrott always managed to look so impeccably dressed – as if she had just stepped out of the pages of a fashion magazine – Pips never ceased to wonder.

'Gas masks,' Marigold said promptly. 'At least something that might help as a temporary measure until someone back home can come up with the design and manufacture of something of a more permanent nature. But I'm guessing that could take at least two months, though I've already been in touch with one of my contacts back home who will set the ball rolling. I'm trying to get the British newspapers involved. However, in the meantime, I've got a lot of the local women in Poperinghe making up pads with string ties using lint bandages made in the convent there.'

'Mrs Parrott – you're a positive marvel. I don't know how you do it.'

Marigold smiled at the compliment. 'That's my job – to support you in your work in any way I can. Now, can you help me unload the car?'

Within hours, supplies were issued to the troops in the trenches with advice from Giles and Robert that if afflicted, the soldiers should not lie down on the ground as the gas was more concentrated there.

'What about the wounded on stretchers?' Pips asked worriedly. 'They haven't got a lot of choice.'

'We'll just have to get them moved away as quickly as we can,' William tried to reassure her, but he knew it was an impossible task to rescue all of them before the gas took effect.

This was the second time a battle had occurred near Ypres, and it seemed that the corps was now dealing with more casualties from the effects of gas than from actual wounds.

'It's disgraceful,' Pips railed. 'It's an insidious weapon to use, but I've no doubt we'll have to follow suit and use it too.'

'Of course,' Giles said. 'Isn't the whole point of war to kill more of the enemy than we lose by any means possible?'

Pips shuddered. 'What a dreadful outlook on life,' she murmured. 'Where will it all end?'

Forty-Four

Four days after the battle had begun, Giles asked anyone who had time to listen, 'Have you heard the news? Italy's joined the war.'

Several pairs of eyes gaped at him and eyebrows rose.

'On the side of the Germans, I suppose,' Robert said.

'No. Surprisingly, on our side.'

'Really? Now that might give us a bit of a break if the enemy has to remove resources from here. Let's hope so.'

But there was to be no respite as the German guns pounded the town of Ypres and beyond.

'They're shelling Poperinghe now.' William was obliged to tell Brigitta what he'd heard. 'They must have found out that the town is full of troops.'

Her eyes were fearful. He touched her hand. 'We'll try to visit your grandparents again as soon as we can.'

But the battle raged on and there was no time for anyone to take leave.

'Nurse Maitland,' Sister Leonore asked in her perfect English. When on duty she called Pips and the nurses by their formal names. Only in private did she use their Christian names. 'You know a little French, don't you?'

'Yes. Why?'

'There's a poor boy at the far end of the tent dying. He's holding on to wait for his mother, but I doubt she'll get here. He's in dreadful pain – I have nothing to give him to relieve it. We have to keep the morphine for operations.'

Pips nodded and pursed her lips. It was disgraceful, she thought, that they had so little to relieve the suffering of the terribly wounded. But there was nothing she could do about it. Daily, they requested more medicines but only the bare essentials ever reached them, despite Marigold Parrott's best efforts.

'Will you sit with him and hold his hand?' Leonore said.

'Pretend to be his mother, you mean?'

'Not exactly, but I think holding a woman's hand will bring him comfort.'

Pips sat by the casualty's bedside and took his hand into hers. 'My poor boy,' she murmured in French. 'Sleep now.'

The hand lying in hers relaxed and, for a while, the young soldier seemed to sleep. Then, after about an hour, he suddenly opened his eyes, stared at the ceiling and whispered, 'Kiss me, *Maman.*'

Pips glanced behind her. There was no one coming into the tent who could be his mother arriving, so she leaned over him and gently kissed his forehead. 'My brave boy.'

There was a small smile on his mouth as he sighed deeply and Pips knew he had gone. She rose and stood for a moment, looking down at him. He was so young, she thought, so achingly

261

young. She had played out a lie, which was not in her nature, but if it had eased his passing – as she believed it had – then it had been the right thing to do. As she covered his face with a blanket and turned away to fetch someone to help her remove him from the tent, she realized that she did not even know his name.

'Good heavens,' Pips exclaimed as she drew up just behind the front line. 'I didn't expect to see you here again.'

Captain Allender smiled up at her, though the worry never left his eyes. 'We keep getting posted to different areas but we always seem to end up back at Ypres, don't we? Both of us.'

There was a pause as they stared at each other, then the captain seemed to shake himself mentally and said, 'Anyway, to business. The shelling seems to have stopped for the moment. Can you come straight into the trench? I've a boy who's seriously wounded, but I think if you can take him immediately, he might survive.'

'Lead the way, captain. I'm right behind you.'

They hurried as fast as they could through the network of trenches until they found the young boy in a deep dugout in the reserve trench. Pips knelt beside him. He had a serious facial wound. His left jaw was smashed and his eye damaged. He was moaning softly, trying his hardest, Pips could tell, not to make a sound, but his pain must have been indescribable.

'We'll get you to the first-aid post as quickly as we can. Now, I'm going to put a clean dressing over your eye and bandage it.'

He made a noise that she had to take as agreement. When she had done all she could, two of his comrades carried him out of the dugout and through the trenches to her car.

'I'll take him straight away, captain, I won't stay to pick up any others, but once I've handed him over, I'll come straight back so, if you'd like to get a few more walking wounded rounded up, I'd be grateful.'

When she returned to the front line again, there were three casualties with minor wounds waiting for her.

'There's another still in the trenches, Nurse Maitland,' Captain Allender greeted her. 'But he won't leave without his pal, who's more seriously injured and needs an ambulance.'

'William's just behind me. He can take him and a few more besides.'

As they walked into the trenches once more, George explained, 'The soldiers I'm talking about are both with one of these pals' battalions that have been set up at home. I don't agree with them myself.'

'What are they?'

'It's where men from the same village, town, workplace – even places of education like schools and colleges – have formed battalions in the hope of serving together. And many of them do, but the problem, that no one yet seems to have realized back home, is that if there are heavy casualties, they're going to be from the same place. Think of the devastation that causes to a community.'

'Yes, I see what you mean,' she began, and then stopped suddenly, looking up at the edge of the trench above her. 'Oh my!' Just above their heads, on the parapet of the trench and a little way down the side, grew a profusion of poppies. She touched the delicate red petals. 'How can they grow in such an awful place?'

They moved on to where the two soldiers were, one sitting with his arm in a rough sling, the other lying on the ground.

'I aren't going without my mate, nurse, so don't ask me to.'

'We can take you together, though you will have to travel separately, but I promise we will keep you together as far as our first-aid post. After that, soldier, I can't promise anything. Your friend looks as if he needs more care than you do. Now, you wouldn't want to stop him getting that, would you?'

''Course not, but—'

'Ah, here's William with the stretcher.'

As carefully as they could in the confines of the narrow trench, they lifted the semi-conscious man onto the stretcher and William and another soldier carried him out to the ambulance.

'Now, you lean on me, soldier, and we'll follow them.'

'I'm a big fella, nurse, I didn't oughta...'

'Here, let me.' George moved forward and put his arm round the man's waist. 'Put your arm along my shoulder, Thompson.'

'By heck, I nivver thought I'd have an officer helping me. You're a good 'un, Captain Allender, that you are.'

As they drove back to the first-aid post, George beside her, Pips said, 'If I hadn't seen it with my own eyes, Captain Allender, I wouldn't have believed it.'

He smiled. 'What? Me helping an injured man?'

Pips laughed aloud. 'Heavens, no! I meant the poppies growing on the tops of the trench parapets.'

'Poppy seeds can lie dormant for years and then bloom when the earth is disturbed. Have you seen them in the war cemeteries that are springing up everywhere?'

Pips shook her head.

'Then I'll take you. I need to visit the grave of a pal of mine who was killed last week. I wasn't able to attend his burial, so I want to go and pay my respects. I had thought to go on my own, but now I find that I'd appreciate the company of just one person. You. Would – would you do that for me? Would you come with me?'

Coming from the straight-backed, strict and rather staid dedicated soldier, the tentative request was a surprise. She'd seen his concern for the welfare of the men in his charge – knew that he put that above even his own safety – but she'd not seen his sensitive side before; a man who was mourning the death of his friend and who could not face visiting the freshly dug grave alone.

Her voice was husky as she said, 'I'd be honoured.'

'Where are you going?' Giles demanded very early the next morning when he saw Pips walking away from the tents towards the edge of the field. 'To the front?'

'No. I promised to go with Captain Allender to

visit the grave of one of his friends and he said he'd pick me up early this morning.'

'Why d'you need to go with him?'

'I think he wants some company, and also, he's going to show me the poppies growing amongst the graves.'

Giles frowned. 'I don't think you should go.'

'Why ever not?'

'Because I don't want you to.'

Pips stared at him for a moment and then she laughed. 'I think my reputation will be quite safe. We're hardly following the conventions of a society drawing room out here, are we, Giles?'

Pips turned and marched away.

'Pips, I...' he called after her, but she did not look back.

Before the fighting was likely to start, Captain Allender drove the vehicle himself and took her to a cemetery very close to where the corps had their tents.

'Of course, at the moment there are only rough crosses to mark their graves,' he explained as he helped her from the car. 'But I'm sure, after the war, proper headstones will be erected.'

As they walked to the area now set aside as a burial ground, Pips asked, 'Was your friend one of our patients?'

George shook his head. 'No, he was killed outright as he stood beside me. It was a shock and I am left feeling so dreadful that he should have been killed and I escaped unharmed.'

'It happens all the time, George,' she said softly. 'We get so many casualties racked with guilt that

266

they have survived and their pals have not. I patched up a soldier last week who was absolutely distraught because he'd been fighting alongside his younger brother, shoulder to shoulder, he said. And then the brother was shot before they even reached the wire. He wasn't concerned about his own injury. All he kept saying was, "I promised our mam I'd take care of him. She'll never forgive me." So, you see, you mustn't feel that way. There's nothing you could have done to save your friend. And there's nothing you can do to save the countless thousands who are going to die before this is all over.'

'When will it be over, Pips?'

'I don't know. I wish I did. But there's one thing I do know, George.'

'What's that?'

'That however long it takes, however many lives it costs, we will win in the end.'

'I wish I had your faith,' he murmured.

'It's the courage of our soldiers that makes me so sure. They never complain, they're not bitter and they try – as much as they can through their pain – to remain cheerful. Sometimes a man's face is grey with agony, but through it all he will crack a joke or try to comfort a younger man beside him. Their stoicism is incredible. But we've nursed a few German prisoners – you know we have...' For a moment, she paused until George prompted, 'And?'

'Some of them have not got the certainty of victory that our lads have. Oh, they do their duty and they're just as courageous, but they have an air of pessimism about them – at least the ones

I've met have – that our boys do not.'

George was thoughtful as they walked on in silence. As they neared the cemetery, Pips stopped and gasped in surprise at the scene before her.

'Oh George! I never thought to see such a beautiful sight, not amongst the horror we witness every day. The trenches were a surprise, but this...'

Amongst the grave markers, a sea of bright red poppies bloomed, their delicate heads fluttering in the breeze.

'It's strangely peaceful just now, isn't it?' There was no sound of shelling or gunfire. 'I'm glad that Arnold is here.'

Pips stood amongst the markers and read some of the handwritten names. On a few there was just the word 'unknown'.

'How sad,' she murmured, 'that we don't even know who they were. I suppose we'll never know now, will we?'

George Allender shook his head. 'No, there was no identification on the bodies when they were found. We sometimes know what regiment or battalion they're from. That's all.'

They paused at several of the graves before George held out his hand and said, 'This way.' Without thinking, she took his hand and stepped over the rough ground, scattered with wild poppies, until they came to a particular grave where the soldier's name was given in full.

'This is my friend,' he said quietly.

They stood together looking down at the crude cross surrounded by the delicate blood-red flowers.

'Somehow it seems fitting that it should be

poppies, don't you think?' he murmured. 'Or am I being over-sentimental?'

'Not at all. How could you be? These fine young men have given their lives in the cause of freedom. And, sadly, there will be a great many more lives lost before the end.'

They stood for several moments in silence before George said, 'Pips, will you promise me something?'

'Of course.'

'If I'm killed, and you can arrange it, will you see that I am buried here?'

A lump came to her throat at the thought, but she said huskily, 'Of course I will.'

They stood a few moments longer and then George took her arm and led her away.

'Thank you,' was all he said, but she didn't know whether his gratitude was for her company at his friend's grave or for the promise she had just made him.

As they walked back towards the car, Pips noticed small clumps of poppies growing here and there.

'Do you think it would matter if I picked a few? They're not near the graves now. I didn't want to take them from there.'

'They won't live for long, though.'

'They'd brighten the tents we jokingly refer to as "wards", even if only for a day or two.' She pinned one to her white apron just above her left breast.

George gazed at her and said solemnly, 'I'm sure you're right. Come, we should be getting back.'

She could not fail to hear the reluctance in his tone.

269

As they neared the car, a lark began to sing somewhere high above their heads.

Pips stood very still. 'Oh, listen.'

'Yes, we hear them often, even when there is shelling going on. They're brave little birds.'

'How lovely, though, that there's one singing here.'

Forty-Five

Before the second battle of Ypres was really over, the British were involved in assaults on either side of Neuve Chapelle in an attempt to secure Aubers Ridge as a supporting operation to the French battle in Artois.

'We stay here,' Robert decided. 'If we keep moving about, we're not serving anyone properly and besides, there's still fighting here.'

His decision had been the correct one, for the Battle of Aubers lasted only a couple of days and cost many casualties for no gain.

The fighting in the second battle for Ypres stopped on 25 May.

'Now what do we do?' Pips asked, anxious, as always, to be where they were needed the most.

'There's not a lot happening here now, I agree...' Robert began.

'Precisely. We really should move.'

'Then we'll go.' He smiled. 'To the Artois region. There's still fighting there.'

'I'll tell Captain Allender...' Pips began.

'No need,' Giles said. 'His battalion has already gone. He came last night to say goodbye.'

Pips glared at him. 'And you didn't think to find me?'

Giles shrugged. 'I thought you were asleep. It was pretty late.'

Pips said no more, but she frowned as she turned away to help Alice pack up their belongings and their tent.

They stayed near Neuve Chapelle for a month but by the end of June the Battle of Artois seemed to have come to an end.

'You know, Robert,' Pips said, 'you should take some respite.' The members of Dr Hazelwood's unit had worked tirelessly for months with only a few hours' break here and there. Brother and sister now had a few moments alone for the first time in weeks. 'You're always making sure we all get away for a bit, but you don't seem to go as often as the rest of us. Why don't you take Sister Leonore to the coast? It wouldn't be improper, would it?'

Robert grinned at her. 'I think the world we're living in has blown away improprieties. Life as we knew it, Pips, is never going to be the same again.'

'That's a good thing, isn't it?'

He pulled a face. 'For some, possibly. But for the older folk – like our parents, especially Mother – it's going to be hard. But you're right, I should get some rest, though the person I would take with me – if she'd come – is Alice.'

'Alice!' Pips was shocked.

Robert nodded slowly. 'I've seen her in a very

different way since we've been out here. She's proved herself every bit our equal, Pips.'

'Well, yes, I know, but...' She blinked. 'Do you mean you've become – *fond* of her?'

'Yes, I really think I have, though I don't know if she could ever feel the same way about me.'

Pips threw back her head and roared with laughter. 'Oh, you men! Sometimes you're so blind, it's unbelievable. Alice has been in love with you for years, Robert.'

He raised his eyebrows and a slow smile spread across this mouth. 'Really?'

Serious now, Pips said, 'But, Brother dear, please don't lead her on until you're sure you are serious. I'd be very upset and angry with you if you broke her heart. Out here, it's not a normal life. At least Giles and I met back home.'

Robert laughed. 'And you think we didn't.'

'Oh phooey! You know what I mean. She was our servant then. Out here, she's not, as she herself reminded me. And,' she grinned impishly, 'what on earth would Mother say?'

'Exactly!' Robert said wryly. 'I'll certainly be in trouble there; the former lady's maid becoming mistress of the hall one day. Oh dear me!'

'You do whatever your heart tells you, Robert, but, like I've said, please don't give her false hope.'

'I won't. I can promise you that.'

Robert and Alice set off to Poperinghe, where they spent two nights wandering the streets surrounded by soldiers taking some well-earned rest, determined to enjoy themselves whilst away from the trenches. At one point, they were forced to step to the side of the road as a convoy of

London buses passed them, crowded with soldiers on their way to the front. Officers on horseback rode alongside them and behind them came a line of horse-drawn gun carriages. Cafes and shops teemed with life and suddenly, beside him, Alice began to laugh and point to the sign above one of the shops. 'Oh look, Robert. How perfect.'

He followed the line of her finger and read: Tommies' General Supply. Outside were several soldiers – even one dressed in a kilt – looking in the windows.

Unlike Pips and Giles, Robert booked two separate rooms. They had a wonderful rest and grew closer in friendship, but Robert held back on declaring his feelings for Alice. He respected Pips's reasoning. Life out here was not normal. Emotions were heightened by the danger and the horrors they faced each day, and, more than anything, he didn't want to hurt the girl he now believed he loved.

By July, news came that British troops were being reinforced.

'At last!' Bernard, who'd chafed continuously at the inaction, said. 'We're finally on our way. Now we'll get at 'em, Roy. War'll soon be over when us Lincolnshire lads get out there.'

Forty-Six

'Mrs Dawson, could I have a word with you, please?'

Peggy Cooper was standing uncertainly on the back doorstep of the Dawsons' cottage.

'Come in,' Norah said, though her tone was hardly welcoming. She had still not forgotten that Peggy had withheld information about Harold from them; knowledge that could have helped them to stop him volunteering. She led her into the kitchen, where Ma was sitting near the fire that constantly burned in the grate of the range, winter and summer.

'Hello, Peggy.' The older woman was more friendly and the girl gave her a weak smile. 'What brings you here?' she said and inwardly added, *As if I didn't know*. Aloud, she said, 'Have you heard from that rascal, Harold?'

Peggy shook her head and blushed.

Ma sighed. 'Sit down, lass. Norah, mek us all a cup of tea, will yer? I reckon Peggy's got summat to tell us.'

'Eh?' Norah looked startled and glanced from one to the other. As Peggy sat down, dropped her head into her hands and began to weep, Norah's shoulders sagged. She too sank into a chair by the table. 'Oh no!' she breathed. 'Not that.'

'Tea, Norah, duck,' Ma prompted firmly. 'We're going to need it.'

With shaking hands Norah made tea for the three of them, thinking, thank goodness Len's not home yet, though how I'm going to tell him, I don't know.

'So, Peggy, you're going to have a bairn, are you?'

Dumbly, the girl nodded.

'It's Harold's, I take it,' Ma said, still taking the lead. 'I won't insult you by suggesting it could be someone else's.'

Norah seemed lost for words in the face of this particular trouble.

Peggy lifted her face and met their disapproving looks squarely. 'Yes, it is. I swear to you, the baby's Harold's. It – it was on the last night of his leave. He – he said he didn't want to die without having – having loved me.' Now she declared stoutly, 'And I didn't want him to either.'

'Aye, well,' Ma said wisely, 'it's amazing what young fellers will do and say to get their way. We've all been in that position at some time, Peggy, lass. It's whether you have the strength to resist them that matters. Obviously, you hadn't.'

Fresh tears flowed as Peggy said haltingly, 'Oh Mrs Dawson, I'm sorry, but – but it was so sad, knowing he – he might never come back. And I love him so much.'

'Did he promise to marry you?'

'Well, sort of, but he seemed so sure that he wouldn't come home again. And I wanted something to remember him by.'

'Well, you've certainly got that now, love, haven't you?' Ma said bluntly.

All through the conversation, Norah had said

nothing, but now she asked, 'What do your parents say?'

'They're very angry with me, and disappointed, but they're standing by me. They're not turning me out.'

'Aye, well, that's good of them,' Ma said and her brief glance at her daughter-in-law spoke volumes. This family had turned out one of their own just because he didn't conform. At least the Coopers were more forgiving than they had been. 'You're not the first to have a bairn out of wedlock, and I doubt very much you'll be the last. We'll do what we can to help when the time comes, Peggy.'

'Oh now, Ma, don't be promising something we can't do. We've got to hear what Len says first.'

Ma glared at her daughter-in-law. 'For once, Norah, Len will do as I say. Even though I'm living in his house and on his charity, I'm still his mother. Besides, this is women's business.'

To Norah's surprise, Len seemed to agree with his mother when, that evening, his wife nervously told him the news. 'Aye, well, these things happen. He's a young feller who wanted to sow a few wild oats before he went to war. Can't blame him for that. It's Peggy who's to blame. She should've said "no". Right, I'm away to my bed. I've an early start in the morning. I'll want me breakfast half an hour earlier, Norah. Goodnight to you, Ma.'

The two women were left in the kitchen staring at each other as they listened to his heavy footsteps climbing the stairs.

'She's been to tell ya, then?' Bess Cooper stood in

front of Ma with her arms folded, but her glance took in Norah standing uncertainly behind her kitchen table.

'She has, Bess, yes.'

'So – what are you going to do about it?'

Ma frowned. 'I don't understand what you mean. What can we do?'

'Get that little tyke back here to marry her before she begins to show, that's what.'

'D'you know, Bess, if I could, I would, but we haven't an address for him. We don't even know if he's still in this country. He never writes.'

Bess sniffed her disapproval and her expression showed that she doubted Ma was telling the truth. But then she seemed to relent a little. 'Aye, to be fair, he doesn't write to our Peggy either.' She was thoughtful for a moment before saying, 'Can you write to his commanding officer?'

'I don't know who he is.'

'But you do know what regiment he's in, don't you?'

'Better than that. I know what battalion he's in. The Tenth Sherwood Foresters, but that doesn't mean I know who to write to.' Ma paused and then added, 'But I do know someone who might be able to help you. Mrs Maitland.'

Bess's face was a picture. 'You mean, you expect me to go traipsing up to the hall and admit to her that me daughter's going to have a little bastard?'

Ma winced at the crude name. 'Everyone's going to know sooner or later and, believe me, word will get back to her eventually. There's not much that goes on in this village that she doesn't know about.'

Bess was thoughtful for a few moments before sighing and saying, 'I expect you're right, Ma. You usually are.'

'Go and have a chat with her, Bess. I'm sure she'll do whatever she can to help you.'

The following afternoon, Bess donned her best Sunday hat and walked to the hall.

'I'm sorry to bother you, Mrs Maitland, ma'am, but Ma – I mean, Mrs Dawson Senior – thought you might be able to help me.'

'Come in, Mrs Cooper. Do sit down. I'll get the maid to bring tea for us.'

'Oh well, I don't want to put you to any trouble, Mrs Maitland, ma'am.'

'No trouble, I assure you. I'm ready for tea and cake myself. I've been busy with fund-raising activities this morning and I am quite worn out. Now, how can I help you?'

Bess settled herself on the easy chair Henrietta indicated. 'It's me daughter – the younger one.'

'Peggy?'

'That's right. She's got herself in the family way.'

Henrietta hid her smile. It was a phrase that always amused her – as if the poor girl had done it all on her own. Gently, she asked, 'Who's the father?'

'That young scallywag' – Bess moderated her language when talking to someone she considered gentry – 'Harold Dawson. I didn't know there was owt serious between them. They're just kids. I knew they were friends, of course. Been friends for years, along with all the other youngsters in the village.' She shook her head. 'But I really didn't know it had got this far. Now, our Betty,

278

she's walking out with Roy Dawson with our blessing. If it had been her ended up in the family way, I could have understood it, but she's disgusted with her sister. Says her and Roy haven't – well, you know.'

Henrietta sighed. 'These are difficult times, Mrs Cooper. Young men are going off to war not knowing if they'll come home again or, if they do, they might be terribly maimed. Perhaps it's to be expected that they're going to ask their girlfriends for things they wouldn't normally. It's always happened, we're all adult enough to know that and, in these times of heightened uncertainty, I'm afraid there are going to be a lot more unwanted pregnancies.'

'Oh, I won't say this bairn's unwanted, Mrs Maitland. I'd never say that about any bairn. Unexpected, mebbe, but never unwanted.'

'I'm glad to hear you say that, Mrs Cooper. So you're standing by her.'

'Oh aye. We're cross with her, but no, we'll look after her. And the bairn.'

'So, how can I help you?'

'Ma Dawson told me that you wrote to the army folk for them when Harold went off. I wondered if you could find out where he is and ask if he can come home and marry her.'

'Is she sixteen yet?'

'Last month.'

'And Harold?'

'Yes. He's nearly seventeen.'

'I'll do what I can,' Henrietta promised.

But when word came back from Harold's commanding officer, it was to give the news, unwelcome for both families, that Harold had now been posted abroad. He had left England only the previous day and was on his way to Boulogne.

Forty-Seven

At the end of July, William said, 'Kitchener's called for more volunteers. They say over two million men have enlisted already, many forming units from their own home towns.'

Pips nodded. 'Yes, I'd heard that. There's a battalion that's already been formed at Grimsby, isn't there? They call themselves the "Grimsby Chums".'

'There've been several. "The Sheffield Pals" and "The Accrington Pals", to name but two.'

William and Pips looked at each other solemnly.

'And they go into battle side by side, don't they?'

'I think that was the idea. That they'd go together, fight together...'

'And die together,' Pips whispered. 'Just like George said.'

Though neither said any more, they were both thinking about William's brothers who had joined up together.

Towards the end of September, six divisions of the British army took part in an offensive at Loos. Although this was still in support of the larger French attack in the third battle of Artois, it was the biggest offensive by the British in the war so far.

'Our side are going to use poison gas this time,' Giles told Pips.

'It's despicable. It should be banned as a weapon of war.'

'War's not a sport, Pips,' Giles snapped. 'It's kill or be killed.'

Pips glared at him, trying to think of an answer, but there was none.

The next few months found Dr Hazelwood's team following various battalions of the British army wherever there was serious fighting. There was limited success at Loos, but eventually the battle petered out in the middle of October.

'Why don't we take it in turns to go home on leave this time?' Robert said. 'Surely you'd like to go to Scarborough, wouldn't you, Giles? And you, Alice, wouldn't you like to be at home for the birth of your nephew or niece? It's due about the beginning of December, your mother said in her letter, didn't she?'

'It would be nice,' Alice murmured. 'But what about you and Pips? I'm sure your parents must be longing to see you. We've been gone over a year now.'

'Tell you what, why don't you and Giles go first, Pips – for a week or so – and then Alice and I will go when you get back. If we're lucky, we'll catch the birth, but we must leave a skeleton staff here in case something hots up again, although I doubt it now winter has set in.'

'That sounds like a plan.' Pips grinned, her eyes shining at the thought of spending a week or so with Giles. Although later, she told him laughingly, 'I'm afraid it will be separate bedrooms at the hall, under Mother's eagle eye.'

This time, William was not even asked if he wanted to go home; sadly, they all knew what his answer would be.

'Philippa! And Giles too. What a wonderful surprise,' Henrietta greeted them as the maid showed the two into the parlour. She threw down her knitting and rose to greet them, arms outstretched. 'But why didn't you let us know you were coming?'

'We wanted to surprise you and we know you always keep the rooms aired, so – here we are.'

'I'll be going on a brief visit to Scarborough to visit my parents,' Giles told her.

'Of course.' Henrietta's face sobered. 'I was so sorry to hear about the attack on the town. It must have been terrifying for everyone.'

Giles smiled thinly and nodded.

At dinner that evening, they deliberately tried to avoid talking about their work, but instead plied Henrietta and Edwin with questions about life here at home.

'We've had our first casualty – fatality, I should say – in the village. One of the lads who volunteered at the same time as the Dawson brothers has been killed.'

'D'you know where?'

Henrietta shook her head.

'Who was it? Oh no – don't tell me it was Sam Nuttall?'

'No – it was Mrs Layne's only son and she's a widow too, poor woman. I've been doing what I can to comfort her and the other villagers are being very supportive, but nothing helps, really, does it?'

Pips shook her head, unable to speak. All those brave young men she'd witnessed dying – they were all someone's sons. Now she was seeing the other side of the tragedy; the families coping with the loss.

She sprang up from the table. 'I don't suppose we've any horses left at all now, have we?'

'Sadly, no,' Edwin said.

'Then I'll take Robert's motorcycle out for a spin.'

'Oh Philippa, do...' Henrietta began, but her daughter was gone before she uttered the final words, 'be careful.'

Giles smiled down the table. 'Don't worry, Mrs Maitland. She'll be fine.'

'That must be Miss Pips home,' Ma remarked as the noisy machine passed the cottage. 'No one rides that thing like she does.'

'I wonder if she'll call to see us. I'd like to know how Alice is getting on. We haven't had a letter from her in ages.'

'No,' Ma murmured and forbore to add, *Nor from William.* She doubted they'd ever hear from him again. Even if he survived the war, she didn't think he would ever come home.

On her way back, Pips stopped outside the cottage, propped the motorcycle against the wall and sat down beside Ma.

'Nah, then, Miss Pips. How are you?'

'Fine, Ma. And you?'

283

'Not so bad for an owd 'un. How's our Alice?' She bent closer to Pips and whispered, 'And how's William? The others make out they don't want to know, but I do.'

'They're both fine. Alice is coming home in a week or so for a visit, when Giles and I get back. We can't all be away together.' She too lowered her voice as she added, 'And William works very hard and does a wonderful job. And a dangerous one too, I might add. It's so sad that his family don't realize just what he *is* doing. You'd all be very proud of him if only you knew.'

'Ah well, Miss Pips, you're not going to change their minds, so it's not worth you trying. But I'm glad you told me. I can think of him again with love and pride – like I always have.'

'You most certainly can, Ma,' Pips said softly. 'And now, I'd better be off or my mother will be having seven fits that I'm lying on the roadside somewhere.'

Pips did not go with Giles to visit his parents. 'Plenty of time for me to meet them when the war's over,' she told him, 'and we can plan our future.' She squeezed his hand and whispered, 'We'll stay overnight in Boulogne or wherever we land on our way back. That's a promise.'

Forty-Eight

The day after Pips and Giles got back to the first-aid post, Robert and Alice left. They arrived in Doddington on the second day in December and Alice went at once to see her parents.

'Miss Pips told us you were coming, so I've got your bed ready,' Norah said as she hugged her. 'I suppose you'll be staying with us, won't you? Surely they won't expect you to work at the hall?'

Alice chuckled. 'No, Mam, they won't. I don't think I'm regarded as employed there any more.'

Norah frowned. 'Oh dear. So what are you going to do when it's all over, if you haven't got a job to come back to? The mistress is doing so much to help the war effort, I thought at least she'd keep your job for you.'

Alice shrugged. She didn't want to get into a lengthy discussion with her mother. The last thing on her mind at the moment was what she was going to do after the war. She couldn't think beyond surviving each day and doing all she could to help the wounded and dying.

'Ma – how are you?' Alice said, turning to kiss her grandmother's wrinkled cheek. 'And what news is there of Peggy and her baby?'

'I reckon she's going to drop any day now. She's the size of a house.'

'I hope I'm still here when it's born.'

'Will you be able to stay for Christmas?

Bernard and Roy got home last year, but I think they're abroad now.'

Alice shook her head. 'No, Mam, we've only got a week.'

'We? Who's we?'

Alice blushed faintly. 'Robert – Master Robert – and me.'

Ma and Norah exchanged a glance.

Two nights later, there was a banging on the door in the middle of the night.

'Norah – Norah, duck,' came Bess's loud voice. 'Babby's on its way. We need your help. Alice, too, if she'll come.'

Norah – in her nightgown and with her hair in curling rags – hurried down the narrow stairs of the cottage and flung open the door. 'Of course we'll come, but I don't know what use Alice might be. Her training was nowt to do with birthing babbies. Come in a minute, Bess, whilst I get dressed...'

'No. I must get back. Poor lass is in agony and Betty's worse than useless when it comes to the sight of blood.'

'We'll be there as soon as we can.'

Ten minutes later, they were hurrying up the lane. They could already hear Peggy's cries as they neared the Coopers' cottage.

'Oh dear,' Norah said worriedly. 'It doesn't sound too good.'

'She's only a young girl, Mam,' Alice said. 'She'll be frightened. Let me deal with her.'

As they entered the shadowy bedroom, lit only by two candles, both Bess and Betty were standing helplessly at the end of the bed.

'She's bad, Norah. I don't know what to do.'

Alice moved to the side of the bed. 'Now, Peggy, you can stop that noise. I know you're in pain, but if you tense yourself against it, it makes it worse.'

Peggy wailed all the louder, but Alice shouted above the noise, 'Listen to me, Peggy. I can help you, if only you'll do as I say.'

'What d'you know about it, Alice Dawson?' Peggy screamed at her. 'You've never had a babby.'

'True, but I've seen a helluva lot of soldiers in all sorts of agony this past year. I do know about pain, so just listen to me. Now, try to relax. Yes, I know it's hard' – she put her hand on Peggy's stomach in readiness to feel the next contraction – 'but between the contractions, just try to relax your whole body. Now, breathe in and out slowly.' She paused and then said, 'There, now that's better. You won't bring this little lad or lass into the world if you fight against it.' Beneath her fingers she felt another contraction building and the girl began to tense again. 'Try to stay calm and relaxed, Peggy; breathe in and out slowly. Think of the pain as a wave breaking on the sea-shore. Ride on top of it. Good girl, now you're doing so much better.'

She turned to the girl's mother and sister. 'Betty, get dressed and run to the hall. Ask Master Robert to come. I'm not experienced enough to examine her to see how far on she is.'

'He'll not know,' Bess put in.

'I think he will. He did two months on the maternity ward at Lincoln hospital as part of his training.'

'Right,' Betty said and scuttled away before her mother could object, thankful to be released from witnessing her sister's distress. 'If that Harold Dawson was here right now,' she muttered to herself as she ran up the lane in the darkness, 'I'd bloody well hang for him.'

Her banging on the door of the hall brought Wainwright in his nightshirt down the stairs.

'Master Robert. Alice said to fetch Master Robert,' she panted at the startled man. 'Peggy Cooper's babby's coming and–'

'I don't think that's the sort of thing I can disturb the young master's sleep for,' Wainwright said loftily. 'It's something you women ought to be able to cope with. Are there complications?'

'I don't know, but I do know she's yelling the place down and Alice said he would come.'

'Alice had no right to...' he began, but a voice spoke behind him from the door leading into the Great Hall.

'What is it, Wainwright?'

'It's Betty Cooper, sir,' Wainwright turned to answer Robert. 'Her sister's baby is coming and Alice has had the temerity to say that you would go, but I've said that–'

Robert glanced beyond the butler and nodded to Betty. 'If Alice has said I'm needed, then I'll come at once. I'll just have to ask my father if I can take his medical bag. I won't be long – I promise. You go back and tell them I'm on my way.'

It seemed an age to the four anxious women gathered round Peggy's bedside for Robert to arrive, but, in fact, it was only about twenty minutes. Swiftly, he washed his hands and examined her.

'You're doing very well, Peggy. Not long now and you'll have a baby in your arms. Alice, carry on doing what you're doing.' He gave her a quick smile, then turned to Bess, Betty and Norah. 'Perhaps you ladies might give us a little more room in here. I'll be sure to call you if I need anything. You've done a sterling job getting hot water and towels ready.' His smile widened. 'Maybe a cup of tea wouldn't go amiss. If I'm not mistaken, Peggy is soon going to be ready for one, to say nothing of the rest of us.'

'What a nice young man he is,' Norah murmured as the three went downstairs.

'Aye, that's all very well, but what's it all going to cost me?' Bess grumbled. 'The likes of us have a woman from the village, not a doctor.'

'Just be thankful he's come to help her, Bess,' Norah snapped, then she softened enough to say, 'We'll all chip in, if necessary. After all, me and Len are the bairn's other grandparents, aren't we?'

'You are,' Bess said grimly. 'It's that young rascal of yourn that's caused all this, Norah. I 'aven't forgotten.'

It was on the tip of Norah's tongue to say that it took two and that Peggy herself had admitted she'd given in to him willingly, but at that moment, she actually felt for Bess. Childbirth was never easy and Peggy was so young. So, Norah kept silent.

It wasn't long before they heard the cries of a newborn infant and the bedroom door open upstairs. 'It's a boy, Mrs Cooper,' Robert called down. 'A healthy baby boy. Give us a few minutes and you can come up and see him.'

'Is Peggy all right?'

'She's fine. Tired, but very happy.'

Minutes later, they were all crowding back into the bedroom to see Peggy cradling her son in her arms, tears of joy flooding down her face. 'I just wish Harold was here to see his son.'

'He will be, love,' Norah said, feeling choked herself. 'I'll try to get word to him. Maybe they'll give him leave to get home.'

Robert and Alice exchanged a glance but said nothing. They didn't want to dash the woman's hopes, but they had their doubts, added to the fact that no one seemed to know exactly where Harold was at this moment.

'Mrs Maitland'll write to his commanding officer again,' Bess said, with utter faith. 'Now, come on, our Peg, let's be 'avin a hold of him.'

Much later, when Peggy was drowsy and the infant was asleep in the bottom drawer of the chest, Robert escorted Alice and her mother home to their cottage, one on either arm, whilst Alice carried his medical bag.

'D'you know what I found strange?' he said. 'Mr Cooper never showed his face.'

Both Norah and Alice began to laugh, so hard that they had to stop walking for a moment.

'What? What have I said?'

'Charlie Cooper wouldn't be seen having anything to do with that sort of thing. No, it's no surprise that he didn't even show his face out of his bedroom, though how he managed to sleep through all that racket, I don't know.'

'I'm so glad I was there to see Peggy's baby born,' Alice said to Robert as they travelled back to Belgium a few days later. 'And it was so kind of you not to make any charge for your services. It was a huge relief to them.'

'They're going to be hard pressed to manage. Peggy won't be able to work for some time, though I presume Betty works. What does she do?'

'She's got a job now in one of the factories in Lincoln. It's all very hush-hush, she says, but she did tell me that the firm are making something that could alter the whole course of the war.'

'Really? I wonder what that could be? Let's hope she's right, because I've got a horrible feeling that 1916 is going to be a very difficult year.'

Forty-Nine

'You'll never guess what,' William told them excitedly when they arrived back and he'd heard about the arrival of his nephew.

Whilst they had been away, it had been decided that the unit should move back to Brandhoek.

'I understand what you mean about this place now, Pips. It does feel like coming home,' Robert had said.

'There's a large house being turned into a soldiers' club in Pop,' William went on.

'Really? How's that come about?' Robert asked as he and Alice listened; it was the most animated and talkative they'd ever seen William. 'The house – somewhere on the Rue de l'Hôpital – is owned by a wealthy brewer. In the summer it was damaged by shells and he moved his family and his belongings out. Anyway, it seems he offered it for rent to the British Army and an army chaplain, the Reverend Clayton, had the idea of using it as a place for the soldiers when they're on leave.'

'Pop has always been the centre for men arriving to go to the front or leaving it,' Alice said. 'What a brilliant idea.'

'And the best thing is,' William went on, 'everyone's to be treated as equals. No pulling rank, nothing like that. Of course, the house needs to be refurnished, but Mrs Parrott's already on to that. She's a miracle worker, that woman. There's stuff arriving from England every day and enough books to fill the library. And, despite their own troubles, the locals are very generous.'

'Will medical staff be allowed to go, d'you think?'

'Oh yes. I've already asked. The folks running it say anyone involved in the war will be made welcome.'

'What's it going to be called?'

'Talbot House, after the brother of Padre Talbot. He was killed at Hooghe at the end of July.'

'We'll have to take a look at it, Alice,' Robert said.

'I'm taking Brigitta as soon as we can go,' William said. 'Why don't we all go together?'

The six of them went the day before Christmas Eve, taking gifts with them.

'We'll visit the trenches tomorrow like we did

last year,' Robert decided, 'but today we'll go and have a look at this house the troops are already calling Toc H.'

'I wonder if there'll be a spontaneous truce at Christmas on both sides like there was last year?' Pips murmured.

'I doubt it,' Giles said. 'There was distinct disapproval from the brass last time. I'm actually surprised your captain wasn't in serious trouble for taking part.'

Pips frowned as she glanced at him. She was about to ask him a question and then decided against it. Pips could be outspoken and impetuous at times, but she also knew when it was wise to keep her counsel. George had told her in strictest confidence that he had had a dressing-down from his superior officer – the lieutenant-colonel commanding the battalion – over the fraternization of the troops on both sides.

'I can't think how he got to hear about it,' George had said. 'My men certainly wouldn't have said a word.'

Now, Pips began to wonder...

If there was an oasis of tranquillity in the middle of the battlegrounds, then it was Talbot House. Local volunteers welcomed anyone who came through the door, plying them with tea and cake. It had been the soldiers' idea to turn the upper floor into a chapel and furnish it themselves. Many a troubled soul found a few hours' peace there. One of the volunteers showed them around, chattering in her own language, which Brigitta translated for them.

'This has just opened but already we're thinking we might have to expand. We plan to hold concerts and the soldiers hope to put on plays. But mainly, they'll be able to come to rest.'

'It's wonderful,' Pips said. Brigitta translated and the lady volunteer beamed and pressed them to have more cake.

On her first outing after the birth of her baby, Peggy wheeled the old pram that one of the villagers had given her down the lane towards the Dawsons' home. As she passed Len's workshops, she hesitated. She hadn't seen or spoken to him since she'd told the family about her pregnancy. Yet, the baby was his grandson, surely...?

His gruff voice, coming out of the dark interior of the wheelwright's, startled her.

'What d'you want?'

'I – er – thought you might like to see the babby, Mr Dawson.'

'Whatever gave you that idea? I want nowt to do wi' it. And when Boy gets home he'll feel the back of my hand for bringing shame on our family. As if we haven't had enough to contend with.' He turned away from her and picked up an iron bar.

Peggy, with tears in her eyes, walked on until she came to the Dawsons' cottage.

'Nah then, duck.' Ma's voice from her bench outside greeted her. She laid aside her clay pipe. Peggy brushed her tears away and tried to summon up a watery smile. 'Mrs Dawson, whatever are you doing sitting outside in this weather? It's winter.'

'Eeh, lass, you've known me long enough to know that the seasons mek no difference to me. Winter and summer, unless it's raining or snowing – I don't like the wet – you can find me sitting out here at least for a little while each day. I've got to get me fresh air.'

Peggy smiled tremulously. Yes, she did know. Ma Dawson was thought an eccentric – but a nice one. And she'd been good to her, Peggy thought, since the news about her pregnancy had broken.

'I've brought the babby to see you.'

'That's nice, duck. Come on inside, then. It is too cold out here for the little mite. Norah's indoors, busy as usual, I shouldn't wonder.'

Moments later, Norah had picked her grandson up from the pram and was nursing him in front of the range. 'He's a grand little chap, Peggy. I can see Boy in him, though, funnily enough, I can see our Bernard too. Can you?'

Ready tears filled Peggy's eyes. She was still a bit weepy, as her mother called it, since her confinement.

'Did you have a nice Christmas?' Norah asked conversationally. 'It'd be grand having a little one in the house again, though he won't have known much about it this year. But you wait till this time next year, then he'll be sitting up and takin' notice.'

'It was all right.' Peggy bit her lip and then burst out, 'Me dad won't hardly look at him, and just now – when I came past the workshops – Mr Dawson told me he wanted nowt to do wi' him.'

Ma gave a snort of contempt. 'That's men for

you. They're not good around little ones. You tek no notice of either of 'em. Wait till the little 'un grows up a bit, then you'll see.'

Peggy shook her head. 'Me dad, maybe, but not Mr Dawson. He said when – when Boy gets back he's going to feel the back of his hand for bringing shame on the family.' She didn't add Len's final words, hinting at William.

'Ne'er mind, duck. There's plenty of us women to fuss over him. You bring him here whenever you like.' She didn't add, 'When Len's out the way.' She thought the girl had enough sense to know that.

'If only Boy had been able to come home for Christmas,' Peggy murmured. 'I reckon he'd even have put up with getting a thick ear from his dad if only he'd had the chance to see his son.'

Fifty

Robert had been right in his intuition that 1916 might prove to be a very difficult year.

'They've introduced conscription at home,' he told the rest of the team in January.

Hugh, Peter and William glanced at each other. 'Will that affect us?' Hugh asked.

'I shouldn't think so for a minute,' Robert said. 'You're already out here, doing your bit.'

The three of them breathed a collective sigh of relief. 'Besides,' Robert said, by way of further reassurance, 'we could apply for exemption, if you were called up.'

By February, however, there was even more worrying news.

'The Germans have launched a huge offensive at Verdun in an attempt to demoralize the French. The area has several large forts and the whole area is symbolic to their nation. The enemy thinks that by taking Verdun, all French resistance will collapse.'

'Do you think we should go there?' Pips asked.

'I really don't know,' Robert said worriedly. 'The French will have their own medical units.'

'Surely – if it's as bad as you think – they'll need all the help they can get,' Pips insisted.

'Why don't you get in touch with Dr Hazelwood? He'll say what he'd like us to do.'

'That's a good idea, Giles.' Relief showed on Robert's face. 'I've always felt able to take decisions before, but this time, I'm really not sure what we ought to do.'

Word came back eventually via Mrs Parrott when she visited the unit. 'Dr Hazelwood sent word that he wanted to meet me in person. He had information that he dare not put in writing to either of us. I went to Boulogne three days ago and he travelled across the Channel to meet me there. This is all very confidential, you understand. There's been a suggestion from General Joffre, Commander-in-Chief of the French Armies, that a major offensive should be launched by the British and French in a combined effort at the River Somme. Through the spring and early summer there is to be a huge build-up of supplies, men and horses in preparation.'

'When will this happen?' Robert asked. 'The actual attack, I mean.'

Marigold shook her head. 'We don't know a date yet. Maybe there is one, but they're keeping that under wraps. Understandably. However,' she continued, 'because of the offensive at Verdun, which is occupying thousands of French troops, the Somme offensive may not actually happen for a few months, though Dr Hazelwood did think that eventually the decision will be taken to launch it even if only to take valuable German troops away from Verdun and so help the French. They are, by all accounts, having a dreadful time there.'

'But what about us? Are we to go there?' Pips asked, impatiently.

'At the moment, no. Dr Hazelwood wants us to make our own preparations in readiness for this "big push" at the Somme. When the time comes, he will want you to go there. He suggests an area near a place called Thiepval. He's already putting together two more flying ambulance corps to send out to support you.' She smiled. 'He knows that you are fearless in your efforts to be as close to the trenches as possible and he is proposing to have backup for you.' Her face sobered. 'He rather fears that the number of casualties will be far higher than anything you have seen to date, and a comparatively small unit like yours would soon be overwhelmed.'

The members of the team listened in silence until at last Giles asked quietly, 'Are the authorities hoping that a big offensive like this will bring about the end of the war?'

Marigold sighed. 'I suppose it's what we hope with every battle that occurs. No doubt, it's what the Germans are fighting for right now at Verdun. But, from what I hear, they have reckoned without the tenacity and the devotion that the French have for that part of their country. I believe they will fight to the last man to save it.'

'Perhaps,' Robert said quietly, 'we are to have the same motive on the Somme.'

Over the following months, through spring and early summer and the blooming of the poppies once more, the unit made their own preparations to move when the time came. Each day, Pips brought bunches of poppies to the tents to brighten the day for the casualties, and she also presented each of the nurses with a single bloom to pin on their aprons. Soon the wounded soldiers were watching out for the nurses' arrival each morning.

'Here come the poppy girls.'

Towards the end of May, Dr Hazelwood brought out two more corps and they set up close by.

'You will all move together, but yours, Robert, will be the forward first-aid post and the other two will be a little distance behind the front lines.'

'It's a very good idea, Dr Hazelwood. We don't know as yet where the nearest hospitals will be when we get to Thiepval, and to have support near at hand will be a godsend.'

The jovial little man laughed heartily. 'Now, I wouldn't presume on the Almighty's territory, but I do my best. I think the nearest large town will be Albert, but we'll have to check on that.'

They met the members of the two teams which had arrived. Each group was made up very much like their own: two doctors, four nurses and several drivers and stretcher bearers. One team even had a dedicated cook.

'I'll never remember all their names,' Brigitta said, as they walked back to their own tents.

'No need.' Giles grinned. 'Just say "Eh-up, lad", like we do in Yorkshire when you meet them.'

'Or "Wotcha, me old china",' Hugh put in.

'Or even "Nah, then",' William laughed. 'That's a favourite greeting of Ma's.' For a fleeting moment there was pain in his eyes as he remembered his home, but it was gone in an instant and only Pips had noticed it.

'Well, I've noted Mike and Phil, the two leaders. The rest we'll learn by degrees. They seem a good bunch,' Robert said. 'I'm sure we'll work very well together.'

'I think,' Giles said, as the levity died, 'we're going to need to.'

Before they were likely to be moved, Pips laid flowers on the grave of George's friend. Poppies were in full bloom amongst the temporary wooden crosses that she was sure would one day be replaced by proper stone markers. She marvelled at the persistence of these delicate flowers that could keep blossoming amidst the ravaged land. She wondered where George was now. He was a strict officer – she had seen that – yet beneath that serious exterior, there was a good, kind man. Though she loved Giles dearly, she wasn't blind to his faults. He had shown flashes of jealousy and possessiveness, which, though flattering in a way, were hard to deal with at times. She didn't think George would ever be like that. She frowned and silently castigated herself. You shouldn't be comparing them. Giles is the man you love, she reminded herself, but still, she couldn't quell the hope deep within her that somehow, somewhere, she would meet George Allender again.

Fifty-One

'Hetty my love,' Edwin said over breakfast. His face was solemn and at once she feared bad news.

'I saw Basil yesterday. He was home for a brief visit. He told me that there is to be a "big push", as he called it, in a few weeks' time. A huge offensive, he said, near the River Somme. It's been planned since the beginning of the year, but it's become imperative now to try to relieve some pressure on the French at Verdun. They are having a bleak time there.'

'I know. I've read the papers.' She paused and then added quietly, 'And you think Robert, Pips and the rest of the team will go there.'

'I'm sure of it.'

'I'm not surprised. To be honest, I've been half-expecting to hear that they'd gone to Verdun.'

'Yes, so had I, but I think you should go and tell the Dawsons. They won't have access to news of

301

this nature, like we have.'

'I expect you're right, but I don't relish telling them.'

'Would you like me to go?' he asked.

Henrietta shook her head. 'No, I'll do it. It would frighten them to death if you turned up on their doorstep. They'd think at once it was bad news.'

'It is, in a way. Because it's very likely that Bernard and Roy – and possibly Harold too – will be sent there.'

'D'you think I should tell them that?'

Edwin shook his head. 'No. No point in worrying them unnecessarily. We don't know that for sure.'

'But you think it's a possibility.'

Edwin paused before saying gravely, 'More like a probability.'

'Oh Mrs Maitland, do come in,' Norah said as she opened the front door. 'We've got the babby here. Would you like to see him? He's growing so fast. Six months old already and sitting up and taking notice.'

She led the way into the kitchen where Ma was nursing the little boy.

'Oh, what a grand little chap,' Henrietta exclaimed. 'How bonny he is. You're doing a fine job, Peggy. May I hold him? I never could resist little babies.' She laughed. 'It's when they get older your problems start.'

They chatted for a few moments about the child until Henrietta told them what her husband had heard.

'Alice won't be near the actual fighting, will she, Mrs Maitland?' Norah asked.

Henrietta hesitated for a brief moment, deciding to be economical with the truth. 'Advanced first-aid posts do get as near as they can to the trenches, but they're well behind the shelling and the gunfire. They shouldn't be in real danger.'

Ma caught and held her gaze and Henrietta was unable to look away as the older woman said, 'But the stretcher bearers go in, don't they? They follow the soldiers to pick up the wounded.'

It was the first time even an oblique reference to William had been made.

'I – believe so,' Henrietta was obliged to admit.

'And it's a "big push", you say? So they'll need a lot of troops there.'

'Yes.'

'Then it's likely that our boys – Bernard, Roy and maybe even Boy – could be sent there.'

No one spoke but Peggy, her eyes wide, gave a sob and covered her mouth with trembling fingers.

'We're to move tomorrow,' Robert said, 'All three units.'

'There'll be quite a convoy of us.'

'We won't be the only ones. Have you seen the double-decker buses taking troops up to the front already?'

Peter laughed. 'They were London buses. I reckon there was one I used to drive.'

'Don't be daft,' his brother scoffed. 'How likely is that?'

'No, I'm serious, mate. It looked very familiar.

If I could have got nearer for a look in the cab, I'd've known for sure.'

'It seems we won't be there a moment too soon. They're starting some sort of countdown already.'

'I wish George was still here to ask,' Pips murmured, and she earned herself a glare from Giles.

'Right, let's start packing.'

They arrived near a wood that lay behind Thiepval and Ovillers and set up the three camps on 22 June. A nearby railway line ran close to the town of Albert. Robert's advanced first-aid post was positioned just behind the line of British artillery with the two newer first-aid posts further back, where they hoped they would be well out of the range of enemy shellfire. They arranged between them that the stretcher bearers from the advanced post would bring wounded there first and then those who were fit enough to travel further would be taken to the next stage.

'I suggest we don't unload the ambulances here,' Robert said to the two men who were in charge of the new posts, 'but use each other's vehicles. All right with you, Phil – Mike?'

'You mean, your guys will sort out who wants to be where when they pick them up at the front, do you?' Mike said. 'That seems very sensible. Less work and also less upheaval for the casualties than to keep transferring them from one ambulance to another.'

'Have you heard what's going to happen?' William said that evening. 'I've just been talking to one of the soldiers.'

'Go on,' Giles said. William was white-faced

and obviously shocked.

'They've dug saps right under the enemy lines and planted nineteen mines that are going to be set off on the morning of the first assault to blow gaps in the German line. And before that they are to be subjected to five days of constant shelling to try to destroy their defences and smash their barbed wire.'

'It sounds ruthless,' Robert murmured.

'It's war,' Giles said. 'They'd do the same to us. In fact, they might well be planning something similar.'

'When's the infantry attack going to start?'

'On the twenty-ninth,' William said. He glanced back over his shoulder towards their own lines and then beyond to the distant line of enemy trenches. 'You know, there are going to be an awful lot of casualties on both sides.'

'Then we'd better make sure we're ready.'

Wet weather in the final week of June postponed the infantry attack until Saturday, 1 July, but added another two days of bombardment of the enemy's defences.

'There can't be anyone left alive over there now,' William said at dusk on the evening of 30 June.

'And don't forget the mines are going to be exploded in the morning,' Pips murmured as they stood near the tents and listened to services which were being held by the chaplains in the fields nearby. And then they heard a band playing and saw men marching as if on parade. As darkness fell, hundreds of troops marched past them towards the trenches, and they realized that this was being repeated all along a zig-zag line to the north and to the south as far as the river itself.

'You know, I think we're right in the middle of it,' Pips said.

'Then we're in exactly the right place. We'll send our non-urgent casualties to Albert. Phil's and Mike's ambulance drivers can undertake the longer journeys whilst we concentrate on getting the wounded out of the trenches.'

'Now we'd better try to get some sleep. I think we have a busy day ahead of us.'

The sound of the soldiers' marching feet went on until five o'clock in the morning. Pips lay awake, praying for an Allied victory, but she had the awful premonition that this was going to be a long and bitter battle.

Robert and the rest of the team were awake and dressed just before the hour they understood the attack was to start. The sky was lit with flashes and then they heard and saw the mines exploding, throwing tons of earth into the air, and heard the whistle that signalled that the men were to 'go over the top'. After a few moments, they heard the dreaded sound of rapid enemy gunfire that went on and on. A shell exploded quite near to them and two horses, pulling a general service wagon, panicked and bolted, the driver clinging desperately onto the reins.

Robert stood on a piece of higher ground and watched through binoculars.

'My God!' he muttered in a hoarse whisper. 'They're being mown down like wheat before a scythe and yet those behind them are still climbing out of the trenches and going forward. It's a slaughter. Our bombardment and the mines can't have done what they were supposed to do.'

Shocked, he lowered his field glasses and thrust them into Giles's hands. 'I can't watch any more. William, Hugh, Peter – we must get up there now. We must be ready as soon as they start bringing in the wounded. Pips – take the car and warn Mike and Phil. Tell them to expect the very worst – because that's what it's going to be.'

Fifty-Two

Just after midday on a beautiful summer's day, William and the other stretcher bearers were taken to a field of dead and dying. Hundreds of corpses lay amongst the injured under the hot sun. Flies buzzed around the wounds of those who had no strength left to flick them away. Others were able to take a drink of water or accept a cigarette before being borne away to the nearest first-aid post or straight to the trucks on the railway, which would take them to the casualty-clearing station.

Robert and Giles gave orders for some of the casualties to be taken to the Hazelwood first-aid post immediately. Others, with relatively minor wounds, who were able to walk, followed Pips to the car.

'We'll have to leave you to it now,' Robert told her. 'We're needed back at the post. We've already sent several through who need immediate surgery if we're to save their lives. Although for some it

307

might already be too late after a day out there under a hot sun.'

By nightfall, the guns on both sides fell silent. William, Hugh and Peter climbed out of the trenches, passed through the Allied barbed wire and stepped into no-man's-land. Verey flares from both sides lit up the ground as they searched for those who could still be helped. Soon, all the stretchers were used up and William began to carry casualties, one at a time, on his back. He took them to the Allied trenches and then set out again to find more. The task was never-ending. The three of them worked all night just taking men into the trench, whilst Pips and Brigitta, with the help of other soldiers, carried them to the ambulances and took them the mile or so back to their first-aid post where Leonore received them and assessed the needs of each casualty. Those who could be moved on at once were taken by Phil's and Mike's ambulances to the next post, whilst Robert and Giles performed emergency treatment or operations.

It was a long night, and the tragedy of it all was that they all knew that, with the dawn, the killing and maiming would begin again.

'Jim?' Boy's voice was weak. He was lying in the bottom of a trench and he couldn't remember how he'd got there. 'Jim? Are you there?'

There was a movement beside him and a hand was clamped over his mouth. 'Ssh, Harold,' came an urgent whisper. 'There's a good lad. We're in an enemy trench and if they hear us... Now, I'll tek my hand away if you promise to be quiet.'

Jim Leatham took his hand away but hovered a moment to be sure the boy wasn't going to make any noise.

'What are we doing here?'

'We've captured their trench, but now we're pinned down and can't get out. Are you hurt bad?'

'Me foot.'

Leatham looked down. At the end of the boy's leg was a bloody mess of torn and mangled flesh, totally unrecognizable as a foot. Before he'd lost consciousness, Harold must have pulled his boot off, for it was lying beside him.

'I'll try and get your boot back on and then hoist you up,' Jim said. 'Where's your field dressing?'

'In me pack.'

Jim put a pad over the boy's foot and then wrapped a bandage round it, but there was little he could do for that wound. 'When it gets dark, we're out of here, lad. I reckon we're the only two left alive.' He nodded towards several crumpled figures further down the trench. 'They're all goners.'

'Roy? Roy, you there?'

'Here, Bernard, what's up?'

'We've got orders. They've sent scouts out to the German front line near the wood. They reckon there's some Sherwood Foresters still holding out in the enemy trenches. Roy, Boy could be there.'

'Can we go and look for him?'

'Not now. We've got to await orders.'

'Damn orders, if Boy's there...'

Bernard gripped his arm. 'Don't be a fool, Roy. There's nowt we can do till we're told. D'you want to get shot by our own side?'

'No, but–'

'No "buts", Roy. Just let's be patient, but once we get over there, then they won't know we're looking for someone, will they?'

Just after 11 p.m., Bernard said, 'They've just changed the orders, Roy.'

'Aren't we to go?'

'Yes. We were to attack the trench and hold it, but now we've to make contact with the Sherwoods and bring 'em back.'

'That's more like it. I'm ready.'

'Right, it's dark now – and quiet,' Jim whispered. 'Let's give it a go. There'll be some of our boys somewhere across there, if only we can reach them. Now, I'm going to put your boot on and lace it up real tight.'

The pain was excruciating, but Harold clamped his own hand over his mouth now to stop himself from making any sound.

'Good lad. Now I'm going to tek one of those rifles from over there. Poor feller won't be needin' it again. You can use it as a crutch.'

Slowly, they climbed out of the trench and crawled forward. They reached the enemy's barbed wire. 'Damn, it's not been cut. Lie down, Harold. I've got me clippers.'

Jim worked as quietly as he could, snipping at the wire, until there was a hole big enough for him to drag Harold through.

Once through, he said, 'There's no sound anywhere. I reckon we could stand up...'

At that moment, flares lit up the landscape and

they saw platoons of British soldiers advancing towards them.

'We'll be all right, now, Harold. They're coming for us.'

At midnight the front line of platoons had moved forward, Bernard and Roy side by side. Half of them had reached the enemy's wire, which they began to cut. But then, the Germans opened fire with machine guns and rifles and the whole area was illuminated by flares.

The order came out to the Lincolns to lie down and to keep their position.

'Not before I've bagged me a German. Look, Bernard, there's two coming out of the trench now.'

'Wait, it might be–'

But Roy had fired and both figures fell to the ground.

'You silly sod,' Bernard muttered. 'You might hit one of ours. Get down.'

Fifty-Three

'Pips–' Brigitta came into the tent where she was tending a patient after his operation to remove his leg. 'There's a young boy asking for you.'

Pips straightened up. 'Me? By name?'

Brigitta nodded. 'Yes. He asked, "Is Alice or Miss Pips here?" Alice is still assisting Robert – I can't ask her to leave what she's doing just now.'

311

'Is it someone who's been wounded before?'

'I don't know.'

'I'll come as soon as I've finished here. Where is he?'

'He's just been brought in from near Gommecourt. He was found by one of the Lincolns who risked his life to fetch him from no-man's-land. There was another soldier with him, but he was dead – shot through the head. At midnight the front line of platoons from the Lincolns moved forward to try to reach some soldiers in the Sherwoods who were trapped in enemy trenches. The boy's in a bad way, Pips. He has an abdominal wound and he's lost his left foot. I don't think...' Her voice trailed away into silence, but Pips understood.

'But why's he been brought all this way? I know it's not that far away, but if you're badly injured it's far enough. Why wasn't he taken to a first-aid post nearer to where he was wounded?'

'Because he was asking for you or Alice and one of the Lincolns knew you were with Dr Hazelwood's ambulance corps.'

As soon as she could, Pips went in search of the soldier. They were overwhelmed with casualties arriving every few minutes by any means of transport that could be utilized. Lorries, cars, horse-drawn carts. Some were even being carried all the way from the trenches by their comrades as well as by the official stretcher bearers. They lay in rows awaiting attention from the nurses or doctors. Pips hurried along the lines, looking for a face she recognized. And then she caught her breath as she saw William squatting down beside a stretcher on the ground. She swallowed hard as she moved forward, almost afraid to see who was lying there, and when she recognized him, she almost cried out aloud. He was the last person she'd expected to see in this awful place.

Jake halted the pony and trap outside the Dawsons' cottage and helped Henrietta to climb down.

'Morning, Mrs Maitland.' From her seat outside the door, which she occupied for most of the day during the warm weather, Ma greeted their visitor.

'Good morning, Mrs Dawson. May I sit beside you?'

The old woman nodded and shifted along the bench seat a little.

'I'll tek the pony to Mester Dawson,' Jake said. 'He needs shoeing.'

'That's all right, Jake,' Henrietta said. 'I'll walk back to the hall. You come back when you're ready.'

The boy touched his forelock and clicked to the pony to make it move on. The two women's gaze followed him along the road.

'He's a good lad. What'd've become of him if you hadn't taken him in, ma'am, I don't know.'

'He's turned out very nicely.'

'How old is he? Will he be called up soon, d'you reckon?'

Henrietta laughed. 'No one's quite sure of his age – least of all Jake – but we think he's about sixteen now, so, hopefully, not yet.'

'Have you had any news?' Ma asked quietly.

'Not recently.'

'We haven't heard from Alice for a while.'

'As far as I know, she's fine,' Henrietta said and was bold enough to add in a low voice, 'William too.'

'Thank you,' Ma whispered as Norah appeared round the corner of the house carrying two cups of tea.

'I saw you arrive, ma'am. I thought you might like a drink.'

'That's most welcome. Thank you, Norah. How are you?'

'I've been better, Mrs Maitland, to tell you the truth. It's the worry about our boys – and Alice, though I don't expect she's in real danger. Not like the other three.'

Henrietta pursed her lips. Still no reference to William. It annoyed her, but she kept silent, though it was hard when she guessed that the ambulance corps was in just as much danger.

'But the constant anxiety just eats away at you,' Norah went on. 'I've lost weight because I can't eat properly and I'm not sleeping well either. But it's the same for anyone who's got loved ones away fighting. I mustn't grumble.'

'Have there been any more telegrams delivered in the village?'

'One yesterday to the Dixon family. Their son has been wounded. He's got what the lads call a "Blighty" wound.'

'Ah,' Henrietta said, 'so he'll be on his way home.'

'If he makes it,' Ma murmured.

For a moment the three women fell silent.

'Any news of Samuel Nuttall?' Henrietta asked.

'His mam had a letter yesterday. He writes regularly.' Norah sniffed contemptuously. 'Which is more than can be said for our lads, though we did hear from Bernard last week. He said that they're going to a place called Somme.'

Gently, Henrietta said, 'It's a river, Norah. The River Somme. There's a battle going on in that area. It started yesterday.' She bit her lip, stopping herself from saying more. Edwin had heard from Rosemary Fieldsend that the early accounts of the huge offensive weren't good – there had been huge British losses on the first day – but it seemed that the news had not yet reached the village. Maybe that was just as well, Henrietta thought.

Norah nodded. 'Oh, I see. Well, at least him and Roy are still together. I'm glad about that. They can look out for each other.'

Henrietta felt a stab of fear for the two brothers, but she tried to be positive. 'I know just how you feel about letters. We don't hear very often, but Edwin says we have to think that "no news is good news".'

There was another silence between them and then Norah jumped up. 'We've got a stack of things for you to send out, Mrs Maitland. They're all packed up in boxes. I don't expect gloves and balaclavas will be needed out there in the summer, though I expect they'll all need socks.'

'We'll send everything out in readiness for winter. It'll come soon enough.'

'I'll see Jake and get him to bring them all to the hall when he comes back,' Norah said. She stood for a moment looking down at her mother-in-law and Henrietta. 'When's it all going to end,

Mrs Maitland? When are our lads coming home?'

Henrietta's reply was heartfelt. 'I only wish I knew, Norah.'

Pips moved forward slowly. Young Harold Dawson – 'Boy', as his family had always called him – was lying on the stretcher, his face glistening with sweat, his features twisted in agony. There was no blanket and his uniform had been torn aside to reveal his wound; his intestines were spilling out of the gaping opening in his abdomen and his foot was a mangled mess. Brigitta had been right; there was nothing that could be done here in these primitive conditions to help him. Perhaps they could keep some of the pain at bay, but he would die an agonizing death. Pips prayed it would be quick. He was hanging onto William's hand as if he would never let it go. And perhaps he wouldn't, Pips thought. Maybe they should release William from his duties and allow him to stay by his brother's side until–

'Miss Pips. That nurse said she was here. I want to see Miss Pips,' Harold was moaning, though his eyes were closed.

'Brigitta, fetch Alice at once,' Pips whispered. 'Tell her it's her brother – the one they call Boy.' She squatted down beside William. 'I'm here, Harold.'

For a moment the boy thrashed his head from side to side and sweat ran down the side of his face. 'Miss Pips – you must tell them – tell them back home – that William is a hero. He's braver than any of us. I'm sorry for what we did. Tell William, Miss Pips. Tell him I'm so sorry.'

'He's here beside you, Harold. He's holding your hand and he's hearing what you say.'

'Is he?' His eyes, dark pools of suffering, opened and he tried to focus on the man beside him. But then he cried out. 'I can't see him, Miss Pips. I can't see – anything. It's so dark – and – and cold.'

'I'm here, Harold. I'm here,' William said hoarsely at last. 'I'm with you.'

'I'm sorry, Will, so very sorry. We shouldn't have treated you the way we did. You're a braver man than the rest of us put together.' A small smile quivered on his mouth. 'As Ma would say.'

'Listen, Harold,' William said urgently, leaning towards him. 'You've got to hang on. You've got to get home. Peggy has had your baby. A little boy. She's called him Luke Harold Cooper.'

For a long moment, Harold didn't speak and they wondered if he had understood, but at last he whispered, 'I've got a son?'

'Yes, you have and you must get home to see him.'

Harold winced as pain overwhelmed him again, but he pulled in a deep breath. 'Poor Peggy. I didn't mean to shame her, Will. Tell them that. I wouldn't have hurt her. I'd've married her, if only I could have got home.'

Alice arrived beside them, her hand over her mouth when she saw her young brother and in time to hear William say, 'You'll get home. Master Robert will help you. Just hang on, Harold.'

The boy's eyes closed, but then they flickered open and, with a glimmer of hope, he asked, 'You've heard from them then? Have they written to you?'

317

William glanced at Pips, silently asking how he should answer such a question, but she took the decision – and the burden – from him. 'Yes, Harold,' she said firmly. 'Your mother's written to William and told him about Peggy.' She stroked his brow gently. 'Don't you worry any more. We'll get you home and you can tell them yourself how brave your brother is.'

He let out a long, deep sigh. They watched him for a moment and then Pips gently closed the boy's staring eyes. 'He's gone, William. I'm so sorry.'

William bowed his head and pressed his brother's hand to his forehead. Pips put her hand on his shoulder and stayed with him until William raised his head again and murmured, ''Tis for the best, Pips. He's out of pain now. There was no hope with an injury like that, was there?'

'No, William,' Pips whispered. 'There wasn't.'

She rose and put her arms around Alice, who was weeping openly now.

'We'll see to him, Alice.'

'I'm sorry, I just can't do it. Not this time, Pips. Not my brother.'

Together Pips and William tended him and when he had been carefully carried away for burial, William said, 'Pips, I don't think I've ever known you tell a lie before.'

Pips sighed. 'Not before coming here, no, I don't think I have – not even when I was little. I always owned up to things, but now...' She paused and her voice broke a little as she added, 'That wasn't the first untruth I've told in the last few weeks, but I think I'll be forgiven. It's best that these poor boys go peacefully. Harold needed to believe that you and your family were in touch again and, who knows, maybe one day, you will be.'

William looked sceptical, but he just gave a brief nod and turned away. Even though he'd just lost his brother, there was work to do. There was always work to do. He could do nothing more for Harold, but there were plenty more wounded he could help.

Fifty-Four

'That'll be Mrs Maitland again,' Norah said to Ma as a knock sounded on the front door of their cottage. Henrietta was the only caller who ever entered their home that way. Everyone else in the village always came to their back door, knocked and walked in. Norah dried her hands on a towel and hurried to open the door.

It took a moment for her to register that it was not Henrietta standing there, but a young boy in a post-office uniform with a yellow envelope in his hand. As realization sank in, Norah gasped and put her hand to her chest. When she didn't take the telegram immediately, the boy thrust it towards her. He was anxious to be gone. He'd had to deliver far too many of these telegrams now in the district and he hated seeing the distress his brief visit brought. With trembling fingers, Norah reached out and took the envelope. The boy turned, mounted his bicycle and pedalled as hard

319

as he could down the lane.

Slowly, Norah closed the door and, on leaden feet, returned to the kitchen. Seeing the envelope in her hand, Ma turned white. 'Open it, lass,' she said huskily. 'Let's see which one it is.'

Norah passed it to her mother-in-law. 'You do it,' she whispered. 'I – I can't.'

Ma tore it open and read the words:

'...deeply regret to inform you that Private Harold Dawson died of his wounds on 2 July 1916...'

There were more words of condolence, but Ma couldn't read them for the tears blurring her eyes.

'It's Boy,' she said hoarsely. The telegram fluttered to the floor as she covered her face with her hands. Norah sank into the chair opposite Ma, the tears rolling down her cheeks, and that was how Len found them when he came home from the workshop for his midday meal.

Len picked up the telegram from the floor and read the dreadful news.

'Silly little bugger. He had no need to go. I blame William for this. If he hadn't refused to go, Boy would at least have waited until he was old enough.' It was the first time that Len had spoken William's name since his son's refusal to join up.

'I don't know if he would have, Len,' Ma said quietly. She was filled with unbearable sadness, but she couldn't bear to hear William blamed for everything that happened, but Len rounded on her angrily. 'Don't you dare stick up for that – that *shirker*. D'you know what they're calling 'em now? Conchies. But it's just another name for coward. And you know what they do to them, don't you? They put 'em up against a wall and shoot them, that's what. And quite right too. So, Ma, don't you dare mention his name again else you'll find yarsen in the workhouse.'

'Oh Len, don't say such things to your mother. You don't mean it.'

Len grunted and turned away, flinging the telegram onto the table. 'Where's me dinner, Norah? I've work to do and no one to help me do it now.'

'William would have helped you if—' Ma began.

Len swung round and pointed his forefinger at her. 'I warned you, Ma...'

When Len had scoffed his dinner and gone back to his workshop, Norah said softly, 'Take no notice of him, Ma. He's taking out his hurt on us. He can't shed tears like us women and his heartbreak comes out in anger.'

Ma sighed. 'I know, lass. I know. But to tell you the truth, after the news we've had today, I'm past caring. I really don't care what he does to me. Not now.'

There was a silence between them until Norah said quietly, 'I'll have to go and tell Peggy, won't I?'

'Aye, you will. And I shouldn't leave it long, duck. Folks will have seen the telegram lad come to our door and rumours'll be rife.'

Half an hour later, Norah had plucked up the courage to visit the Coopers' home. As she passed her husband's workshop, she saw him wielding a big hammer and crashing it down on his anvil. But there was no piece of metal beneath his blows. He was just smashing his hammer against his anvil again and again.

Norah sighed and walked on. She would have liked to have gone to him, have tried to comfort him, but there was no reaching out to Len. He would deal with his grief in his own way and entirely on his own. And it sounded as if he would turn his pain into even more resentment against William.

'Hello, Bess,' Norah said flatly when her knock at their back door was answered. 'Is Peggy in? I've got bad news.'

'Aw, lass, no! Not Harold. Tell me it's not Harold.'

'I'm afraid it is. He was killed at the Somme.'

'Come in, Norah, duck. I'll mek tea for all of us. Peggy's in the kitchen giving the babby his dinner. She's breastfeeding him, but you don't mind that, do ya?'

Norah shook her head and followed Bess.

At the sight of their serious faces, tears welled in Peggy's eyes. They didn't even need to speak as she clutched the baby closer to her and began to cry, loud, heartrending sobs. Luke, his mouth dislodged from her breast, began to whimper, his cries mingling with his mother's until, gently, Bess took him from Peggy and leaned him against her shoulder, patting his back and walking around the kitchen table with him.

They gave Peggy time to calm herself a little until, through her tears, she asked, 'Is he – is he dead?'

'I'm so sorry, love, but yes, he is. He was killed a few days ago on the Somme.'

Peggy crossed her arms over her waist as if she had a physical pain there. 'I don't want to live any more if he's not coming back. I want to die. Just let me die...'

'Now, our Peggy, I won't have such talk,' Bess said firmly. 'I know you've had a terrible shock, but you've this little one to think about and all your family. You've got to bring Luke up. Young Harold's son. Never forget that. We'll stand by you. We've said we will.'

'And we will too, Peggy,' Norah said. 'He's our grandson too.' She glanced at Bess as she added, 'And Harold would have expected you to be strong and look after his son, now wouldn't he?'

The young girl's sobs subsided a little, but tears still streaked her face. 'I'll always be an un-married mother now. Luke'll be so ashamed of me when he grows up. If only Harold had come back and married me.'

'Don't fret, love,' her mother said. 'It'll not be easy, but you won't be the only one to have a bairn by a soldier who's been killed before he's had chance to do the decent thing.'

Norah winced at Bess's words, but said nothing.

'And besides, you're still young. Maybe you'll meet someone...'

Peggy shook her head adamantly. 'I'll never love anyone else.'

Norah left the Coopers about an hour later, feeling drained.

'Was it very bad?' Ma asked.

'Dreadful. Poor girl's distraught, but Bess is strong. She'll pull her through this.'

But who is going to pull me through? Norah

323

thought. I'll never get over this. A fresh fear clutched at her heart as Ma said, 'Just let's hope the others come back safe and sound.'

Fifty-Five

'I don't suppose you're writing to your parents, are you, William?' Pips asked him. 'About Harold?'

Tight-lipped, William shook his head.

'Then I will. They should be told what Harold said.'

'I can't stop you,' he said stiffly. 'But I'd be obliged if you don't mention me. Don't even say I was with him at the end.'

Pips sighed. 'William, I have to. He wanted them to know about you.'

He turned away without another word.

Pips found it difficult to write to the Dawsons, but eventually she found what she hoped were the right words.

You will have heard from Harold's superior officer by now, but I wanted you to hear this from me.

Here she paused and wondered how to tell the truth without causing them even more anguish. The usual way was to say that he died instantly and suffered no pain, and though Pips didn't always agree with this tradition, when it came to writing about their son's suffering, she found she couldn't be completely truthful, and began to understand why officialdom adopted the wording it did. With a heavy heart, she wrote:

William carried him from the battlefield to our first-aid post, which is only yards behind the front line. We – and Alice too – were with him and he died only a few moments later. Please believe me that he didn't suffer, but he wanted you to know that he and his brothers had been wrong about William. William is no coward. As a stretcher bearer he must go out into the battlefield, completely unarmed himself, to bring in the wounded. Harold asked me to tell you that William is 'braver than the rest of them put together'. He said that this is one of Ma's favourite sayings.

I am deeply sorry for your loss.

She felt the letter was rather stilted, but she didn't know how else to word it.

When Pips's letter arrived at the Dawsons' home, Norah showed it to Ma and then burned it in the grate. She neither showed it to Len nor even told him about it.

'When the whistle goes, Roy, you stick close to me. You hear me?'

Roy nodded. He dared not speak. He was afraid that his teeth would chatter with fear and be seen as cowardice. Roy, younger than his brother by six years, had always looked up to Bernard. He would follow him to the ends of the earth and into the jaws of hell. In fact, he probably was doing just that in this dreadful place.

It had been all right at first. But the night when

they'd tried to rescue the Sherwoods had left its mark on Roy. Now, here they were, supposedly going yet again in support of the Sherwoods near a place called Longueval.

'Do you – do you think we might see Boy this time?'

When they'd volunteered along with all the other Kitchener recruits, it had seemed like a merry jape, a chance to go abroad, to see a bit of the world and an opportunity to serve one's country. Now, it was anything but that.

They were 'standing to' on the fire step, a long line of them waiting for the signal that would send them up the ladders and over the parapet of the newly dug trenches. Behind them were the stretcher bearers, standing quietly against the back wall of the trench with their first-aid bags and stretchers. The men about to go into battle studiously avoided talking to them, or even looking at them, as if by doing so they could ignore the reason they were there. The soldiers believed they wouldn't be the ones to get injured or killed; that would be the other fellow. No, in a few hours' time they'd be back in the trenches, sitting cosily in a dugout cooking up bully beef on a small primus stove and laughing and joking about how they'd routed the enemy, how they'd sent him packing...

The whistle shrilled all the way down the line and up the ladders they went, across the ground to cut their way through the barbed wire and then into the open ground between the two lines of opposing trenches. The enemy opened fire and the slaughter began again.

'Come on, Roy,' Bernard shouted. 'Stay close,

weave from side to side, firing as you go, like we was taught.'

They had as little chance as they would facing a firing squad. The hail of bullets mowed them down.

'Bernard! I'm hit.'

Through the noise and the smoke, Bernard heard his brother's voice. He stopped firing his gun and turned to see Roy on the ground, reaching out his hand towards him. Then he felt a thud in his back and fell forward, right beside his brother. Roy was crying, pulling at Bernard's sleeve. 'Bernard, help me. I'm hit.'

'It's all right, Roy,' Bernard gasped. 'I'm here. We'll be all right. We'll crawl back to the trench... Aah!' His words ended in a groan of pain, but, stoically, he dragged himself to his knees and then to his feet. With a gigantic effort, he pulled Roy up and they staggered like two drunks back towards their own trench. But the earth gave way between them and they both felt themselves falling forwards, rolling down the sides of a shell hole. Roy cried out and Bernard felt the air knocked out of his lungs. They lay together in the bottom of the hole. Bernard moved his arm, wincing with pain as he did so, and put it over his brother.

'We'll be all right, Roy. Just hang on. The stretcher bearers will find us. You saw them all standing behind us, didn't you? That's what they were there for. When the shooting stops, they'll come out looking for us. It won't be long. Just hang on...'

Roy was whimpering. 'I'm hit in the stomach, Bernard. I can feel the blood...'

'Don't, Roy. Don't touch it. They'll come soon.'

'The pain, Bernard. I can't bear it.' There was a pause and then, 'Will William come and find us, Bernard? I want William to come.'

'He will, Roy. 'Course he will. He'll come looking for us.'

But William was further down the line, waiting in the trench until he could begin to bring in the wounded from no-man's-land. He had no idea that his two brothers were less than six miles away and desperately in need of his help.

As dusk came the guns fell silent and the stretcher bearers began their gruesome task.

Weak now, from loss of blood and the terrible pain, Roy was delirious. 'William, William,' he cried incessantly.

With still a little strength, Bernard began to shout, 'Help, help. Over here.'

It seemed an age before they heard voices at the edge of the crater.

'There's two down here, Wilf,' a voice said. 'Let's go down and have a look. I reckon I saw one moving.'

Two figures slithered down the side of the shell hole.

'Nah, mate,' a cheerful voice greeted them.

Roy reached out a trembling hand. 'William – William, is that you?'

'Sorry, mate. I'm Alf and this 'ere's Wilf.'

But Roy didn't understand. 'I knew you'd come and find us. William, I'm so sorry about what happened...'

'S'all right, mate, take it easy. We'll get you

back. Now, who's going first, 'cos there's only the two of us?'

'Take Roy,' Bernard gasped and winced in pain again.

The stretcher bearer who'd said his name was Alf regarded them both. 'I reckon we ought to take you first,' he said to Bernard. 'He won't last...'

'Don't say that,' Bernard groaned. 'He's me brother. Please, take him.'

'All right,' Alf agreed and he and Wilf lifted Roy onto their stretcher. 'We'll be back for you as soon as we can, mate.'

'I knew you'd come and find us, William,' were the last words Bernard heard Roy utter as the two strangers struggled up the side of the shell hole with their casualty.

After they'd gone, Bernard felt himself let go. Believing that his younger brother was now in good hands, he slipped into blissful unconsciousness. When the two stretcher bearers, true to their promise, returned, it was to find Bernard in a deep coma and, although they took him back to their trenches, he died before they could even get him to a dressing station.

'That's a shame,' Alf said to Wilf. 'We did our best, though, didn't we, mate?'

'We did. Brothers, they said they were, didn't they?'

Alf nodded. 'It'll be hard for their parents to hear that they've lost both their sons on the same day, won't it? I knew the first one was a goner, but I did think this one had a chance. Oh well, come on, we'd best get back out there and see if there's anyone we *can* save.'

The two bearers went back out into no-man's-land and continued their daunting task. By dawn the following day, after a strenuous night of carrying the wounded and dying from the field of battle, the deaths of the two brothers had become just two more amongst the many losses they witnessed that night.

Fifty-Six

This time the deaths of both his sons, on the same day in August, affected Len deeply. It wasn't that he loved them more than he had Harold, it was just that the accumulation of loss tipped him over the edge of his resilience. He sat in his chair near the range, on the opposite side of the hearth to Ma, day after day, unable to eat or sleep or go to his work. He sank into silence and wouldn't speak to anyone. He only left his chair to answer the call of nature.

Dr Maitland was called, but he was unable to rouse the man from his great sorrow.

Once again, it fell to Norah to visit the Coopers and tell Betty of Roy's death. The girl shed tears and the two sisters hugged each other and cuddled baby Luke.

'He's extra special now,' Betty said, wiping her tears. 'I'll try to be the best ever aunty to him. He's all we've got left of Harold and Roy now.'

Norah watched the two girls fussing over the baby, who, ignorant of the sadness in the house, crowed and smiled with delight at all the sudden attention.

'Len's taken these last two very hard, Bess. As far as he's concerned now, that's all our sons gone. He's sitting by the range and won't move. Won't eat or go to his work. Won't even go upstairs to his bed.'

Bess put her hand on Norah's shoulder as they watched the baby together. 'You know, I was wondering,' Norah said slowly, 'if Peggy would bring the baby to see him. Like Betty just said, he's all we have left of the boys now.'

'We can try, Norah. It can't do any harm, duck, can it?'

'Come with me, Mam,' Peggy asked Bess. 'I daren't go on me own. I'm frit of Mr Dawson.'

'He won't bite, love. I reckon poor feller's lost all his bite now.'

'That's what I'm afraid of. I'm not used to seeing Mr Dawson like his missus said he was. Besides, he's not taken much notice of Babby before now. He might not want to have owt to do with him, seeing as he's a – well, you know. He told me so himself a while back.'

'All right. Come on, then. Let's get it over with.'

Bess rapped sharply on the back door, opened it and walked in. 'It's only us, Norah, duck. We've brought your grandson to see you.' She walked into the kitchen with Peggy behind her carrying Luke. 'Here he is. Hello, Ma. Would you like to hold your great-grandson?'

Deliberately, she ignored Len, sunk in his armchair, and gestured to Peggy to place the baby on Ma's lap.

'My, he's grown, Peggy, lass. You must be feeding him well.'

'I was, but I lost me milk when we heard about Harold. Mam said it'd be the shock. But Luke's taken to cow's milk just as if he'd never known anything else. Mrs Maitland's been ever so kind. She sends fresh milk every day and won't take a penny for it.'

'Aye, she's a good woman.' Ma glanced across the hearth at her son. 'Now, Len, stir yarsen and look at this little chap. He's your grandson. Don't you reckon he's got the look of our Bernard, even though he's Harold's bairn?' Ma turned the baby towards him and Luke waved his arms and smiled a toothless grin.

'He's very like Bernard was when he was little,' Norah murmured.

Bess moved forward, picked up the baby and plonked him on Len's lap before he could make any protest. She stood back, forcing Len to steady the child. Luke reached out and tugged at Len's hair.

'Ouch, young feller,' Len said, pretending to be in pain. 'That hurts. How would you like me to pull yours, eh? That's if you had any.'

Slowly, Len smiled and the four women in the room heaved a collective sigh of relief. Len stood up, the child still in his arms. 'I reckon I'd better stir mesen and show you the workshop that's likely to be yourn one day now.'

He walked out of the room, still carrying the baby, then out of the cottage and down the lane towards his workshop, Peggy scurrying after him, pushing the empty pram.

'By heck,' Bess said, sinking down into the chair Len had just left. 'I could do with a cuppa after that, Norah, duck. I didn't think it was going to be that easy.'

'But it worked, Bess, it worked,' Norah said as she bustled about the kitchen, setting the kettle to boil and reaching for cups and saucers. 'He's a funny feller, Bess, though I mebbe ses it as shouldn't.'

'Well, I can, Norah,' Ma said. She tried to smile but the sadness that would now stay with her for the rest of her life never left her eyes. 'When the bairns were little I used to watch him. He'd pretend not to take any notice of them. It was woman's work, he always said, looking after the home and the family. But then I'd see him taking them down to the workshop, saying he was only going to show them what their future'd be. Just like he has just now. But I sneaked after him one day and found him playing football with the three of them – the oldest three boys, that is – on that patch of ground behind the wheelwright's. But, d'you know, he never told us that's what he was doing, did he, Norah?'

Norah shook her head. 'No, and we never mentioned it to him. It would have belittled him, you see, in his own eyes.'

'He never took a lot of notice of Alice – not the same. His lads were everything to him.'

'I can understand that.' Bess nodded. ''Course, he'd never admit it, but I reckon my Charlie was always secretly disappointed because we didn't have a lad. He loves the girls – 'course he does – but I reckon he'd've liked a son. But now maybe we're the lucky ones.' She gave a huge sigh. 'I'm more sorry than I can put into words for your great loss. Let's just hope your Alice stays safe.'

'Oh, she'll be all right,' Norah said confidently. 'She'll be well away from the action. She won't go anywhere near these trenches they talk about.'

And nor, they were all thinking, would William.

'Alice, will you come with me to the front line?' Robert asked. 'There are so many wounded still being brought in too late for us to be able to save them. Now the shelling's stopped for a while, I want to get to them earlier.'

'Of course.'

'Bring a stretcher bearer's pack. I've got my medical bag and we'll go with William. If we can reach one or two, then you can come back with William when he brings them to Giles and Leonore. Where's Pips?'

'She's driven the car to see if she can bring back the walking wounded.'

'Right. Let's go.'

None of them spoke as William negotiated the rough track to the trenches. They passed the artillery and went down into the reserve trench, then wound their way through the communications trenches and the support trench until they came to the front line. They climbed the ladders into no-man's-land. Everything seemed quiet. Stretcher bearers were working tirelessly to bring in the casualties, but the ground was littered with the dead and dying from both sides. Only a few yards away the enemy were fetching in their wounded too. Robert held out his hand to help Alice up the last few steps. As she straightened up, she gasped at the sight before her. They stood a moment, looking about them. The ground was ravaged and mutilated bodies lay everywhere. Moans and cries from the wounded reached them.

'What a terrible waste of human life,' Robert murmured, before adding strongly, 'Come on, Alice, let's see what we can do. Look, there's William and Pips. Oh, and there's Hugh and Peter too, carrying someone.'

In fact, there were several stretcher bearers trying to ferry the wounded back to safety and to receive treatment as quickly as possible.

They worked for the next hour, bandaging minor wounds, staunching the flow of blood on more serious injuries and helping to carry the casualties back to the waiting ambulances.

'You shouldn't be here, Robert,' Pips said. 'You ought to be back at the post helping Giles.'

'You take the next load of walking wounded, Pips. Alice, you go with her now, help get them patched up and moved on. Phil and Mike will take them on to their posts. I'll come back with William on his next trip back, I promise.' He glanced around him. 'But there is still a lot I can do here yet. It can make the difference between survival and losing them.'

The two girls glanced at each other, shrugged and did as he suggested. Back at their first-aid post, Giles, Leonore and Brigitta were over-whelmed.

'Thank goodness, you've come back. Where's

Robert? He's needed here.'

'Coming back with William on the next trip. He'll be here soon.'

Fifty-Seven

'Pips? *Pips!* Where are you?'

Alice's voice was frantic. Pips finished the dressing on a soldier's arm and turned to see Alice weaving her way between the stretchers on the ground, their occupants still awaiting attention. The unit was overwhelmed with casualties and soon there would be even more; Robert would do what he could in the trenches but he would send the casualties back to the unit as soon as possible.

'Pips – come quickly. William has come back alone. Robert's been hit – wounded. Shot by a sniper. We have to go back with William to get him. He couldn't manage to carry him on his own and there are so many wounded out there...' Alice's voice faded away and she shook her head, unable to comprehend what was happening. It was all a terrible nightmare.

'Oh no,' Pips breathed. 'Is it – is it bad?'

Alice bit her lip and nodded. 'His arm – his right arm, Pips. William said it's – it's hanging off. That's why he couldn't pick him up and carry him on his back, else he would have done.'

Pips closed her eyes as her heart thudded painfully. For a moment, she felt she would faint but then she pulled in a deep breath. Robert! She must think of Robert. No time for the vapours. Her brother needed help.

'We'll go with William. Tell Leonore and – and Giles. He ought to know.'

As Pips sought her medical satchel and swiftly told Brigitta what had happened, Giles appeared. 'I'll go with Alice, Pips,' he said. 'You stay here.'

Pips shook her head. 'No,' she said hoarsely. 'I need to go. Please – don't try to stop me.'

'Then we'll all go. William can take Alice to attend to other wounded. We'll bring Robert in.'

'There isn't another vehicle. They're all ferrying the wounded back.'

'Then we'll take the car. You brought that back, didn't you? We'll manage something, but we must get him attended to as quickly as possible by the sounds of it. Come on, let's go.'

In that moment, Pips believed she had never loved Giles more than when he was willing to go out into danger to save her beloved brother.

Alice climbed into the ambulance beside William, and Giles, driving Dr Maitland's car, followed him with Pips.

The sound of shelling and gunfire grew louder as they neared the front line.

'I didn't realize it had started up again. It was all so quiet when I was here. Both sides were retrieving their wounded,' William said.

Leaving the vehicles, the four of them entered the trench system, hurrying through the channels, twisting and turning until they reached the very front line.

'Keep yer 'eads down,' a soldier, appearing from a dugout, yelled at them. 'God Almighty –

it's a couple of nurses. Wot you doin' here?'

'We've come to fetch a casualty,' Pips said. 'Dr Maitland. William...' She turned back to him. 'Where is he?'

'Out there, Pips. Up this ladder and just the other side of the barbed wire. There's a hole been cut. We can get through all right,' William said.

'You're going nowhere, sunshine. Can't you hear? There's a war going on. My captain'd have my guts for garters if I let you go over the top.'

'Sorry, sergeant,' Pips said, catching sight of the grubby insignia on his arm, 'but your captain isn't my captain and he can't stop us.'

'Well, I think he could, but he probably won't, seein' as you're rescuing our lads. I don't give much for your chances out there, though, but just so long as you know what you're doing, that's all.' He nodded grimly. 'Good luck – you're going to need it.'

William was first up the ladder leading the way. 'Keep as low as you can. Crawl, if you have to. That way, you're not such a target for snipers.'

One by one they climbed the ladder and, following in the steps of thousands of their countrymen, they went over the top of the trench side and crawled towards the barbed wire. Briefly, the shelling seemed to have stopped, but there was still the danger of snipers watching out for any movement that they could aim at. Now a pall of smoke drifted over the ground between the opposing trenches, hiding them briefly from the enemy.

'Oh my God – that's not gas, is it?' Pips muttered.

'Don't think so,' William panted, dragging a

stretcher after him. 'Keep going. We're nearly there.'

Reaching the barbed wire, William parted the vicious fencing for them to pass through without getting torn to shreds. 'About another ten yards and to the left of here. I left him in a shell hole.'

They stumbled in the direction William indicated, still keeping as low as they could. All around them they could hear the cries of wounded men, shouting for help. It tore at Pips's heart.

After only a couple of minutes, William said, 'This is it,' and Pips slithered down the side of the hole and landed beside Robert. He was lying on his back, his eyes closed, his face deathly pale. For a moment, Pips thought they were too late, but, as Giles arrived on his other side, she saw Robert's eyelids flicker.

'Robert, old chap, we're here,' Giles said. Quickly, he assessed the situation. William had fastened a tourniquet near Robert's shoulder, but his arm was hanging loosely beside him, scarcely still attached. It was clear that there was no saving the limb.

Giles loosened the tourniquet, allowing the blood to flow freely before reapplying it. 'We need to get him out of here.' But as he spoke a shell landed only a few feet away, scattering earth over them all.

'Pips, take off your headgear and wave it above the side of the shell hole. Maybe – just maybe – they'll respect it.'

'They'll think we're surrendering, won't they?'

Grimly, Giles said, 'We are – for the moment.'

William, crouching in the bottom of the pit with

339

Alice beside him, said, 'They're usually pretty good at respecting the stretcher bearers.' He smiled wryly. 'Else I doubt I'd still be here. We do the same for them when we know they're picking up their wounded and dead.'

'Right, I'll give it a try,' Pips said, putting her hands up to her head to remove her nurse's cap. But before she could do so, Alice had whipped her own from her head and said, 'Let me.' And she began to scramble up the side of the hole.

'Alice – Alice...' The word was a whisper from Robert's cracked lips, but the girl heard him and turned briefly, her eyes wide. 'Be – be careful,' he whispered, but then his eyes closed again and he lost consciousness. Pausing only a second, Alice stared at him, but then she scrabbled her way to the top and waved her white nurse's cap.

After a moment, they heard a voice shout loudly in German and Alice ducked her head before sliding back down. 'What's he saying?'

Scarcely able to believe it, Pips murmured, '"Hold your fire". That's what he said.'

'Are you sure?'

'She's right, Alice,' William said.

His sister stared at him. 'And when did you learn to speak German?'

'Since I've been out here – the important bits, that is.' Despite the seriousness of their situation, he grinned sheepishly, 'Brigitta's been teaching me.'

'Right, let's give it a try.'

It wasn't easy getting the dead weight of the unconscious man out of the shell hole, across the brief stretch of ground, through the barbed wire

340

and into their own trenches. It took the strength of all four of them to manage it. And even carrying him through the narrow passageways was difficult. How on earth did William do this? Pips was in awe not only of the young man's courage, but at his tenacity in doing such a perilous task day after day. And, she marvelled, never a word of complaint passed his lips.

Once back at the vehicles, they manoeuvred Robert onto the back seat of his father's car.

'I'll drive,' Pips said, 'you sit in the back with him, Giles.'

'Alice, I need you to stay with me,' William said. 'There are no other stretcher bearers available and you've seen for yourself just how many wounded are still out there.'

'But I...' Alice began, but then bit her lip. Her gaze was still on Robert, but bravely she nodded and stepped back as Pips climbed behind the wheel. William started the engine for her and then, with a brief wave, Pips turned the car round and drove away, aware that Alice was standing very still watching them go.

As they left, the shelling began again.

Fifty-Eight

Back at the unit, Robert was swiftly carried into the operating tent.

'You do realize I'm going to have to amputate his arm, don't you, Pips?' Giles said.

Dumbly, she nodded, tears glistening in her eyes. Would he survive and, if he did, what would he do for the rest of his life with only one arm? It was a future that Pips dared not contemplate; the only thing in her mind at this moment was to save her brother's life.

Giles worked swiftly. Leonore stood by, but Pips wanted to be the one to assist in the surgery and the older, more experienced, sister understood her reasons.

Alice and William returned late that night. Both were at the point of exhaustion, but Alice still found the strength to go to Robert's bedside to see how he was. She sat down beside him and took his left hand in hers. It was there that Pips found her at two o'clock in the morning, asleep with her head resting on his bed, his hand still firmly clasped in hers.

'Come along, my dear. You should get some proper rest.'

'But I...' Alice began again, but Pips was insistent. 'You're no good to him or to anyone else if you wear yourself out. We're all watching over him and I promise I'll tell you at once if there's any change.'

'You'll wake me up?'

'Of course,' Pips said and knew she would have to keep her promise.

Over the next several hours they watched for any sign of infection.

'I tried to clean the wound as much as possible,' William said, 'before I came back and he wasn't out there too long – not like some poor fellows – though he was covered in a shower of earth.'

'That's what can cause infection. If he gets gas

gangrene...' Giles said, but left the rest of the sentence unspoken. They all knew the consequences of that.

At three o'clock in the morning, Pips shook Alice gently awake. 'He's calling for you, Alice. He's delirious, but it's you he wants.'

'Is – is it infection?' Alice asked, as she scrambled out of bed and dressed hurriedly.

'We don't think so. But – but Giles says if he survives the night, then he'll pull through. He's seen this before. It's the shock of the injury and the aftermath of the amputation, he thinks.'

'He'll come through,' Alice muttered, more to herself than to Pips. 'He *has* to.'

She ran to the tent where Robert lay amongst other wounded; there was no space for him to be treated any differently. 'He wouldn't want it anyway,' Pips had said firmly. 'He'd want to be with the men.'

Alice sat with him through the rest of the night, sponging his face and giving him sips of water. She held him when he thrashed about in the bed, crying out in his delirium. Giles, Pips and the other nurses came often to look at him, glance sympathetically at Alice and then silently walk away. The girl, though officially unqualified, was doing everything that could be done. No one could do more for him than the devoted former lady's maid.

As dawn broke, Robert fell into a deep sleep. He was calmer now and not sweating so much. Giles came to take his pulse and feel his forehead. Pips was standing just behind him, holding her breath. At last, Giles stood up and he was smiling as he said, 'The fever's going. I really think he's going to be all right.'

Tears of relief and thankfulness ran down Alice's face and Pips had to swallow hard.

Robert had been lucky – if it could be called lucky to lose his right arm – he had not developed the dreaded infection.

Now Alice refused to leave his side. 'I'll take it as leave of absence, if you wish,' she told Leonore, who was responsible for drawing up the nursing duty rota.

'No need,' the sister said briskly. 'Pips has said she will do extra duty to cover for you.' She lowered her voice. 'And with all due respect to our other patients, he is rather special, being our doctor.'

Alice's face fell as the enormity of Robert's injury sank in. 'But he won't be any more, will he?'

'Sadly, no.'

'Have you – will you be sending for a replacement?'

'I have sent word to Dr Hazelwood through Mrs Parrott and he will make arrangements. Pips has informed their parents.' She paused and then added kindly, 'You do realize that as soon as he is fit enough to be moved, we will have to send him to a hospital and then home?'

'I – hadn't thought that far, but, yes, of course.'

Sister Leonore regarded the young girl. 'I expect you would like to accompany him?' It was a statement rather than a question, but Alice's head shot up and she gazed at the sister.

'Could I? I mean – aren't I needed here?'

Leonore smiled. 'Of course you are. You are a very valuable member of our team, but you've

344

been out here since the beginning, apart from that one trip home and the odd day or two's leave here. I think it's high time we got another nurse and allowed you some extended leave to take him all the way home.'

'We'd need to ask for Dr Hazelwood's approval, wouldn't we?'

Leonore's face lit up as she chuckled mischievously. 'I already have.'

'We must get him on a train home,' Pips declared. 'Alice, you must go with him.' Pips grasped her hand. 'Sorry, I mean, Alice, will you *please* go with him?'

Alice smiled tremulously. 'Of course, Pips. I've already agreed it with Sister Leonore.'

'Oh, that's good. I – *we* – don't want him left unattended for hours on end in a railway siding or on a platform.'

Worrying stories had filtered back to them of how the wounded on their way across France were left unattended for hours whilst priority was given to trains carrying troops, ammunition and supplies to the front. The wounded, it seemed, were at the bottom of the priority list. 'And you could help others nearby too, couldn't you?'

'You know I could, but I won't leave Robert alone.'

Pips gazed into the younger girl's eyes. Bluntly, she said, 'I do know you're in love with him, you know.'

For a moment, colour suffused Alice's face, but then she raised her head proudly.

'I've loved Robert for years, Pips, but I've

345

always known it could never come to anything.' She grimaced. 'After all, back home, I'm only a maid.'

Pips patted her hand absent-mindedly. 'You never know, Alice. This war will change everything. It really depends on what Robert feels for you and that is not for me to say. But just remember, it was you – not me – he was calling for when he was injured; it was you he wanted by his side after the operation and to tend him since.'

Alice shook her head. 'Oh Pips, half the men here fall in love with their nurses. I'm not going to start hoping based on that.'

'You're very sensible, but, like I say, you never know. But just for the moment, please get him home safely, won't you?'

'Hetty, my love, come into the parlour for a moment, will you?'

Henrietta's heart seemed to miss a beat as she saw her husband's serious face. Closing the door behind them, Edwin said, 'I've had a telegram...'

Before he could say more, she let out a cry and covered her mouth with her fingers.

'Robert has been seriously wounded, my love, but he is alive.'

'How?'

Edwin's voice was heavy with sorrow as he said, 'He has lost his right arm.'

Henrietta turned white and fell back against the sofa cushions.

'What happened? Why on earth was he in such danger?'

Edwin shook his head. 'I don't know, but Pips

has sent the telegram and she says a letter will follow.'

'That could take days,' Henrietta moaned. 'I need to know *now*. Can you get in touch with the authorities to see if they know any more?'

'I'll try,' was all Edwin could promise.

Thankfully, the letter reached them amazingly quickly.

When it was delivered, Henrietta carried it through to her husband's surgery waiting on tenterhooks until the patient he was seeing had left the room.

'I'm sorry, I must just have a word with the doctor,' she apologized to the two women who were still waiting.

Seeing her anxious face, they nodded. As she went into Edwin's room and closed the door, the two women whispered to each other. 'Reckon it's bad news by the look on her face, don't you?'

Inside the room, Henrietta said, 'You open it, Edwin. I just can't.'

Edwin tore it open and read the first few lines swiftly. 'He's all right. Giles amputated his arm with Pips assisting and, very soon, he'll be on his way home.'

'Oh my,' Henrietta murmured, her eyes filling with tears. 'How brave she is to do that for her brother.'

'She says that they're all sure he's going to be all right. There was no infection, which is the curse for all the wounded out there. Alice is to accompany him all the way home.'

'Not Pips?'

'No, she says Alice is coming with him.'

When he was well enough to be moved, Robert was taken by ambulance, with William driving, first to the casualty-clearing station at Poperinghe. Although it was a longer journey, they had chosen to take him there rather than to Albert, as they all knew the area, and the route home, so well.

'You're still here?' He smiled at Alice as she tucked him into a proper bed in the huge tented ward.

'Yes, you don't get rid of me that easily.'

'I don't want to, Alice,' he murmured, but then added more strongly, 'Aren't you needed at the unit?'

'Sister Leonore said I was long overdue a home leave, so I'm going to see you all the way back to Doddington Hall, spend a little time with my family and then – and then return to the unit.'

Robert grasped her hand tightly. 'No, Alice. Don't leave me. Stay with me. Please.'

'I'll stay as long as you want me to,' she whispered, 'but once you're home with your family, you won't need me.'

Slowly, he turned his head on the pillow towards her, his dark brown eyes gazing deeply into hers. 'I'll always want you beside me, Alice.' Then his eyes closed and he slept.

Alice felt as if her heart had turned over in her chest with love for him, but she was sensible enough to realize that this was a sick man clinging to his nurse for care and support. Despite what he said – and she believed that at this moment he meant every word – once he was back at home with his family, his need of her would evaporate.

But for the moment, he wanted and needed her, Alice Dawson. It was little comfort for the young woman, who had loved him devotedly for as long as she could remember, but it would have to be enough. No one could ever take away these precious few days she would spend with him.

As she turned away to see how she could help around the hospital now that Robert was well enough to be left for a while, she saw William hovering in the doorway.

'I must go back, but I just wanted to see that you were both all right.'

Alice smiled. 'We'll be fine. I'm going all the way home with him to see him safely settled back at the hall. And then I'll spend some time with our family. Have you any messages for them?'

He stared at her incredulously before saying harshly, 'No, I have not.' He turned on his heel and would have walked away from her without another word if she had not run after him and caught hold of his arm. 'William – don't go – not like that. You've no need to be bitter towards me, now have you?'

He stopped, turned and hugged her tightly. 'I'm sorry, Alice. I didn't mean it to be against you.'

'It's all right,' she said, returning his hug, but she said no more about their family. Instead, she added, 'Just take care of yourself. Promise me? And look out for Pips and all the others too.'

'I will,' was all he said.

Fifty-Nine

The journey across France to reach a coastal port and a ship to take them home was tortuous. But Robert's experience – and that of those on the same train – was made easier by Alice's presence. Her first duty was to him, but Robert himself insisted that she should help others too.

'They're my comrades,' he said. 'Do whatever you can for them, Alice.'

So Alice, with the help of the other nurses and orderlies travelling on the hospital train to care for the wounded, dressed their injuries, handed out soup and sandwiches and stayed with them if they were de-trained and had to wait for hours on a draughty platform for a connection that would take them to the next stage.

At last they boarded a ship.

'We'll soon be home now, Robert. We've sent word and your father is coming down to meet us.'

Robert reached for her hand and clasped it. 'Dear Alice. I wouldn't have survived without you by my side. You will stay with me, won't you? You won't go back straight away?'

Huskily, Alice said, 'I'll stay with you as long as you need me.'

Robert turned his head to look into her eyes as she leaned over him. 'I'll always need you, Alice.'

Dr Maitland was waiting at Charing Cross

Station to greet them.

'My boy,' he said gently as he knelt beside the stretcher as it was set carefully on the platform.

'Father,' Robert murmured and closed his eyes to blot out the anguish on Edwin's face.

'Let's get you home,' Edwin said. He looked at Alice for reassurance. 'Will he be all right sitting in the car?'

'He has to go to the hospital here in London first, Dr Maitland, just to be checked over before he travels any further, but I'm sure they'll transfer him to Lincoln hospital very soon.'

Edwin nodded as he stood up. Now, he could not speak. There was this great weight of sadness in his chest and yet there was joy too that his son had at least survived, albeit maimed for life. But Robert was home now – home for good – and they'd work together as a family to build a life for him.

At last, he found his voice and turned to clasp Alice's hand. 'My dear girl. How can I ever thank you for bringing him home? Now, once we've seen him to the hospital here, I will take you home to your parents. They need you. I can come back to fetch Robert when the hospital says he can be discharged.'

Robert's eyes flickered open. 'No, she stays with me. Don't leave me, Alice.'

She touched his shoulder and said softly, 'You know I won't.' Then she turned back to Edwin and said gently, but with a hint of firmness that he could not fail to notice. 'I have promised Robert that I will stay with him as long as he needs me and I will. I'm sure the hospital here will have plenty of work I can do for them so that I can be near him and yet be useful too.'

For a moment, Edwin was startled by the change in the family's former maid, but then his kindly nature recognized that all she had seen and endured had changed her, had given her a new-found confidence, and he respected her for it.

At that moment, two stretcher bearers came to carry Robert to a waiting ambulance. Alice touched Edwin's arm. 'We'll soon be home, and then you and Mrs Maitland will be able to see him as often as you want.'

Edwin nodded, his gaze never leaving his son as Robert was borne away and put into the back of the ambulance.

'I must go with him. Goodbye.' And without waiting for a response, she hurried away.

When Edwin arrived home, his face was sombre.

'Where is he?' Henrietta greeted him anxiously, her hands clasped together to stop them shaking. 'I thought you were bringing him home.'

'He had to be taken to the hospital in London first. We'll have to abide by the rules.'

'How is he?'

'Much as I expected, my love, but at least he is alive and he'll soon be back home. I hope they will release him into our care very shortly.'

'Is Pips with him?'

'No. Alice has accompanied him all the way like Pips told us she would. He seems to be relying on her heavily, but I suppose it's only natural.'

'He'll be better once we get him here,' Henrietta said confidently. 'I expect Alice will want to go back to Belgium, won't she?'

'Nothing's been said about that, but she did say she thought we'd be allowed to see him often when he's transferred to Lincoln hospital.'

'Allowed!' For a moment Henrietta was angry that anyone should even think of keeping her from her son's bedside. 'And what authority has *Alice* got, might I ask?'

Calmly, Edwin said, 'The authority of his nurse. You will notice a big change in your lady's maid, my love. I don't expect that she will ever return here in her former role. She has matured and found a new confidence and, I think, a new purpose. I suspect that will have happened to a great many young women who have been nursing in the war zone. Life will never be the same again for them as it was before the war started. Nor for the servicemen either. This will change the way of life as we have known it, Hetty, I fear, for ever.'

Sixty

Robert was greatly missed by his colleagues in Dr Hazelwood's flying ambulance corps, for it was two weeks before the great man himself came out to visit them and to bring a replacement doctor and another nurse with him.

'This is Dr Stephen Portas and Nurse Primrose Hill.'

Pips tried to keep a straight face, but failed.

The girl, a fresh-faced blonde with blue eyes

and a broad smile, grimaced. 'Yes, I know, it's a ridiculous name, isn't it? What my parents were thinking of, I don't know. I suppose they thought it cute when they were naming a little baby, but failed to realize I'd have to live with it all my life. By the way, I prefer to be called just "Rose", if that's all right.'

Pips liked the new arrival and warmed even more to her as she showed her the sleeping arrangements. 'We girls sleep in two tents,' she said, throwing back the flap and indicating the bed that Alice had vacated. 'You'll be in here with me.'

Rose bent and peered inside the tent. 'Mm,' she said, 'cosy.' And she laughed.

'Are you a trained nurse?'

'Yes. I've been nursing the war casualties in London, but when I heard Dr Hazelwood was looking for someone, I volunteered. I think I know what to expect as regards the injuries, but, of course, being out here will be very different to working in a clinically clean hospital.' She gazed at Pips with admiration. 'You've been out here since the very beginning, haven't you?'

Pips nodded. 'Almost. We came out here at the end of September 1914. We move around a lot too. Dr Hazelwood's idea is that we should always be where we're needed the most and that, of course, is wherever there's heavy fighting. Now, come along, we'll find you some tea and you must meet the others.'

Dr Stephen Portas was an older man, in his late forties or even early fifties, Pips judged. He'd recently lost his wife and as his two children were grown up, he'd decided to offer his services somewhere at the war front. He, too, hearing that Dr Hazelwood was looking for a replacement, had volunteered. He was quiet but friendly, and said at once to Giles, 'I want you to be regarded as the senior doctor out here, Giles. This is going to be very different for me, so, please, just tell me what you want me to do.' He held out his hand to Giles. 'I think we'll get along very well together. You seem to have a very strong team around you and I wouldn't want to disrupt that in any way. I'm sure Nurse Hill feels exactly the same.'

Rose nodded at once. 'Yes, just–'

At that moment the sound of a shell burst drowned whatever she had been going to say. She let out an involuntary squeal and even Stephen was startled. The sound of a shrill whistle in the distance followed and Pips said seriously, 'You'll get used to it. But that whistle means they're going over the top. I'll see you later.'

Hugh, Peter and William were already running to their ambulances.

'William, wait for me,' Pips shouted, as she scooped up her medical satchel and ran across the grass towards him.

It was two weeks before the hospital in London would release Robert to be taken to Lincoln hospital and a further week before he was discharged into his parents' care. 'And that,' the ward sister explained to Edwin, 'is only because you are a doctor.'

Alice came with him and settled Robert into his old bedroom. He was getting up each day now for a few hours, but soon grew tired. Henrietta spent several hours a day reading to him and talking with him, but it was always Alice he asked for, his gaze following her as she moved quietly about the room. Soon, Henrietta grew impatient with his reliance on the girl.

'Alice should go to see her parents before she goes back abroad.'

He turned his head sharply on the pillow. 'Go back? Alice isn't going back. She's staying here with me.'

'There's no need, Robert. She would be much more use at the front alongside Pips and the others. We have the means in place now to care for you here.'

'But I want Alice,' he said, in a petulant tone his mother had never heard him use before. 'She promised me she would stay with me as long as I needed her. And I do need her.'

Henrietta regarded her son thoughtfully. He was a damaged young man, not only physically, but mentally and emotionally too. She didn't quite know how to handle this situation and decided she must talk to Edwin.

'Very well, my dear,' she said softly. 'But I feel you should let her at least visit her family for an hour or so. Perhaps whilst you have your afternoon rest. Would that be all right?'

'Well, yes, I suppose so. As long as she promises not to be away long.'

'Is this normal behaviour, Edwin, in the circumstances?'

Edwin sighed. 'Possibly, my love. Many patients, especially the wounded, who perhaps owe their

356

lives to the ministrations of their nurses, imagine themselves in love with the one who has had the caring of them.'

'You mean – you mean, you think Robert believes he has fallen in love with Alice?'

'At this moment in time, yes, I do.'

'And I suppose she will, no doubt, be in love with him.' Her tone was heavy with sarcasm. 'But what will happen when he recovers and realizes it was just a fleeting infatuation because of the unusual circumstances?'

Edwin regarded her solemnly. 'But who, my love, is to say that it is? Perhaps they really are in love with each other.'

His wife's face was a picture of horrified incredulity.

Sixty-One

'I've heard from my father,' Pips told Giles. 'Robert's safely home.'

'Is Alice coming back?'

'He doesn't say, but it doesn't sound like it. He says that Robert will hardly let her out of his sight.' She pulled a face and chuckled. 'Oh dear, that is going to be such a shock for my mother.'

'A shock? What do you mean?'

'My brother falling in love with a lady's maid. A *former* lady's maid,' she corrected herself.

'Mm, I see what you mean. Do you think they are in love?' He touched her face with gentle

357

fingers. 'Like us?'

Pips grasped his hand and looked deep into his eyes. 'Oh, I think so.' She paused and whispered, 'When can we get away again?'

'Not until this is all over.'

'What! You mean the war?'

'No – no, here on the Somme. We can't take leave just now, especially as Stephen and Rose are still settling in. He's very good – very competent – but he does look to me for leadership.'

'You're right, of course. It's just that – I miss you.'

'I know,' he said softly, and his eyes caressed her.

She shivered with frustrated excitement and turned away. 'I'd better be about my work before I make a fool of myself.'

Alice walked down the road from the hall towards her parents' cottage. Autumn was in the air and, whilst she would not wish to be anywhere else other than where she was at this moment, her thoughts turned to those back at the front and the winter that faced them. She was feeling strangely nervous, but couldn't really put into words why. Perhaps it was because there had been a huge shift in her relationship with the Maitland family. Not only had her position changed radically with Pips, but now Robert seemed so dependent on her. Though Mrs Maitland had not altered; she still treated Alice as the servant she'd always been. Alice smiled a little at the thought. Poor Mrs Maitland; she wasn't coping very well with a rapidly changing world, even though her fund-raising efforts and war work were unsurpassable.

Robert had told her that his mother had begun visiting the convalescing soldiers, whose families did not live locally, in Lincoln hospital.

Ma Dawson was sitting outside puffing at her pipe and well wrapped up against the autumnal chill.

'Well, well, fancy seeing you here.' She smiled at Alice. 'We heard you was home.'

'Sorry I haven't been down before, but Robert needed me.'

'Robert, is it now? Not *Master* Robert any more?'

Alice sat down beside her on the wooden seat. 'No, nor is it Miss Pips, though I still call the mistress Mrs Maitland and slip in the odd "ma'am" to keep her happy.'

'Is there owt between you and Master Robert?' Ma laughed throatily. 'Sorry, but I can't call him owt else, lass.'

'To tell you the truth, Ma, I don't know. I've loved him for years, but I don't know how he feels about me. You see, a lot of wounded soldiers grow close to their nurses. They're vulnerable, far from home and they need – oh, I don't know – a woman's affection, I suppose.'

'And how many fell in love with you, Alice?' Ma laughed.

'Oh dozens, but I never took it seriously.'

'Good lass. You did right. Besides,' she sighed, 'if you fancy yourself in love with the young master… But don't get hurt, me little love. He's way above your station in life, and his parents – well, certainly his mother – wouldn't take kindly to it.'

'No, I realize that. Don't worry, Ma. I know exactly how the land lies and I won't get my heart broken. But there is someone I do worry about. Pips. I just wonder if, when the war's over, things'll still be the same for her.'

'Nothing'll ever be the same again,' Ma said sadly. 'How can it be now we've lost three of our boys?'

'What?'

'Oh duck, didn't you know?'

Alice's heart hammered in her chest as she asked shakily, 'Know what?'

'About Bernard and Roy?'

Alice shook her head and asked hoarsely, 'Tell me.'

'No disrespect to Alice,' Giles said as he and Pips took a walk in the dusk after another hard day, 'but this new nurse is proving a godsend. It's really good to have three fully qualified nurses in the unit. She's even better at assisting with operations than Leonore is. I've tactfully suggested that she should help me most of the time, leaving Leonore to oversee the nursing side. We've so many serious cases now that cannot be moved straight away, Leonore really is more useful caring for the post-op patients.'

'What about Stephen?'

'He's very good, though he's not a surgeon and won't touch a scalpel, so all the ops are falling on me. I know Robert wasn't a trained surgeon as such, but out here he'd watched me so often and had learned to do minor ones that relieved me a bit. He'd have made a very competent surgeon one day.'

'Stephen's skills in treatment and care are great, though, aren't they?'

'Absolutely.'

'Ought you to ask Dr Hazelwood if he can find another surgeon to join us?'

Giles wrinkled his brow. 'I could, I suppose. We'll see how it goes up to Christmas. I expect Dr Hazelwood will come out again then as usual.'

Out of sight of the unit, Pips linked her arm through his. 'How much longer do you think this particular battle will go on? We're into October now, and I really thought when those monstrous tanks arrived that it'd all be over pretty quickly, not just here on the Somme, but the whole war.'

Pips had felt incredibly proud the first time she'd seen a tank – designed and manufactured in Lincoln – thundering across no-man's-land towards the enemy in the middle of September.

She'd laughed out loud. 'That'll *frighten* them to death.'

But, for a few precious moments, all thoughts of the war were forgotten, as, hidden by some trees, Giles took her in his arms and kissed her. 'Let's hope this particular skirmish is over very soon and we can get away together for a break,' he murmured against her lips. 'Oh Pips, I want you so much. If only...'

Sixty-Two

'Robert, you're so much better now,' Alice said. 'I really should be getting back.'

'Back where?' he asked sharply.

'To the front, or at least to some kind of war work. Since I heard about Bernard and Roy, I need to keep busy. I need to *do* something. If you don't need me quite so much, maybe...' She waited, holding her breath in case he should say no, I don't need you any more. 'I could help out at Lincoln hospital.'

Robert gazed at her lovely face and held out his hand to her. 'Please – come here and sit beside me. What I do need is to talk to you.'

She sat down, her heart beating a little faster. Was this it? Was he going to tell her that he was, like she'd said, so much better that he could release her from her promise?

'Alice,' he said softly, 'my darling Alice, you must know how I feel about you.'

Her heart felt as if it flipped over and then began to beat rapidly. Unable to speak, she shook her head.

'I love you, dearest girl. I can't let you go because I want you to stay with me. Alice Dawson, will you do me the honour of becoming my wife?'

Alice gasped and felt colour flood her face. She stared at him with wide eyes. 'Oh Robert – *Master* Robert – I – we can't possibly. What would your mother say?'

Robert laughed. 'It's what *you* say that matters, darling.' His face fell for a moment. 'Don't you love me? Is that it?'

'No, no, of course not. I mean – of course I love you. I think I always have.'

'If that's true, then I've been a blind fool.'

She shook her head. 'We've been together – out there – thrown together in extraordinary circumstances. Then you were injured and I nursed you. I want you to be sure it's not just a – a wartime romance.'

'No, Alice, I know it isn't. I promise you it isn't.'

There was silence between them as they gazed at each other, the love shining out of their faces. At last he said softly, 'You haven't answered my question.'

'It'll cause trouble.'

He shrugged. 'So? If we can get through what we've experienced out there, we can weather a few storms at home, now, can't we? Is it my mother you're thinking of?'

'And your father. And my family too. They'll think I'll get hurt – Ma – my grandmother – has already said as much.'

Robert chuckled. 'And how come she knows about it?'

Alice blushed again. 'Because I told her I was in love with you, but that I didn't think it could ever come to anything.'

He squeezed her hand. 'Oh, it's come to something, Alice Dawson, you'd better believe it. But please – please, put me out of my misery. Are you going to say "yes"?'

'Of course I am.'

'It won't do, Robert. Have you taken leave of your senses? She's a maid in this house, for heaven's sake.' Henrietta was angry. Very angry. But the angrier his mother grew, the calmer Robert became.

'Dearest Mother, I wouldn't want to hurt or upset you in any way. You must know that. But Alice is no longer a maid of any sort. We have shared danger together and grown close and–'

'Exactly!' Henrietta said triumphantly. He had unwittingly played into her hands. 'You've been out there under enormous pressure, so of course your emotions are heightened and you've imagined yourself in love with her. Added to which, presumably there were no other girls there of your class–'

'Mother!' Now Robert was angry too. They faced each other as she stood at the end of his bed. Deliberately, he tried to calm himself. He had no wish to fall out with his mother but he was determined to marry Alice, even if it meant they would have to leave the hall and live elsewhere. But Henrietta was not finished yet.

'Robert, you're not thinking logically. You are the heir to the hall and its estate. Do you really think Alice can become the "lady of the manor"?'

Robert smiled wryly. 'Is that how you think of yourself, Mother?'

'It's how the villagers see me,' she shot back. 'You would be taking Alice out of her class. She would be lost and lonely because no one would know how to treat her.'

'They would treat her as *my wife* or I'd want to know the reason why.'

Henrietta glared at him, not knowing what to say next. 'I'll have to ask your father to speak to you.'

'You do that, Mother, but my answer will be the same.'

Henrietta stalked towards the door and pulled it open.

'Oh and by the way, if you're thinking of disinheriting me, then go ahead. Pips would make a much better heir than me.'

Henrietta muttered something beneath her breath and went through the door, slamming it behind her.

'Oh no, I'm not going to allow that,' Len said. 'Whatever are you thinking of, girl? How much more shame is to be heaped on my head? First William disgraces us, and now you.'

Alice gasped and stared at him. 'How can accepting a proposal of marriage from the future master of the hall be a disgrace?'

'Because you're stepping out of your class. Marriages like that never work. Norah,' he rounded on his wife, 'have you been filling her head with romantic nonsense?'

Norah cringed under his anger, but it was Ma who spoke up, 'This is the first your wife has heard of it, Len, so pipe down, will you, and let's discuss this rationally.'

Len swung round on her, pointing his finger at her. 'I've warned you before. I'm head of this house and you live here under my benevolence.'

Ma stared at him. 'D'you know, lad, over these last two years since this wretched war started, I've sometimes thought it might be a lot pleasanter living in the workhouse than here and that says a lot, doesn't it? I've been grateful to you, Len, giving me a home all these years, but I'm still your mother and I won't be spoken to like that or threatened. So, if that's how you really feel, I'll go upstairs right this minute and pack my bags.'

'Aye well, you can go, then.'

'Len!' Now it was Norah who was shocked.

He rounded on her. 'And you can go, an' all. I blame the pair of you for all the trouble we've had. You made a coward out of William, encouraging him to work at the hall instead of with me and his brothers where I could have made a man of him. And then you let *her* go abroad with Miss Pips. I knew no good would come of her getting too close to that family. And now look what's happened.'

The three women stared at each other in turn. There was nothing any of them could think of to say in the face of Len's anger.

'I'd better get back,' Alice murmured at last.

'Aye, go back,' Len shouted, shaking his fist at her. 'Go to him, but don't come running back here when he changes his mind. You've made your bed, you'd better lie on it.'

'I wonder how Robert is getting on,' Pips said. 'I haven't had a letter from home in ages.'

They were on their way to the coast for a two-day break. The slaughter of the Somme had eased, but all the members of Dr Hazelwood's corps were exhausted, none more so than Giles, who'd taken on the sole burden of surgery after Robert's injury. It had been a soul-destroying experience for all of them.

'Mm.' Giles seemed distracted and the rest of the journey was completed in silence.

When they arrived at their favourite hotel, Giles threw himself on the bed and fell asleep. Pips moved quietly about the room unpacking her belongings, then she lay down beside him, but sleep eluded her. She longed to be in Giles's arms, to love and be loved, but he was snoring gently beside her. At last, she dozed. Later, when he is rested, she promised herself...

But Giles did not wake, not even for dinner, and Pips ate alone in the dining room, after which she took a brief walk in the dark November night along the beach. Back in the room, Giles was still not awake. Gently she covered him with the eider-down without disturbing him, undressed and slipped into the bed beside him. She lay awake for a long time, staring into the darkness and longing for his touch. But Giles slept on.

In the morning, he was apologetic, but Pips brushed it aside. 'You were shattered, I could see that.' She put her arms around him. For a moment he resisted until she said, 'It's all right, Giles. I understand. Really. We'll just use this as a complete rest, if that's what you want.'

'It's not what I want,' he muttered, 'but I'm just so damned tired.'

'Hardly surprising.' She kissed the top of his head as he leaned his cheek against her breast. 'We've been going non-stop since the beginning of July and then we've had to cope with Robert's injury. It must have been hard for you to operate on your friend.'

'It was, but even harder for you to assist when he's your brother.'

'Alice was a brick. It wasn't easy for her either, not when she's in love with him.'

Giles looked up at her. 'Is she? I hadn't realized until you mentioned it.'

Pips chuckled. 'Men don't notice these things. Even Robert had been unaware until I told him.'

'You told him? Why?'

'Because he's in love with her too. Surely that was obvious from the way he wouldn't let her out of his sight after the operation, and insisted she go all the way back to England with him. And she hasn't come back, has she?'

Giles was thoughtful for a moment before murmuring, 'I wouldn't be in Robert's shoes when your mother gets to hear about it.'

Pips wrinkled her brow. 'You're right. I really hadn't given much thought to Mother's reaction. Oh dear!' She collapsed in gales of laughter. 'Poor Robert.'

Though they took gentle walks on the beach despite the wintry weather, and lay in each other's arms at night, they did not make love. Pips was disappointed and not a little hurt, but she tried to tell herself that it was merely because Giles was worn out. Next time, everything would be all right.

When they returned to the unit there was a letter waiting for Pips from home and, to her surprise, it was from her mother. Henrietta had never written to her. Edwin had written regularly, sending loving messages from Henrietta, but this was the first time she'd written herself. Pips tore open the letter anxiously, fearing something must be wrong. Had Robert taken a turn for the worse, or was her father ill with the burden of carrying on his practice alone when he had expected to be able to take things a bit easier with Robert working alongside him?

The letter was surprisingly, short but to the point.

Pips, you will have to come home. Robert is being ridiculously stupid, saying he is going to marry Alice. We need your support to stop this catastrophe.

Pips sought out Giles. 'Do you think you could spare me for a week or so? I really must go home to support Robert and Alice.'

'You're going to side with them against your parents?' he asked, sounding surprised.

'I most certainly am,' Pips said, determinedly.

Giles pulled a face. Obviously, he didn't agree with her, but all he said was, 'We can manage here, now things are quieter. Let's hope they stay that way for a while.'

'It usually quietens down during the worst of the winter. This'll be the third one we've faced. When is it going to end, Giles? When will we be able to get on with our lives?'

Giles shrugged. 'I only wish I knew,' he said flatly. He put his arms around her and kissed her cheek. 'Safe journey.'

Sixty-Three

Pips arrived in England on 27 November and decided to stay the night in London before travelling to Lincolnshire the following day. Next morning, as she walked along the street to the station, she heard a noise above and glanced up to see a single aeroplane in the sky. She stopped to watch it. Several more pedestrians followed suit and even traffic slowed to a halt, drivers leaning out to look up.

Something fell from the plane and hurtled to earth some distance away. No one moved, but they watched in horror as it exploded on impact. The plane banked and flew away, its mission – to drop a bomb on London – accomplished.

'We've had Zeppelin raids,' she heard one man say, 'but I reckon that's the first aeroplane that's reached us.' He shook his head. 'I don't like the look of this.'

Pips hurried to the railway station, hoping that they wouldn't have cancelled the service. The trains did keep running, but suffered delays and she didn't reach Lincoln until late evening. She took a taxi to Doddington Hall.

'My dear girl,' Edwin held out his arms to her as he emerged from the parlour, 'why ever didn't you let us know you were coming? I'd've met you at the station. I have another car now. I really need one in the winter for my rounds.'

For a moment, Pips clung to him, not realizing until this moment just how much she had missed her father. Then she pulled back and kissed his cheek. 'I couldn't let you know because the train service was disrupted. There was an air raid on London. Just a single plane, true, but it must have caused damage and probably loss of life.'

'An aeroplane, you say? I'd heard they'd had Zeppelin raids, but not a plane.'

'I overheard someone saying he thought it was the first time a plane had reached the city.'

'Come along in. Sarah will take your suitcase up to your room. Are you hungry?'

'Starving.' Pips grinned.

'Then we'll get something on a tray for you.'

She turned as her mother came into the room.

'Thank you for coming, Philippa. We have to put a stop to this nonsense. I thought he might listen to your common sense.'

For the moment, Pips said nothing. She would wash away the grime of her travels first and then have something to eat. And before launching into an argument with her mother, she would see Robert.

A little later, she entered his bedroom. Although he was now able to come downstairs in the daytime, by evening he was weary and retired to bed early. Alice was sitting by his bedside holding his hand. As Pips opened the door and entered the room, they both looked startled.

'What on earth are you doing here?' Robert smiled. 'Is the war over and we haven't heard?'

She moved towards them, hugged Alice and kissed Robert's cheek.

'I only wish it was,' she said, sitting down on the opposite side of the bed to Alice. 'But after what they are beginning to call the Battle of the Somme, things have quietened down. I expect they'll remain that way through the winter. Let's hope so.'

Robert's face clouded. 'It was horrific, wasn't it? So many killed and wounded.'

'Did you know about my brothers, Pips? Bernard and Roy? Killed on the same day somewhere on the Somme.'

'Yes. Father wrote to tell me soon after you and Robert had left. I'm so sorry. And I told William.'

Alice nodded and tears filled her eyes. Pips noticed that Robert squeezed her hand.

'They've sort of lost all their children now,' Alice said, with a catch in her voice.

'Are they still adamant about William?'

'Yes, and now, they're going to disown me if – if I marry Robert.'

Pips gasped. This was something she had not expected. She wasn't surprised by her mother's reaction to the news, but she couldn't understand why the Dawsons would disapprove.

'Why?'

'They think I would be marrying above myself. Out of my class, my father said.'

Pips laughed wryly. 'Don't they realize that this war will most probably destroy such barriers? A generation of young men from all classes of society will have been wiped out.'

'I don't think any of them realize yet what a totally different world we're going to be living in,' Robert murmured. He paused and then added, 'But you haven't answered my question, Pips.

372

Why are you here?'

'I was summoned – by Mother – to come home and talk some sense into you, Brother dear.'

He frowned. 'And are you going to try?'

'Certainly not. I heartily approve of you marrying Alice, but that's only if you're both absolutely sure that you truly love each other and that this isn't just because you were thrown together in such emotional circumstances.'

'We are sure – we've discussed it.' Robert tried to reassure her, but seeing the look of adoration in his eyes when he looked at Alice, Pips knew there would be no separating them, however hard her mother and Len Dawson tried.

Pips couldn't help a moment's envy. It was the same look that Giles had had for her when they'd first declared their love for each other, but just recently... Hastily, she quashed her own doubts. Their last few days away together hadn't been as blissful as earlier trysts, but Giles, she conceded, was feeling the weight of the sole responsibility for operations. But if Robert and Alice felt for each other half of what she and Giles did, then no one would prevent this marriage. And she certainly wasn't going to try.

When she returned downstairs, her mother greeted her. 'Have you seen Robert? Have you managed to talk some sense into him?'

Pips sat down on the sofa between her parents' seats on either side of the fireplace.

'I have seen him, yes. In fact, I've seen them both,' Pips said carefully. What she was about to say was going to hurt her mother, she knew.

Henrietta gave a click of exasperation. 'She's up

373

there again, is she?' She sighed. 'So?'

Pips ran her tongue around her lips. 'Mother, I'm sorry, but I can't agree with you. They are obviously so in love. It would be cruel – and I believe useless – to try to stop them being together.'

Henrietta glared at her daughter. 'I might have known I couldn't count on you. I don't know why I bothered asking you to come home. I thought – obviously mistakenly – that now you'd found a nice young man of your own class, you would understand. Philippa, Robert is heir to the hall and all that that entails. Can you really see Alice Dawson as mistress of all this?' She waved her hand to encompass the room and the house and lands beyond.

Before she could answer, her father put down the newspaper he had been pretending to read and cleared his throat.

'Hetty, my love, this marriage is going to take place whether you or the Dawsons approve or not. I think you should resign yourself to it, or I fear you may lose your son.'

'Don't tell me you approve of it, Edwin?'

'I'm sorry, Hetty, but yes I do. I want whatever makes Robert happy. His life – if not exactly ruined – has been drastically altered by his injury. We must allow him to make his own choices.'

Henrietta glared at him for a moment and then stood up suddenly. 'Then I have no more to say on the matter.' With disapproval and disappointment in every movement, she left the room.

'Oh dear,' Edwin said mildly, picking up his paper again. 'I think I'm going to be in the doghouse for some time.'

Pips chuckled quietly. 'Well, we'll be there together, Father.'

To her great surprise, Edwin actually winked at her.

A little later, when Henrietta had retired, Pips asked her father, 'Are you really happy about Robert and Alice?'

Edwin folded his newspaper and laid it aside. 'I am, Pips. I was impressed by her when I first met them at the station in London and I have watched her since. Her devotion to him is obvious. I just hope that his love for her isn't just because she has – in my opinion – saved his life. Oh, I know Giles did the operation and you assisted–' he glanced at her – 'that was very courageous of you, my dear, but it's her care since that has brought him safely all the way home to us.'

'I agree, Father, but I don't think you need have any qualms about his feelings. I saw it start – out there – before he was wounded. I'm as sure as I can be that it's mutual.'

Edwin nodded and smiled. 'Thank you, Pips. You have eased my mind.'

There was a pause as the fire settled in the grate, sending a shower of sparks up the chimney.

'How are you coping with the practice on your own? There must be even more work for you in the village with the returning wounded, to say nothing of the illnesses brought on by the anxieties – and sometimes heartbreak – that the families of soldiers are having to live with every day.'

Edwin sighed. 'It's not easy, I'll admit. But perhaps, as Robert recovers, he'll be able to help me in some way, if not exactly as we'd planned.'

'I hope so, Father, but I'm afraid his recovery is going to take some time.'

'I very much fear you're right, Pips.'

The following morning, Pips sought out Jake.

Averting her eyes from Midnight's empty stable, she asked him, 'How are you? Still finding plenty of work now – now there are no horses?'

'I've taken over looking after the garden and the grounds, Miss Pips, like William used to do. How is he?'

'He's fine. Doing a grand job.'

Jake nodded. 'I aren't going to volunteer, miss, but if I get called up, then of course I'll go.'

'Very wise, Jake. Let's hope it's all over before then.'

He grinned suddenly. 'Trouble is, miss, no one knows me real age, so when they'll call me up is anyone's guess.'

Pips laughed as she turned away to take a walk through the gardens before returning indoors. The atmosphere in the house was uneasy, to say the least. She contemplated visiting the Dawsons, but she didn't want to get into an argument with them. With the loss of their three sons and now the news that Alice intended to marry Robert, they had enough to deal with.

And sadly, there were no messages for them from William.

At the beginning of December, Pips was surprised to receive a letter from Leonore.

I'm writing to let you know that we are moving back to Brandhoek, to our old stamping ground, so you will know where to come to when you come back. We are all delighted to hear that Alice and Robert are to be married and understand that you will want to stay for the wedding if it is to be soon. But please, don't stay away too long. We need you here and we all miss you. Oh, and I nearly forgot, Captain Allender is also back here with his company...

Pips folded the letter thoughtfully. She was surprised to hear from Leonore – not that her letter wasn't welcome – but she wondered why Giles had not written to her at all during the time she had been at home.

Robert and Alice were married quietly a week later, before Pips felt she must return to Belgium. The ceremony took place in the church close to the hall and there would be no official honeymoon. Robert was not fit enough to travel far. Breaking with tradition, Ma Dawson gave the bride away. Len refused to attend the ceremony, though Edwin had managed to persuade his own wife to attend.

'Hetty, you will regret it for the rest of your life if you don't go to Robert's wedding. And remember, my love, Pips will undoubtedly give you the wedding of the year when she and Giles come back from the war.'

At last, Henrietta had seen his reasoning and had grudgingly given her consent to Robert and Alice having rooms of their own within the hall.

At the marriage ceremony, no one noticed Norah sneak into the rear of the church. When the bride and groom disappeared into the vestry, she slipped out again. No one had seen her come or go, but Norah was not going to miss her daughter's wedding whatever the consequences might be. She told no one, and after a couple of weeks, she began to breathe easily. Len had not found out.

Perhaps the most embarrassing time for Alice had been facing her former colleagues, the rest of the servants at the hall. It had been worse, she thought, than facing Mrs Maitland's disapproval. When the news of her impending marriage to Robert had broken, she'd gone to the kitchen to talk to them. Mrs Warren and Mrs Bentley were a formidable pair to face, but Alice took a deep breath. 'I expect you've heard the news.'

'Aye, we have.' Their expressions were disapproving and yet there was a look of apprehension in their eyes too.

'You've done well for yourself, lass. You kept that dark.'

Alice shrugged, feeling a little braver now. 'It happened out there, Mrs Warren. We worked together and grew close.'

'Are you sure, lass, really sure, that he loves you?' the cook asked, and now her tone was gentler, more concerned. 'That it's not just because you were thrown together and then his awful injury...'

'Mrs Bentley, I've loved Master Robert secretly for years. Even if – even if he doesn't love me in quite the same way as I love him, it's a risk I'm prepared to take.'

The cook shrugged. 'There's nowt more to say then, duck. We wish you well. Of course we do.

378

But it's going to be difficult for us, having to take orders from you.'

Now Alice laughed. 'I hope that won't be happening for a very long time. Nothing will change in the running of the household. Robert and I are to have our own rooms, that's the only difference.'

'It'll mean more work for the housemaids...' Mrs Warren began, but Alice interrupted her. 'I'll be quite happy to clean our rooms myself and to help out in the kitchen when needed. I'll need something to keep myself occupied.'

'Oh, that would never do,' Mrs Warren said primly. 'You'll be mistress of this house one day and–'

'But not yet and, like I said, hopefully not for a long time.'

'Not until we're in the workhouse, Mrs Warren, to end our days,' Mrs Bentley said.

Alice was shocked. 'I am sure Mrs Maitland would never see that happen.'

'Aye, but what about you, when we can no longer work?'

'Robert would never let that happen – and neither would I.'

'Aye, well, only time will tell.'

'Will you all come to the wedding? It's only going to be very quiet, but we'd like you to come.'

Mrs Bentley smiled. 'We'll be there, and I'll do you a grand spread for your wedding breakfast. That we can do for you.'

Sixty-Four

The marriage of the future master of the hall to his mother's lady's maid was, of course, the talk of the district and, on the day, most of the women of the village had lined the path to the church. Some had even been bold enough to go into the church and to sit at the back, Bess Cooper amongst them. But not one of them noticed Norah come and go; they were too intent on watching the ceremony.

Pips planned to return to Belgium just before Christmas.

'Can't you stay until the New Year?' Henrietta asked.

'I'd love to, Mother, but I must get back. And there are all these wonderful parcels for me to take too. Your fund-raising is amazing. I can't tell you how much everything you send is so needed and appreciated. And now, I must go and see if I can have a few moments with my brother.'

'How – how do you think he is, Pips? Be honest with me.' Henrietta's face was creased with anxiety and sadness at her son's dreadful injury.

Gently, Pips said, 'Give him time, Mother. He'll be fine. It was the right thing for him to marry Alice, you know.'

Henrietta bit her lip and whispered, 'But what is he going to do with the rest of his life?'

Moved by her mother's distress, Pips put her

arms around her. 'Learn how to run the hall and its estate, for one thing. And I'm going to see him now to ask him to keep writing to me.'

'But he can't write – not now.'

Pips chuckled. 'He'll have to learn to write with his left hand. That'll be a challenge in itself.' Then her tone sobered as she added softly, 'He has come back, Mother. Just hold on to that. So many don't.'

For a moment Henrietta clung to her. 'I know. I know how thankful I should be. And, Pips, do take care of yourself, won't you?'

Pips kissed Henrietta's forehead and promised, 'Of course I will.'

It was a rare display of affection between mother and daughter and both of them would remember it.

'And now,' Pips said briskly. 'I must find Robert.'

Henrietta sighed. 'He'll be where he spends most of his time. In his bedroom.'

'Then we must prise him out of there.'

A few moments later, Pips knocked on his door and entered the room that Robert and Alice now shared. 'Are you decent?' she called out, laughter in her voice.

'Come in, Pips,' Alice called out.

Robert was sitting near the window, fully dressed, but obviously with no intention of venturing from the sanctuary of his room. Now that he had gone through the ordeal of appearing in public for his wedding, he was sinking back into depression.

'I have a suggestion,' Pips said, coming straight to the point as she sat beside him on the window seat. 'You know how it is out there. We're in the thick of it, and yet we never hear the news as to how the war is really going. Now, I want you to write to me and tell me all that you read in the newspapers – *and* what you hear from dear old Basil.'

'How can I? One, I can't write and two, it'd never get past the censor.'

'Item one,' Pips said. 'Learn to write with your left hand, and two, surely you haven't forgotten our code?'

Robert stared at her, then, slowly, a smile spread across his face. 'No,' he said softly, 'I haven't.'

When either of them had been away from home – Robert at medical school and Pips at boarding school, which she'd hated – they'd devised a code between them based on their mutual love of chess. They'd pretended they were conducting a game by post and they had written any sentences they didn't wish prying eyes to see at the end of a normal letter as if it was a list of chess moves.

'There you are, then. Until you get practised at writing with your left hand, Alice can write for you, but that's only at first.' Pips wagged her finger at him. Then she turned to Alice, who was looking mystified. Even she hadn't been privy to this particular secret. 'Help him out, Alice, but make him persevere with the writing.'

'I will,' the new Mrs Maitland promised.

The night before Pips's departure, the five of them had dinner together. Pips had bullied Robert into leaving his room, and so it was the first time Alice had sat at the table as a member of the family and

Pips could see that she was nervous. She decided to make light of it to ease the tension.

'You know, Alice, you're like a cat on hot bricks. I keep expecting you to leap up at any minute and help Mr Wainwright serve.'

Alice giggled nervously. 'I just don't feel right, Pips, sitting here with the master and the mistress.'

'They're not your master and mistress now, Alice,' Pips leaned forward and tried to keep the laughter from her voice, 'they're your father-in-law and mother-in-law.'

Alice's face was a picture and everyone around the table laughed, even Henrietta.

As the main course was served, Robert murmured, 'Darling, could you...?'

At once, Alice moved his plate in front of her and deftly cut up his meat so that he could eat with just his fork in his left hand. It was done with no fuss, no calling attention to his predicament, and Pips saw his grateful wink at his wife as she neatly replaced his plate in front of him and took her own.

And, as Alice gazed at him, adoration in her eyes, no one sitting around the table could have any doubt of the love they had for each other. Seeing it, Pips couldn't wait to leave the following morning to begin her journey back to Giles.

'You know, Mother,' Pips said, as dinner came to an end, 'there's one thing I don't think you have thought of.'

Henrietta frowned. 'Oh, and what's that?'

'With Alice now part of the family and destined to live here at the hall, probably for the rest of her life, the tapestries will always be well cared for.'

Edwin's eyes widened and even Robert glanced nervously at his mother, whilst Alice whispered worriedly, 'Oh Pips!'

Pips met her mother's stare calmly and then, to everyone's surprise, Henrietta began to smile and then to laugh until she had to reach for her handkerchief to wipe away the tears of merriment.

'Oh Philippa, you're incorrigible.'

Sixty-Five

Pips arrived back at the unit, now back at Brandhoek once more, late at night. There had been disruptions and delays at every part of her journey. Troops going home on leave, new troops arriving on their way to the front. She travelled on one such train and was pleased she was not wearing her nurse's uniform. It didn't do to remind those going to the front – especially those on their way for the first time – that a nurse's services would be required. For the final part of her journey, she begged a lift on a London bus taking soldiers to Ypres. They were all surprisingly jolly and she joined in their raucous rendition of 'It's a Long Way to Tipperary'.

All was quiet at the post. No sound of guns or shellfire. The ambulances were parked side by side and no one seemed to be about. She went to the tent she now shared with Rose, but she wasn't there either. She hesitated to go to the men's tent in case they were taking a well-earned rest. It was gone ten and the stretcher bearers often retired early after long, hard days. Even though there didn't seem to be fighting going on, there was always illness and disease to contend with.

She stood listening, but could hear no sound from anywhere. Where was everyone? Had they gone into Pop to Talbot House for an evening of entertainment? Then she saw a glimmer of light coming from the large tent where the operations took place. Maybe Giles was working late. Her heart leapt at the thought of seeing him. She strode across the grass and quietly lifted the tent flap.

There was no operation in progress, but there were two figures in the shadows at the rear, locked in each other's arms and kissing passionately. Thinking it was William and Brigitta, Pips was about to turn away when she realized with a shock that it was Giles and Rose. She stared at them, unable to believe what she was seeing. She gripped the side of the tent flap until her knuckles were white and hung onto it as her legs threatened to give way.

They must have heard her gasp for they both looked up and then sprang guiltily apart. For what seemed a long moment, the three of them just stood staring at each other, their faces shocked.

With a supreme effort, Pips pulled in a steadying breath, but her knees were still trembling, her heart pounding. Her forehead felt clammy as if at any minute she might faint. She couldn't, at this moment, confront them, so she let the flap fall and turned away, stumbling blindly towards the sleeping tent, but then she veered away from it. She couldn't bear to share a tent with Rose, not now.

And then she began to run and run, not knowing or caring where she went...'

It was the early hours of the morning before George Allender found her, huddled near the canal bank, some distance from the post.

'What – are – you – doing – here?' she asked, shivering with cold.

'My battalion – like your unit – seems to keep coming back to Ypres. Thank goodness we did.' He was carrying a blanket and wrapped it round her at once. He sat down next to her and put his arms around her, holding her close and rubbing her back to warm her.

'How – did – you – know – where I was?' she asked through chattering teeth.

'I didn't. When the word spread that you were missing, we got search parties out scouring the countryside for you. It's just luck that I'm the one to find you.' He laughed wryly. 'Even the Germans are looking for you, though we didn't think you'd go across no-man's-land.'

'The – the Germans?'

'Oh yes. You see, they don't regard you as an enemy. You're a nurse. Now, let's get you back to the warmth.'

'I can't go back there.'

'Yes, you can. It's them that are in the wrong, not you.'

'You – you know?' She looked up at him. In the darkness, she couldn't see him properly and was thankful that he couldn't see her tear-ravaged face. Pips, who rarely cried, had given way to a storm of weeping such as she could never remember having experienced before, not even when she had received the news about Midnight.

'I do. William told just me, but not the rest of my company. The men don't know. They were just told you'd gone for a walk in the dark and must have got lost.' His tone was grim as he added, 'Dr Giles Kendall should be horsewhipped.'

She was silent for a moment and then she said quietly, 'No, I'm glad I've found out, though it was a shock. It shows his feelings for me weren't deep enough. But,' she hiccuped miserably, 'I didn't know something like this would actually hurt physically. There's such a pain' – she touched her chest – 'here.'

'I know.' Gently, he touched her hair with his lips and held her even closer.

Then Pips began to laugh, a little hysterically, but she was laughing between her tears. 'And to think he was jealous of my friendship with you.'

Quietly, George said drily, 'Was he now?'

They sat a few moments longer before he said, 'Come on, we must get you back to the unit, or at least to the trenches. You need a hot drink and somewhere to rest.'

'The trenches. Please. They must all know at the unit, and I need a little longer before I can face them.'

'Very well. I'll get one of my men to take word to them that you've been found.'

'Thank you,' she said in a small voice. 'I'm sorry if I've caused you trouble. I didn't mean to.'

'Don't mention it. It's given the lads something to do, though I have to say we were all scared witless.'

As he helped her to her feet, she asked, 'How did the Germans hear about it?'

'There's a section where our trenches are only yards apart and one of our lads shouted across and told them that one of our nurses was missing. They were out of their trenches in a flash, completely unarmed and offering to help look for you. They were the ones who searched no-man's-land.'

'Isn't all this ridiculous, George? Why, oh why can't those in authority see this wretched war for what it is? Just a waste of young lives on both sides. And look at the ravaged land. However are the poor French and Belgians ever going to rebuild their shattered lives?'

They were walking back towards the trenches as a figure loomed out of the darkness. 'That you, sir?'

'It is indeed, Corporal Brown. I have Nurse Maitland here, safe and sound. Will you run to the first-aid post and inform her colleagues that she is all right and will return in the morning? We'll find her a nice cosy dugout for the night.'

'Right away, sir.' He paused only briefly to say, 'Are you really all right, nurse?'

'I'm fine, thank you. I'm sorry if I've been a nuisance.'

'No bother, nurse. Just glad you're safe. I'll shout to Fritz when I get back, sir. Let them know, an' all.'

And he was gone, disappearing into the darkness.

Slowly, with his arm about her, not caring who might see, George led her to the support trench and into a deep dugout. The sides and floor were covered with hessian and the 'door' was a blanket. She curled up on his camp bed, drawing her knees up to her chest and fell into a fitful sleep. He covered her with a rough blanket and stood looking down at her for several moments. Gently, he smoothed a stray strand of her lovely hair from her forehead.

'We're a casualty of war, you and I,' he murmured.

Then he pulled up a battered chair and sat beside her where he remained for the rest of the night.

Sixty-Six

After a night's rest, even though her sleep had been troubled by nightmarish dreams, Pips felt much better. She breakfasted with the soldiers in the trench, sharing their biscuits and canned meat, listened to their banter and marvelled at their good-humoured resilience. It did her good; whatever had she to make such a fuss about when daily they faced death? she asked herself sharply. Just a broken love affair. She felt rather foolish now for having caused so much trouble.

As she stood up to leave, George said, 'I'll come with you,' but she shook her head. 'I can never thank you enough for your kindness, George, but this is something I have to do on my own.'

'You're a very brave girl, Pips, but now you've got to use that courage for a private battle. You've got to hold your head up high and carry on with the work you do so wonderfully. My men – and many more on the Western Front – need people like you.' His forehead creased with concern. 'Will you really be all right?'

She smiled up at him and, to her surprise, found that her smile was genuine. 'I'll be fine. Honestly. Now I'm angry – and that will carry me through. Believe me.'

He saw the spark in her green eyes and thought, I wouldn't want to be in Kendall's shoes right now. But all he said was, 'If you're sure...'

With determination in every step, Pips lifted her chin and marched back towards the first-aid post. Leonore came out to meet her.

'My dear girl,' she said, holding out her hands. There was genuine concern and sympathy in the sister's eyes.

Pips stared at her and then asked quietly, 'How long have you known?'

Leonore sighed. 'It only became apparent to all of us whilst you were away. I had heated words with Giles, but it doesn't seem to have done any good. When I wrote that letter to you, I was tempted to say something then, but I wondered if it would all blow over. I'm sorry, my dear, if I should have told you.'

'Don't be, Leonore, but I'm glad I know now, because I don't want to be with a man whose thoughts are elsewhere. Where is he? I need to speak to him.'

'Of course. Will you – will you be leaving us?'

'Heavens, no. I'm not going to be driven away from the work I love.'

'But...' Leonore bit her lip. 'Won't it be – painful for you?'

'Probably, but I've just had breakfast with the lads in the trenches. Listening to them talk and laugh and joke when they must know, deep inside them, that this could be their last day alive, rather puts my little problems into perspective, don't you think?'

Leonore squeezed her hands. 'You're a very special girl, Pips. I do so admire you. Would you like me to come with you?'

'Thank you, but no. I must do this on my own.'

It was the second kind offer of support she'd had within the space of an hour.

'Giles, can you spare me a moment?'

He looked up from the table where the instruments for operations were spread out. Guilt spread across his handsome features.

'I – of course,' he murmured and came, reluctantly, she thought, towards her. 'Pips, I am so very sorry. I've behaved like a cad. Can you ever forgive me? I've ended it with Rose. She's leaving, and–'

'There's no need for that.'

He blinked and searched her face. 'Why? D'you mean, *you're* going?'

'Heavens, no. I've no intention of missing Christmas here. Besides, there's no reason for any of us to leave. We're all desperately needed here and we work well together.' She allowed herself a wry smile.

391

'I don't think Rose will stay. She's very upset.'

'Why?'

'Because – because she says she loves me and because I've told her that it's you I really love and want to be with, if only you'll forgive me.'

Pips put her hand up, palm outwards. 'Oh no. No, no, no. There's no going back, Giles. Whatever was between us, is over.'

'Oh Pips, please, I...'

She shook her head vehemently. 'No, Giles. There's no way back.'

'You – you really mean it?' His face was stricken, but Pips felt no sympathy for him. Even if she took him back – and at this moment that was the very last thing she could think of doing – she would never be able to trust him again.

Quietly, she said, 'I don't condone infidelity, Giles. Not ever. Not under any circumstances. Now, you go and find Rose and tell her that all is well. There's no need for either of you to leave. And, if you want to be together, then' – Pips found she was actually smiling – 'quite frankly, she's welcome to you.'

The way Pips had dealt with the situation surprised everyone around her – not least herself. The shock of seeing the man she loved kissing another girl so passionately had been like a physical blow. She had run away blindly, not caring where she went or, in that moment, what happened to her. But the kindness and understanding of George and his men had made her see, very swiftly, just how unimportant it was. On waking that morning in the dugout and seeing George dozing in the chair beside her, she realized he must have stayed there all night watching over her. She had waited for the pain to come again and for the tears to start. But there was nothing. And when his men plied her with breakfast, sharing their own meagre rations with her, she was humbled by their concern.

But she did feel something: anger. She was furious that she had been made such a fool of, that she had given herself wholly to someone who had betrayed her so easily when she'd been away for only a few weeks. But the worst thing would be that she would be unable to trust any man again for a very long time – if ever. And that made her very sad.

Sixty-Seven

Pips worked alongside Leonore and Brigitta at the unit, but most of the time she helped William, Hugh and Peter bring the sick and wounded back to the first-aid post. Rose now assisted Giles with operations and Stephen with treatments, and so Pips saw little of them. Stephen was quiet and reserved and didn't speak to Pips about what had happened, though she caught him glancing at her once or twice with sympathy in his eyes. But when Dr Hazelwood visited them as usual at Christmas, Giles spoke to him and told him that he and Rose were leaving the corps. 'We will stay until you can find replacements for us, but we both wish to return to England.'

'I'm surprised,' he said to Pips. 'Has something happened?'

Briefly, Pips explained.

'Ah, I see,' Dr Hazelwood said. 'I'm sorry to hear that, but maybe it's best that they should go.'

Tersely, Pips said, 'They needn't go on my account. We don't see a lot of each other in the course of our work now.' She didn't add that still sleeping in the same tent as Rose was a little awkward at times.

'It's not been the same for any of you since your brother was injured, has it?' Dr Hazelwood said sadly. 'That seemed to break up the dynamics of the team that was working superbly well.'

'I think you're right,' Pips murmured and sighed inwardly, realizing that she still had to write to her family to break the news of the split between Giles and herself. She dreaded to think what her mother would say.

By the time New Year 1917 arrived, the news of the broken romance, imparted by Pips in a letter to her brother, had filtered out of the hall and around the village.

'Have you heard about Miss Pips and her young man?' Bess asked Ma, sitting down on the opposite side of the hearth with her grandson on her lap. Bess brought Luke regularly to see the Dawsons, and the little chap certainly brightened their sombre days. 'It's all off, then.'

'So it would seem,' Ma said shortly. She didn't like gossip. 'She's better off without him if that's the kind of young man he is.'

'And him a doctor, an' all.'

Trying to steer their visitor away from the topic, Ma said, 'Now, are you going to let me nurse my great-grandson, Bess?'

At the hall, Henrietta remained tight-lipped about the news. Things were not going the way she wanted with either of her children, though, she had to admit, Alice had settled into her new role. Even the staff – her former workmates – had accepted the new situation. She was certainly coping with Robert much better than Henrietta could. He had never been an irritable man, but now he was often morose and short-tempered with dark mood swings. Alice dealt with him admirably, never losing her patience or taking his sullenness personally. On such occasions when he was sunk in gloom, neither Henrietta nor Edwin could reach him.

'He's best left alone,' Alice told them gently. 'It's hard for him to find a purpose in his life now, but give him time.' She was in the drawing room with the two of them. Robert had retired early, pleading a headache, but they all knew it was an excuse. A black mood was descending and he wished to be alone. 'But there is something I've been thinking about that might help him.'

Edwin put down his newspaper. 'Then tell us, my dear. You know we'll do all we can.'

Alice ran her tongue nervously around her lips. She still wasn't entirely at ease sitting in the parlour, especially when Robert wasn't there. But she took a deep breath; this was for her beloved husband.

'I was wondering if you would consider taking

in a few convalescent soldiers here at the hall – ones who no longer need much nursing care, but who are not quite fit to return home and certainly not to duty.'

'Amputees, you mean?' Edwin said.

'Yes, and maybe those suffering from shell shock and trauma too. The constant bombardment, the fear of facing death on a daily basis for those on the front line – it all took its toll on the bravest of soldiers. And Robert has changed, hasn't he – we can all see that? It's not only the loss of his arm, it's the dreadful memories he has too. He still wakes up from nightmares, sweating and shouting. Oh, I know we weren't in the fighting, but we saw such dreadful injuries and mutilations and, sadly, death. Each time Robert couldn't save a casualty, he seemed to take it personally, as if somehow he'd failed. And now, because of his own injury, he can't see how he can ever be useful again.'

'Wouldn't it make him worse to have others here like him?' Henrietta asked.

'I don't think so. I think he needs to be able to help others. He can't practise as a doctor any more – and that was his life's work, wasn't it? – but he could perhaps help others come to terms with what's happened to them. They'd listen to him, because he's one of them. He understands the after-effects of serious injury. Oh dear, I don't think I'm explaining this properly.'

'You're doing very well, my dear. I understand perfectly what you mean,' Edwin said. 'Perhaps he could study the patients too, and eventually write a paper on it.'

'And I could do whatever nursing was needed

with your backing and advice, Dr Maitland.'

Edwin looked at his wife. 'It sounds like a very good idea. We do have rooms that are unused. What do you think, Hetty, my love?'

'I have heard that there are quite a few large houses throughout the country doing something similar. It would take a lot of organizing, but yes, I think it's something we could do. Anything, to help Robert.'

'And you'd be helping so many others too, Mrs Maitland.'

Henrietta smiled at Alice. She was warming to the girl every day. She was quiet and unassuming and hadn't tried to take advantage of her new position in any way. And her every waking hour was devoted to Robert. There was no denying that.

'You know, my dear,' Henrietta said gently, 'Dr and Mrs Maitland sounds so very formal. Would you consider calling us "Mother" and "Father"?'

Alice blushed and said softly, 'I'd like that very much. Thank you.'

Sixty-Eight

Her family and friends would not have thought Pips was suffering a broken heart had they seen her in Belgium. In an effort to take her mind off things, Hugh said, 'You'll never guess what? With this icy weather, William and I have found a field not too far away with a frozen pool of water and we think we can go skating there.'

'We haven't any skates.'

'Don't need them. Didn't you ever make a slide along the ice in the school playground?'

Pips laughed wryly, 'I was sent to the most awful boarding school where there was never an ounce of fun to be had.'

'Ah sorry, me ol' china.'

She beamed at him. 'I forgive you. You weren't to know. Come, show me.'

'Some of the lads in the reserve trenches are there.'

For the rest of the afternoon, until it grew dusk, they had great fun on the makeshift slide the soldiers had made. Pips fell a couple of times, her skirts flying. But she got up again, laughing. Corporal Brown, who had been one of the soldiers searching for her when she'd gone missing for a few hours, grinned. 'It's good to see you, nurse. Are you quite well again now?'

'I am, thank you, corporal. And – thank you for your help that night.'

He shrugged. 'Think nothing of it, nurse.'

'Oh, but I do. I think a lot of it.'

'We was all concerned, 'cos you're very special to us, you know. You an' all the team. We know you're volunteers. You've no need to be here, none of you.' He dropped his voice. 'And William, he's a braver man than any of us. We're here because we have no choice. But he had. You might like to tell him some time, nurse, that we all respect him and we're very grateful to him.' He grinned. 'Even if we do ignore him when he stands behind us with his stretcher when we're about to go over the top.'

Pips's voice was husky as she said, 'Thank you, corporal. If I get the right moment, I'll let him know.'

In the middle of January, the two replacements for Giles and Rose arrived. They were a middle-aged husband and wife, Matthew and Grace Wallis; he a qualified surgeon, she an experienced nurse. They were lively, energetic and friendly and, with their two children grown up, they had time to spare.

'We're thrilled to be here,' Grace told Pips and Leonore. 'Now, you must tell us exactly what we have to do. We want to fit in with all of you.'

The newcomers had brought a small tent for themselves so that no extra strain was put on the existing number of tents, but Leonore said, 'Once Rose has gone, Pips, we'll make room for you in our tent.' But it seemed that arrangement would not last long. The following day, Leonore sought her out again. 'It seems we are to have another nurse. Grace Wallis has been telling me that her niece, Millicent Fortesque, is absolutely desperate to come out here.' The sister pulled a face and laughed. 'It sounds as if she's one of these English upper-class girls who imagine themselves holding a soldier's hand and smoothing his brow. I really don't know what use she'll be, but Grace has insisted that she'll be responsible for the girl. And it seems that Dr Hazelwood has already given his consent, so we can't very well say "no", can we?'

Pips pulled a face. 'I doubt she'll last long, but an extra pair of hands will be useful. She can fetch and carry and keep the supplies in order, if nothing else.'

Two days later, Giles and Rose were due to leave. Giles sought Pips out and took her hands in his.

'I'm so sorry, Pips, for everything.'

'I'm not going to lie to you, Giles. You hurt me very deeply, but I don't wish either of you any harm. Just go and be happy together.'

Giles pulled a face. 'I'm not sure we will be. It's you I truly love. I know that now. I've been a fool.'

Pips shook her head. 'It'd never work, Giles. Even if I could have forgiven you, which, at the moment, I can't, I couldn't ever forget. And there's a school of thought that says if you can't forget, then you haven't truly forgiven.'

There was nothing more to say between them, and Giles turned away looking more sick at heart than when she'd first caught them in an embrace. Watching him go, Pips had the feeling that his new romance would not last very long either.

The day after Giles had left, George came to say goodbye too.

'We have orders to leave. There's not much happening here at the moment, and there's unlikely to be before spring.' His gaze searched her face. 'How are you?'

'I'm fine. Like you say, we've little to do. The casualties are now suffering from disease rather than injuries. She paused and added quietly, 'They've gone – Giles and Rose.'

George nodded. 'Have you time to take a walk with me? There's something I'd like to say to you.'

'I must just tell Leonore, so that she knows

where I am.' She smiled wryly. 'I mustn't run off again.'

'Of course.'

They walked away from the post and found their way to the small cemetery where George's friend lay.

'I'll look after his grave for you, at least whilst we're still here.'

'Thank you,' he said quietly, and then he was silent for a long time. He seemed to be struggling with something. Then, suddenly, the words burst from him. 'There's no knowing if our paths will ever cross again, and I can't leave without telling you that I have fallen in love with you.' As she opened her mouth to speak, he put up his hand. 'Please don't say anything. Just – hear me out.' They walked a little further, side by side but not touching.

'Even if you could ever feel something for me, there can be no future in it. I'm so much older than you and – I'm married. I have been married for nineteen years. My wife is an invalid. She has a sickness' – he touched his head – 'of the mind, but I would never leave her, never even be unfaithful to her, but we haven't lived as man and wife for several years now. Our daughter looks after her at present, but once this war is over, and if I survive, then I must leave the army and take over that responsibility. Rebecca – she's seventeen now – deserves a life of her own.'

'George,' Pips whispered, 'I'm so very sorry.'

He acknowledged her sympathy with a nod and then continued. 'But one can't help one's feelings, and I just wanted you to know that somewhere in the world, there is always someone who loves you devotedly and would never, ever have treated you in the way you have been treated. We're not all' – he paused and bit back the impolite word he'd been about to use – 'philanderers.'

They stopped walking and turned to face each other. George took her hands into his and gazed down at her as if he were committing her lovely face to memory; a memory that would have to last him a lifetime.

'There's something I want to give you.' He reached into his pocket and pulled out a small jeweller's box. 'Please accept this as a memento of our meeting.'

Pips opened it and, nestling against a black velvet cushion, was an enamel brooch in the shape and colours of a poppy.

'I know how much you love to see them grow, even in this godforsaken land...'

'George, it's truly beautiful. I will treasure it always.' She reached up and kissed his cheek and, as she pulled back, she could see the huge inner conflict he was having not to sweep her into his arms.

'I will never forget you, George,' she whispered. 'May God bless you and keep you safe.'

Sixty-Nine

The new girl arrived in a flurry of excitement and with more luggage than the rest of the unit had brought put together.

'Where are we to store it all?' Pips murmured.

'Goodness knows.' Leonore hid her laughter. 'But you can't help but like her.'

It was impossible to dislike Millicent – or Milly, as she insisted on being called. She was bright and bubbly with golden curls framing a pretty face and bright blue eyes.

'She's like an enthusiastic puppy bouncing around,' Leonore said indulgently.

'And probably about as much use out here,' Pips said, but even she was smiling as she said it.

'But just think how the soldiers love pets. Maybe that's how they'll view her. She'll certainly raise a smile.'

'I know I'm a bit much for some people, darling,' Milly had trilled in a sweet voice as she introduced herself to everyone. 'But Aunty Grace will keep me in check.' She smiled widely. 'And I'll never take offence if you tell me to pipe down.'

As it turned out, although she had little nursing knowledge, just as Leonore had predicted, she was a tonic to the troops. She kept the less seriously ill or wounded in fits of laughter – she was a natural mimic and didn't seem to mind acting the fool to raise a smile. And, despite what she had said of herself, around the desperately ill casualties, she was quiet and calm and yet exuded a positivity that those in the first-aid post who had been at the front since the beginning, were finding hard to show now.

'We're all a bit jaded having been here so long,' Pips admitted to Leonore and Grace when they were alone. 'She's brought a breath of fresh air. She's good for us all, and her impression of the music hall star, Marie Lloyd, is just amazing. The lads love to hear her sing "A Little of What You Fancy Does You Good". She's so saucy with it, but in a nice way.'

'I'm glad you think she'll be useful,' Grace said. 'I did have my doubts about her coming out here, but she has surprised me, I have to admit. She's always been indulged by her doting parents, being the only girl in the family. We've always thought of her as being very spoiled. But, so far so good, is all I can say at present, though I don't know how she will fare when we get into another big battle.'

Leonore sighed. 'I'm sure we won't have long to wait to find out. With the coming of spring, the fighting is bound to start again.'

Once they'd all agreed to Alice's suggestion, events moved very quickly and Henrietta was not too proud to turn to Alice for advice on what was needed for the patients.

'The Long Gallery on the second floor can become a dormitory for about eight beds, I thought, with screens around each one to afford the men some privacy,' Henrietta said. 'They can have the Blue Drawing Room on the first floor for their recreation room. It's large enough to have comfortable seating at one end for quiet pursuits – reading, and so on – and we could make the far end a games room of sorts. What do you think, Alice?'

'I think that's an excellent idea. On fine days, I think they'll spend a lot of time in the grounds. They'll love the peace and quiet and to hear birdsong again, but on cold, wet days they'll need some indoor activities.' She paused and then asked, 'Where will they eat?'

'I thought we'd let them have the Great Hall. The family can manage with a dining table in the Brown Parlour, don't you think?'

Alice nodded.

'Now, there's one more thing. I know you're not fully qualified as a nurse, Alice, but your experience must far outstrip many a nurse who is. I have talked to the matron at Lincoln County and she thinks that, with both you and Dr Maitland here, there is no need for us to employ a qualified nurse. She did say, though, that if we needed extra help at any time, she'd gladly send someone from the hospital. I want you to be regarded as in charge here. Would you like that?'

Alice was pink with pleasure. 'But won't you...?' she began, but Henrietta shook her head. 'I know what my forte is, Alice dear. I'm good at organizing things, but I'm certainly no nurse. Oh, I can go and chat to the patients – and I will do – but you've seen how I am with my own son when he sinks into depression. I haven't the faintest idea how to deal with it.'

The whole household became enthusiastically involved. Cook revelled in planning suitable menus, and Alice and Mrs Warren worked happily together reorganizing the rooms and obtaining furnishings and household goods that would be needed. Edwin planned to restock his dispensary. Only Robert took no interest in the plans to bring more wounded soldiers into the hall.

'Haven't you got enough with me?' he asked Alice morosely as she helped him undress for bed.

'You will always be my priority, darling, but you don't need me twenty-four hours a day.'

'Yes, I do. I hate it when you're out of my sight.' He climbed into bed and lay back, propped up against the pillows. 'I don't want you nursing other soldiers. Not any more. I want you here with me.'

When she had undressed and put on her nightdress, Alice sat on the end of his bed and regarded him solemnly. 'The ones who will be coming here won't need much in the way of nursing. They'll be convalescents. But you could do so much to help them, Robert, especially those suffering mental anguish. You saw for yourself that so many poor fellows suffered trauma that was misdiagnosed as cowardice. Shell shock ought to be recognized as an injury, just like a physical one.'

She and Edwin had talked at length about how to rouse Robert from his apathy.

'Somewhere deep inside him, Alice, there must still be the desire to help others that he had when he wanted to become a doctor,' Edwin had said. 'We've just got to find it again. We'll work on it together, my dear.'

Now an opportunity had arisen where she could begin her side of the bargain. She ran her tongue nervously round her lips; she was moving into dangerous waters.

'And, sadly, you know what it's like to be devastatingly wounded. But first and foremost, you're a doctor, Robert. It's what you trained for.'

'Not any more, I'm not.'

'Of course you are. You haven't been brain-damaged. You're a clever man, Robert. You can still use all your medical knowledge to help others. Oh, perhaps not in the same way as you had planned, I realize that. But don't let all that studying go to waste, my darling, not when there is so much you could do. And you won't even have to leave your home to do it. They're coming to you.'

Robert stared at her for what seemed, to the nervous young woman, a long time.

'You know, Alice, I thought I knew you, but every day I find out something new about you. I knew you were kind and caring – and loving – and courageous in the face of extreme danger – and oh, how I love you for all that. But until now, I hadn't realized that you're brave enough to stand up to all of us for something you believe in. My darling, I love you even more now than the day I asked you to marry me.' He reached out to her with his left hand. 'I've been such a selfish pig, wallowing in self-pity, believing my whole life is useless. But it isn't, is it?'

Alice chuckled as she climbed into bed beside him and nestled her cheek against his chest. 'It most certainly is not.'

Then she lifted her face to be kissed...

'Robert,' Edwin said the following morning on entering his son's bedroom. 'I really need you to advise me on what extra medical supplies I need to stock. Won't you come down and help me?'

'It's all right, Father.' Robert grinned. 'Alice has given me a good talking-to.' There was the old twinkle in his eyes as he added, 'I'm guessing that you and my wife have been in cahoots to stir me into doing something.'

Edwin chuckled. 'You're too sharp for your own good sometimes, Robert. You'll cut yourself one of these days.'

Robert's face sobered as he said, haltingly, 'I still have nightmares about what happened out there – all the terrible injuries we saw and my own, of course. And sudden noises – if someone bangs a door downstairs, I nearly jump out of my skin and begin to sweat. I can't sleep properly, and as for trying to take an interest in anything...' He stopped and shrugged. 'Alice understands and I'm sure you do, but I worry that I'm upsetting Mother.'

'I'll explain it to her, my boy.'

'I'm doing my best to fight it, Father, but it's not easy.'

'I know, but that's precisely why we think you could be such a help to others in your situation.' He paused and then added, 'So, what do you say, Robert? Will you help me sort out my supplies?'

'I say, that if you'll ask Alice to come up and help me dress, I will then come downstairs and we can go through your current stock together and we can make a list of what you're likely to need.' He let out a bark of wry laughter. 'I might even start to learn to write with my left hand.'

'Doctors are notorious for their illegible handwriting,' Edwin said, with a chuckle. 'I don't suppose anyone will notice the difference.'

Seventy

'Have you heard what's happening at the hall?' Bess said on one of her frequent visits to bring Luke to visit his other grandparents.

'No,' Ma said, reaching out to take her great-grandson onto her lap. At just over a year old, the little chap was walking well and, as Ma said, 'into everything he can reach'. But they all delighted in him. 'Who's been daft enough to volunteer now? Young Jake, I suppose. Or has he been called up?'

Bess shook her head and took great pleasure in imparting the latest village news as she explained the Maitlands' plans to take in convalescent soldiers. 'I'm telling our Betty to go up there and see if there're any jobs going. You knew she'd left that factory job she had in Lincoln, didn't you? It was making her ill. Dr Maitland sent a letter to her employers. But they're bound to want more staff at the hall now, wouldn't you think?'

Ma nodded. 'What about Peggy? We could have little 'un now and again to help out. You'd like that, wouldn't you, Norah?'

Norah was dewy-eyed for a moment, remembering the time when her own boys had been little. And now they were all lost to her.

'Aye, I would. And I don't think Len would mind either. He's taken to the little chap. Keeps talking about him being his only heir now.'

Ma and Bess glanced at each other. There was still one somewhere, but no one ever spoke of William. Not any more.

'I don't know if they'd consider Peggy, though,' Bess said in a low voice. 'She's a fallen woman now, in't she?'

Ma shrugged. 'She can only ask. I don't reckon Mrs Maitland would mind. The world's altered, Bess.'

The following day, Betty and Peggy walked up to the hall and went round to the back door.

'Is the mistress in?' Betty asked boldly. 'We've come to see if there're any jobs going.'

Mrs Warren looked them up and down. 'Come in, both of you. I'll send Mr Wainwright to see if madam will see you.'

They sat in the kitchen. Betty was bolder than her sister and engaged in conversation with the housekeeper and cook. Peggy sat quietly, her eyes downcast. She hadn't expected to be allowed in, let alone considered for a post.

Mr Wainwright returned in a few moments. 'Madam would like a word with you first, Mrs Warren, if you'd go to her, please.'

She was gone for what seemed like a long time and both girls grew increasingly nervous. Peggy was about to leap up and run out when Mrs Warren returned and invited them to follow her to the parlour.

'We've heard about what's happening here, ma'am, and we just wondered if you had any jobs going. On'y cleaning and such. We couldn't do no nursing. Peg here faints at the sight of blood.' Betty grinned. ''Specially if it's her own.'

Henrietta hid her smile.

'I'm sure we'll be needing more help about the house, Betty, but I'm not sure exactly what yet. Leave it with me and I'll let you know. How much time can each of you give a week, d'you think?'

Betty and Peggy glanced at each other. Peggy turned back to look at Henrietta. 'You – you mean, you'll take me?'

Henrietta regarded her solemnly. 'Peggy, my dear, it was a mistake to give way to young Harold, but I expect he was very persuasive and, in the circumstances, it's understandable that you felt compassion for him. There'll be many a young lass in your predicament before this war is over, sad to say, but we're a close community. We'll all stand by you, so, yes, I am offering you employment here, but I do understand that, because of your little boy, you might not be able to work full-time.' Now Henrietta smiled. 'But we'll work something out. I only wish...' she began and then stopped. She sighed and said no more. But what she had been about to say was, I only wish the Dawsons could have been more understanding towards William.

In February 1917, America cut off diplomatic relations with Germany.

'Surely that must mean they're going to come into the war,' Pips said, as they continued with their daily routine. Pockets of fighting and spasmodic sniper fire still occurred, creating casualties for the team, but there was no word of any major battle where they were.

In March, they heard that the Germans had begun to withdraw to what they called the Hindenburg Line.

'I think they're going to dig in there and hold on to that, come what may,' Stephen said.

'So, at some point, we're going to have to break through that, are we?' Pips said.

'If we're to win the war, then, yes, I expect so.'

'Mm. I'll write and ask Robert what he thinks.' Despite the fact that she liked the three newcomers, Pips still missed meaningful conversations with her brother, and, if she was honest, with Giles too.

But Robert's reply, when it came, was full of news about what was happening at home. The letter was in Alice's handwriting, but obviously written under Robert's dictation.

We'll be ready to receive our first patients soon. We're in touch with Lincoln hospital and they'll be glad to send convalescents to us when they have suitable patients. Mother has employed Betty and Peggy Cooper, and they're fitting in really well. We thought it might be painful for them in the circumstances, but I think they feel they'll be helping to carry on the fight. Alice says I'm to tell you that I am much better and that this has given me a purpose too. And, yes, she's right!

Pips smiled and sent a silent prayer of thankfulness for Alice. But with regard to her comment about America, Robert's reply was brief and in their prearranged code:

Severance of relations between the US and Germany might well be a prelude to the Americans entering the war. Let's hope so. With regard to the Hindenburg Line, I fear they will entrench there and it will be even harder for the Allies to break through such strong defences. Our regular source of information...

Pips smiled as she read on. Good old Basil!

...tells us that the enemy have rebuilt the line with barbed wire one hundred yards deep and a row of concrete pill boxes. Although by doing this they have shortened their own front by fifty miles or so, they are confident that the Hindenburg Line will be unassailable. As they retreated, they devastated the land, the roads and razed towns to the ground. Rumour has it that they even poisoned the water.

At the beginning of April, William ran excitedly around the camp.

'Pips, have you heard? The Americans have come into the war.'

The winter of 1916 into 1917 had been bitterly cold. Mrs Parrott had obtained leather jerkins and greatcoats for the soldiers.

'Animal skins don't work,' she'd laughed. 'They're lovely and warm at first, but they encourage lice and the men say they already have enough of those to contend with. Oh, and by the way, I remembered what Robert told me last year. I've obtained quantities of whale-oil grease to help the boys protect themselves against frostbite. You

413

can take some to the trenches.'

But now, spring was in the air and already Pips was looking forward to seeing the poppies bloom. At William's news, she flung her arms wide and hugged the bearer of the glad tidings.

'That's wonderful. Surely, with their might, it'll soon be over now, don't you think?'

William shrugged. 'To be honest, Pips, I don't even think about the end. I just concentrate on getting through each day. There are rumours flying about amongst the troops that there's going to be a British attack near Arras, and that the Canadians plan to take Vimy Ridge. So, the fighting's all going to begin again.'

Pips shrugged. 'It's inevitable, now the better weather is here. I'd better talk to Stephen – see if he thinks we ought to move camp.' She was silent for a moment and then asked suddenly, 'What are you going to do when it *is* all over, William?'

'Marry Brigitta,' he said promptly and grinned, his whole face lighting up.

'So you'd stay here, would you? With her and her family?'

He nodded. 'Her grandparents are very good to me. In fact, her grandfather has already hinted – well, actually no, he's more than hinted – that I'm very welcome to live with them. They've got a farm, Pips. A small one, granted, but I'd love to work on getting it back to how it was before. He's getting on a bit now, and this war's devastated them. He won't be able to do all the work it'll need on his own. But I could.'

There was a light in William's eyes that Pips hadn't seen for a long time. It seemed that William had more to look forward to than the rest of them – if only he dared to hope that they would make it through to the end of the war unharmed.

'So, you won't go back home, then?'

For a moment, the light died. 'There's nothing for me to go back for now, is there, Pips? And besides, d'you know what I'd really like to do? Apart from help Monsieur Dupont, that is.'

Pips shook her head.

'There are going to be an awful lot of war cemeteries around here. I'd like to look after one or two.'

Tears sprang to Pips's eyes and she brushed them away hastily. 'Oh William, what a lovely thought. You've helped save so many lives, and then you'd be tending the resting place of those who can never go home.'

'Despite what happened, I'd like to look after my brothers' graves. They didn't deserve to die. Though I expect I'll have a lot of red tape to go through before I get permission to live here permanently.'

'There'll be a way,' Pips said confidently. 'We'll find it.'

'I love the Belgian people and the country,' William went on. 'It does remind me a bit of Lincolnshire, being so flat around here. But more than anything, Pips, I love Brigitta and, amazingly, she loves me.'

Pips chuckled. How modest and unassuming William still was. So, she mused, William will be settled. Robert and Alice were married. Hopefully, they would have children and one day they would take over the reins of the hall and its estate, and its

415

future would be assured. But what would she do after the war ended?

The future for her, Pips felt, was very uncertain.

Seventy-One

In early April, the hall received its first convalescents; a captain with a broken leg, which was mending well but still not out of plaster, and three privates, two of whom would most likely be sent back to the front eventually and one who was suffering from shell shock. The poor fellow shook constantly and walked with a drunken gait. He wandered around the grounds, avoiding contact with anyone. But Robert sought him out and tried to talk to him. It wasn't easy, for the soldier, whose name was Donald Travis, was morose and locked in his own private hell.

'It's going to take a long time,' Robert told Alice.

'I hope you're making notes,' she said.

Robert pulled a face. 'I am, but it's hard trying to write with my left hand.'

'You should persevere.'

'No one'll be able to read it – my writing's so bad. Even I can't make out some of the words now, and I wrote them!'

Alice picked up a few of the sheets of paper that Robert had scribbled. 'We-ell, I can decipher most of it. I'll borrow your mother's typewriter and type it up for you.'

Robert's face was animated. 'Would you? That'd

be wonderful. But will you have time? You have so much to do now.'

Alice perched herself on his knee, put her arm around his neck and kissed his cheek. 'And I'll soon have a lot more to do.'

'Are there more patients expected?'

'More than likely,' Alice said cheerfully, 'but, no, this is something different. I'm pretty sure, though I haven't seen a doctor yet, that we're going to have a baby, Robert.'

For a moment, Robert looked bewildered and then joy spread across his face. 'Oh Alice, I never thought that could happen. Not after...'

Alice laughed. 'And you a doctor! Didn't anyone teach you about the birds and the bees?'

His response was to tickle her waist gently. 'When are you due?'

'About November, I think.'

'And you haven't seen a doctor yet?'

Alice shook her head.

'Then you must. Would you be happy for Father to attend you, or would you prefer someone outside the family?'

'I'd love it to be your father, if he doesn't mind.'

Edwin was delighted and confirmed Alice's suspicions. 'You're fit and healthy, my dear – remarkably so after all you've been through – but you must still take care and not overdo it. Plenty of good food, gentle exercise and fresh air. And rest. You mustn't feel guilty about resting.'

'What about my work?' Alice was running the convalescent home at the hall with dedicated efficiency.

'We-ell,' Edwin said thoughtfully. 'I don't believe in my expectant mothers being idle – that brings problems of its own when they think it's a good idea to "eat for two" and take little exercise. They put on far too much weight. I suggest that you carry on running the home as long as you feel able, but no heavy lifting. I'll talk to Hetty and we'll employ another nurse. Oh, she's going to be so thrilled at the thought of being a grandmother.' He smiled broadly. 'But I'll leave that to you or Robert to tell her. I won't steal your thunder.'

'I'll let Robert do it.'

They smiled at each other, perhaps quite surprised about the fondness that had already grown between both Edwin and Henrietta and the girl who had been their former maid.

Henrietta was ecstatic. 'Oh, how wonderful. An heir for the estate. It'll be a boy, I know it will. I'm so pleased for both of you.' She stretched out her hands to them. In her eyes, Robert could see the relief; no doubt his mother had feared that perhaps, after the trauma of his dreadful injury, he wouldn't be able to sire children. It had been something that had been in Robert's own mind.

'Pips will be thrilled too.'

'I hope so,' Robert murmured and for a moment they were all silent, thinking of her.

It had taken Pips a long time to write to tell her family that she and Giles had broken up and still, she had not told them the full story. Rose had not been mentioned, though she did say that Giles had gone to work elsewhere. The rest of her letter had been about their work within the corps and none of them could even read between the lines as to how she was feeling about her broken love affair.

'I really thought she had found someone nice at last,' Henrietta murmured.

'I thought so too,' Robert said. 'He was a fine chap – a good friend to me. I'm convinced he saved my life – even if he did have to chop my arm off.'

'There was no possibility of saving it, Robert,' Alice said quietly, 'but, yes, he did save you because his speedy operation prevented the dreadful gangrene.'

'I don't remember much about what happened, only waking up without my arm and you being there.' He touched her hand. 'And you've been there ever since. And now you're to give me a son or a daughter. I couldn't be more proud of you, Alice, or love you more.'

'It'll be a boy,' Henrietta said firmly. 'It's got to be a boy.'

'I really don't mind, Mother, as long as it's fit and healthy. And I wouldn't mind a little girl who looks just like her mother.' He kissed Alice's fingertips and smiled at her. 'Just you mind you don't overdo it, that's all. But, at least, I have Father on my side over that.'

'Me too,' Henrietta said. 'I'll watch she doesn't try to do too much.'

Alice smiled. Despite everything, she was happier than she'd ever dared to hope she would be. She was adored by the man she'd loved for years and the final drop to fill her cup of happiness was not only the expected child, but also that her husband's family had accepted her wholeheartedly. And because of her kind and sensitive nature, she still treated all the household staff with the deference she always had done. And in doing so, she had won them over too. They all, without exception, now treated her with the respect her elevated position deserved, but also with the friendliness they'd always shown her.

Alice had earned herself a special position within the household.

Seventy-Two

During the second week in April, Stephen called the team together. 'I would like your opinion, but I think we should move nearer to Arras. A battle started there a few days ago and it looks like lasting a while. What d'you all think?'

Pips glanced at Leonore. She and the sister now seemed to be regarded by the rest of the team as senior members. Leonore was certainly in charge of the nursing side, and they all looked to Pips to organize the vehicles and the recovery of casualties.

'I agree with you, Stephen, I think we should go,' Pips said and Leonore nodded. 'Dr Hazelwood formed us to be a *flying* ambulance corps that would go wherever we are most needed.'

'Are we all agreed, then?' Stephen asked, glancing around and receiving a chorus of 'yes'.

'Then I'll get in touch with Phil and Mike and see what they want to do. They'd be good as backup, but that decision must be theirs.'

'Right, then,' Grace said, 'Milly, you're with me. Come and help me pack, there's a dear.'

'Oh, and Milly,' Pips said, 'when you've finished helping Grace, come and help me sort out all the medical supplies the stretcher bearers use, will you? We need to make sure they have everything in their packs ready for use the minute we get there.'

'And after that, you can help Brigitta and me.' Leonore smiled.

Milly beamed. She loved being busy, and everyone was making her feel so needed.

As she trotted after her aunt, Pips murmured, 'You know, she really is an adorable girl. I just hope she doesn't get taken in by some lovesick soldier.'

Leonore chuckled. 'Have you noticed how she calls them all "dahling"?'

'*Does* she? Oh dear. I hope that doesn't give them the wrong idea.'

'I don't think so, because she says it to everyone. I even heard her call Stephen it yesterday. He looked a bit startled at first and then smiled as if to say, "Oh, it's just Milly".'

Pips laughed, but then she sobered. 'Well, we'll soon find out if she can cope with battle conditions. She's had a fairly easy induction so far. But now, things will get serious...'

The move to Arras went smoothly, but, on their arrival, they were soon inundated with casualties. As William unloaded the first ambulance, Milly stood and stared at the bandaged men, heard their cries of pain and saw two more ambulances coming into the field with yet more wounded.

'Oh my!' she murmured, but then she moved suddenly towards the rear of the vehicle and reached out to help William lift the stretcher. 'We'll soon have that leg seen to, dahling,' she said to the young soldier with a deep gash down the length of his left leg.

By the end of the first day, the front of Milly's dress was soaked with the blood of others and her hands were blistered from carrying the stretchers, but she was still smiling and moving amongst those lying on the ground, waiting for attention. She made them as comfortable as possible, helped them to drink or to eat and spoke soothingly.

'I'm so sorry I'm not a nurse, but is there anything I can do for you?'

She did not leave the field until the last patient had been carried into the treatment tent.

Later, Milly was missing and Pips went in search of her. She found her in the tent they shared at night. She was in tears and holding her hands out, palms upwards, in front of her. As Pips entered the tent, she tried to wipe the tears away but not before Pips had seen them. She sat down on the camp bed and put her arms around the girl's shoulders. 'You did wonderfully well today, Milly. I'll find you some ointment for your hands and, tomorrow, you must wear gloves.'

She leaned her head against Pips's shoulder. 'I didn't know it would be so awful. I feel so useless.'

'But you weren't. You fetched and carried, gave them drinks and comforted them until one of us could attend to their wounds. Now, come on, dry those tears and come with me to find Sister Leonore for that ointment.'

As they left the tent, Pips slipped her arm through Milly's. 'You'll do, Millicent Fortesque. You'll do.'

The Battle of Arras lasted a month and was considered one of the more successful offensives of the war, particularly the capture of Vimy Ridge in which the Canadians played the significant role.

At the beginning of July, the team heard that the first American troops had landed in France and had paraded in Paris. Bad news reached them at the same time that a casualty-clearing station near Bailleul had been attacked in an air raid and doctors and patients had been killed and injured.

At the very end of the month Stephen told them, 'We're going back to Ypres. There's going to be a third battle there in an effort to consolidate our gains – so I'm told. Field Marshal Sir Douglas Haig's aim is to capture the ports of Ostend and Zeebrugge.'

'I presume,' Pips said, 'that's because the German submarines and destroyers menace our shipping from those ports.'

Stephen smiled at her. 'Exactly right, Pips.'

'Then we'd better do our best to help him do it.'

'I'm suggesting we don't go back to Brandhoek this time, but to a place called Essex Farm about five miles from there as the crow flies and not far from the Ypres-Yser canal.'

Pips shuddered. Had she really walked all that

way in the darkness the night that she had discovered Giles's infidelity? For it had been near the canal that George had found her.

She pulled her attention back to what Stephen was saying.

'Why's it called Essex Farm? Unusual for an English name to be used, isn't it?'

'I understand the British took over that area from the French in the spring of 1915 and started to give English names to various locations, one of them being the dressing station and,' he added soberly, 'the cemetery that sadly became necessary there too.'

He paused briefly and then went on, 'I've been told that there are some well-constructed bunkers there that have been used as operating theatres, wards, kitchens and also dugouts for our personnel. We'll still take our tents with us, of course, they'll always come in useful. Mrs Parrott has obtained gas masks and tin hats for all of us, as we shall be pretty close to the fighting.'

'Gas?' Milly's eyes were wide. 'Are there likely to be gas attacks?'

'Their new weapon is mustard gas. It burns the eyes and comes over from the enemy in shells, so there's no warning.'

They reached their new home on 30 July and having inspected – and approved – the new accommodation, set everything up.

'We'd better get as much sleep as we can,' Stephen advised.

Early in the morning, the gunfire started and further sleep was impossible. Instead, they dressed and went outside to watch the searchlights, the star shells and gun flashes.

'Oh, the noise,' Milly said, putting her hands over her ears. 'Will it go on like this non-stop?'

'I wouldn't be surprised,' Pips said ruefully. 'Come on, Milly, we'd better get ready. We're going to have a busy day...'

About mid-morning came the high explosives. 'These are what the tin hats are for,' Pips said, pulling hers on. 'Oh, very fetching, Milly.'

'At least they're not gas shells,' Milly said.

'No, but the flying shrapnel is just as deadly. Come on, I'm driving the ambulance today. The others have already gone. If only this wretched rain would stop.'

'Is it ever going to stop raining, William?'

'I've never known weather like this in July and August, Pips. The locals say that it's not rained like this for over thirty years. The mud is the worst enemy in this battle. It takes eight of us sometimes to carry one casualty through it. And even if we get to our first-aid post, the motor ambulances are getting bogged down. And the horses...' He shuddered. 'It's pitiful to see the poor creatures struggling and just sinking. The look in their eyes...'

'Don't, William. I hope I don't witness any of that.'

'We've lost no end of men that way too. If they slip off the duckboards and there's no one on hand to help them, they're gone.'

But, of course, she did see it all. Day after day, they trudged from the trenches back to the advanced first-aid post, scarcely knowing how they kept going. And then out again they went. Whilst there were men to tend, somehow, they would carry on.

Pips wrote home to Robert, using the code as they'd planned where she felt it was necessary:

The Somme was bad enough – and of course, the tremendous loss of life was appalling – but this is just soul-destroying. The countryside is a wasteland as far as one can see. Ravaged and devastated for generations to come, I shouldn't wonder. And there are so many who've been lost and who have no known grave – blown to pieces and never found or lost in the mud. We're all so weary and can't see an end to it all. The one bright spark is Milly. At first, we all thought she was rather scatty and empty-headed, but she keeps so cheerful through it all and isn't afraid of anything. Looks can certainly be deceptive. The soldiers absolutely adore her...

But it's the mud, Robert, that's making life so difficult here. To see the men brought in caked with mud and to know that it will have infected their wounds when we're trying so hard – and putting ourselves in danger in the effort – to get treatment to them so much earlier is heartbreaking. We get the odd fine day now and again but it never seems long enough for the ground to really dry out and then we get rain and thunderstorms again. Everyone here is doing sterling work, but I do miss you and Alice...

Seventy-Three

'Edwin, you don't mean to tell me that Pips is in that lot?' Henrietta held out the newspaper to her husband and jabbed at the picture on the front page of seven stretcher bearers struggling to carry one casualty through mud almost up to their knees. 'Haig's talking about successful operations and the capture of various fortified locations, but then concedes that the actual ground gained is only a few hundred yards. Edwin, if my schoolgirl arithmetic serves me correctly, that's less than a mile. And according to this report, there are air battles going on overhead now and several British aircraft have been lost.'

'It's a bad business,' he murmured, folding his newspaper. 'Hetty, my love, I have tickets for a concert tonight. Why don't we...?'

'Edwin, how can you even think of going out when our daughter is in such danger? I couldn't settle – I can't settle – until I know she's safe.'

It wasn't until the beginning of November that the long, weary battle, the third near the town of Ypres, but which would always be known as Pass-chendaele – a name that would become synony-mous with the mud, blood and carnage of Flanders fields – seemed to be coming to an end. For over three months, Dr Hazelwood's team had worked non-stop, without anyone taking so much as a whole day off. In early November, the British and the Canadians captured the devastated village of Passchendaele and drove the Germans back.

'This has been the worst one yet, hasn't it?' Pips said to William as they made their way yet again into the trenches and through the winding, water-logged channels to reach the front line.

'It's the mud,' William muttered, as he splashed through the brackish water, leading the way. 'We must have lost hundreds of men who drowned in it. And the number of horses they've lost that way, well, I reckon they've lost count.'

Pips shuddered. She'd seen one poor creature perish that way, thrashing helplessly in the mud and sinking further with each desperate effort. No one could help him, though one or two men tried to put a rope round him and haul him out. But the mud had sucked him down and threatened to take his would-be rescuers with him.

But there was still spasmodic gunfire, still men being injured. They reached the front-line trenches and passed behind the men standing to on the fire steps. No one took any notice of them; they were the faceless stretcher bearers, whom no one wanted to acknowledge.

There was a faint buzzing in the sky. Everyone glanced up and watched as a lone aircraft flew down the length of no-man's-land, between the two lines of trenches. He was only thirty or forty feet above the ground. As he came closer, they heard his engine splutter and then die. The nose of the aircraft dipped.

'Oh my, he's coming down,' Pips breathed and watched in horror as the aircraft hit the ground, bounced twice and then settled into the mud almost level with where Pips and William were standing.

'Come on,' Pips said, grasping the nearest ladder. 'We've got to get to him before the Germans do.'

'Wait, Pips. It might go up if he was carrying a bomb.'

'If he had been, it'd've blown up before now.'

'You can't go up there, miss,' a sergeant said. 'They'll start firing.'

'Just watch me, sunshine,' Pips muttered as she climbed almost to the top, dragged her nurse's cap from her hair and waved it above her head.

'Stretcher bearers,' she yelled, but there was no response this time from the enemy line. 'Oh phooey,' she muttered and climbed over the top.

'I'm right behind you, Pips, but for God's sake, keep low.'

Pips glanced back briefly at William. 'There's a break in the wire with a plank over it, just to the left. I'll make for that.'

Without waiting for any further objection from anyone, Pips climbed over the edge of the parapet and, stooping as low as she could, ran to the gap in the barbed wire. A shot zapped close by her.

'Bastards,' she muttered and yelled again. 'Stretcher bearers,' but yet another bullet buried itself in the mud close by. She was through the wire and running zig-zag across the ground towards the aircraft lying drunkenly on one buckled wing. Close behind her, she could hear splashing footsteps and knew William was following. She reached the aircraft and ducked down beside it to shield herself from the enemy's gunfire. William threw himself down beside her, panting heavily.

'Right, let's get him out, if we can, before they get here.'

'Sergeant said our lads'll cover us.'

She glanced back quickly and could see a line of soldiers, their helmets just above the top of the trench, their rifles pointing at the enemy. Already they were firing consecutively to stop the Germans leaving the safety of their trenches. Cautiously, they moved to the cockpit. The pilot was leaning to one side, his head against the side of the air-craft. His eyes were closed. Pips wriggled her fingers beneath his flying helmet and scarf until she could feel a pulse in his neck.

'He's still alive. Let's get him out.'

Together they stood up, leaned into the cockpit and struggled to release his straps.

'Ease him out steadily, William. We don't know what injuries he's got yet...'

The pilot groaned and moved.

'What – where...?' he moaned.

'Are you hurt?'

A bullet pinged against the far side of the aircraft and Pips and William's reflex action was to duck down.

'It's my right leg, I think.'

'Can you lever yourself up, so we can pull you out?'

Another bullet hit the aircraft.

'Hell fire!' the pilot muttered and pushed him-self up.

With their help, he toppled sideways out of the plane and lay on the ground.

'My plates,' he gasped. 'You must get my plates.'

'Can't worry about that...' Pips began, but he was insistent.

'They mustn't get their hands on my box of plates. They're photographs of their lines – and ours.' He winced in pain, but persisted. 'It's on the floor of the cockpit on the left-hand side, beneath where the camera is mounted.'

'William, can you carry him on your back and I'll look for this damned box? It's obviously very important to him.'

William was doubtful, but he knew Pips couldn't carry the casualty on her own. Reluctantly, he agreed; he had no choice. 'All right, but don't hang about. If you can't find it, leave it.'

She helped hoist the pilot onto William's broad back, then turned back to the aircraft. Reaching into the cockpit, her fingers found a box shape. 'This must be it,' she muttered. It was heavier than she'd thought.

Hearing a shout behind her, she looked back at the British lines to see several of the soldiers waving frantically. William had almost reached the barbed wire and two soldiers had climbed out of the trench to help him cover the last few yards.

'They're coming, they're coming. Hurry, nurse, hurry!'

She glanced over her shoulder and saw three Germans climbing out of their trenches. One fell immediately, shot by a Tommy, but the other two began firing at the crashed aircraft – and her. Hugging the box to her chest, she began to run back towards the British line, still remembering to zig-zag. Through the barbed wire and towards the trench. She was almost there when she felt a searing pain in her leg and knew she'd been shot.

Pips pitched forward, face down in the mud.

Seventy-Four

'You know, Alice, I don't like the tone of the letters we're getting from Pips now. She sounds utterly exhausted. I wish she'd come home for a while.'

'She won't leave whilst there's still work to be done, you know that, Robert. And this offensive at Passchendaele isn't over yet, is it?'

'Surely it must come to an end soon. We're into November and another winter.' He paused and then added, 'I'll write to her and suggest it. She might listen to me.'

Alice chuckled. 'Pips won't listen to anyone, darling. You should know that.'

'Well, what would bring her home?'

Alice smoothed her hand over her growing bulge. 'The arrival of her nephew or niece, perhaps.'

'What a good idea. I'll write at once.'

'Your handwriting is improving each day. The last batch of your notes I typed up for you – though to be honest I can hardly reach the keys now – was much more legible.'

'You shouldn't be doing so much now.' Robert frowned. 'I think I should confiscate the typewriter.'

'Don't you dare! It's all I have left to do. Your

father's banned me from involving myself with our convalescents until after the baby is born, the staff won't let me do so much as a little light dusting. And as for your mother...' She rolled her eyes. 'She's making me drink the most disgusting things, saying it's good for the indigestion I've been getting. She's a dear, and I'm thankful she's forgiven me for marrying you, but just sometimes, I wish Pips was here.'

'Then I'll tell her that too. Actually, that's the one thing that might work...'

Willing hands lifted her and carried Pips through the barbed wire and down into the trench. She was still clutching the heavy box of photographic plates.

'William? Where's William? Is he all right? And what about the pilot?'

'I'm here, Pips.' She was thankful to hear William's voice. He was squatting down beside her. 'Where are you hurt?'

'My left calf.'

Gently, William lifted her skirt. 'It doesn't look too bad. Just a flesh wound, but it's bleeding quite badly. I'd better dress it.'

'The pilot. See to him first.'

'He's already on his way to our ambulance. Some of the lads have taken him.'

As William put a temporary bandage round her leg, they heard the order given to stand down.

'They've scuttled back to their trenches,' the sergeant told them. 'I'll have to ask my captain what I'm to do about the plane. I suppose we ought to bring it in or at least set fire to it so they can't capture it.'

'Sorry, mate.' William grinned. 'We'll have to leave that to you. Now, Pips, can you stand?'

'We'll carry her,' came a chorus of voices before she could move. A burly soldier stepped forward and said, in a broad Yorkshire accent, 'I can carry t'lass.' And so saying, he placed his right arm beneath her knees and his left around her back and lifted her into his arms. 'She's as light as a feather.'

He manoeuvred his way through the network of trenches and placed her in the ambulance alongside their other casualty.

'Have you got my plates?' was all the pilot asked her.

Despite the stinging pain in her leg, Pips fell into a paroxysm of laughter.

'What? What did I say?'

'Pips, I need to talk to you,' Stephen said. 'First, how's the leg feel?'

'Not bad. A bit sore, but I'm sure I could go on light duties...'

But Stephen waved aside her suggestion. 'No, I think you should go on leave for a few weeks until it's properly healed. And because of that,' Stephen went on, 'I've had an idea. There are four casualties with what we call "Blighty" wounds, including your pilot. His leg is quite badly smashed up. I hear that the hospitals here are overflowing with all the casualties, particularly after Passchendaele, and I'm suggesting that these four should go straight back to England, and I'd like you to go with them and then stay a while at home until you're fully fit again. However careful we are, your wound could become infected out here. You know that, don't you? And these patients will still need a modicum of nursing care on the journey, which I'm sure you could give them without any harm to yourself.'

Although she was reluctant to go, Pips could understand his reasoning. 'Is this an order?'

Stephen smiled gently. 'If it needs to be, Pips, then yes, it is.'

The day before William was due to drive Pips and the four patients to the coast, Pips went to meet them. Her leg was hurting and she was limping, but she refused to use a walking stick. Two of the men she would look after on the journey had shoulder wounds. Not serious in themselves, but they would take some time to heal well enough for them to return to duty.

'I can't hold me rifle properly, nurse. Beggars got me right where the butt rests,' Norman told her, then he grinned broadly and waved a piece of paper in the air. 'But it's got me a "Blighty" ticket.'

Pips reached out as if to take it. 'Would you like me to take care of that for you?'

Norman snatched it away and held it possessively against his chest. 'Not likely. No offence, nurse, but the only place this ticket is going is in my pocket.'

Pips laughed and turned to speak to the soldier sitting beside him, whose name was Terry.

'My collarbone's smashed. Doc says it'll tek a while before I'm fit to come back.' He nodded towards another soldier sitting a short distance away. 'But I reckon that poor lad's going home for good, don't you, nurse?'

All three turned to look at the private, who was no more than a boy, Pips thought. He reminded her poignantly of Harold Dawson. If only, she thought, it could have been him she was taking home to his family.

'Shell shock – that's what we call all that dreadful shaking, nurse,' Norman said.

'And he was gassed too. His breathing's bad.'

'But if you can get him home, nurse...'

'What's his name?'

'Joe – that's all I know. He doesn't say much.'

Pips walked to him and put her hand on his shoulder. His whole body was shaking and when he looked up at her, his eyes mirrored his suffering.

'I'm taking you home, Joe. Back to England. I'll see that you're cared for.'

Joe – he couldn't be much more than seventeen or eighteen, she thought – appeared to nod, though Pips could not tell if it was merely part of the constant shaking or whether he really understood.

'And now, I'd better go and find my pilot.'

'He's in the tent over there.' Terry pointed. 'Still clutching that blasted box you nearly died for.'

It seemed everyone at the unit had now heard the story.

His name was Mitchell Hammond. 'Mitch to my friends,' he told her. He was very handsome, with raven-black hair and the darkest brown eyes she had ever seen. When he laughed, his eyes twinkled with merriment.

'You've got a very nasty injury,' Pips said, with sympathy.

Mitch grimaced. 'Doc said my leg's broken in two places. I need to go to the hospital to have it put in plaster. So, I won't be flying again for a while. But I must get my pictures back to the authorities as soon as I can.' He tapped the box-like shape sitting beside him. 'Have you any idea how I can do that?'

'Dr Portas is sending four of you all the way home. The hospitals here are overcrowded now. William is taking you and three others to the coast.'

'If that's the case, then I think I'll take it all the way home with me. Are you coming with us?'

She hesitated and then smiled. 'As it happens, yes. I haven't been home for almost a year and Dr Portas has suggested that I accompany the four of you to hospital in England.'

'Once I get my leg in plaster, maybe I could go home. I won't need to take up a valuable hospital bed.'

'Mm,' Pips said thoughtfully. 'Or, maybe you could go to a convalescent home. I think I know just the place.'

Seventy-Five

William drove them to the nearest hospital, where Mitch had his leg put in plaster. When it was over, he was grey with the pain, but still he was holding tightly onto his precious box.

'I just daren't let it out of my sight until we get across the Channel,' he told Pips. 'If I hand it over to someone here, I've no way of knowing how long it'll take to get back to England, so, as soon as we land, I'll have to find someone in authority who will understand its significance.'

'I'll see what I can do to help you,' Pips promised. She was beginning to understand just how important these photographs might be.

It seemed to Pips that Mitch Hammond's charm was working for all of them – that, or his need for speed. There were few hold-ups on the trains and they were quickly on board a ship to take them to England.

As soon as they landed, Pips went in search of someone who could help Mitch. She found the port authorities and asked to see someone in a senior position.

After half an hour's wait, she was shown into someone's office. The man behind the desk, middle-aged and kindly, was wearing some sort of uniform, though she couldn't be sure what it was.

'Come in, nurse. Do sit down,' he said at once,

noticing her limp. 'How can I help you?'

Swiftly, she explained their dilemma.

At once he picked up a telephone. 'We have an RAF camp quite close. I will speak to the station commander there.'

After a short conversation, he replaced the receiver. 'He's coming over straight away to meet Lieutenant Hammond and to take the photographic plates into his safe keeping. Now, I will have someone drive you back to your patients.'

An hour later the group captain arrived in person, proved his identity to Mitch's satisfaction and was handed the box.

'This nurse almost lost her life rescuing me and these from my crashed plane, sir,' Mitch told him. 'Right in the middle of no-man's-land. If it hadn't been for her and the stretcher bearer with her neither I, nor these photographs, would be here. We'd be in German hands. Please see that they get to the right people as soon as you can. The photographs are of the enemy's fortifications along a stretch of the Western Front.'

'Very valuable information,' the group captain murmured. 'I shall take it there myself.' Instead of saluting, he held out his hand to Mitch. 'Well done, Hammond, and thank you too, nurse.'

After he'd gone, Mitch lay back and closed his eyes as if, at last relieved of the huge responsibility, he could relax.

The two soldiers with shoulder wounds were to stay in a hospital near the coast, but it had been decided, on Pips's insistence, that she should take Joe and Mitch to Doddington Hall.

'My brother is a doctor and was badly wounded

himself. He is making a study of the trauma caused by the constant shelling and of other serious injuries. The Fourth Northern General Hospital is situated at Lincoln, so help is at hand if we need it.'

Approval was given and Pips and her two patients were taken to the station.

She was on her way home.

'Have you heard?' This had now become a regular greeting when Bess stepped through the back door of the Dawsons' cottage. 'Miss Pips is home. She's been injured out there.'

Ma and Norah paused in their knitting and turned anxious eyes towards their visitor. 'Badly?'

Bess shook her head. 'Just a flesh wound on the back of her leg. Nowt serious, they say. Our Betty told us.'

Now that both her daughters were working at the hall, Bess got the news first-hand.

'She knows everything even afore the *Lincolnshire Echo*,' Ma had commented with a sniff. 'I reckon they'd give her a job as a local reporter, if she asked.'

'And,' Bess went on, 'she's summat of a heroine, it seems.'

'We don't need to be told that,' Ma said, picking up her knitting needles. 'All them nurses and doctors are. Look what's happened to poor Master Robert.'

'Aye, but it's more than that. Miss Pips went out into the strip of land between the opposing armies to rescue a pilot from his crashed aeroplane. That's when she got shot in the leg, and now she's

440

brought him all the way back to the hall to con-
valesce along with another poor lad who's got the
shakes bad. The pilot's got a smashed-up leg.
Betty says he's ever so handsome.'

'They let her go out there on her own? Into
danger?'

'She wasn't on her own,' Bess said, with a note
of triumph in her tone. This was the choicest
titbit of news. 'Your William was with her. He's a
hero, an' all.'

Seventy-Six

Pips had known the inquisition would come.
Ever since her arrival home three days earlier, her
mother had been tight-lipped and disapproving
glances had been cast in her direction.

'So, Philippa,' Henrietta said, as they sat down
in the parlour after their evening meal and when
she could hold back the questions no longer.
'What did you do to upset Giles?'

'Mother,' Robert said, before Pips could answer,
'that's hardly fair. Their romance started in very
unusual circumstances. Not all of them are going
to survive.' He smiled at Alice as if to say, 'We're
lucky. Ours did.'

There was a silence in the room. Edwin picked
up his newspaper and hid behind it, though they
all knew he was listening intently to the conversation.

'No, it didn't, Robert,' Henrietta insisted. 'It

started here – in this house. We all saw it.'

'No doubt,' Pips said drily in answer to her mother's question, 'I was just being me and he decided I was not the sort to make him a suitable wife.'

'Mm.' Henrietta eyed her daughter thoughtfully. 'That's understandable, though with all your experience as a nurse now, I'd've thought that, at least, would have been a point in your favour. But you're too wayward, Philippa, too independent. You should have shown him that you would be obedient to your husband in all things.'

The newspaper shook and from behind it there came what sounded suspiciously like a chuckle, though it was turned swiftly into a cough. Henrietta glared at the back of the paper, but went on, 'I want to know if there's anything we can do to get him back. If I invite him to stay with us...'

Pips shook her head. 'There's nothing that can be done, Mother. Please – just leave it.'

'But he was such a nice young man, so suitable.'

'I wasn't going to say anything,' Robert said, 'but perhaps I should.'

Henrietta and Pips both turned to look at him. Alice bowed her head as if she already knew what Robert was about to say.

'Giles was in many ways a good man. He was an excellent doctor and a very skilled surgeon, but, even before you told us what happened, Pips, I had begun to have my doubts about him. Since I've been home, I've done a little digging. It seems his parents don't live in Scarborough, nor is his father a teacher. He is in fact a coal miner from a small Yorkshire village.'

442

Pips stared at him. 'You mean – you mean, he's ashamed of his parentage?'

'Seems like it.'

'That's despicable. Miners are the salt of the earth.'

'I agree with you there, Pips,' Edwin said, lowering his newspaper. 'Where would we all be without them? But it seems to me that what has happened is for the best after all, though I'm sorry if you've been hurt, Pips.'

Before her mother could say anything, Pips jumped up and left the room. She climbed the stairs to the drawing room that was now the patients' lounge.

'Hello, there.' Mitch greeted her with a wide grin. 'Please come and talk to me. I'm dying of boredom.'

Pips stood in front of him, her arms akimbo. 'Do you play chess?'

Mitch's eyes lit up. 'I do. Not very well, but no doubt I could beat you.'

Pips smiled, the confrontation with her mother forgotten as she planned her campaign to put this conceited young man firmly in his place. 'I'll fetch the chess set.'

She was obliged to go back into the parlour to fetch the board and pieces. There was still an uncomfortable silence.

'Mind if I take the chess set, Robert? Mitch Hammond plays.'

'Be my guest.'

'Oh now, I don't know about that, Philippa,' Henrietta said. 'He's a very brash young man. He flirts with all the maids and–'

443

'Yes, Mother, that's what handsome young men do,' Pips murmured bitterly as she picked up the game and headed back towards the door.

'But, Philippa, I wouldn't like you to–'

'Never in a million years, Mother. You needn't worry on that score, I promise you.'

After half an hour's play, Pips said, 'Checkmate.'

Mitch stared at the board. 'How on earth did that happen?'

Pips laughed. He'd been an easy conquest, but it was exactly what she needed just now. She didn't want long, complicated and therefore taxing games.

'I'll show you,' she said, as she set up the board as if to begin another game, but instead she took him through all the moves they had both made in the game they had just played.

'You see, if you'd moved your knight there and your bishop there, you would have thwarted my plan, which was this–' Deftly, she moved the pieces about the board.

'How on earth can you remember all the moves we *both* made? I can't even remember my own, let alone yours as well.' He looked up into her eyes. 'You must have a remarkable memory, Miss Maitland. You're wasted as a nurse. You ought to have been a spy.'

'And be shot for my trouble, like poor Edith Cavell? Thanks very much.'

'I'm a bit tired now,' Mitch admitted and, indeed, there were dark shadows beneath his eyes. 'But will you play again tomorrow?'

'Of course. I'm planning to go back abroad soon, but Robert is a good player. He'll give you a game now and then.'

'Is he better than you?'

'Heavens, no!' She grinned and then added generously, 'But just as good.'

Mitch grimaced as she packed the pieces into their wooden box and folded the board. 'I don't expect I'll have any chance of beating him then, either.'

'Try the tactics I've just shown you.'

'I'll never remember them.'

'We'll go through them again tomorrow. It'll give you a fighting chance.'

Seventy-Seven

Pips woke with a start. Dawn was just beginning to filter through the gap in her bedroom curtains, when the noise that had disturbed her came again. A gentle knock on her door and an urgent whisper, 'Pips! Pips!'

Pips threw back the covers and reached for her dressing gown from the end of the bed. 'Coming,' she said softly and crossed to the door. Opening it, she found Robert in his nightshirt.

'It's Alice. She's in labour, but she says not to waken Father yet. Her waters have broken, but the pains are only ten minutes apart.'

'Right. I'll come and see her, then get dressed and mobilize the troops.' They exchanged a glance. Would they ever be able to drop phrases that reminded them of wartime?

Alice was sitting up in bed, beaming with pleasure.

'Well, I've never heard of anyone looking quite so happy when they're in labour,' Pips said.

Alice's grin only broadened. 'Our baby's coming, Pips. Soon, we'll have our baby–' But then her face twisted as the pain began again.

'Should we send for the midwife?' Pips began, but Alice shook her head. 'No. No midwife. Just you and Father. And I want Robert here too.'

'Right, you're the boss. Robert, go and wake Father now. I think he should be warned.'

When Robert returned, Pips went to dress hurriedly and then ran down to the kitchen where the maids were already at work. Swiftly, she told them what was needed upstairs. As she climbed back up the stairs, she realized that her leg was no longer hurting.

Back in the bedroom, Alice said, 'The pains are coming about every five minutes now. I've timed them.'

Pips was amazed at how calm and organized Alice was. She placed her hand on Alice's abdomen and, after three minutes, she felt the contraction. Then she timed the next one and said, 'Only four minutes now. This little one's in a hurry to make his entrance into the world.'

'Now, here we are, then...' Edwin came into the room carrying his medical bag. He was fully dressed and washed his hands in the ewer and bowl on the washstand in the corner of the room. Then he examined Alice and said, 'Now, my dear, you must do exactly as I say. Pant when I tell you and then push when I tell you. All right?

446

We've been through it together, haven't we, but now it's for real.'

Alice nodded and then screwed up her face again as Robert slipped back into the room. He had managed to put on his dressing gown over his nightshirt, but dressing properly was still impossible for him unaided. Tiny shirt buttons presented a problem. He sat beside Alice and held her hand, glancing every so often at Pips and his father for reassurance that all was going well.

After only twenty minutes of pushing and panting alternately, Edwin said, 'The head's presented. Now, my dear, take a breather and when the next contraction starts, push as hard as you can.'

Seconds later, Alice said, 'It's coming, it's coming. Aah!'

'There!' Edwin said triumphantly as if he had done it all himself. 'Alice – Robert – you have a baby girl.'

'Is she – all right?'

'She's perfect. Now, wait a moment whilst I cut the cord and then you can hold her. Pips, fetch that warm towel from the fireguard to wrap her in. Mother must hold her straight away.'

Edwin placed the baby into Alice's arms and both she and Robert bent over their daughter.

'A girl! I really wanted a girl,' Robert said. 'And she has black hair just like you.'

'Not a boy? You're not disappointed?'

'Not for a moment. How clever you are, my darling,' Robert murmured as he kissed Alice's damp forehead.

'Pips, you get a bath ready for the little one,' Edwin said. 'I'll test the water and then you'll know what it needs to be for the next few days whilst Alice recovers. How fortunate it is that you're at home.'

When Alice surrendered her daughter, Pips looked down at the tiny baby and love flooded through her whole being. Tears of joy filled her eyes and fell onto the towel. 'Alice, she's beautiful,' she said huskily. 'What are you going to call her?'

'Daisy,' Alice said promptly.

At that moment, Pips gave away her heart to the little baby wriggling in her arms. 'Hello, Daisy,' she whispered. 'I'm your Aunty Pips.'

Later that morning, Alice said, 'Pips, please will you go and tell my parents and Ma?'

'Of course. I'll go this minute.'

'Have luncheon first...' Alice began, but Pips shook her head. 'No, I'll go now. I don't want them hearing via the Cooper girls. You know what Bess is like.'

Alice, still pink-cheeked from her exertions, laughed.

Pips walked down the road, hardly limping at all now. Her father had examined the wound yesterday and pronounced that it was healing well.

'Soon be time to go back,' she murmured. 'There's nothing to keep me here...' But a little voice inside her head said, *But what about that beautiful baby girl? How can you bear to leave her now?*

'She's Alice's baby, not mine,' Pips said the words aloud as if to tell herself it was so.

Ma was sitting outside the cottage in the watery December sun.

Taking the clay pipe from her mouth, she said, 'Nah, then, Miss Pips. How are you?'

'I'm well, thank you. And you?'

'Aye, well enough.' There was a pause before she asked, 'Have you brought us some news? Have I got another great-grandchild?'

Pips sat down beside her. 'Indeed you have, Ma. A great-granddaughter, this time.'

''Spect that's a disappointment for you all. You'd've wanted a boy, no doubt.'

'Certainly not! What I mean is, none of us minded what it was, as long as it was healthy.'

'And is she?'

'Oh Ma,' Pips said, dreamily, 'she's absolutely perfect.'

The old lady chuckled. 'Sounds as if you've fallen in love with her.'

'Yes, Ma, I think perhaps I have.'

'Aye well, lass, your time will come. It's a shame it didn't work out for you with that nice young man. Dr Kendall, was it?'

'Mm,' was all Pips replied.

There was a short silence between them but Ma asked no more questions. Instead, she said, 'Give Norah a call for me, will you, lass? She should hear the news.'

Norah shed a few tears. 'It's happy news, I know, but I just can't help thinking about my boys at a time like this. Wouldn't they have been tickled pink, Ma?'

'Aye, and 'tis sad Boy never even knew he had a bairn.'

Startled, Pips said, 'But he did know. William and I were both with him at the end. Alice had

449

had a letter from you and we told him he had a son and he understood, because he said, "I have a son".'

Norah nodded. 'I'm glad. I must tell Peggy. She'll be pleased that at least he knew.'

'And he also said that if he could have got home, he would've married her.'

'Did he? Did he really say that?'

'Yes, he did.'

'That'll mean the world to her. Perhaps, Miss Pips, if it's not asking too much, would you tell Peggy yourself? She'll believe it more if it comes from you, 'cos she knows you were with him.'

'Of course I will.'

'So, poor lad knew he was dying, then,' Ma said. 'Did he?'

'We tried to get him to believe we could save him, but his injury was such that–' Pips paused, recalling the words she'd put in her letter to them, telling them that he hadn't suffered. She ran her tongue round her lips and added, 'If he'd lingered, he would have suffered terrible pain then.'

Ma nodded, but Pips could see in her wise old eyes that she wasn't deceived. Norah, however, clung to the belief that her boy had gone quickly and without any real agony.

Pips hesitated, then said, 'There's something else. Perhaps I should have told you this before – when I was home for Alice and Robert's wedding – but you all seemed quite upset then–'

She paused and didn't continue until Ma prompted, 'Go on, Miss Pips.'

'Harold wanted to be sure you knew that William was a hero – not a coward. He told William he was so very sorry about how he and his brothers had treated him. I did – I'm afraid – tell a little white lie.' One of many at that time, she thought ruefully. 'Harold so wanted to believe that you were in touch with William and – to let him die happy – I told him that you' – she glanced at Norah – 'had written to William to tell him about Peggy. I said we'd get him home so that he could tell you about his brother himself. But then, he gave a long sigh and died, though he went peacefully in the end. I – I hope I did the right thing.'

Both Ma and Norah spoke at once.

'Of course you did, Miss Pips.'

'You eased my boy's passing and I thank you for that.'

'And William?'

The two older women glanced at each other before Ma said, 'We understand what he's doing, but it's Len that's the problem. I don't reckon he'll ever believe it, however much anyone tells him.'

'Then I'm sorry,' Pips said.

There was a silence in the room until Pips rose. 'I'll be leaving in a few days' time, but I'll make sure I speak to Peggy before then. And Mother said that you're welcome at the hall any time to see Daisy.'

'Daisy? Is that her name?'

Pips nodded.

Slowly, Norah smiled and murmured, 'Daisy. Daisy Maitland. And fancy, my little Alice being a mother. Please tell her we'll come and see her tomorrow afternoon.'

'I'll get Jake to bring the trap to fetch you. And

now, I must go. I have some packing to do.'

'I really think you should stay until the New Year, Pips,' Edwin said seriously. 'And it's not just because we'd all like you here for Christmas. I'd be much happier about your leg if you stayed a little longer.'

'But it's healing well, Father. You said so yourself.'

'I did, my dear, and it is, but not quite well enough to go back where there's such a lot of infection. Dr Portas is unlikely to let you go back on duty yet. And – be honest – you're still limping a little when you think no one else is watching.'

'But I was hoping to take back a lot of the gifts Mother has collected for Christmas.'

'She can send those through the usual channels.'

'Well,' Pips said slowly, 'it would be rather nice to be with you all for Christmas, especially now that we have a little one in the house.'

'Yes, it rather adds meaning to the whole celebration, doesn't it, though I fear, as a nation, we haven't much to celebrate.'

'Maybe 1918 will be the year it all ends.'

Edwin's wish was heartfelt as he said, 'I'll raise a glass to that, my dear.'

'You'll be delighted to know,' Henrietta announced, 'that Basil and Rosemary are able to dine with us on New Year's Eve.'

Pips clapped her hands. 'Oh, I'm so glad I stayed, then. I haven't seen him for what seems years.'

'It is years,' Henrietta said. 'He hasn't been at home much since before the war started.'

Pips was suddenly concerned. 'He's all right, isn't he? I mean, he's not ill, is he?'

'No, no. It's just a long leave, I think.'

'Not before time,' Pips said tartly and then smiled, just thinking of the ebullient character.

Pips dressed with care for dinner that evening. The convalescents were having their own celebration in the drawing room that they now used as their sitting room. She went to wish them all a Happy New Year before joining her own family.

'You look absolutely ravishing,' Mitch said, with a saucy wink. 'Do I get a New Year kiss?'

'No, you most certainly do not.'

He grimaced but continued to gaze at her with undisguised admiration until she said goodnight to them all and left the room.

Mitch might have been a little put out if he had seen her enthusiastic welcome for Major Fieldsend. She flung her arms around him and kissed him soundly on both cheeks, and he was delighted to reciprocate.

'My dear, dear girl. How good it is to see you. And still looking so beautiful, despite all you've been through. And Robert. Dear boy. How are you?'

Tactfully, he held out his left hand to Robert, who smiled and shook it firmly.

The dinner party was a merry one, but inevitably, it grew more serious towards the end of the meal when the war could no longer be kept from the conversation.

'Now tell me, my dear, are you really going back?'

'I must, major. There's still such a need out there for what we do.' She glanced apologetically at her mother before saying, 'It is imperative that we have an advanced first-aid post as close to the trenches as possible. It's the infection, you see. Robert was extraordinarily lucky that he didn't develop gas gangrene.'

Solemnly, Robert said, 'Only because, as I now know, the four of you came out into no-man's-land to fetch me straight away. Much longer out there and I would not have survived.'

Henrietta gasped and turned pale. Though the news of the dramatic rescue had filtered into the village, everyone had been careful to keep the details from Henrietta. But now she was hearing them for herself.

Her eyes filled with tears. 'Oh Pips – and you too, Alice – how courageous you were.'

Pips shrugged. 'He's my brother.' She glanced at Alice and smiled. 'And we all know why Alice was first up the side of the shell hole waving her nurse's cap to try to stop the Germans firing at us.'

'And did they?'

'Yes, they did, but not when William and I fetched Mitch Hammond from his plane. That's why I got shot.' Her smile widened. 'I called them a few choice names that are not repeatable around the dinner table.'

Basil's booming laugh filled the room, but then he became serious once more. 'I think I should warn you that the war is far from over yet. Through intelligence we have received from our spies and from one or two prisoners and even, I have to say, from a couple of deserters from the German Army, we think that the enemy are likely to mount a series of offensives through this year. Pips, you were wounded just as the village of Passchendaele fell into Allied hands at the beginning of November, so you may not have the very latest news.'

'I get letters from Leonore, and she tells me that all three units have moved to near Cambrai.'

Basil nodded. 'Towards the end of November, the plan was for our Third Army, under General Sir Julian Byng, to begin a tank-led offensive against the Hindenburg Line.'

Pips grinned. 'Tanks!' she murmured. 'Oh, I love those tanks.'

'The early attacks were very successful in the main,' Basil went on, 'but, sadly, the tanks began to suffer mechanical failure, got bogged down or were put out of action by German artillery. Unfortunately, by December, the Germans launched successful counterattacks.' Basil's face was solemn. 'So, we gained little or nothing for about forty thousand casualties. Still,' his face brightened a little as he added, 'the good news is that the US declared war on Austria-Hungary at the beginning of December. But no doubt you know that.'

'Was anything learned from the Battle of Cambrai?' Edwin asked.

'As a matter of fact, yes. We realized that to be successful, offensives don't necessarily need to be started with a long artillery bombardment and, second, tanks can achieve an initial breakthrough even though their long-term reliability is still an issue.'

'What's happening now?' Pips was anxious to know. 'What am I going back to?'

'Nothing much at present. The bad weather of winter will play its usual part, but come the spring...' The major spread his hands in a gesture that said: *who knows what will happen?*

'So, you're really going back, then?' Robert said, hugging her as Pips stood in the hall with her suitcases at her feet.

They had enjoyed a quiet Christmas and New Year. Being all together and with the baby to dote on, it had been a happy time cocooned in their own little world. Pips had monopolized Daisy, wheeling her out on fine days in her perambulator, showing her off around the village and taking her to visit her other grandparents and great-grandmother. And seeing the major and Rosemary, despite the serious conversations, had been a delight. But now, in the second week in January, Pips felt the pull to return to duty.

'I can't stay here, Robert – though I'd like to, now we've got little Daisy – but there's still so much to do out there. I've had a letter from Dr Hazelwood. He says the unit are somewhere near Arras until they find out where they are needed next. He asked when I'd be returning, so they obviously still want me.'

'Of course they do, but do take care of yourself, darling Sis. You're a bit rash at times. Saving Mitch like you did was foolhardy, to say the least.'

'That reminds me, I'd better go and say goodbye to the boys.'

Swiftly, she went from bed to bed in the long gallery, leaving the drawing room until last.

Mitch was alone. 'Come for a last game?'

'Sorry, but no, Jake is waiting to take me to the station. I have to go.'

She held out her hand. He took it and pulled her towards him. Caught off balance, she pitched forward, almost on top of him. His hand held the back of her head and he kissed her firmly on the mouth. She tried to pull back, but he still held her, his face close, his dark eyes gazing into hers. 'There,' he said softly, 'that's just so you don't forget me.'

She wriggled out of his grasp, but she was laughing as she stood up. 'I'll do my best to do just that.' She turned and walked towards the door.

'I'll see you again,' he called after her.

'In your dreams, Mitch Hammond.'

As the door closed behind her, he stared at it and then murmured to the empty room, 'You can be sure of that, Miss Maitland. You can be *very* sure of that.'

Seventy-Eight

For many reasons, Pips was glad to be back; she was kept busy and she felt wanted and needed, though she missed Daisy painfully. But at least she was able to talk about her often, for William wanted to know all about his niece. Eagerly, she awaited any news from home and scanned hurriedly through the letters to reach the paragraphs about the baby. Luckily, each member of her family wrote regularly and they, too, never tired of giving her regular updates on her niece. Even Robert, finding a good reason to practise writing with his left hand, sent frequent letters full of news about her. With each letter, she could see an improvement in his handwriting and told him so.

And then, he sent a photograph. 'Look, William, oh do look! Isn't she just adorable?'

'She is,' William said, gazing at the photograph. 'I wonder if I will ever see her.'

'Of course you will,' Pips said firmly. 'When she's old enough, I will bring her to see you and Brigitta.' She chuckled. 'To meet her uncle and aunty – and her cousins.'

For a moment, William looked startled and then he grinned. 'I hope you will, Pips.'

'Oh I will, make no mistake about that.'

'D'you know what they've done now?' Bess demanded.

458

Ma glanced up at her with a smile. 'Who and what, Bess?'

'The Government, I suppose. They've only gone and brought in rationing. What's that supposed to mean, anyway?'

'Oh aye, Norah did mention it, but I don't expect it'll affect us here in the country very much, will it?'

Bess folded her arms. 'Why won't it? They're saying every man, woman and child is only going to be allowed so much to eat each week.'

'Only certain items, I think.'

'That's as maybe, but it won't keep a mouse alive.'

Ma tactfully averted her eyes from the large woman standing in front of her and hid her smile. Bess Cooper would hardly waste away.

Norah came into the kitchen carrying a large basket of washing she had just collected from the clothes line in the back garden.

'I'll do a bit of ironing later, duck,' Ma said. 'Just you fold it all and leave it on the table.'

'You've heard about this rationing, Norah?' Bess went on. 'They reckon it's going to apply to meat, butter and sugar.'

'Yes, Bess, I have. We should be all right for meat and butter, living near farms, but sugar might be in short supply.'

'What I don't understand is why it's necessary.'

'The German submarines have sunk a lot of the ships bringing supplies to this country, but more importantly, Bess, have *you* heard that President Wilson has suggested a fourteen-point peace plan?'

Bess gaped at her. 'Who's he when he's at home?'

'The President of the United States.'

'Oh.' Bess wriggled her shoulders. Matters outside her own back yard didn't really concern her – except, of course, the war, which was affecting everyone. Wasn't it the fault of this war that she now had an illegitimate grandson? This war had a lot to answer for. 'Let's hope he can do summat, then. Whoever he is.'

Norah hid her smile and dared not meet Ma's eyes for she knew they would both fall into fits of laughter.

In March, Robert wrote almost a full letter in code to Pips. It held worrying news.

The Peace Plan doesn't seem to be having any effect. Like he suspected at New Year, Basil says it is thought that the enemy are planning a series of offensives. At present, because of armies released from the Eastern Front, they are superior in numbers to us and yet they know the Americans are to arrive shortly. Basil thinks that Ludendorff's plan might be to attack at the weakest points, probably along a fifty-mile front. He believes that the French will defend Paris to the last man, whilst the British will defend the ports because of the supplies and troops coming through them.

So goodness knows where Stephen will decide you should be...

'So, are we staying here or going further south to Thiepval?' Pips asked Stephen when she'd told him the news.

'I think you could take a skeleton first-aid post there first. You can get in touch with the casualty-clearing stations at Albert. It's only about five miles from Thiepval, whereas we're about twenty from there. I'm reluctant to move us all – we have three units now to think of moving – at least until we see how long it's going to last.'

'It could be a while,' Pips said. 'Like Robert says, the Germans have got more troops to reinforce the Western Front now that Russia has withdrawn from the war.'

The events in Russia throughout 1917 had appalled everyone and had robbed the Allies of a strong partner.

'Then we'll just keep moving wherever we're needed the most,' Stephen said. 'Let's just hope the Americans aren't too long in getting here.'

It was a bad time for the Allies. General Erich Ludendorff planned a major offensive known as the Kaiser's Battle along a fifty-mile front from Arras southwards to St Quentin, just as the major had predicted. The bombardment of high-explosive and gas shells began on 21 March and lasted for five hours. That was followed by storm troopers and the enemy made significant advances, and all Pips and her colleagues could do was move to relative safety and attend to the wounded as they always had done. But Pips could tell from the mood of the casualties that the men were losing heart, and this concerned her more than anything. The Allied armies were stretched so thinly. Two days later, the Germans began a bombardment of Paris and they started to march towards Amiens.

At the end of March, Pips wrote to Robert.

The Germans launched an attack on Arras so that our advanced post went scuttling back. The offensive failed, but the casualties were high. We've been run off our feet... And now they're bombarding Paris again.

His reply to her at the beginning of April told her:

The British Third Army have halted the Germans north of the Somme with the help of air support. The Royal Air Force has come into being. I wonder where your pilot, Mitch, is now. He left here a while ago...

Ludendorff had abandoned the German offensives along the River Somme and, by 12 April, concentrated his attacks on the area around the River Lys, one of their objectives being Hazebrouck, to the south-west of Ypres, in an effort to command the Channel ports. Sir Douglas Haig, the British commander-in-chief, issued a 'fight on to the end' statement.

'It's serious when the top brass start issuing orders like that,' Pips muttered.

'You know the Brits.' William was determinedly optimistic. 'It'll toughen their resolve. You mark my words.'

'Poor Ypres. I think there's always going to be fighting there,' Pips said. 'Right, that settles it. I must talk to Stephen. I think we need to go back to Ypres.' She smiled wistfully. 'Back home.' And silently, she thought, I wonder if George will be there again.

The British, aided by French troops, halted the Germans along the River Lys, though there followed attacks and counter-attacks until, by the end of the month, it was accepted that the German attempt to reach the ports had failed.

'He's not done yet,' Pips remarked wisely. 'He'll just move his offensive elsewhere.'

It came soon enough near the River Aisne, and brought the enemy ever nearer to Paris. Through June and July there were more attacks but, forewarned by German deserters, the Allied defences were prepared.

Ludendorff's fifth offensive of the year was a diversionary tactic near the River Marne to draw the Allies away from northern France so that he could still seize the Channel ports. But, through aerial reconnaissance and the questioning of enemy deserters, the French began an attack and Ludendorff was halted. British, French and now US forces combined to launch an attack in what became known as the Second Battle of the Marne River. By early August, the battle proved to be a disaster for the Germans when they were forced to abandon Soissons and fall back, losing recently captured land. But worse was to come for them when Field Marshall Haig launched the Amiens Offensive, led by General Sir Henry Rawlinson's British Fourth Army, the first day of which became known as 'Black Day for the German Army'. The Germans were forced back over ten miles and many of their soldiers were captured or fled from the fighting.

By the beginning of September, the German Army began falling back to the Hindenburg Line.

A letter from Robert in the middle of the month heartened Pips:

Old Basil is convinced this is the beginning of the end. He has heard – though how and from whom your guess is as good as mine – that even Ludendorff no longer believes that Germany can win the war. With the combined attack by the Americans and the French on the area to the south of Verdun, which has been held by the Germans almost from the beginning, the enemy's resistance is futile.

Various offensives were taking place along the Western Front, but the one that affected Pips and the teams was the one at the end of September by the Group of Armies of Flanders who drove the Germans from the high ground near Ypres. The push by all the Allied armies continued and by the beginning of November, the German resistance had collapsed.

'What an irony it is,' Pips said to William. 'They're saying that the last shot fired in the war was in almost the same place as the first shot that was fired four years ago. What a tragic waste of young lives, and for what?'

The team packed up all their equipment and medical supplies, making sure that there was no one else needing their immediate attention.

'The RAMC will have to cope now,' Dr Hazelwood said when he came out to say a final farewell. 'We've all done our bit. And now I'm going to take the whole team into Poperinghe for a farewell meal.'

The members from the original team sat together.

'It's so nice to see you, Mrs Parrott,' Pips greeted her. 'We didn't see much of you through the war, but I don't know how we'd have managed without you.'

'Marigold, please. Well, I just hope we can meet up in England some time in happier circumstances.'

'I'd like that,' Pips said.

'I'll take you for a ride on my bus,' Hugh said. 'Show you the sights.'

'That's if you get your bus back – and your job,' Peter reminded him.

'Boss said before we left that our jobs'd be there for us. Mind you, me ol' bus might not be, specially if the old girl's been out here.'

Pips smiled across the table at the two cockney brothers. She'd grown very fond of them both. Their unfailing cheerfulness had kept the corps going in the darkest of times. But tonight, they all tried to reminisce about the good times they'd had, for, strangely, there had been some even amidst the horror. More than anything it had been the comradeship that had carried them through. At the end of the evening, there were hugs and kisses and a few tears.

'Leonore,' Pips murmured. 'I can't thank you enough for all you've done. You've held us together many a time.'

'And you – and Alice – were a revelation to me.

I never thought you'd stick it.' She laughed. 'Is that the right English word?'

Pips laughed through tears that threatened to fall. 'Perfect and, yes, I'm sure we did surprise you.'

Pips found the hardest goodbye was to William.

'I'm not even going to suggest you coming back to England because I can see how happy you both are,' she said to William and Brigitta as they stood with their arms around one another. 'But if you need any references or anything when you apply to stay here – I'm not quite sure what you're going to have to do – be sure to let me know.'

'We will, Pips. And thank you for everything. Give my love to Alice, won't you?' William hesitated and then added haltingly, 'and – if you get the chance – to Mam and Ma.'

Pips squeezed his hand. 'I will, William. I promise. And don't forget to send me an invitation to the wedding.'

Brigitta blushed. 'Of course not.'

'*Dahlings*, you weren't going off to your new home without saying goodbye to me, were you?' Milly flung her arms wide and embraced an embarrassed William and a smiling Brigitta together. Then she turned to Pips. 'And as for you, Miss Maitland, I want a solemn promise that you will come and stay with me in London. Daddy said he'd buy me a flat in town if I came home in one piece, so I'm determined to make him keep his promise. I'll show you all the sights and take you dancing. *Do* say you will? I've got your address, so I'll write to you. And if you don't come, I'll turn up on the doorstep and drag you back with me.'

Pips laughed. 'Milly, I couldn't think of anything nicer to do after all we've been through. A little frivolity will do us the world of good.'

Apart from William, Brigitta and Leonore, they all said their final goodbyes when they reached England, all promising to keep in touch; and then, at last, Pips was on her way home – this time for good.

Seventy-Nine

'I can't believe it's finally over,' Robert greeted Pips. 'You've missed all the local celebrations.'

'I'm surprised there was much in the way of celebrating. Robert, we've lost a whole generation of fine young men and left a raft of single women who will never marry and have children.' Pips pulled a face. 'Probably including me.'

Robert didn't know how to answer that, so instead he said, 'I'm surprised you weren't needed to stay out there longer. There must still be wounded needing care.'

'There are, but they're all in the hospitals now or being shipped home. Obviously, there are no new casualties coming in from the front line any more. Dr Hazelwood has disbanded all the flying ambulance corps he set up. Besides,' she laughed wryly, 'Mrs Parrott's sources of funding have dried up. Folks don't want to give money now it's all over.'

'I can see their point, but what they don't realize

467

is the dreadful ongoing suffering of all the wounded and those maimed for life. Not everyone is as lucky as me, with a supportive family. There'll be a lot of hardship.'

'Nonsense, haven't the Government promised "a land fit for heroes"?'

'And you really think that will happen? Where's the money going to come from? We're probably bankrupt as a nation after the last four years. Anyway, let's not dwell on that just now. Let's just give thanks that the whole dreadful business is over and hope that it's true what they say, that this really has been "the war to end all wars".'

'How many have we lost from the village?'

'Aside from the three Dawson brothers, there were four more besides them.'

'What about Sam Nuttall?'

'He's home. Got a "Blighty wound" in August, but he'll make a full recovery. Oh, and talking of Dr Hazelwood, did you know that he's written to Father and asked if he can visit and stay a couple of nights?'

'No, I didn't. When's he coming?'

'Next week, I think.'

'Will we still have any patients here by then?'

Robert shook his head. 'No, the last one is leaving tomorrow.' For a moment, his face was bleak. 'So what I'm going to do with my time then, I don't know.'

Pips grinned as she said promptly, 'Play with Daisy, of course.'

Robert smiled half-heartedly. 'I'll always enjoy that, but it's hardly a career, is it?'

'Haven't you been studying the after-effects of

468

the war on the men you've had here?'

'Well, yes, but once that's done—'

'Then you'll have to learn all about running the estate. You are the heir and now,' she added pointedly, 'you too have an heir. You must leave it in good order for Daisy.'

Now Robert smiled genuinely as he looked at Pips fondly. 'You're besotted with her, aren't you?'

Pips laughed. 'Yes, that's a good word to describe how I feel about my niece, but I realize that I too must find something useful to do. First, however, I intend to have a little fun.'

The war had demanded so much of them, had made them feel needed and useful, but now its end had left them both – and many like them – without a definite purpose.

Dr John Hazelwood arrived in the last weekend in November. At dinner on the first evening, he gazed around the table with a beaming smile.

'My dear friend,' he said to Edwin. 'What wonderful children you have. As you know, they were a major part of the first flying ambulance corps I set up. It became my flagship, and all the subsequent ones followed their fine example.' His face sobered. 'But I'm devastated that their involvement caused such heartache. Robert's injury and,' he nodded towards her with sympathy in his eyes, 'Pips's betrayal.'

Henrietta's sharp ears missed nothing and Pips sighed inwardly.

'Whatever do you mean, John? Who did Philippa betray? You?'

'Heavens, no, dear lady. Perish the very idea. I

have never known such dedication and loyalty in one so young. No, she was the one who was betrayed by Dr Kendall.'

Henrietta's face was a picture. 'I – don't understand.'

'Oh dear.' Dr Hazelwood was contrite. 'Have I put my foot in it?' He sighed heavily. 'My late wife always said that, for a doctor, I could be very tactless at times. She often told me that I only opened my mouth to change feet.'

There was a murmur of polite laughter around the table, but neither Henrietta nor Pips were laughing.

Attempting to change the subject, Edwin said, 'Robert has been making a particular study of the patients we have had here with particular reference to shell shock and the ongoing trauma of a serious, life-changing injury.'

John Hazelwood nodded. 'I would be very interested to read your findings, my boy, and if there is any way in which I can help you to get your work published in the right places, you only have to ask.'

The conversation had been successfully steered away from Pips, but she knew her mother would not let the matter rest there.

'Philippa, my dear, come and sit beside me.' Henrietta's voice was unusually gentle. The three women had retired to the parlour, leaving the men to enjoy a glass of port – or even something stronger.

Alice hovered uncertainly near the doorway. 'I'll – um – go and...'

'There's no need, Alice. You might as well hear

470

this too. I don't have any secrets from you.' Pips smiled. 'I never did have, did I? Well, not many.'

Alice chuckled and moved to sit opposite them.

'Now, tell me, what did happen between you and Giles?' Henrietta asked.

Pips sat down and took the cup of coffee her mother handed to her. Alice helped herself from the tray. 'It's quite simple, really, though I have to admit that I was very hurt at the time. That's really why I couldn't talk about it before, Mother. He fell in love with someone else. That's all.'

'Who?'

'Rose.'

'Rose!' Alice was shocked.

'Who's Rose?'

'The nurse who joined the team when Alice left to bring Robert home.'

'It happened whilst you were still here at home?' Henrietta asked.

Pips nodded.

'Then it's a pity you came home. I'm sorry now that I asked you to come home, particularly,' her glance rested fondly on Alice, 'as you were all quite right about their marriage and I was wrong. Maybe, if you'd stayed...'

'No, I don't see it like that. If – if what he felt for me was so easily put aside for another pretty face, then I'm glad it happened then and not later. And besides, after what Robert told us, I'm relieved. I can't stand deceit of any sort – at least' – she hesitated as she remembered her own white lies to the dying – 'not when there's no good reason. And there wasn't in this case.'

'That's true, I suppose.' Henrietta was silent for

several moments. 'I'm sorry, Pips. I wouldn't have believed it of him.'

Pips held her breath, hoping that her mother wouldn't ask any more searching questions, but at that moment they heard the menfolk leaving the Great Hall and entering the room. Pips gave a sigh of relief.

'I almost forgot to tell you,' John Hazelwood said, as he accepted a cup of coffee. 'I met a friend of yours recently. It was funny how it happened. I was leaving the hospital and this chap was obviously hanging about outside as if he was waiting for me. I didn't recognize him at first because he was in civvies.' He paused as if for dramatic effect. 'It was Captain Allender.'

'George? Oh, I'm so glad to hear you've seen him. Was he all right?' Without thinking, Pips touched the poppy brooch she always wore just beneath her left shoulder.

'He'd been invalided out of the army two months before the war ended with a serious leg injury. I'm pleased to say he was recovering, though I suspect he will always walk with a limp.'

'What did he want?' Robert asked. 'You said it seemed as if he was waiting to speak to you.'

John wrinkled his forehead. 'He just wanted to know about all of you. He was so sorry to hear of your injury, Robert, but delighted that you and Alice had married and that you have a baby daughter.'

And me, Pips wanted to ask. Did he mention me? But instead she murmured, 'He was such a lovely man.'

John turned towards her now. 'And he wanted

472

to know if you were well, Pips, and he asked me particularly to give *you* his very best wishes.'

She saw Henrietta's eyebrows rise with an unspoken question. There was a huge temptation to tease her mother, yet she knew it wasn't fair, so she said swiftly, 'Did he say how his wife is now?'

'Yes, she's much improved since he's come home and is able to be with her all the time. His daughter, now relieved of having to care for her mother, has gone to college and is pursuing a career in nursing.'

The conversation moved on, but Pips was left with mixed feelings. She was happy to hear that he had survived the war and had come home, but saddened to think that his future was bleak, shackled to an ailing wife.

And yet, that was what she had admired about him. He'd made a commitment to her for life and he would honour it. If ever a man deserved the title 'an officer and a gentleman', then it was Captain George Allender.

Eighty

'Robert, I need your help.'

'Well, as long as it doesn't involve a strong right arm, I'm your man.'

'Oh phooey!' Pips laughed, delighted that Robert could now begin to joke about his dreadful injury. Then she explained. 'I nursed a young German boy and was with him when he died. He asked me to write to his parents after the war to tell them he didn't suffer.'

Brother and sister exchanged a solemn glance and Robert nodded slowly. 'They were all the same, weren't they? Wanting their families to believe they felt no pain.' He paused and then asked, 'So, what are you going to do?'

Pips ran her tongue around her lips. 'Robert, I told a lot of lies to the dying and their families, even to the Dawsons. Maybe this will be the last one I need to tell.'

'So, why do you want my help?'

'Although I used the language occasionally out there, my German is still not nearly good enough to compose a letter. Can you help me?'

'I'll try, though I shouldn't think mine's much better.'

For the next hour, they drafted a letter together and, when they were happy that it was the best they could do, Pips put it in an envelope and left it on the table near the front door to be posted.

Two weeks later she received a reply, written in English. It expressed the parents' gratitude that she had been with their boy and had cared for him. The letter ended with the words: *You sound like a lovely young woman and we thank you from the bottom of our hearts. It is a tragedy that our two countries ever went to war against each other.*

'Amen to that,' Pips murmured as she folded the letter and tucked it away in the drawer of her dressing table.

A week before Christmas, there was another visitor to the hall, his arrival heralded by a noisy sports car. He swung it round in front of the main entrance, leapt out and bounded up the steps.

Before he could ring the bell, Pips, hearing the engine noise, opened the front door.

'*You!* What are you doing here?'

Mitch Hammond grinned up at her. 'I've come to show you my pride and joy and to take you for a spin. I'll even let you drive her, if you're very good.'

'She's a beauty.'

'I'm going to race her when the tracks get under way again after the war.'

'*Are* you? How thrilling,' Pips said, her eyes sparkling.

'You must come and watch me sometime. Though, knowing you, you'd want to take part, wouldn't you?'

Pips laughed. 'More than likely.'

'Come on – get your coat and I'll take you out.'

The little blue open-topped sports car tore through the lanes, startling hens and geese and even the cows in the fields, and causing the villagers to look up and smile.

'That'll be Miss Pips. Not changed, has she?'

Ma, sitting outside the cottage, smoking her pipe, waved to the cloud of dust left by the disappearing car. 'There she goes,' she murmured to herself. 'It's good to have her back safe and sound.'

'That was wonderful,' Pips said as they drew up again in front of the hall and she climbed out. 'Are you coming in for lunch?'

'No, sorry, I've got to fly. Literally. I've got a flying session, later.'

He held out his hand and when she put hers into his, he raised it to his lips and kissed it gallantly.

'I'll see you around, Miss Maitland.'

Pips laughed loudly. 'Not if I see you first, Mitch Hammond. Not if I see you first.'

With a cheeky grin and a mock salute, Mitch settled himself behind the wheel and the car roared down the driveway, through the archway of the gatehouse and out into the lane. Pips followed him down the drive and stood at the gate watching until he turned the corner and disappeared from her view. But she could still hear the noise of the engine. She stayed there until the sound faded away completely and he was gone. With a wry smile, she remembered that she had once before stood on this very same spot, listening to the sound of a motorcycle engine disappearing into the night. And look how that had turned out!

With a little shrug, as if to throw off the whole business of young men and their motors, Pips lifted her head, marched back up the drive, entered the house and went in search of Daisy.

The publishers hope that this book has given you enjoyable reading. Large Print Books are especially designed to be as easy to see and hold as possible. If you wish a complete list of our books please ask at your local library or write directly to:

Magna Large Print Books
Magna House, Long Preston,
Skipton, North Yorkshire.
BD23 4ND

This Large Print Book for the partially sighted, who cannot read normal print, is published under the auspices of

THE ULVERSCROFT FOUNDATION

THE ULVERSCROFT FOUNDATION

... we hope that you have enjoyed this Large Print Book. Please think for a moment about those people who have worse eyesight problems than you ... and are unable to even read or enjoy Large Print, without great difficulty.

You can help them by sending a donation, large or small to:

**The Ulverscroft Foundation,
1, The Green, Bradgate Road,
Anstey, Leicestershire, LE7 7FU,
England.**
or request a copy of our brochure for more details.

The Foundation will use all your help to assist those people who are handicapped by various sight problems and need special attention.

Thank you very much for your help.